HOT DUKE SUMMER

A Regency Historical Romance Anthology

Scarlett Scott, Alexa Aston, Annabelle Anders,
Meara Platt, Kathleen Ayers, Chasity Bowlin,
Sara Adrien, Jude Knight

Dragonblade Publishing, Inc. is an imprint of Kathryn Le Veque Novels, Inc.
P.O. Box 23
Moreno Valley, CA 92556
ceo@dragonbladepublishing.com

Produced in the United States of America

First Edition August 2024
Print Edition

ARE YOU SIGNED UP FOR DRAGONBLADE'S BLOG?

You'll get the latest news and information on exclusive giveaways, exclusive excerpts, coming releases, sales, free books, cover reveals and more.

Check out our complete list of authors, too!

No spam, no junk. That's a promise!

Sign Up Here

www.dragonbladepublishing.com

Dearest Reader;

Thank you for your support of a small press. At Dragonblade Publishing, we strive to bring you the highest quality Historical Romance from some of the best authors in the business. Without your support, there is no 'us', so we sincerely hope you adore these stories and find some new favorite authors along the way.

Happy Reading!

CEO, Dragonblade Publishing

Anthology Contents

Welcome to a rollicking summer in Regency England, where the weather is warm, the ladies warmer, and the dukes sizzling-hot!

It's the scorching tales of a Hot Duke Summer Regency Anthology!

For lovers of historical romance, lose yourself in this collection of **never before published** Regency stories. From gambling halls to ballrooms, you'll enjoy a cast of unforgettable characters from tales inspired from some of your favorite summer movies. A Regency Gidget? Yes, please! Or the hottest duke in London with a penchant for a fancy conveyance? Absolutely!

It's glamour, passion, and adventure in one magical summer in Regency England, so join the hottest dukes for the hottest summer around!

THE DUCHESS BRIDE

by Scarlett Scott

After the death of her true love the Duke of Westley, Lady Celandine Raynell has been left with no choice but to marry the odious Earl of Humberton to protect her family from ruin. On her wedding day, she's kidnapped by a dashing, masked stranger whose eyes seem hauntingly familiar. Celandine is drawn to her captor and increasingly convinced he's her Westley. But is he, or has she been spirited away by a villain determined to obtain a ransom from her wealthy fiancé?

CHAPTER ONE

LADY CELANDINE RAYNELL couldn't keep herself from weeping as she rode her favorite mount through the familiar landscape of her father's country seat. Just as she did every morning at dawn, she rode Buttercup as if they were one with the wind.

Only this time, she wished she could fly into the wind and disappear.

The occasion should have been a joyous one, cause for celebration. It was her wedding day. A day she had once longed for with hope in her heart, a day she'd been looking forward to from the moment the man she loved had left on his Grand Tour, leaving her with a promise to return soon so they could wed. A day when she should have met the man she loved in her family's chapel and promised herself to him forever.

But the man she loved was dead.

And the man she was marrying in his stead—the icy-hearted Earl of Humberton—was a cold, distant, loathsome substitute. He would never own her heart. Humberton had been determined to marry her, and this morning, he would finally get what he wanted. The future rose before her, grim and unhappy.

As another rush of dread fell over her, Celandine slowed Buttercup to a trot, holding the reins with one hand as she dashed at her tears. She should have been marrying Westley today. Instead, he had taken her heart with him to his watery grave. And now, she was being forced to marry another.

Another sob welled up, impossible to contain.

Her life with Humberton would be a mockery of what it should have been. But Papa's debts had mounted, and Humberton's wealth was vast. The earl had offered a more than handsome sum for Celandine's hand in marriage. To save her sisters, her brother, and her family, she had reluctantly agreed to this farce of a union, knowing she was casting herself into misery. Knowing she hadn't any other choice.

She rode Buttercup into a grove of trees, following the familiar path that would soon no longer be hers to follow. Cool shade enveloped her, the high boughs of the ancient trees blotting out the sun. As her eyes adjusted to the lack of light, she almost didn't see the man, dressed all in black, wearing a mask.

He was tall, broad of shoulder, lean of hip.

And he was pointing a double-barreled flintlock at her.

"Halt, my lady."

Icy fear trilled down her spine, making her lungs seize in her chest. So many times, she had ridden this path without a groom for accompaniment. It was one of many liberties Papa had allowed her. She'd never had reason to fear being alone. She was an excellent horsewoman, and she could outride the devil himself.

But not when the devil had a pistol.

Celandine reined in Buttercup, who shied at the stranger, dancing to the side as if she understood the peril they faced.

"Who are you?" she demanded, inwardly cursing herself for the quaver in her voice.

"Perhaps I'm a highwayman come to rob all the pretty maidens riding alone this morning," he drawled.

And for a moment, she swore she heard the trace of something familiar in his voice. The timbre of it, not the derisive edge. She'd heard it before. Was he someone she knew? Who was he, and why was he here in the woods of her father's estate? Had he been waiting for her?

The questions rose inside her, endless. But Celandine knew she had to concentrate on the most important question of all—how she could escape him.

"We don't have highwaymen here at Bradley Abbey," she said, trying to distract him.

At least, they hadn't before. There was something distinctly menacing about the man before her, however. And the fear blossomed into dread, replacing all the sorrow she'd been wallowing in over her impending nuptials.

The stranger's lips curved into a sardonic smile. "Then perhaps I'm Hades, come to spirit sweet Persephone to the underworld."

Good heavens, mayhap he was a madman. Or worse. Perhaps he truly was a highwayman. Or someone intent upon somehow doing her harm.

She considered her options. If she spurred Buttercup into a gallop, the mare could easily take her far from the stranger. But if he shot at them, and if he had good aim, then she'd not only be putting her own life at risk but her beloved horse's as well. She couldn't bear to chance it.

"I wouldn't try to escape if I were you, my lady," he said, almost as if he had been privy to her thoughts, striding toward her, one hand extended whilst the other still held the pistol.

His gloves were as black as the rest of his attire. She stared at that hand as if it were a venomous snake intending to strike.

"I'm not dismounting," she told him. "And you had best carry on before someone comes looking for me."

"Why should anyone come looking for you when they don't know you're missing yet, Lady Celandine?" he asked.

His question was like a knife directly between her ribs. He knew her name.

How?

"Who are you?" she asked again, her grip on Buttercup's reins so tight that her knuckles ached with the strain.

"Hades or a highwayman," he quipped. "Or anyone else you wish me to be. It hardly matters. All that does matter is that you obey me. Get down from your horse."

She hesitated, unable to shake the feeling that leaving her saddle would be the worst sort of mistake. "Please, sir," she begged, deciding upon a different tactic. "I'm to be married this morning to the Earl of Humberton. He's a most wealthy man, and I'm certain he would be indebted to you for returning his bride to him safely. If you take me to him, I've no doubt that he will reward you handsomely."

The man's lip curled. "Humberton can keep his coin. There is only one reward I'm interested in, my lady, and it's you."

"Me?" she sputtered, confused. "I don't understand."

"You will in time," he promised darkly.

When she failed to place her hand in his, he grasped her wrist and tugged with more strength than she had anticipated. He was far stronger than she and able to outmaneuver her with ease. She lost her balance instantly, tumbling not to the ground, but into the stranger's arms. She fell against his hard, broad chest, the impact and the feeling of his well-muscled frame against hers robbing her of breath.

He clamped a hand on her waist, moving her from him, the pistol between them now. "Tell me, my lady. Will you come with me of your own free will, or must I bind you and take you as my captive?"

The dread and fear turned into horror. If he took her with him, she would be ruined. The earl would refuse to marry her, and Papa's debts would not be paid. Her family would be cast into penury, with nothing left and no way to save Bradley Abbey.

And what would become of Celandine herself? Without her family, it wouldn't matter. She had to do something. To stop him somehow.

"I won't go anywhere with you," she told him defiantly. "I've told you that I'm about to be married. Please, sir, release me. I beg you. Whatever reward you think to find in taking me, I can assure you that my betrothed will recompense you a hundredfold for my safe return."

Actually, she wasn't certain of that. Not at all. Humberton had been clear in his expectations for his future wife. She was to be above reproach, her reputation nothing short of faultless. Being unchaperoned with a stranger would no doubt cast question on her virtue. But she was desperate enough to try anything to save her family. Desperation—and the knowledge that her true love was forever lost to her—had been her reason for accepting the earl's proposal in the first place.

"You hardly looked like a happy bride when you rode into this forest," her would-be captor pointed out harshly, cutting through her wildly vacilating thoughts. "You looked as if you'd lost your favorite pair of slippers. Could it be you aren't as eager to attend your nuptials as you claim?"

"Of course not," she lied, all too aware of the pistol that continued to be trained upon her, its menacing barrels making her heart pound and her mouth go dry. "I want nothing more than to marry the earl, and I promise you that he'll pay handsomely for my return."

"Even if I believed you, I still wouldn't take you to him. I've told you, I neither want, nor need, the Earl of Humberton's blunt." He extracted a length of rope from inside his voluminous greatcoat. "Give me your hands, my lady."

He intended to tie her up, as he'd threatened. Her instinct took over, and she attempted to jerk away from him, to flee. But he was faster. He caught her in an unforgiving hold, keeping her from going anywhere.

"Your hands," he growled. "And don't do anything foolish."

He was too quick for her, too strong. He had a weapon. All she had to defend herself was her wits, and she knew she had to keep them about her. To bide her time. To plan her escape and make it when the time was right.

Celandine offered him her wrists with a meekness that her determined thoughts belied. "If you must."

"Oh, I must," he said grimly. "It's for your own good."

With that pronouncement, he looped the rope around her.

CHAPTER TWO

T HEY RODE, HER captor's muscled chest a wall at her back, his arms wrapped around her in a hold that rendered escape impossible unless she wanted to risk a fall and a broken neck.

They rode until Celandine's body was sore and aching. Until the rope binding her wrists had chafed them raw and red. Until her stomach grumbled embarrassingly with protest from lack of food. For some reason, it was the latter that had the most potent effect on her. It was silly, for she had far more pressing concerns than whether her kidnapper overheard her body's impolite response to the fact that she had forgone breaking her fast that morning.

And yet she shifted on the saddle, seeking a position that would lessen her discomfort, hoping he hadn't heard the loud rumble.

"Hungry?" he asked, his voice deep and pleasant.

"Not at all," she lied, because she refused to show him a hint of weakness.

"Your body betrays you."

He sounded almost amused. Or perhaps as if he were taking pleasure in her disquiet.

"I'll thank you not to speak to me with such unwelcome familiarity," she snapped, stiffening her spine so that she might escape from the warm strength of him at her back.

So that she could escape too from the vague sense that there was something about him that she recognized.

Because that was also foolishness. How would she be acquainted with a masked ruffian who stooped so low as to steal a marquess's daughter on her wedding day? He was a villain who bound her with crude rope without a thought for her comfort, who had pointed a flintlock at her, forced her to ride for hours, taking her far from the bosom of her family. And only heaven knew what his plans for her were. No, she did not know this vile creature at her back. Did not know him at all.

"And how would my lady have me speak to her?" he asked.

She held herself away from him as best as she could—no easy feat, given that they shared the saddle. "I would have you not speak to me at all."

"How does your betrothed speak to you? Perhaps I'll earn your favor if I aspire to such courtly charm."

There was an undeniable sharp edge of mockery in his tone.

"I don't wish to speak of my betrothed with you," she said icily.

Humberton possessed appallingly little charm. He spoke to her with the supercilious air of a man who expected his wife to be docile and biddable. Or as if she were a child incapable of complex thought.

"Why not? You must love him, if you are marrying him today. One would think a new bride would be ready to extol all the virtues of the gentleman who owns her heart."

He didn't speak like she imagined a vagabond would. His words were crisp, enunciated with the polished perfection of any lord at court. How strange he was, her captor. It was almost as if he had been waiting for her in the woods. As if he had somehow known the route she took on her morning rides. But how could that be?

And he had known her name. But then, perhaps he had somehow heard of the wedding from some coaching inn or another traveler. It was possible he had hoped he might capture the wealthy Earl of Humberton's bride and hold her for ransom. If so, there was hope he might release her without harm.

"My lady?" he prodded when she didn't answer him. "Tell me about Humberton. Why do you love him?"

"I don't love him," she blurted before she could think better of it.

"No?" her captor asked softly, his lips perilously near to her ear. "Why not?"

Was it her imagination, or had he shifted in the saddle so that their bodies were pressed closely together again? He radiated such heat at her back. The air bore a chill, and that was why part of her longed to lean into his warmth, to settle herself against him as if it were where she belonged. There was no reason for her to be drawn to her captor, a man who had ruthlessly taken her prisoner.

None at all, she reminded herself firmly.

"It's hardly any of your concern, sirrah," she told him sharply.

"But it *is* my concern. If I'm not spiriting away a brokenhearted bride, I ought to know why."

"Where are you taking me?" she asked instead of answering his question.

"Wherever I like. Now, tell me—whom does your heart belong to, if not to your betrothed?"

She didn't want to speak of Westley with this callous stranger. It felt desperately wrong. The tears that always rose whenever she thought of him returned, welling in her eyes. Celandine blinked at them furiously.

"I won't speak of it."

How she missed her beloved. She would mourn him forever. Neither time nor death had changed the way she felt for him. And she knew nothing would. She would never love anyone as she had loved her Westley.

"Tell me," her captor demanded, his voice harsh.

"The man I truly love is gone," she said, a tremor in her voice that she couldn't control as more tears rose, pricking her eyes, making her vision blur. "And that is why it's no concern of yours."

Gone.

How she loathed that word. Such a simple, bloodless means of conveying the vast chasm of emptiness inside her. Westley was gone. One day, he had been in her life, in her arms. And the next, he had ridden away, never to return. She had told herself for weeks after the ship he'd been on had sunk on his way to his Grand Tour that it had been a mistake. That somehow, he might have escaped and survived. That he would return to her. But as the weeks had turned into months, she'd had to reconcile herself to the fact that her Westley—her handsome, charming, wonderful Westley—was dead.

And a part of her had died with him.

"Gone, you say? Where?"

"He died," she forced out, tears clinging to her lashes, rolling down her cheeks.

"Ah, and your idea of mourning your love was to marry someone else? May God spare me from the inconstant heart of a woman who claims to be in love. How long did you mourn him before agreeing to become another man's wife?"

This time, there was no mistaking the bitterness lacing her captor's voice.

She cast an angry look at him over her shoulder. "You dare to judge me? You, a criminal who has taken an innocent woman as your captive? You don't even know me, sirrah."

His blue eyes were cold behind his mask. "You are correct in that, Lady Celandine. I don't know you. Not at all."

There was a dig in those words that she didn't understand. Now that the initial fright of her kidnapping had worn off beneath the grueling pace of their journey, she took a moment to study him. To truly look at him, from the angular jaw to his finely molded lips. Lips that reminded her of another's. Much like his eyes.

Her heart seized. Her captor bore a startling resemblance to Westley. She hadn't seen it in the forest, shade from the centuries-old trees and her fear mingling to obscure the features hidden beneath his mask.

"Who are you?" she whispered.

But no, how could that be? This stranger, this villain who had captured her, was not the man she loved. Westley had gone overboard at sea. He'd drowned. Likely, it was just her desperate heart wanting her to believe.

His mouth curved into a disdainful smile. "I've already told you, my lady. I'm Hades, come to spirit fair Persephone into the underworld."

She stared at him, disbelief warring with dawning realization. Her neck pained her from looking over her shoulder, but she couldn't wrest her gaze from him, this stranger dressed all in black who looked—and sounded, now that she thought upon it— remarkably similar to her Westley. Although almost a year had passed since she had last seen him, she hadn't forgotten him. As impossible as it seemed, she swore that it was him.

"Westley?" His name was torn from her, part plea, part demand.

But his grim smile remained firmly in place. "Is that his name, this lover of yours?"

She longed to reach for him, to touch his face, to rip off his mask. But her hands were bound together and he'd fastened the rope to the saddle, making it unachievable.

"Westley," she repeated, desperation making her voice rough. "Is it you?"

"Of course not. Your Westley is dead. Now turn around, my lady, lest your lovely neck cramp. We've a long journey yet ahead of us."

He spurred Buttercup on, and they continued riding.

But that incipient burst of hope remained stubbornly lodged in her breast, and with each fall of her horse's hooves, it grew.

CHAPTER THREE

"**W**HERE HAVE YOU brought me?" Celandine asked as her captor dismounted in the stables behind what appeared to be a small hunting lodge, hidden deep within the woods.

They'd traveled far from the main road, and for a time, she'd feared they were hopelessly lost until the edifice had at last loomed before them, at once a welcome and forbidding sight.

"To a place where you can rest and I can provide that rumbling stomach of yours with some much-needed sustenance," he replied, untying the rope binding her to the saddle with calm, efficient motions before securing Buttercup.

With the darkness in the stables bathing them in shadows, he remained an enigma. A dark figure, clad all in black. Tall and strong and lean. Was it her own desperate heart that so wanted Westley to come back to her that she fooled herself into seeing him in this harsh stranger?

Her stomach rumbled again, and she pressed her bound hands against it, shame heating her face. She was ravenous and thirsty, and she also needed to have a moment alone to tend to other needs.

"I'm not hungry," she lied again.

"Hmm," was all he said, a noncommittal hum as he finished his task and then reached for her, his strong hands settling on her waist.

She tried to dismount with as much grace as she could muster, but it was no easy feat, given the state of her legs. Their many hours of riding had left her muscles sore and weary. She slid from the saddle in a twist of riding habit and weak legs, falling.

Her captor caught her against him, settling her on her feet with a gentle care that was distinctly at odds with the morning's kidnapping. "Steady, Lady Celandine."

She grasped at the lapels of his greatcoat with her bound hands, struggling to keep from tumbling at his feet. Her head swam with dizziness; her stomach gnawed with hunger. For a moment, she feared she might swoon.

He scooped her into his arms, as if sensing her sudden weakness, carrying her from the stables and then across the distance to the hunting lodge. He shouldered his way into the door, and she was relieved to find the interior hall neatly swept and clean. Her captor carried her into a room that was lit from the meager light filtering through the windows from the sun high above the trees. He lowered her to a Grecian divan.

After so many hours of traveling in an unforgiving saddle, she couldn't contain the sigh that left her at the cushioned comfort beneath her.

He loomed over her for a moment, frowning. "I need to tend to your horse. Don't move from this spot until I return."

He needn't fear she would flee him. At the moment, in her weakened state and with her hands bound before her, she was incapable of it.

"I'll have your promise, my lady," he pressed at her silence.

And heaven help her, but his voice sounded more like Westley's than ever. Perhaps her hunger was rendering her delusional.

"I shan't move," she reassured him. "At the moment, I rather think I'm incapable of it."

And even if she weren't, where would she go? She had no notion of where she was, she hadn't eaten in hours, and her hands were bound.

He nodded and then swiftly quit the room, leaving her alone. She heard his booted footfalls in the entry hall and then the sound of the door opening and closing, followed by the crunch of his steps beyond. At least he was being kind to Buttercup, but then, his motives were likely selfish. He needed the mount to get them to wherever he planned to take her.

Unless this lodge was as far as he intended to go?

Celandine took in her surroundings. This room—perhaps a breakfast or sitting room—was as tidy as the entry hall. It was decorated with overstuffed furniture, the walls hung with pictures bearing scenes of the hunt. There was a hearth at the opposite end of the chamber, fire stacked neatly in the grate as if awaiting the hand that would set it aflame. The hunting lodge certainly didn't appear abandoned. It didn't smell of must or damp, as homes so often did when they were shuttered for a lengthy expanse of time.

The silence surrounding her told her that they were alone. No servants toiled here. But none of her observations answered the mystery of where he'd brought her and why. Nor was there any hint that might reveal who her captor truly was.

The door opened with a creak, telling her he had returned before his strides carried him over the entry hall and back to her side. He loomed over her, frowning, almost as if he were surprised to find she had kept her word and remained where he'd left her.

"Hold out your hands," he commanded.

She did as he asked, extending her arms, tensing when he extracted a wicked-looking blade from his greatcoat and began sawing at the rope. To her great relief, he inflicted no harm, not even touching her reddened skin with the blade.

When the ropes fell, she flexed her fingers, relieved at the freedom of movement. "Thank you."

"Your wrists are raw," he said, sheathing the knife and returning it to its hiding place. "Why did you not say so?"

"Would you have cared if I had?" she asked tartly.

Her stomach gave another indignant rumble then.

"You're hungry, despite your protests to the contrary. I'll fetch you some food and something for your wrists."

When he made to leave her again, she stopped him. "If you don't mind, sir, I would like a moment of privacy." And a chamber pot, but her ingrained manners refused to allow her to admit as much aloud.

"Of course. Come with me."

He helped her to her feet and led her to a staircase. Her legs were more accustomed to functioning now, but every part of her ached. Still, there was no helping her current dilemma. It was either follow him or ask him to carry her, and her pride wouldn't allow that.

He led her to a small bedroom that was every bit as neat and comfortable as the rest of the lodge. "You'll find what you need on the other side of the screen."

She thanked him and went inside, making haste to perform the necessary functions before straightening her riding habit again. The chamber had a large window, and for a moment, she hovered at it, tempted to open it and attempt an escape. But it was a rather dizzying height. The fall would leave her with broken bones at best. Her stomach reminded her that she had yet to eat.

A knock sounded at the door almost simultaneously. "Lady Celandine, are you finished?"

She froze.

That voice.

It was his, she was sure of it. Westley's voice.

But if her captor was Westley, why had he not simply made himself known to her? Why the mask, the ruse? Why the bitterness in his voice? Why take her captive at all? He must have known that she would go with him willingly, anywhere he chose to take her.

The latch moved. The door opened.

He spied her by the window, and his lips settled in a forbidding line. "I wouldn't, were I you, my lady. Humberton won't want a bride with a broken neck."

"Of course," she said, moving toward him. "Will you not take off your mask, now that we are away from the road?"

"And why should I wish to do so? I can't have you describing me to your beloved after he comes charging to your rescue."

She stopped before him, holding his stare, so sure those were the same eyes she had gazed into hundreds of times before. "I have only one beloved: the Duke of Westley."

Celandine said it firmly, watching him for a hint of recognition. For the tiniest betrayal of emotion. But he gave her nothing.

"Come, my lady," he said dispassionately. "Let us find some sustenance."

THEIR REPAST WAS a modest one, but Celandine ate heartily

nonetheless. Crusty bread and jam, cold tongue, buttery cheese, and to wash it down, a bottle of wine. As she took another sip from her glass, watching her captor over the rim, she plotted.

At the first opportunity she had, she would tear the mask from his face.

And she would either prove to them both that he was, indeed, her Westley returned from the dead. Or the last, fragile hope that had been summoned from the darkest depths of her heart would crumble into dust.

"Are you going to tell me why you've taken me captive?" she dared to ask him now that she was sated.

There was a tense silence as he said nothing, merely took a draught from his own wine goblet, watching her with an intensity that threatened to steal her breath. At last, he lowered the glass.

"I'll be asking the questions, my lady. Not you."

Fair enough. Although it galled her to admit it, he was the one who held all the power. Her presence here was a testament to that fact.

"Then perhaps you should ask them," she said, emboldened.

"Fine." He sat back in his chair, surveying her coolly. "Why are you marrying a louse like Humberton?"

"He's not a louse," she felt obligated to say, even if she wasn't particularly fond of her betrothed.

"The earl is known for certain predilections that an innocent like you undoubtedly isn't privy to," her captor said grimly. "Still, I cannot fathom why you would bind yourself to him forever, particularly when you claim to be in love with another."

"I don't claim it." Her chin went up in defiance. "I *am* in love with another. But my father has debts the earl is willing to pay, and it falls upon me to protect my younger siblings. I have no choice but to marry Lord Humberton and save them all."

Her voice trembled on the last, much to the dismay of her pride. She had vowed that she should be strong today. That she would marry the earl despite her every misgiving and the protestations of her heart. But the longer her captor kept her with him, the less likely her chances of Humberton accepting her as his wife. And if the earl refused to marry her, he could choose to call in Papa's vowels, which would mean utter ruin not just for Celandine, but for her family as well.

"I didn't know your father to be a wastrel," her captor said then, his tone gentling. "I was unaware he had debts."

"Gambling debts," she clarified bitterly. "They've been steadily mounting, unbeknownst to us all, and the Earl of Humberton holds all his vowels. But how do you know my father, sir, if you are indeed the stranger you claim to be?"

"Perhaps I'm not a stranger after all," he said.

Hope returned, a fervent ache that would not release her from its grasp. Could it be that he was truly Westley?

"Then lower your mask," she urged. "Show me your face."

He inclined his head. "If it pleases my lady."

Her hand trembled on her glass, overturning it and sending wine spilling across the table linen. But she paid it no heed, because *those words*—good heavens, those sweet, wondrous words.

She had heard them uttered so many times before. In the same smooth, deep voice that could be softer than velvet when he wished. Those words had charmed her. Lured her. Those words and the man who had spoken them had claimed her heart as his. And her heart recognized him now. Her heart knew.

"Westley," she whispered. "It *is* you."

He untied the mask and allowed it to fall.

Celandine found herself staring at a ghost.

A ghost who possessed the same angular, well-defined jaw, the same sky-blue eyes and high cheekbones. Only, he wasn't a ghost at all.

He was real.

Somehow, she was on her feet, and so was he. They collided halfway around the table, and she threw herself into his arms, where she belonged. Her captor, her stranger, her love, her Westley. They were all the same. And he was somehow, miraculously, *alive*.

He held her tightly, lifting her feet from the floor.

She clung to him, burrowing her face into his neck, half afraid she was dreaming and she would wake, trembling and alone in her lonely bed, only to realize that Westley was still gone and that she would have to marry the Earl of Humberton.

But she wasn't asleep. She was awake. And breathing in his scent, leather and crisp country air and spice.

"You're alive," she choked out, overwhelmed by emotion—so much of it, swelling like a raging tide within. "You're here."

There was joy. There was love. Sheer amazement commingling with relief.

"Yes, my love. I'm alive." He stroked her hair, holding her as if she were made of glass, and in that moment, she felt as if perhaps she were.

That at the slightest touch, she might shatter into a thousand pieces. Because the man she loved had returned from the dead, and yet she was still promised to marry another.

"How?" she managed, tipping her head back so that she could see him again, her eyes roaming hungrily over his handsome face, committing each masculine angle, every detail, to her memory. "How are you alive? I thought you had drowned at sea."

"I nearly did," he said. "On the passage to France, there was a man who had been sent to kill me. He tried to push me overboard, but I was stronger than he expected, and I managed to fight him off. He confessed to me that he had been hired by my uncle to murder me so that my uncle would inherit the title, being the heir presumptive. I paid the man to send word to my uncle that the deed had been done, and I plotted my return."

Horror filled her at his revelation, her heart clenching painfully.

"Dear God," she whispered, trying to make sense of the unimaginable evil his uncle must possess to have wanted him to drown at sea.

To pay a man to have him killed.

Westley stroked her cheek reverently, his gaze roaming her face as if he too were trying to memorize every detail should they be torn apart again. "I'm damned lucky I survived the attempt on my life. I was meant to be thrown overboard and never seen again so that my uncle could be the next Duke of Westley."

"How could he do something so evil, so wretched?"

"I cannot speak for my uncle." Westley's countenance was grim as he paused, as if the weight of what had happened to him was almost too much to bear, before continuing. "It would have been the perfect plot. Unfortunately for him, I survived. But he doesn't know that just yet."

"Does anyone know?"

Westley shook his head. "Only you, my love. I painstakingly made my way back to England, but I had to take great care in keeping my identity a secret. If he discovers I'm alive before I have sufficient proof of his plot against me, I fear he'll try to kill me again. It's been best for everyone to believe me dead."

"Is that why you were masked?"

"In part. When I learned of your impending marriage to Humberton, I was devastated. I told myself that perhaps you were better off without me, that if you were in love with a scoundrel like the earl, you weren't the woman I believed you to be. But the thought of you marrying him kept me awake at night, plaguing me, until I knew I had to speak with you. I needed to understand why, but I couldn't allow you to know who I was."

"You feared I would betray you."

"I didn't know what to think, Celandine. When we parted, you promised you would wait for me forever when I left on that blasted Grand Tour my uncle insisted upon, but not even a year had passed and you were marrying another."

"And I would have waited forever for you. I intended to. Surely you see that I had no choice. All the world believes you're dead, and I believed it too. I had to do something to save my family. I convinced myself marrying Humberton was for the best—I already knew I would never love again. That my chance for happiness had gone to the bottom of the sea with you."

"But I'm not at the bottom of the sea, my darling. I'm right here. I understand the terrible circumstances you found yourself in, and I'm sorry I couldn't have come to you sooner. If I had known—"

"No," she interrupted. "Don't say it. You came for me when you could, and just before I gave myself to him forever. I'm still yours, Westley. I'll always be yours. Nothing and no one can change that. Not time, not death, not Humberton. I love you with all my heart."

"And I love you. Marry me, Celandine," he said hoarsely. "Don't marry the earl. Be my duchess."

They stared at each other, faces close, breath mingling, wonderment and long pent-up yearning burning fiercely between them.

She didn't hesitate in her response. "Yes, my love."

"Thank God," he growled.

His lips found hers then, hungry, hot, and demanding. She needed no urging. Nor did she need wooing. Celandine was every bit as desperate for him as he was for her. And he kissed her boldly, with a commanding passion that made her knees tremble and sent desire crashing over her like the waves in a storm-tossed sea.

This was not the sweet kiss of her beloved suitor she had known before. It was the kiss of a man who had cheated death and returned to her. It was the passionate, consuming kiss of a man who was laying claim to her. And she wanted that claim.

Wanted him.

Celandine's arms, already twined around his neck, tightened. She rose on her toes to press herself more firmly against him. Still, it was somehow not enough. She wanted to wrap around him, to hold him close, to never let him go.

She opened for his questing tongue, tasting wine and Westley, a most divine flavor she'd thought up until that morning she would never know again. He was alive. Not just alive, but here, in her arms. He had rescued her.

Her Westley was *alive*.

Her tongue moved with his, and he groaned, the sound low and rough, as if it were torn from him. His hands flexed on her waist, holding her possessively, drawing her against him, the straining ridge of his erection rising thick and hard against her belly. She should have been shocked, and yet she wasn't. She wanted more.

There was an ache inside her, a restless need that grew increasingly demanding by the second. Each press of his hungry mouth over hers, every place their bodies made contact, only served to heighten that feeling.

He ended the kiss abruptly, staring down at her, his breathing ragged. "Not here, my love. Come with me upstairs."

CHAPTER FOUR

WESTLEY OFFERED CELANDINE his hand, and she took it. She would follow him anywhere. Do anything he asked of her.

She allowed him to lead her as he had not long before.

Through the entry hall, up the staircase. This time, he took her to a different bedchamber. It was larger, the bed within dominating one wall. She knew without asking what would happen here. He was going to make her his.

He cupped her face in his hands, looking at her with such love and tenderness that fresh tears rose to her eyes. Not tears of sorrow or mourning, as she had wept so many times before. But tears of true happiness. Tears of joy.

"Don't cry," he said softly. "We're together now, and no one will tear us apart."

"No one," she repeated. "I'm yours, Westley. Always."

"Forever," he vowed.

And then he kissed her again, with every bit as much passionate intensity as the last time. His hands were on her then, gentle and tender, soothing and caressing. Tapes came undone. Her riding habit fell to the floor. She returned the favor, acting instinctively, for she hadn't disrobed a man before. Her fingers found buttons and plucked them free. His waistcoat dropped. He tore his mouth from hers long enough to haul his shirt over his head, and for a moment her eyes feasted on the solid strength of his bare chest before his lips were back on hers.

The rest of their garments fell away. They kissed in a flurry of lips and tongues, their mouths never parting as they moved toward the bed. And then Westley guided her down onto the softness of the mattress and bedclothes. He followed her, his lips chasing hers with another string of deep, intoxicating kisses. With his hands, he worshipped her. Loving passes over her hip, along her waist, over her breasts. It was as if he couldn't touch her enough, as if he needed to feel her everywhere.

And she understood, because she felt the same way, her own hands traveling over the broad plane of his muscled chest, along his shoulders, over his back. She found the queue holding his golden hair away from his face and pulled it free, running her fingers through the thick, silky strands. It was longer than it had been when he left, but she liked the roguish effect—too long for fashion, as if he were some sort of pillaging pirate determined to make her his.

She gasped into his mouth, arching into his touch as his thumb stroked over her nipple, teasing it into a tight, achy point. His lips left hers to trail down her throat, then lower. He nuzzled the curve of her breast and then took the sensitive bud into his mouth, sucking.

"Oh," she gasped out, the sensation so strange, so new.

So wondrous.

He released her nipple, then flicked it with his tongue. "My sweet Celandine. You have no idea how many nights I dreamt of you in my bed. How I ached and burned with longing, knowing you were far from me."

She understood what he meant—the burning, the aching. Because inside her, there was a fire brighter and hotter than any she'd ever known. She brushed a rakish tendril of hair from his brow, her love for him so magnificent and all-consuming that she could scarcely speak.

"Please," was all she managed.

A plea for him to continue. To take her. To unite them in body and soul.

He kissed his way back to her mouth, and then sealed their lips, giving her the sinuous glide of his tongue. Molten heat poured through her, settling between her thighs, where she burned hotter still.

He had settled between her parted legs, but he had not fully pressed his naked body to hers. He did so now, and she knew the glide of his thickness over her most tender intimate flesh. He groaned into her mouth, rocking his body into hers. His erection was stiff and insistent against her, sliding through the wetness between her legs that seemed to somehow be caused by everything Westley was doing to her. It was as if her body had been fashioned for his, for this moment, this joining.

He reached between them, leveraging himself on one forearm as his lips moved over hers, his fingers dipping to unerringly find the hidden knot of pleasure within her folds. Bliss streaked through her, so sudden and shocking that she cried out, bowing from the bed, seeking more.

Westley kissed her harder, giving her what she wanted, more pressure, faster strokes, his tongue inside her mouth, the weight of his body, welcomed and strong and so very alive. She was still reeling from the realization her Westley wasn't lost to her forever, the press of his masculine flesh against hers a miracle that her mind couldn't seem to make sense of, even as the rest of her knew. Instinct took over. Instead of thinking, she felt.

Felt everything inside her lighting up at his knowing touch. Felt his fingers working her, stimulating her, driving her to an exquisite edge of something wicked. She flew apart with a gasp he swallowed with his kiss. Pleasure burst over her, sharp and delicious, wave after wave, beginning in her core and radiating outward. Celandine clutched him to her, reveling in the heated strength of his arms, his broad shoulders.

Her beautiful Westley, alive.

Here with her.

His lips left hers, and he dusted worshipful kisses over her cheekbone, to her ear. "I need you, my love."

She ran her fingers through his hair, down his back. "Yes. I need you, too."

A new sensation then. His fingers left her aching bud, and the thick, rigid length of him passed up and down her folds. Once, twice. The intimacy of the act might have embarrassed her were she not so desperate for more of the sensations he'd already visited upon her. What a wanton she was, her hips chasing his touch, an aching hollow deep inside her that could only be filled in one way. But she didn't care. Her body was his just as her heart was. She'd been his when she had thought him gone, and she was his now that he had returned to her.

He guided himself to her entrance, lifting his head to stare down at her with a pained expression, the cords in his neck taut and pronounced.

"It was my intention to wait until we were wed, but I can't wait another second," he rasped.

"I don't want you to wait." She took his face in her hands, letting him see all the unfettered love burning inside her, buried for so many agonizing months by grief. "Make me yours, Westley."

He smiled tenderly. "If it pleases my lady."

Those words, always his for her. Once, they had been teasing. Flirtatious. Now, they held so much more meaning. They were the words that had brought him back to her.

"Nothing would please your lady more," she murmured.

He lowered his mouth, covering hers in a kiss that was passionate and deep. And as he kissed her, he shifted, the movement increasing the pressure at her entrance. Her body tensed at the unfamiliar invasion, expected and yet wholly unlike anything she'd ever felt before.

"Let me in," he whispered against her lips.

She took a slow breath, filling her lungs with his beloved scent as she twined her arms around his neck. He kissed her again, rocking against her, and the sensation grew as he slowly, slowly sank inside her. Another gasp stole from her, and he claimed it as he claimed her, mouth feasting on hers, his rigid length fitting somehow deeper, finding a place that was acutely sensitive. A place where he alone belonged. She clung to him, a feverish need taking over her.

She felt exquisitely aware of everything—his breathing, his movements, the rhythmic thrusting taking her away from the initial pain and into the dizzying heights of pleasure again. It was too much, a myriad of sensations more profound than she could have imagined, and at the center of it all was the man she loved, his body atop hers, inside her, until finally his cock was moving swiftly in and out of her, sped by the wetness between her legs, by her frenzied need and the ever-tightening knot of pleasure threatening to break again.

Celandine felt the moment that he lost control, surrendering himself to the same desire that had her hips pumping in rhythmic time to his thrusts as she chased more of the pleasure he'd given her. He moved faster, the muscles in his back tensing under her questing fingertips. One more stroke of his shaft inside her, and she shattered again.

With a groan, he moved inside her. Faster, faster, and she was mindless now, her body aflame. There was no Westley and no Celandine. They were joined, hearts beating frantically as one, skin slick with perspiration. Her inner walls tightened around him, clinging to him, wringing every last drop of pleasure she could. He stiffened, thrusting into her one last time as he tore his mouth from hers and buried his face against her throat. A rush of warm wetness pulsed within her.

Celandine held him tightly, her breathing ragged, her body worn and weary and yet deliciously sated. The day had begun in misery, but now she had a reason to hope.

Her beloved Westley had returned from the dead. This time, she wouldn't let him go.

CHAPTER FIVE

"CELANDINE?" A GENTLE hand was on her bare shoulder. "Celandine, you must wake, my love."

But Celandine didn't want to open her eyes. Didn't want to awaken. Because when she did, then the marvelous dream would be over and she would realize Westley's return to her hadn't been real. That he was still as lost to her as he'd been these many long, dark, lonely months.

"No." She rolled over, weary and desperate to cling to her precious dream that her Westley was alive and that he'd rescued her from having to marry Humberton.

"My love, we've company. You need to dress."

The voice at her ear was deep and wonderfully familiar.

It hadn't been a dream.

Her eyes flew open, and she sat up, the bedclothes falling to her waist, the kiss of cool evening air on her bare breasts.

"It wasn't a dream," she said, wonder and awe taking hold, chasing any concern for modesty.

All that mattered was him.

Her love.

But he wasn't smiling at her with tenderness and love just now. Instead, his handsome face was lined with worry, his angular jaw rigid. There was something in his eyes as well, shadows and worry. His words gradually pierced the haze of slumber and love clouding her mind.

We've company.

"Who is it?" she asked, her belly tightening with dread.

"I'm not certain," Westley said grimly. "I heard hooves approaching in the distance, then silence, suggesting that whomever he is, he's tied his mount far enough away in an effort to elude notice. He'll be walking the rest of the way on foot, so we have a few minutes to prepare ourselves. I don't want you hurt. You'll need to hide in the garret until I've made certain it's safe."

Good heavens. He bore the resolute expression of a man going to battle, prepared to give his life for his cause.

"You fear it's your uncle, don't you?" she asked, her mouth going dry at the notion.

"I don't fear him. But my first concern is your welfare. You'll need to dress with all haste and get yourself to the garret."

Her denial was instant. "I'll not hide in the garret while you defend yourself."

"Celandine, you must."

"But—"

"This isn't a discussion," he interrupted sternly. "I'll not put you in danger because of me. The longer we argue, the less time I have to prepare for whoever it is who has found us here."

"Perhaps it's a passing rider," she suggested, hoping, even as she slid from the bed to retrieve her chemise and throw it on.

"No." He shook his head. "We're on my estate, and this hunting lodge is nowhere near the main roads. There's only one reason a horseman would be in this vicinity. I've taken great care with whom I trusted since my return, but it would appear I've been betrayed just the same."

"But your uncle tried to have you killed." She found her gown next, pulling it on without a care for its wrinkled state. "If that is who has come here, you cannot face him. We should escape. Take Buttercup and ride."

"I'll not run, my love. I've been waiting for this moment. I never intended to face him with you here by my side. It's my fault that he's found us before I was ready for him to do so. That's why you must hide for me. Above all, I must know you're free from harm."

There was no time to fret over the tapes of her gown. She eschewed her stockings and simply stuffed her feet into her boots. An ominous creak from below suggested that they were no longer alone.

Westley cursed, taking her hand in his.

"Come," he said with quiet urgency. "I'll show you to the garret stairs."

Her heart pounding with new fear, Celandine kept pace with Westley's long-limbed strides as he led her from the chamber. They hastened to the end of the hall, where a small paneled door blended seamlessly with the walls. He opened the latch and the door swung open, revealing a narrow, steep staircase that led to the dimly lit garret above.

Westley pressed a finger to his lips, indicating she should moved quietly.

Celandine went past him, taking the steps two at a time, determined to move as quickly as she could. But whether it was dread or her cumbersome skirts and hastily donned boots that caused her to stumble and fall, she couldn't say. All she knew was that one moment, she was scrambling up the narrow stairs, and the next, she was tumbling down them, striking her head.

Westley caught her in his strong arms before she could tumble the entire way. Wordlessly, he carried her up the stairs, his booted footfalls making too much noise on the wooden boards. When they reached the garret, he gently lowered her to her feet, cupping her face in his big hands as he examined her for injuries.

"You're bleeding, my love."

Her head ached, and at his pronouncement, she lifted her fingers instinctively to find her head wet with warm blood, a gash about a finger in length opened at her temple. But she didn't care about herself in this moment. All she did care about was him.

"I'm fine," she reassured him quietly. "You haven't time to worry over me. Leave me here."

"I can't leave you like this."

"You can, Westley. You must." Already he'd wasted precious time in lingering with her when he should be concentrating on defending himself against his uncle's murderous wrath.

"Here." He reached into his coat and extracted a handkerchief. "Press this to the wound to stay the bleeding. I'll come back to you as soon as I'm able."

She took the handkerchief, more concerned for him than the

blow she'd taken to her head in her fall. "Go. I'll wait here, as you asked of me."

His countenance was resolute. "I love you, Celandine."

She stared into his eyes, committing his handsome face to memory, praying that he hadn't returned to her from the dead only to die again. Her heart couldn't withstand losing him a second time. "And I love you, Westley. God go with you."

"How heartwarming."

The cold male voice tore a gasp from Celandine. Westley whirled about, keeping her behind his back, to face the man who had silently crept up the garret stairs without either of them being aware.

"Uncle," Westley bit out, barely suppressed rage in his voice.

Celandine peered around Westley's shoulder. A few paces away, the usurper Duke of Westley stood, flintlock pistol in hand.

"Forgive me for the interruption," drawled the man, his tone dripping with scorn. "But when I learned there were trespassers in my hunting lodge, I rode out immediately to investigate."

"Who told you?" Westley demanded, his spine stiffening.

Dear heavens. Did Westley have his weapon? How would he defend them if he didn't?

"Rogers," his uncle said. "His loyalty will certainly be justly rewarded." He gestured with his pistol. "Move slowly, both of you. Stand by the window where I can see you more clearly."

"The lady is an innocent," Westley said, remaining immobile despite his uncle's demand. "She's also injured. I would ask that you release her."

"And why should I wish to do so?" His uncle's lip curled. "No, I don't think that I'll be allowing her to flee so that she can carry the tale of what happens here to anyone. Now step into the light, both of you."

He meant to kill them both, Celandine realized, horror making her throat tighten.

"There's no reason to harm her," Westley cajoled. "I'm the one you want. Let the lady go."

"Perhaps you've failed to notice I'm the one holding the weapon," his uncle said sharply. "To the window. At once! Do as I say, and I'll consider sparing her."

"If you harm us, all the world will know you for a murderer," Westley said, moving them slowly, with grave care, toward one of the small windows at the sloped end of the garret. "Killing us defies all logic and reason."

"On the contrary, my dear nephew. It's the perfect plan. You see, everyone already believes you're dead."

They stopped near the window, Westley continuing to keep Celandine shielded behind his body. "The man you sent to kill me knows I'm alive."

"Bah." His uncle dismissed the notion with great disdain. "He's nothing but a criminal. No one would believe his word over that of a duke. Moreover, where is he now?"

"He is in London," Westley said. "Along with all the proof of what you've done. Let us go, and I'll see that you're treated with lenience. There's no need to become a murderer in truth. You'll be hanged."

"You're lying," his uncle snapped. "Do you truly think I'm stupid? You may have succeeded in thwarting death on that ship, but you'll not do so this time, and neither will your whore."

"Don't you dare to besmirch her," Westley growled.

Celandine couldn't remain hidden behind his back any longer. They had to do something to save themselves, or his uncle would kill them both. The double-barrel held two shots without the necessity of reloading, one for Westley and one for Celandine. She couldn't lose him. Wouldn't lose him. Her mind worked to frantically form a plan, some means of distracting Westley's uncle so that he might be able to wrest the flintlock from his grasp.

It was their only hope.

"I'll dare anything I like if it brings me what is owed to me," his uncle said coldly. "*I* should have been the duke. A mere circumstance of birth kept me from what should have been mine. Your father had a weak constitution. I've always been hale and strong. I was my father's favorite.

"And then you came along, to rob any hope I possessed of one day claiming my birthright. I settled upon an easy solution—send you on a Grand Tour. You were so wonderfully easy to sway. With the war over and Boney exiled, it was the perfect time to send you away and then send you to the bottom of the sea."

"You envied my father," Westley said hoarsely. "You coveted what he had."

"I wanted what was mine."

"But it's not yours," Celandine countered, stepping from behind her beloved's back, at his side, facing the monster who had tried to take him from her and who would now attempt to do so again. Her chin went up in defiance. "You aren't the rightful duke, and you never were. You're the second son. A vile, hateful man who would try to kill his own flesh and blood out of greed."

"Celandine," Westley said in soft warning.

He likely feared she would incite his uncle to shoot her. But she would gladly give her own life for Westley's if she must. She would do anything for him.

"You've a barbed tongue on you, don't you?" his uncle snarled, aiming at her now. "Perhaps I'll kill you first, just to make him suffer before he dies."

When she'd moved from behind Westley's protective back, she had loosened her boot by rolling her ankle to the side. Now, she discreetly slipped her foot from the boot, her actions shielded by the hem of her gown.

"I would gladly give my life for his," Celandine declared, meaning those words to her marrow.

And then it was time.

She dropped the handkerchief she'd been pressing to her wounded head, watching it flutter to the floor precisely where she'd intended for it to land. "Oh dear." She pressed her hand to her wound, raising fingers that were red with blood. "I've dropped my handkerchief. May I at least retrieve it? I'm bleeding."

His uncle's eyes narrowed at her, suspicion evident. "I suppose you may. No need for you to bleed everywhere until I've had my say with my nephew."

Thank heavens. She hadn't been certain he would agree. Celandine cast a meaningful glance at Westley, hoping he could read everything she needed to tell him in her eyes. Then she bent her knees, taking care to make certain her skirts obstructed the view of her boot. When she retrieved the bloodied handkerchief, she swiftly reached beneath her hem, seizing the boot. Without thought, she hurled it toward Westley's uncle.

Everything happened with impossible haste. Her aim was true, her boot sending the flintlock clattering to the floor as an explosion went off and shattered glass rained down. With a roar, Westley charged at his uncle, who still stood perilously near to the steep, narrow garret stairs. The two of them went crashing down in a series of horrible thuds.

Celandine ran after them, scrambling down the stairs to where they'd fallen, Westley atop his uncle. His uncle's neck was bent at an unnatural angle, and he didn't appear to be moving or breathing, his eyes open wide, unblinking.

"Westley!" she cried as she reached them.

Had he been wounded? Had he been shot? Had he been otherwise injured in the fall down the stairs?

"My love." He rolled away from his uncle, rising to his feet in haste. "Are you hurt?"

She frantically searched his person for any sign of blood and found none. "No. Are you?"

"A bit bruised, but I'll live." He took her in his arms and held her so tightly that his crushing embrace might have been painful had she not been so overwhelmed by relief.

He was safe.

She was safe.

And his evil uncle…

She stiffened, remembering the villain lying on the floor, the man who had repeatedly tried to kill Westley and who would have murdered her as well. "Your uncle—is he…?"

"Dead," Westley confirmed grimly. "He must have broken his neck in the fall."

"You're safe," she breathed. "He can never try to hurt you again."

"You saved me." Westley drew back slightly, gazing down at her with so much love that her heart ached. "You saved us both, my brave darling."

"We saved each other," she told him, smiling through her tears of love and relief. "It was meant to be, just like we are."

He cupped her face in his hands, catching a fallen teardrop on the pad of his thumb. "I'll secure a special license. I want to marry as soon as we're able. I'll pay your father's debts, and I'll spend the rest of my life loving you with everything I have. We've spent too much time apart as it is."

There was no answer save one for the man she'd always loved.

"Yes," she told him.

Some time later, as they rode Buttercup away from the hunting lodge and toward a future together, Celandine turned to slant a glance over her shoulder.

"Westley?"

He glanced down at her. "Yes, love?"

"Would you kiss me now?"

He gave her a devastating grin. "If it pleases my lady."

"It pleases your lady very much."

Her beloved Westley lowered his head and claimed her lips with his.

The End

Additional Dragonblade books by Author Scarlett Scott

The Sins and Scoundrels Series
Duke of Depravity (Book 1)
Prince of Persuasion (Book 2)
Marquess of Mayhem (Book 3)
Earl of Every Sin (Book 4)
Duke of Debauchery (Book 5)

Also from Scarlett Scott
Sarah (Novella)

About Scarlett Scott

Bestselling author Scarlett Scott writes steamy Victorian and Regency historical romances with strong, intelligent heroines and sexy alpha heroes. She lives in Pennsylvania with her Canadian husband, their adorable identical twins, and one TV-loving dog.

A self-professed literary junkie and nerd, she loves reading anything but especially romance novels, poetry, and Middle English verse. When she's not reading, writing, wrangling toddlers, or camping, you can catch up with her on her website. Hearing from readers never fails to make her day.

LINKS:
Website: www.scarlettscottauthor.com
Facebook: facebook.com/ScarlettScottAuthor
BookBub: bookbub.com/profile/scarlett-scott
Instagram: instagram.com/scarlettscottauthor
Pinterest: pinterest.com/scarlettscott
Twitter: twitter.com/scarscoromance

DILEMMA OVER A DUKE

by Alexa Aston

PROLOGUE

Devonshire—1806

L ADY EVANGELINE EASTFIELD rose and dressed, not bothering to call her maid. She was usually up early most mornings, even before many of the servants began to stir. Evie enjoyed walking Valwood Park, seeing the sun come up. She would dress in breeches to do so, along with one of her brother David's old topcoats, since it was easier to don the garb of a man without assistance. Only after her return home and her bath would she allow her maid to place her in demure gowns, her hair dressed properly and not tumbling to her waist.

As she slipped from the house, she had a destination in mind this morning and headed to the bridge which spanned the stream separating her family's land from that of the Duke of Wentworth's. The duke and Evie's father, the Earl of Valwood, had been close friends since the cradle. Her own brother and Hatch, the duke's elder son, were the best of friends, as well. Today, Hatch would leave them, reporting for duty in His Majesty's Army in the fight against Bonaparte.

And Evie wanted to see her friend once last time before he departed.

The two families had dined together at Davenport Hall last night, a merry group telling stories that spanned decades. But Evie wanted to say her own, private goodbye to Hatch.

Within minutes, she had reached the bridge, spotting Hatch standing in its center, gazing out. He didn't bother to glance at her as she joined him, keeping his eyes to where the sun would soon make its appearance.

"You knew I would be here," he finally said.

She turned to face him, seeing how dashing he looked in his regimental colors. "Yes, Lieutenant. Will it be Lieutenant Davenport—or Lieutenant Hatchley?"

His gaze met hers, his eyes glinting with a bit of mischief. "Since the Earl of Hatchley is my courtesy title, I believe I will stick with Lieutenant Davenport. Most of my fellow officers, though from the aristocracy, do not hold titles themselves. No need to stick out like a sore thumb."

Evie playfully punched him in the arm. "You will always stand above others, Hatch, and not because of your height. You are a true leader. Brave, honorable, and wise beyond your years."

He smiled. "I am glad you have such a high opinion of me, Evie." Sighing, he added, "I shall miss you."

Though Hatch was one and twenty, the same as her brother, and six years her senior, they had always been close.

"Thank you for letting me always tag along with you and David. You've taught me so much. How to swim. Shoot. Ride. I know you are David's best friend, Hatch, but you are mine, too."

He smoothed her hair. "You are forever a breath of fresh air, Evie. I never minded your company." He laughed. "And sometimes preferred it over David's."

She knew he was teasing her now. "Have you and Your Grace made your peace?"

The duke had been furious when his heir decided to enter the army upon graduating from Cambridge, but he had seemed to accept things last night.

"Papa is only mildly annoyed with me now, a nice change from when he roared that he wished he could disown me." Hatch's tone grew serious. "I feel I must fight for my country, Evie. Good leaders are needed. This war with Bonaparte has already gone on far too long. He threatens not only our way of life—but the balance of Europe hangs with the outcome of this conflict."

Hatch chuckled. "Besides, could you imagine Elias going off to war?"

Evie laughed. "Elias cannot stand a wrinkle in his trousers, much less for his hair to be mussed. Your younger brother is a charming man, but he is not one for war."

They both turned back to gaze across to where the sun now broke the horizon. Hatch slipped an arm about her shoulder, and Evie leaned into him. She would miss this man dreadfully.

"I'll write," she promised.

"No, you won't."

"I will," she insisted.

"You will soon make your come-out and forget all about writing. You will wed and have a bevy of brats by the time I return to England."

Evie snorted. "First of all, I am only ten and five and will not make my come-out for a good three years, Lieutenant. As for a husband, don't tell Papa, but I plan to have at least three Seasons before I consider taking one."

"Three?" he asked, laughing.

"Yes. I have spent my entire life in Devonshire, being told what to do. By my parents. My governess. I want to live a little, Hatch. The Season is all about having fun and making new friends. Experiencing life. I shall go to balls and routs. Venetian breakfasts and the theater. Garden parties and musicales. And card parties."

Hatch smiled fondly at her. "I believe you will enjoy your come-out immensely, Evie. You are full of life. You will attract all kinds of gentlemen. They will fall madly in love with you."

She sniffed. "Love is not for me," she declared.

"You are not interested in a love match?" he asked.

"I don't believe in them, Hatch. My parents—and yours—are not in love. They have amiable relationships, however. I think the notion of love is foolish. When I do finally decide to settle down and become a boring matron with a house full of children, I want a man who will like me. Respect me. And let me go my own way. Pursue my own interests. Love, if it exists, would simply muddy those waters. No, I will find an interesting man who doesn't gamble. One who will enjoy my company and that of our children. But love is not something I foresee in my future."

"Then I cannot wait to meet this future husband of yours," Hatch said lightly. "I hope he will treasure you as much as I do."

Evie gazed up at her friend, a constant in her life. "I will miss you, Hatch. And I won't think of wedding any gentleman who would take exception to our friendship."

He smiled at her, the sun now striking his face, lighting up his golden mane of hair and causing his startling blue eyes to gleam.

"I will miss you as well, Evie. I cannot promise I will write you. I know not what war truly is like, and I will have many responsibilities as an officer. But I will read your every letter. They will bring me comfort."

Hatch paused. "It's time I returned home and told my parents and Elias goodbye. Take care, little one."

He clasped her shoulders, his large hands warm, and pressed a long kiss to her brow. Evie closed her eyes, taking in the moment.

Then his lips moved and touched her own briefly.

"I won't say goodbye," he told her. "I will simply say farewell."

Evie gazed up at him, her lips tingling, an odd feeling running through her. "Until we meet again."

She turned, determined to be the one to walk away before she cried, knowing her tears would upset him.

And with every step Evie Eastfield took away from him, she knew she would always remember the sweetness of his kiss.

CHAPTER ONE

London—August 1812

E VIE THANKED AND dismissed her maid before staring into the mirror, assessing her appearance. She studied her image carefully, thinking how she had now been through three Seasons. The first had been exciting, everything new and wonderful. The people. The parties. Her wardrobe. The second year, some of the polish had worn off, and she wasn't quite as impressed with Polite Society or the events she attended. Worse, she made only one new friend, as opposed to three good ones that first year, all of whom had wed at Season's end.

Now in her third Season, Evie was done with the *ton*. Everyone talked about the same, dull things, such as the weather, or they gossiped viciously about anyone not in their immediate circle, savaging reputations for sport. She found herself bored. Uninterested.

And ready to go home to the green hills and coast of Devonshire, where her heart lay.

Since Devon was home, she decided she must wed a gentleman from her home county. That considerably narrowed the list of eligible bachelors, but Evie was a practical woman and had already picked out her groom. She would propose to her neighbor, Elias Davenport, tonight.

Elias was handsome, charming, and as affable as a man could be. Although she had spent more of her childhood with his brother Hatch, they had grown up together and were immensely comfortable in one another's company. While Elias held no title, his father had provided his younger son with a smart townhouse in London, as well as a quarterly allowance. Better yet, Elias would never think to interfere with anything Evie planned. He would lead his life; she would lead her own. He would be the perfect husband for her.

She simply had to convince him to marry her.

Tonight was one of the last events of the Season, which would officially close in three days. While Evie had her pick of beaux over the last few years, most of the men who paid attention to her were tiresome and annoying, not to mention overbearing. While they paid her pretty compliments, she didn't think a single one of them was interested in her as a person. Rather, they were interested in her large dowry. She shuddered to think what her life would be if she wed one of them.

"It must be tonight," she said aloud, knowing her parents grew weary of her unmarried status. Mama had even worried aloud that Evie would soon be on the shelf. She was afraid if she didn't take the initiative and determine her own fate, Papa might get the notion to arrange a marriage for her.

Determination filled her as she left her bedchamber and went downstairs, riding the short way to Lord and Lady Tucker's house with her parents. As her mother babbled on, Evie's gaze met her father's. He shrugged and looked out the window. She did the same.

Always popular at a ball, a bevy of gentlemen flocked to her, eager to sign her programme. Thankfully, one of them was Elias. They always danced one set together, both of them graceful dancers.

"May I?" Elias asked, reaching for her dance card.

"Could we possibly share the supper dance?" she asked quietly.

He looked puzzled but scrawled his name beside it. "You wish to speak to me about something, Lady Evangeline?"

She merely smiled. "I look forward to dancing with you, Mr. Davenport."

When the supper dance arrived, they partnered together. Evie knew they drew looks from others. They would be a handsome couple for years to come, and her heart told her this was the right decision.

Unfortunately, Elias led them to a table of his friends, and she said, "I was hoping for a bit of privacy."

Frowning, he said, "Might we speak after supper? We could stroll the gardens before the orchestra begins playing again."

Wanting to accommodate him, she agreed. While she wasn't fond of the crowd Elias ran with, it wasn't as if she were wedding them. She was pleasant to all, her usual effervescence on display.

When she finished eating, she waited patiently. Elias did not let her down.

Turning to her, he said, "The supper room is overheated. Would you care to take a stroll in the moonlight, my lady?"

"That would be most agreeable," Evie replied, rising and placing her arm on his sleeve.

Once outside, they moved along the terrace. A few other couples had the same idea, but Elias steered her to the far end.

"What did you wish to discuss, Evie?"

She steeled herself, not certain how he would react to her bold idea.

"I have not seen you courting any particular young lady, Elias. Has no woman tugged at your heartstrings?"

He laughed. "You know me better than that. Papa was pushing for me to wed before he took ill last September and left us. Though Mama has taken up the banner, I do not think I will wed for several more years. I enjoy my freedom too much."

"What if you could have marriage—and freedom?" she challenged.

His brows knit together. "Forgive me, for I am clueless. What are you saying, Evie?"

"It is time for me to wed, Elias. I would rather it be someone I know and like." She paused, letting her words sink in, and then saw understanding dawn on his face.

"You wish for *us* to wed?" he asked, incredulous.

"Think about it," she said. "We already know all there is to know about one another, so there would be no surprises in that regard. Our families are close. I feel at home at Davenport Hall, just as you do at Valwood Park. Better yet, we can be frank with one another. I am not that fond of the *ton* and life in town, Elias. I much prefer the country, whereas you loathe the quiet and enjoy being in London. Can't you see—we are a perfect match."

Nodding, he said, "You are suggesting we could lead very separate lives."

"I am. Of course, I want children. You would have to do your duty in that regard, but I would prefer to raise them in the country under my hand. You know your mother and I would always welcome you home. Hatch, too."

The thought of Hatch gave her pause for a moment. She had not seen her old friend since he left for war six years ago. When the Duke of Wentworth passed last autumn, a letter was sent to the warfront, summoning Hatch home to take up his ducal title. From what Evie gathered, it had taken months to reach him, and Hatch had only returned to England in May. He had gone straight to Davenport Hall to assume his duties and had sent word to his mother and brother that he would not partake in this year's Season.

For a moment, she thought what Hatch would think of her scheme to wed his brother. The new duke knew what a strong will Evie possessed, so it probably would not surprise him to know she arranged her own marriage, down to proposing to her future fiancé.

Elias grew thoughtful. "Your offer is very appealing, Evie. We get on well and always have. While you didn't pay much attention to me when you were younger, I have enjoyed being in your company ever since your come-out."

To encourage him, she said, "We do enjoy one another's company. I would be happy to come to town during the Season and stay as long as you wish, accompanying you to events. I know, though, that you would most likely choose to remain in town a good part of the year, while I would be happy to remain in the country. You could pursue your own interests, and I could do the same."

He grinned. "It would be nice, having a beautiful, thoughtful wife who let me live as I choose." Taking her hand, Elias added, "I would never embarrass you, Evie. I would be discreet in taking lovers."

Feeling her cheeks heat, she said, "I appreciate that effort. You would be expected to be home for events, such as our children's births. Possibly their birthdays. But I am willing to give you a great deal of freedom, Elias. If you promise to give the same to me in return."

He took her hand, raising it to his lips, kissing her fingers tenderly. "I think it would be jolly good to have a wife I liked. Who was actually a friend. Who let me be myself and have my own friends, as well."

"Remember, Elias, that I expect the same. While I have no plans to take a lover, I want to follow my own interests."

Beaming at her, he said, "Then we should make this official. It doesn't do for you to have offered for me."

Dropping to one knee—which Evie knew would draw the attention of other couples on the terrace—Elias asked, sincerity in his eyes and voice, "Lady Evangeline, would you make me the happiest of men and marry me?"

For a moment, Evie paused, hoping she was doing the right thing. "Yes, Mr. Davenport. I would be happy to become your wife."

He sprang to his feet and kissed her lightly. As she expected, Evie felt nothing. She had kissed several men over the last three years. Not one time had anything stirred within her.

Unlike long ago . . .

Shoving that thought aside, she smiled at her future husband. "I am glad we came to our arrangement, Elias. It is a respectable match. One where we do not have to worry about love or such nonsense."

"Shall we go inside and speak to your parents?" He glanced about. "It seems we are already being whispered about as it is."

Evie saw they had gained the notice of everyone present on the terrace. "Yes, we should speak to my parents and your mother," she agreed.

As they moved toward the ballroom doors, a few called congratulations to them, and she smiled graciously. Inside, Elias said he would fetch her father, while Evie went to find her mother and the Duchess of Wentworth. They were seated together, ready to watch the dancing which was about to begin.

"Might I ask you to come with me?" she asked, drawing a perplexed look from her mother and a knowing one from Her Grace.

Her father and Elias joined them. From the look on Papa's face, she could tell Elias had formally asked him for her hand.

Papa smiled at her, moving to kiss her cheek. "Well, Evangeline. I hear you and Elias wish to share some good news with us." He turned to his wife. "Look lively, Lady Valwood. Your daughter is about to become betrothed."

Mama gasped. "Oh, Evangeline. How wonderful!"

Mama hugged her tightly, and then the Duchess of Wentworth embraced her, saying, "My husband always wanted for our families to be joined. Not only in friendship, but in marriage." Then quietly, the duchess added, "I only hope you are choosing the right son of mine to wed."

Color flooded Evie's cheeks. "I am most happy to be engaged to Elias, Your Grace."

"We must start planning for the wedding," Mama declared, looking at her and Elias. "Is early October agreeable to the two of you?"

"Whatever Evie wishes," Elias said diplomatically. "I aim to please her always."

"Thank you," she told him. To her mother, Evie said, "October would be wonderful, Mama. Elias plans to stay in town another month, but we can return to Devonshire and plan the wedding."

"Then we shall leave tomorrow," Mama said. "You must come, too, Your Grace. Your advice will be much desired."

"Go see if Lord Tucker will allow you to make the announcement, Valwood," Her Grace commanded.

Papa went scurrying off, and soon the entire ballroom was aware of the wedding to take place between Lady Evangeline Eastfield and Mr. Elias Davenport.

Evie slipped into bed just before dawn. Satisfaction filled her. She would have a husband who was malleable. One who would let her do as she pleased and give her the children she wanted. She fell asleep quickly, but was restless as she slumbered.

Because for the first time ever, she dreamed of Hatch.

CHAPTER TWO

Davenport Hall—Devonshire

EDGAR DAVENPORT, FORMERLY the Earl of Hatchley, awoke with a start. When he slept, nightmares of the war plagued him. Men dying. Crying desperately for their mothers. Bleeding into the soil, limbs mangled, holes shot through them.

He should be grateful he was fortunate enough to come back to the green peace of England after six years on the battlefront. Those years, though, had aged Hatch. Ruined him beyond repair. Even now, guilt flowed through him, knowing that he had left good soldiers behind, ones who had followed him into battle without regard to life or limb.

War was hell. It should be outlawed. It ate a man's soul alive, leaving an empty shell.

Of course, his return had been because his father died, the only event which would have caused Hatch to return home. Take up his title. Look after the tenants at Davenport Hall and the other ducal estates scattered about the country.

And to hope that Evie might have waited for him.

He'd come straight to Devonshire once news of his father's death in September reached him. The letter caught up to Hatch, who'd been constantly on the move the following April, after Wellington had captured Badajoz. He'd requested an audience with Wellington himself, informing his commander of the Duke of Wentworth's death. Wellington had studied Hatch a long moment before telling him Godspeed and sending him back to England.

Duty lay heavily upon him, knowing no one had taken up the mantle of the duke for many months. While every estate manager on each of the ducal properties was experienced and held in high esteem, Hatch had wanted to personally come first to Davenport Hall. Then he traveled to his other estates, staying at each a few days, making certain the transition of authority had gone smoothly and everyone was cared for.

By the time he'd visited each estate and returned to Davenport Hall, the Season was almost over. He'd written his mother and brother, telling them of his plans when he arrived home. He'd never been especially close to either, preferring the company of David and Evie, who seemed more like family to him. In his letter to his mother, he had inquired about Lord and Lady Valwood, along with their children. He learned all four were in excellent health and that Lady Valwood was lamenting the fact that her daughter had yet to wed.

Evie had written to Hatch four times over the years since they'd parted. When she'd promised to do so, he hadn't thought much of it. Evie wasn't one for reading and writing, preferring to be out on the land. The fact she had written that many times touched him. He carried her letters inside his scarlet regimental coat, close to his heart.

Hatch had always loved Evie. He had never spoken those words to her, however. She was six years his junior, on the cusp of womanhood and yet still a child when he went away to the Continent and war. It would have been unfair to burden her with a proclamation, declaring his love for her. At the same time, Evie was practical to the bone. To her, love was nothing but nonsense. He'd hoped one day, though, he could come home and tell her of his feelings for her. Now that she was a woman, still unwed, he prayed that she might give him a chance.

He didn't deserve her. No man did. Evie was sunshine and happiness. And while Hatch might now be a powerful and wealthy duke, he was scarred, both physically and in his soul. His cheek now bore a scar. Half the length of his index finger, a painful reminder of a brief tangle with a French bastard Hatch had dispatched to Hell. Inside him was a black chaos, swirling, making him restless.

Evie could ground him. Evie might give him hope. Evie would show him the way to a better tomorrow.

For the both of them.

That is, if she hadn't accepted a marriage proposal during the last part of the Season. Even Hatch knew how after weeks of social activities, a sudden rush to the church occurred between many couples. Some were men trying to neatly tie up a dowry of the lady they had wooed during the Season. Some betrothals were urged by parents, wanting to see their sons and daughters in a state of matrimony. A few engagements, he supposed, might be actual love matches, men and women who had fallen in love with one another and chose to spend the rest of their lives together in bliss.

He wouldn't hold out hope that Evie hadn't become betrothed. If she had, it was what was meant to be. After all, she had told him she would take three Seasons and then enter matrimony with an agreeable fellow. But if she hadn't chosen a husband—if no one had caught her fancy—then perhaps, scar and all, he might have a chance to make his case to her for why she should become his duchess.

Instead of riding, as he usually did upon rising, Hatch decided to go for a walk. The bridge between his estate and Valwood Park called to him. It had been the last place he had seen Evie, and his thoughts drove him there.

Much to his surprise, he saw a figure at the center of the bridge. As he drew closer, he realized it was a woman. Then he halted in his tracks.

It was Evie . . .

Heart racing, Hatch forced one foot in front of the other, moving silently toward her. She leaned, elbows on the rail, her palms nestled against her cheeks, waiting for the sun to appear.

"Fancy seeing you here," he said, his deep voice breaking the quiet.

Startled, she swung around, facing him. Hatch caught his breath, gazing at her.

Evie Eastfield had grown into a lovely woman. Her caramel hair fell to her waist. Those moss green eyes loomed large in a face of delicate beauty. Her lips parted, and all he wanted to do was latch on to her and drink from them.

"Hatch! You scared me! I mean, Your Grace," she corrected,

casting her eyes down.

His finger went to her chin, tilting it up until their eyes met. "I never knew Evie Eastfield to be afraid of anything."

Her throaty laugh caused desire to shoot through him. He made his finger fall away, wishing he could smooth it against the curve of her jaw.

"I am still afraid of grass snakes," she admitted. "Added to that are women of the *ton* who speak as adders." She shivered.

"You did not find Polite Society to your liking?" he asked, catching the faint scent of lavender coming off her skin.

Wrinkling her nose, Evie said, "I did make a few lovely friends. Unfortunately, they all wed the moment they received a marriage proposal. What I was left with were some very mean acquaintances, Hatch. I mean, Your Grace."

"None of that, Evie," Hatch commanded. "We are old friends. I am still Hatch to you, I hope."

"I still think of you that way. Or Colonel Davenport. Your father passed along news to mine of your rise in rank."

"Do I hear you chastising me in your tone? Because I did not write to you."

She sniffed. "I didn't think you would. You practically told me you wouldn't. And yet I did hope I would hear from you at some point. I do understand that chasing Bonaparte and his allies kept you quite busy, though." Now, her tone was teasing.

Taking her hand, Hatch said, "I would have written if I had anything I could have said to you, Evie."

"You wrote your parents. Your brother. David twice."

"Yes, a handful of letters which said nothing." He paused, their gazes meeting. "I told them a few amusing stories about my fellow officers or my men. But you? I could never have lied to you." Hatch swallowed. "War is deplorable, Evie. It's the greatest blight mankind ever saw. I was miserable the entire time, knowing my death could come any moment as I led men into battle. I hated every minute of it. If I had written you, that is what I would have said, and I would not have had you worry about me."

She squeezed his fingers. "That awful?"

"Violent death always is. I saw my fair share of it. It changed me.

I am hollow inside now. Part of me feels guilty because I survived when so many others lost their lives. Another part rejoiced at the news of my father's death because I knew I would be freed from the bonds of war, something I took on willingly, having no idea of its true horrors."

With her free hand, the pad of her thumb touched his scar. "And this?"

"A never-ending reminder of my foolishness. I was so idealistic, Evie. I went to fight for honor. Glory. I thought it was the right thing, the only thing, and I was meant to lead men." He laughed harshly. "All it did was break me. Damage my soul beyond repair."

He was telling her this because she needed to know. He was broken. Flawed. Cynical. She was still so lovely. Fresh. Untouched. Unmarked by the sights and sounds he had endured.

Her hand fell from his face. She pulled her other hand from his. Standing on tiptoe, she placed her hands on his shoulders.

"You saw the harsh realities of war, Hatch. You survived. I know you did good while you were away. You are a man men trust. I'm certain your soldiers adored you." She squeezed hard. "But you are home now. Leave it to others to fight this war. Somehow, some way, Bonaparte shall be defeated. And you will have been a part of that effort."

Smiling up at him, she added, "In the meantime, you are come home to us. A duke, no less. You will make for a fine one. While your father was conscientious, you are a man apart. You will care for your tenants as no Duke of Wentworth has before now. You will keep old traditions and start new ones." Her eyes grew serious. "You will never forget what you saw, Hatch, but you will learn to set it aside. Close the door on it. Live your life here in peace."

Evie released her hold on him. He caught her hands, bringing them to his lips and tenderly kissing them, causing color to rise in her cheeks.

"Thank you. You have always been wise beyond your years. I value our friendship."

His throat grew thick. Hatch wanted to say more, but the words seemed to stick. He realized he needed to give her time to accept he was back. Grow used to his company again. Even watch to see if his scar was off-putting. Once he determined if things could be good between them, he would then speak his mind to her.

Or stay forever silent.

Her radiant smile bolstered him, though. For the first time since his first engagement in battle, he felt like the old Hatch. Hope sprang within him.

"I treasure our friendship, as well. And I have news for you. Something which I hope will make you happy. We are soon to be related, Hatch."

Confusion filled him. "What . . . do you mean?"

"Elias and I are betrothed. We plan to wed at the beginning of October."

CHAPTER THREE

E VIE RETURNED TO the house, glad she had run into Hatch and given him the news about her upcoming wedding in person. Afterward, they had talked briefly about things Hatch was doing about the estate, which had prevented him from traveling to town for the Season.

While Hatch was still as handsome as ever, she had sensed a hardness in him. Anger filled her, seeing how the war had affected him. Some of the best and brightest men of this generation had gone off to war, never to return. She should be thankful Hatch had come home to them, yet part of him had definitely been left on the battlefield. He had spoken of darkness in his soul, and that greatly concerned her. Perhaps seeing his brother settled in marriage might make Hatch think of claiming a duchess for himself. If he could find a kind, sensitive woman and have children with her, Evie guessed the burden Hatch carried deep within him might lessen.

She returned to her bedchamber, ringing for her maid and dressing for the day. After breakfast this morning, she and Mama were to go into the village and speak with Mrs. Hamshaw.

When she arrived at breakfast, it surprised her to see David. Evie squealed, falling into his arms.

"What are you doing home? I thought you and Elias were coming down together in a few weeks. Why, you had to have left the day after us to already be in Devonshire."

David seated her at the table and took his place across from her. Papa usually ate later, while Mama always took a tray in her room for the morning meal.

"I knew I would be bored with you gone from town," her

brother admitted. "And the fact you are getting married made me want to spend time with you."

Evie laughed. "I will only reside a few miles from Valwood Park for most of the year though I will go to town for the Season. That is, unless I am increasing. The journey to London is far too rough and long to be made in that condition."

A footman poured tea for her and coffee for her brother, as another brought each plates filled with eggs, ham, and toast points. She smeared marmalade on her toast and bit into it.

"I also thought I might visit with our new duke," David continued, stirring sugar into his coffee. "I was disappointed when Hatch did not come to town."

"I saw him this morning," she revealed. "You know Hatch. Filled with concern for his tenants. As responsible as ever. He has a list which must be pages long of all he wants to do at Davenport Hall and on the estate itself. Did you know he's also visited all his ducal properties since his return home?"

"Doesn't surprise me. Hatch will be a role model for every peer in the land. He will be thorough in his duties and a shining example to all. What will be most difficult for him is the way ladies will swarm him next Season. After all, he is now a duke in need of a duchess."

The thought of those vipers clinging to Hatch left a bad taste in Evie's mouth. As his future sister-in-law, she would help him steer clear of certain individuals.

"Will you go see him today?" she asked.

"Probably tomorrow," David replied. "I would like to get settled here first."

She bit back a smile. "Then tell Mrs. Ludlow hello for me."

He had the decency to blush. "Do I have no secrets from you?"

"Mrs. Ludlow is a pretty widow. If you choose to see one another, it is none of my business." Pausing, she added, "But David, you are going to need to find a wife of your own, you know."

"When I am thirty," he declared. "That gives me three years. Perhaps I can talk Hatch into waiting until then, as well." He grinned shamelessly. "Until then, I will frequent Mrs. Ludlow's and others, seeking . . . companionship."

Two hours later, Evie rode with Mama to East Davenport. The village had taken its name from its two best-known families in the area at least two hundred years ago.

"I do not see why you wish for Mrs. Hamshaw to sew your gown, Evangeline," Mama complained. "We could have had one made up in town for you."

"Mrs. Hamshaw's gowns have always pleased me, Mama. Her work makes my heart sing. I want to look my best on my wedding day, and will in one of her creations."

They entered the dressmaker's shop, being greeted fondly.

"I hear there's to be a wedding," the seamstress said.

"I would have no other but you make my gown, Mrs. Hamshaw."

"It does my bones good to hear you say that, Lady Evie. Let's see if any of your measurements have changed."

They took an hour to look at various fabrics, finally settling on a gown of the palest powder blue with a beautiful lace overlay. The square neckline would show an appropriate amount of her bosom, and she adored the capped sleeves.

"I shall start on this at once, my lady," Mrs. Hamshaw told her. "I'll send word when you can come for a fitting. I'll tinker a bit with it before we do a final one. Wedding's the first week in October?"

"Yes. Now, let's look at veils."

After they finished, Mama said she had a headache and would return straight to Valwood Park.

"I am craving one of Mrs. Oatman's scones. I will walk back."

"Oh, it is so far, Evangeline."

"I enjoy the exercise, Mama. Besides, walking allows me to eat all the scones I want," she said breezily.

She saw Mama to the carriage and walked down the main thoroughfare until she reached the bakery. Heavenly smells hung in the air. Evie started to go inside but heard her name called. Turning, she saw Hatch.

"Your Grace!" she greeted.

"Lady Evie," he said, swinging from his horse and tying it to a post. "Are you in the mood for a treat? Lemon blueberry—or raspberry almond?"

"You still remember what scones I like?"

He studied her. "I remember everything about you."

A shiver danced along her spine.

"Then come have a scone with me, Your Grace."

He ordered one of each for her and a cranberry orange scone for himself, as well as a pot of tea. Mrs. Hamshaw had three tables inside the bakery and two outside, and they chose to sit in the late August sun.

"David is home," she informed Hatch after their tea arrived. "He said he would come visit you tomorrow."

"Why not today?" He chuckled. "Don't tell me. Some pretty widow has turned his head."

"You know him well. A Mrs. Ludlow. He has seen her several times over the past two years. They have an understanding. She knows nothing will come of it, but he does buy her a nice trinket here and there. He told me he plans to wed at thirty and wants to see if you will hold out that long with him."

His face solemn, Hatch said, "I have no plans to ever wed."

"But you must," she insisted. "Davenport Hall should be filled with children. After all, a duke needs an heir and a spare."

"Come riding with me," he said suddenly. "This afternoon. I would like to show you some of the things I have done and see what you think."

"You do not need my approval, Hatch."

"But I would like it anyway."

Again, his words caused a shiver to run through her. It was a pleasant feeling—yet it seemed to warn her. She pushed aside the thought. This was Hatch, after all.

"I would be pleased to ride with you. Shall I invite David?"

"He will be keeping Mrs. Ludlow company," Hatch said. "We will make it just us."

They made plans to meet at the Valwood stables. If the end of their ride coincided with teatime, he would stay for it.

"Don't tell Lady Valwood," he begged. "While I like your mother a good deal, I fear now that I am a duke, it will cause her head to spin to entertain me at tea."

"I promise to keep silent as the grave," Evie teased.

She left him in East Davenport, where he said he was going to a fitting with the tailor, and walked back to Valwood Park, taking her time to pick a bouquet of flowers and arranging them when she arrived home.

Evie changed into her riding habit and went down to the stables, where Hatch stood waiting next to a horse she had never seen before. She started to ask him about why he wasn't riding Rex, the horse he had taken to war, and bit back the question. Hatch had been very affected by his time at war. He may have lost his horse during battle. Talking about its absence might upset him.

She also wondered if he might be bothered by the small scar marring his cheek. He hadn't explained how he received it when she touched it. Evie decided to let sleeping dogs lie and simply enjoy their ride together.

Joseph, Valwood's head groom, led her horse from the stables. "Got Starlight all saddled and ready for you, my lady." He gazed up at the sky and then back to them. "Might want to keep your ride short, Your Grace. Looks like rain to me."

Hatch glanced at the sky. "I don't see any indication of rain."

The groom patted his hips with his hands. "Hips don't lie, Your Grace. I can feel in my old bones that a storm is coming."

"We'll keep that in mind," Hatch said, assisting Evie into the saddle and mounting his own horse.

Without asking, he spurred his horse into a gallop, and she followed. They had always enjoyed racing one another and did so until the end of the meadow. He pulled up on his reins as she and Starlight flew by him and then came to a halt.

"I love to give Starlight her head," she said. "It's so good to have you home again, Hatch."

"Let's head to my estate so I can show you some of the changes I'm implementing."

They cantered to his property, and he showed her a new fence being built and another which was in the midst of repairs. They went by some of his tenants' cottages, where he pointed out the ongoing work. Everyone greeted the new duke with enthusiasm, and Evie saw that whether he realized or not, Hatch was in his element. He would make for a wonderful Duke of Wentworth, his people loving him as much as his soldiers had.

The foreman invited them inside for a glass of cider and a tea-cake. By the time they left the cottage, the skies had darkened.

"Joseph has been proven right after all," Evie commented.

As they started for Valwood Park, the bottom suddenly dropped from the skies.

"Follow me!" called Hatch, riding ahead of her.

She followed and saw they came to what looked like an abandoned cottage. They sprang from their horses, Hatch tying the reins to a nearby bush, and sprinted toward the door. Inside, the cottage was dusty and neglected. Floorboards needed repairing. A windowpane was missing. She spotted three places where leaks had sprung in the roof and moved to a corner to avoid the incoming drips.

Evie shivered, cold and wet, and Hatch began briskly rubbing his large hands up and down her arms, trying to warm her. She appreciated the effort. Then her heart began to race wildly. She inhaled the woodsy scent of his cologne, coupled with a muskiness. Suddenly, she was aware of him. As a man.

Their gazes met, and those brilliant blue eyes of his burned.

With desire . . .

No man had looked at her as Hatch did now. It thrilled her. Excited her. Frightened her. Worried her.

Her heart continued pounding, almost seeming to fly from her chest, as she saw him slowly, deliberately lowering his head. Any moment now, his lips would graze hers.

This was wrong. Hatch was her good friend. She was betrothed to another man.

His brother.

And yet Evie wanted to sample whatever he might give her.

Their lips touched. It was as if kindling had been lit. His hands, holding her shoulders, tightened. Fire raced through her.

His lips were firm yet soft. Eager yet restrained. It seemed as if he waited for her to do something. What, she hadn't a clue.

Not wanting to wait, she broke the kiss and stared at him. Heat sizzled in his eyes.

"You want something of me," she said, breathless. "I don't understand. But I want to."

"Have you kissed a man before, Evie?" Hatch asked, his voice hoarse.

"Yes. Several times."

"What was it like?"

She frowned. "I'm not certain what you mean. Pleasant. At least a few times. Awkward on two occasions."

His eyes burned into her now. "But how were those kisses?"

"Just . . . kisses," she said, frustrated. "Ordinary, lips pressed together. What more—"

His thumb silenced her. "Then you haven't been kissed properly."

The most radiant smile lit his face then, taking her breath away. All of a sudden Hatch was no friend. He was a living, breathing, sensual man, heat rolling from him, placing her under his spell.

"I intend to teach you how to kiss."

It was unwise to go along with this scheme. Evie should stop this madness. Yet curiosity won out.

"Go right ahead," she said.

So he did.

CHAPTER FOUR

H ATCH'S LIPS TOUCHED hers again. Soft. Grazing. *Tempting . . .*

Evie wrapped her arms about his waist, stepping into him, their bodies touching, his scent and warmth enveloping her. His lips teased, placing soft kisses against hers. Then his tongue came into play, totally shocking her sensibilities. He ran its tip over her lips ever so slowly, outlining her mouth, causing her to tremble.

Need for more swept through her. Without thinking, her tongue began to mimic what he had done, causing a sharp intake of breath from him. Then his mouth covered hers, and she could feel his smile. His tongue lazily glided back and forth across the seam of her mouth, urging her to open to him.

So she did.

Now, it was Evie's turn to gasp as Hatch's tongue swept into her mouth. Tasting. Taking. Nudging. The kiss deepened, her senses out of control. Her knees weakened, and she clung to him. Slowly, he possessed her. Body. Mind. Soul.

And she wanted even more . . .

He broke the kiss, and she mewled a protest, only to have his lips blaze a trail down her throat. Hatch stopped where her pulse beat wildly out of control, nipping the skin, bringing a deep yearning. He nipped again, then his tongue soothed the spot. His mouth returned to hers, his teeth sinking into her lower lip, causing a burst of flames inside her. Evie moaned. Afraid he would stop. Afraid he wouldn't.

His mouth descended upon hers again, hot, demanding, in-sistent. Their tongues warred playfully, and she sighed. Her breasts seemed to rise, and his palm went to one, kneading it, causing her to sigh.

Somehow, he maneuvered her, and they were sitting. Rather, Hatch was sitting in a dilapidated chair and Evie was in his lap. His fingertips brushed the swell of her breast and then freed it from her bodice. His mouth fixed upon it, sucking hard, making her core pulse out of control. Hot need filled her. Her nails bit into his shoulders, her head tossed back as his tongue toyed with her nipple. She began panting with urgency. Needing relief.

His lips returned to hers, the kisses long and drugging, even as his hand massaged her breast. Then it moved lower, coming to rest upon her thigh. It glided back and forth, coming perilously close to her womanhood. She shouldn't want his hand there.

But she did.

A moan escaped her, and Hatch broke the kiss. His clear eyes pinned hers.

"I'm going to touch you where no man ever has. You will respond like you never have."

"I will like it?" she asked hesitantly.

He grinned. "You will love it," he assured her.

His fingers tickled her ankle, slipping under her gown and up her calf, moving sensually. They traveled higher and though she knew their destination, Evie couldn't quite comprehend it.

Hatch moved her slightly on his lap, giving him better access to her. Suddenly, his scorching touch reached her most private place, which pulsed violently. He ran a finger along the seam of her sex, and Evie whimpered.

Those fingers danced. Stroked. Pushed inside her. Curled in an intimate caress which threatened to devastate her. Her breath quickened. Her senses came alive. Anticipation flooded her.

Then she shattered in his arms, calling his name, half-crying, half-laughing as her body went to unchartered territory. The waves of pleasure overcame her, and her body was no longer her own.

It was his.

And always would be.

Instinctively, Evie knew no man could make her feel the way Hatch did. Yet guilt raced through her. This was how her husband was to touch her. Or a lover, once she had provided the required heir. Of course, with Elias not possessing a title, he didn't even need an heir. Still, she had made clear to him that she wanted children, and he had agreed to give them to her.

The thought of Elias touching her so intimately almost made her ill. He was her betrothed, however. She had already betrayed him and couldn't allow things to go any further with Hatch.

Quickly, Evie scrambled from his lap, her breath coming in short spurts. She wrapped her arms about her, wishing to protect herself from further wrongdoing.

He rose, his gaze steady. "Evie?" he asked huskily, making her want him all over.

"I am engaged, Your Grace," she said shakily. "To your brother. What we did was wrong. It cannot happen again." She looked at him pleadingly. "Please. Say it won't."

He held his hands open to her. "How can I agree to give up the very thing I need to live?" he asked. "I love you, Evie. I have from the time we were children."

"What? Why did you never say anything?"

Stepping toward her, he cupped her face in his hands, making her feel cherished.

"I could not tell you before. You were so young, and I was afraid sharing my feelings would frighten you."

Anger simmered within her. "Then you should have spoken up before you left for war."

"Perhaps. But I was afraid I would not come back." He gazed down at her. "How could I tell you I loved you? That I wished for you to wait for me to return—when I wasn't certain that I would."

He brushed his lips softly against hers. "You were young. Too young. It would have been wrong of me to ask you to keep from making your come-out. You needed the chance to live. To grow. To be free. To become . . . you."

Anguish filled her. "If I had known of your feelings . . ." Her voice trailed off.

"They would have frightened you. Or you would have laughed. I recall our last conversation before I left for the Continent. You were quite adamant about not believing in love."

"I . . . I still don't know if I do," she said.

Hatch kissed her nose. "Ah, that is my stubborn Evie."

Though she wanted to push him away, she was afraid she might die without his touch. His kiss. And so Evie's hand clasped his nape, drawing his mouth to hers.

They kissed a long time, each kiss heartfelt. Deep. Sensual. Loving.

Could she really be in love with Hatch?

She ended the kiss. "Why do you love me?"

He shrugged. "What's not to love? You're clever. Brave. Interesting. Amusing. Charming. Full of spirit. How could I not love you, Evie?"

"No one has truly loved me," she said quietly. "Well, David, I suppose. Papa blithely ignores me because I am a female. Mama has always been absorbed in herself. I met many gentlemen these past three Seasons, Hatch. They have wooed me. Kissed me. Yet none ever made me feel the way you do. I am trying to understand all this."

"Perhaps you love me and didn't even know you did," he suggested.

"I don't know!" she cried, frustration spilling from her. "How can I know what love is? I'm so confused. You seem so certain. Why don't I feel the same?"

"Then you must think on things," he encouraged. "You are also quite practical, Evie. It might be harder for a practical person to fall in love."

Not knowing how to ask him, she blurted out, "Do men and women . . . do they do together what we just did? Would a husband and wife do such a thing?"

He smiled. "That. And more," he said enigmatically.

"I have never felt inside the way I did when any man kissed me," she admitted. "Kissing you was very different."

His brow creased. "What of when Elias has kissed you?"

She snorted. "Elias has never kissed me. Well, one brief kiss, which was barely a kiss at all."

"What?" His shock was evident. "Then why did he offer for you without having kissed you?"

Sheepishly, Evie said, "Actually, I proposed to him."

Hatch roared with laughter. "Why on earth did you do so?"

Wringing her hands, she told him, "After three Seasons, my parents were growing frustrated with me. I discovered I am not one for town. I decided to take control of my fate and choose my own husband."

"Aha! Someone you could manipulate into doing your bidding?"

"Yes," she admitted. "Elias prefers town and his crowd. Most couples go their separate ways in a marriage. At least Elias is known to me. We like one another. I would never be far from home. He promised to give me children. I told him he could remain in town for the most part. We are comfortable with one another. It would work." She paused and corrected herself. "It will work."

His eyes narrowed. "How do you think it will work, Evie? Elias living across the country. You, living in close quarters with me. Knowing I love you and would do anything for you." His eyes darkened with desire. "Knowing I will do anything to you—and that you cannot resist."

She bit her lip. "You and I were supposed to remain friends. *You* are the one who has ruined things, Hatch. I was going to have a pleasant life in the country. Do as I wish." She paused. "Now, I won't be able to stay at Davenport Hall. I will be forced to live in town. Unless you would grant Elias leave for us to live at another of your ducal properties."

He clasped her elbows. "No, Evie. You will not wed Elias. He is not the man for you. *I* am that man. Even if you do not love me, I know you like me." His wicked grin caused her breath to hitch. "And you like what I do to your body."

Exasperation filled her. "How can I break my promise to Elias?"

He yanked her to him, pinning her against his muscular chest. "You will wed only me, Evie. Whether you love me or not. Because I am the one who can make you happy. I make your pulse jump. Your body shiver in anticipation. I will plant my seed within you and give you the children you desire. The life you want is what you will have. As my duchess."

Evie slapped him.

She regretted it immediately, but did not apologize. Instead, she marched from the cottage and untangled Starlight's reins, pushing herself into the saddle and riding away in the rain. From what had happened between them. From the guilt and remorse that filled her.

And from the hot desire that she now knew was so addictive.

CHAPTER FIVE

E VIE DID THE only thing she could think to do.

She wrote to Elias and begged him to come home at once.

Her betrothed was supposed to stay in town with his friends for another few weeks before he came back to Devonshire. Usually, Elias escorted his mother home, but this time, the Duchess of Wentworth had traveled home with her family.

She had yet to see Her Grace—and now pondered what the regal woman meant when she remarked if Evie were marrying the right son.

Had the duchess known of Hatch's feelings for her?

Hatch was a quiet man, unlike his outgoing brother. If he truly had these feelings for her all these years, he had certainly kept them to himself. She liked the fact that he had respected the age difference between them and not frightened her with a declaration of love in her youth.

Evie wondered if that was why he'd given her the brief kiss on the bridge that morning before he'd gone off to war.

She fretted that it would take Elias a good two weeks before he arrived home. By the time he received her letter and then packed and returned to the country, she would have spent more time in Hatch's company—which came to pass.

With David enthusiastic about spending time with his sister, and thrilled his best friend was now home, he wanted the three of them to be together often. They had gone for numerous rides. On these outings, Hatch conducted himself as a perfect gentleman, but Evie now looked at him with new eyes. His hands clasping her waist to toss her into the saddle. The brush of their legs together at tea. All of a sudden, she was more than aware of him as a man.

And her attraction to him.

She still wasn't certain whether she loved him or not, but she was intrigued by how she now responded to him. Evie thought about Hatch constantly. She wanted to pull him into an empty room and kiss him for hours. She needed to explore his muscular frame as his own fingers had explored her body. Evie told herself it was lust, not love.

Yet thoughts of Elias touching her in such a manner disgusted her.

In order for her to bear the children she so desperately wanted, her husband would have to be intimate with her. But now, she wanted the only man touching her to be Hatch. How could she be with a man who didn't have his goodness? His kindness. His courage. His thoughtfulness and care for responsibilities. Where once Evie had thought she would be happy wedding Elias and blithely accepting the fact they would go their separate ways, now she wanted more in her marriage. A closeness. An intimacy. Not only of bodies—but minds.

That moment of realization led Evie to believe that she was, in fact, in love with Hatch.

He and his mother came to tea that afternoon, and she quickly whispered to him they must talk. Though Hatch acted as if he hadn't heard her request, near the end of tea, he turned to her.

"Evie, were you going to show me that book in the library you wished for me to read?"

Oh, he was good.

"Yes," she said brightly. "Would you like to come look at it now?"

"Of course. If you will excuse us," he said to the others.

She thought it amusing that during her come-out and each Season beyond, it would have been totally against Polite Society's rules for her to be alone in the company of a gentleman. She would have been ruined—and that man would have needed to do the honorable thing and wed her. Circumstances were different with Hatch, however. They had been brought up together, and her parents looked upon the duke as another son, thinking nothing of the two of them going off alone together.

Once in the library, Evie became tongue-tied, and Hatch asked, "What is it?"

Not certain she could say what was in her heart, she decided her actions would speak for her. Clasping the lapels of his coat, she yanked his mouth down to hers, and he was only too happy to accommodate her.

Evie kissed Hatch with a desperation born of need. Desire for this man flowed through her veins, and she communicated that to him in her kiss.

The kiss was wild. Wanton. And deeply satisfying, letting her know this was the man she was destined to always love.

Hatch was the one to end the kiss and looked at her questioningly.

Finding her voice, she said, "I think I do love you, Hatch." She swallowed, correcting herself. "I know I love you. If wanting to only be with you is love. I think about you constantly. I yearn for your kiss. I can only see a future with you."

His smile caused warmth to radiate within her, and he embraced her, holding her close, making her feel cherished. He kissed the top of her head, no words between them. Evie thought if he only held her like this until the end of time, it would be enough. He was enough. Together, they could do anything.

Hatch said, "We should tell Elias together."

"No," she protested, breaking away. "I'm the one who got us into this mess. It is my responsibility to speak to Elias."

His gaze showed admiration for her. "When is he to return?"

"I wrote to him, asking if he would come immediately." She smiled weakly. "I thought if he were here, it would give me the strength to avoid you. As these days have passed, however, avoiding you is the last thing I wish to do."

"Then you will wed me, Evie?"

"If you are offering, Hatch, I am accepting."

He kissed her enthusiastically.

"Not a word to our parents," he cautioned. "It is only right for Elias to know first."

"Send word to me the minute he arrives at Davenport Hall."

※

TWO DAYS LATER, Evie and David sat on the front lawn of Valwood Park. Hatch had left a few minutes earlier.

"I see a rider," David commented, taking a sip of tea.

Evie's heart thundered. Instinctively, she knew it was Elias and recognized him as he drew nearer.

Looking at her brother, she said, "I must speak to him alone."

"Of course," David said, standing and kissing her brow, waiting to greet Elias before leaving.

She stood, too, waiting for her fiancé, nerves flitting through her. She was doing the right thing, yet she would hurt this man.

Elias brought his horse to a halt and slipped from the saddle, looking at her hesitantly. "I came as soon as I received your letter, Evie."

David said, "Good to see you, Elias. I'll take your horse to the stables to be watered."

Elias thanked him, and Evie indicated they sit.

Frowning, her betrothed said, "I was ready to leave town for a house party. What is going on?"

"I am sorry you had to change your plans because of me," she apologized.

"It wasn't very sporting of you, Evie. I thought we had made our arrangement clear."

"Do you truly wish to wed me, Elias?" she asked pointedly.

His gaze fell as he flushed. "We have the best of both worlds if we wed," he said stiffly. "We can be married to someone we are fond of and yet pursue our own interests."

"What of love?"

Elias looked shocked. "You, of all people, ask about love? This was your idea, Evie. I merely agreed to it. Love has nothing to do with us."

"What if I wished to break things off?" she challenged. Studying him carefully, she noted relief flashed in his eyes.

Still, he said, "If you cry off, Evie, it won't set well with the *ton*. A broken engagement, no matter who ends things, always reflects poorly on the woman. I won't have tongues wagging about you.

You are as a sister to me."

She reached and took his hand. "And that is why things must end between us, Elias. I want to continue to be a sister to you." Pausing, she added, "In fact, I will be a true sister to you. A sister-in-law."

Watching, she saw the moment he realized the meaning behind her words. Then a slow smile spread across his face.

"Hatch finally spoke up, did he?"

"What do you mean?"

"I suspected how he felt about you. He never voiced it, but I felt it." Taking her hands in his now, he said, "This is the best of news, Evie. I am relieved. I wasn't ready for marriage, but our agreement made perfect sense to me."

"If you knew Hatch had feelings for me, why did you even agree to wed me?"

"Because I didn't think you looked at him in that regard. I can see, though, that you do have feelings for my brother. I couldn't be happier for the both of you."

"The gossip will fly," she noted. "Lady Evangeline Eastfield betrothed to one brother, yet wedding another."

Elias laughed. "Polite Society will say you tossed me aside in order to become a duchess." He squeezed her hands. "But the last laugh will on the *ton*, for I believe a great love story will play out between you and Hatch."

"You are taking this quite well, Elias. I thought you would be upset with me. Even angry."

"I am gaining a wonderful sister while maintaining my freedom." He grinned. "I'm certain the ladies will feel sorry for me and wish to comfort me in my loss."

"Why, you devil!" she exclaimed. "You'll turn this to your advantage."

He shrugged nonchalantly. "We are both getting what we want, Evie." He raised their joined hands and kissed her fingers. "No bitterness on my part. I wish you and Hatch all the best."

"Then I suppose the banns may be read starting this coming Sunday," she mused. "Won't the villagers receive a surprise when they hear the names announced?"

Evie and Elias both laughed, and her former fiancé said, "We must inform our parents of the change in plans. And Hatch. I hope he knows you love him."

She smiled. "He does. I never thought I would love my husband, but I love Hatch, heart and soul. I hope you'll find a love of your own someday, Elias."

"Maybe in a few years. For now, I celebrate my brother's love for you, Evie."

EPILOGUE

London—Twenty years later . . .

E VIE REVELED IN the final kiss her husband gave her, their naked
limbs entwined.

"We must rise and dress," Hatch said. "After all, our daughter's
come-out ball is happening tonight."

She stroked his cheek. "I only hope that Elizabeth is as lucky in
love as we have been, husband. I want all our children to make love
matches."

He kissed her again, long and deep. "Now, out of our bed and go
straight to your bedchamber. Your maid must be having a fit of
apoplexy."

Rising, Evie slipped into Hatch's banyan, the sleeves far too long
for her. "She is used to it. All the servants are," she said flippantly.
"They are happy to work in such a home, where the Duke of
Wentworth adores his duchess."

Hatch climbed from the bed, ringing for his valet. "Out, woman!" he teased.

She went through his dressing room and their shared bathing
chamber before passing through her own dressing room, arriving in
the duchess' bedchamber. Evie never slept here. She stayed each
night with her husband and used this room for changing her
clothing.

"There you are, Your Grace," Martha said, biting back a smile.
"I've got your ballgown laid out for you. Let's get you ready for
Lady Elizabeth's ball."

The Season had started four weeks ago. Tonight, they hosted a
ball for their eldest child, Elizabeth, who had made her come-out

this spring, Evie only wished their two sons, who were away at Eton, could be here for this night, but they were finishing up their term. Hatch had said to let the boys be when she had thought to summon them home early, saying boys that age had no interest in balls.

As Martha put the finishing touches on Evie's hair, she glanced in the mirror and saw Hatch looming in the background, so handsome in his evening wear.

"You have made my duchess look like a queen, Martha," the duke praised, causing the servant to blush.

"She's all yours, Your Grace," Martha said.

After the maid left, Hatch asked, "Are you ready to visit our girl?"

"I am."

They went down the corridor, and Hatch tapped lightly on his daughter's bedchamber door. Another maid answered, and said, "Come in, Your Graces. Lady Elizabeth is ready."

As they entered the room, pride swelled within Evie when she caught sight of their daughter. Elizabeth had her mother's caramel hair and her father's incredibly blue eyes, and those eyes now were lit with excitement.

"Mama! Papa! Oh, I cannot wait for my ball to begin," Elizabeth declared.

Stepping forward, she embraced her daughter. "Your father and I have something to give you."

Her daughter frowned. "But you already gave me that beautiful sapphire necklace the opening night of the Season."

Hatch joined them, opening the palm of his hand, revealing the matching earrings to the necklace Elizabeth mentioned. Her eyes widened.

"Earrings? I love them!" Elizabeth claimed them and placed them on her earlobes, bending to check her image in the mirror. "They are perfect. Thank you so much."

She hugged both her parents, and Evie had to blink back tears. She saw her husband did the same.

In his deep voice, Hatch asked, "Has any particular gentleman caught your eye yet?"

Elizabeth blushed. "Yes. Lord Morrow. He is more than handsome, Papa. He actually listens to me after he asks a question. Most gentlemen seem to lose interest in a conversation quickly, but Lord Morrow always is engaged."

"Does he make your heart sing?" Hatch asked.

"Do you get lightheaded and quick-hearted when he comes near?" Evie added.

"Yes. And yes," their daughter said, laughing. "I think about him all the time."

"Then you need to kiss him," Hatch advised.

"Papa!" Elizbeth said, punching him in the arm. "Fathers are not supposed to tell their daughters to go about kissing men."

"I agree with your papa," Evie said. "One kiss should do it. Then you will know for certain."

Elizabeth placed fisted hands upon her waist. "All right. I shall figure out how to do so. Tonight." She patted her hair. "We should go downstairs. Grandmama will be waiting. You know she does not like it when others are late. *Especially* you two."

They allowed their daughter to leave the bedchamber, then Hatch tucked Evie's hand through the crook of his arm.

"She is exuberant," he said.

"She is magnificent," Evie corrected. "I smell a love match with Lord Morrow. What do you think of him?"

"I like what I know of him. I shall get to know him better," Hatch promised.

They went to the ballroom, where the musicians were warming up. It was as if a garden had been moved indoors, with the scent of roses lingering in the air.

Elizabeth was showing the Dowager Duchess of Wentworth her new earrings.

"They are lovely, my dear."

Evie joined her mother-in-law, who said, "You have raised a remarkable daughter, Evie, as well as two incredible sons." The duchess smiled. "More importantly, you have made my son very happy. I am glad you changed your mind all those years ago and wed the right son of mine."

"Elias is most happy with his choice of a wife," she replied.

"Both Agnes and I found the right partners in your two sons, Your Grace."

Hatch indicated to their butler to allow their guests inside, and Elizabeth came to stand next to her grandmama, chattering away to her.

Evie looked up at Hatch, who joined her. "Thank you for admitting to me all those years ago that you loved me. I think back on the years we've shared—and the ones yet to come. I cannot see myself with anyone else by my side but you, my darling."

Hatch caressed her cheek. "We were meant to be together, my love."

Her husband bent to press his mouth to hers, causing those of the *ton* who entered to chuckle fondly, seeing the Duke and Duchess of Wentworth were still crazy for one another.

And would be so until their dying day.

The End

Additional Dragonblade books by Author Alexa Aston

The Strongs of Shadowcrest Series
The Duke's Unexpected Love (Book 1)
The Perks of Loving a Viscount (Book 2)
Falling for the Marquess (Book 3)
The Captain and the Duchess (Book 4)
Courtship at Shadowcrest (Book 5)

Suddenly a Duke Series
Portrait of the Duke (Book 1)
Music for the Duke (Book 2)
Polishing the Duke (Book 3)
Designs on the Duke (Book 4)
Fashioning the Duke (Book 5)
Love Blooms with the Duke (Book 6)
Training the Duke (Book 7)
Investigating the Duke (Book 8)

Second Sons of London Series
Educated By The Earl (Book 1)
Debating With The Duke (Book 2)
Empowered By The Earl (Book 3)
Made for the Marquess (Book 4)
Dubious about the Duke (Book 5)
Valued by the Viscount (Book 6)
Meant for the Marquess (Book 7)

Dukes Done Wrong Series
Discouraging the Duke (Book 1)
Deflecting the Duke (Book 2)
Disrupting the Duke (Book 3)
Delighting the Duke (Book 4)

Destiny with a Duke (Book 5)

Dukes of Distinction Series
Duke of Renown (Book 1)
Duke of Charm (Book 2)
Duke of Disrepute (Book 3)
Duke of Arrogance (Book 4)
Duke of Honor (Book 5)
The Duke That I Want (Book 6)

The St. Clairs Series
Devoted to the Duke (Book 1)
Midnight with the Marquess (Book 2)
Embracing the Earl (Book 3)
Defending the Duke (Book 4)
Suddenly a St. Clair (Book 5)
Starlight Night (Novella)
The Twelve Days of Love (Novella)

Soldiers & Soulmates Series
To Heal an Earl (Book 1)
To Tame a Rogue (Book 2)
To Trust a Duke (Book 3)
To Save a Love (Book 4)
To Win a Widow (Book 5)
Yuletide at Gillingham (Novella)

King's Cousins Series
The Pawn (Book 1)
The Heir (Book 2)
The Bastard (Book 3)

Medieval Runaway Wives
Song of the Heart (Book 1)
A Promise of Tomorrow (Book 2)
Destined for Love (Book 3)

Knights of Honor Series
Word of Honor (Book 1)

Marked by Honor (Book 2)
Code of Honor (Book 3)
Journey to Honor (Book 4)
Heart of Honor (Book 5)
Bold in Honor (Book 6)
Love and Honor (Book 7)
Gift of Honor (Book 8)
Path to Honor (Book 9)
Return to Honor (Book 10)

The Lyon's Den Series
The Lyon's Lady Love

Pirates of Britannia Series
God of the Seas

De Wolfe Pack: The Series
Rise of de Wolfe

The de Wolfes of Esterley Castle
Diana
Derek
Thea

Also from Alexa Aston
The Bridge to Love (Novella)
One Magic Night

About Alexa Aston

USA Today and Amazon Top 10 bestselling author Alexa Aston lives with her husband in a Dallas suburb, where she eats her fair share of dark chocolate and plots while she walks every morning. She enjoys travel and sports—and can't get enough of *Survivor* or *The Crown*.

Her Regency and Medieval historical romances bring to life loveable rogues and dashing knights. Her series include: *The Strongs of Shadowcrest, Suddenly a Duke, Second Sons of London, Dukes Done Wrong, Dukes of Distinction, Soldiers and Soulmates, The St. Clairs, The de Wolfes of Esterley Castle, The King's Cousins, Medieval Runaway Wives,* and *The Knights of Honor.*

THE DUKE'S DAY OFF

by Annabelle Anders

CHAPTER ONE

Glenbrook Castle, England
1834

"DOES YOUR VALET steam your trousers, darling, or simply hang them from the wardrobe hoping the wrinkles will fall out on their own?" The Duchess of Ferris took a delicate sip of tea and then added, "I so wish you would have hired Mr. Talbot instead of that... Smith fellow—or was it Sloth?"

"His name is Sloan, Mother." Victor Fairchild, the Duke of Ferris, stared into his tea, his mouth set in a grim line. "And he is quite capable."

After all these years, Victor ought to be accustomed to his mother's highhanded nitpicking, especially on important occasions. With Lady Lincoln and her daughter, Lady Lucinda, set to arrive today, he supposed this qualified as such.

He needn't look up to feel the disappointment in his mother's frown.

"What is that you are wearing? I'd prefer the grey waistcoat—the one that matches your eyes." She twisted around to address her companion, seated on a stool behind her. "You relayed my instructions to Mr. Smith, did you not?"

Miss Evalina Sparrow rolled her lips together, drawing Victor's attention to her mouth. Her lips were a dusky rose color, glistening, plump and inviting, but also quite off-limits.

He could appreciate them from a distance, but that was all.

Accustomed to his mother's harsh manner, she remained unruffled, casually flipping through the small journal she carried everywhere before answering. "Yes, Your Grace."

Eyes the color of jade locked with Victor's momentarily. Miss Sparrow blinked and then turned her attention to his mother. "I do not know about Mr. *Smith*, but I did, in fact, inform Mr. Sloan of your wishes. Would you like me to—"

"It's too late now," the duchess snapped, causing Victor to wince. He hated hearing his mother speak with such contempt to anyone, but especially to this particular young woman, who had borne far more than her fair share of these beratings.

Miss Sparrow, for reasons unknown, had lasted in his mother's employ for nearly a year now. None of the companions before her had lasted more than a fortnight.

Even now, any other person would be bristling or cowering. Not Evalina Sparrow.

She leaned forward and, for all intents and purposes, appeared to be quite focused on that little notebook of hers. But Victor couldn't help but notice the way her mouth twitched and the amused little twinkle in her eye.

She hid it well, but underneath that calm, professional exterior, she was smiling.

The woman was either delusional or utterly unconcerned at the possibility of displeasing the duchess. He'd wager it was the latter.

Victor's gaze followed the trail of freckles smattered across her pert nose, over the curve of her cheek and along her jaw. Her complexion was pale and her flashing green eyes sparkled beneath auburn eyebrows. Victor wondered if the hair hidden beneath the white mobcap was a deep brownish-red, ginger, or orange and gold, like the setting sun.

Regardless, his mother's companion defied the stereotypical expectations of a redhead. She also defied the expectations one had of the typical lady's companion.

She was a question wrapped up in an enigma, but as much as she intrigued him, he could never be the man to solve that equation.

Victor turned to his mother. "I chose the black, Mother. The silver waistcoat is too formal for daytime." He held tightly to his patience, a practice that was becoming more and more difficult where his mother was concerned. Furthermore, with Lady Lucinda and her mother's visit upon them, Victor had been feeling unusually tense all morning. He rolled his shoulders and then tugged at his cravat. "Neither Miss Sparrow nor Mr. Sloan is to blame."

"Harumph." Of course, rather than apologize to her companion, his mother would prefer to pout instead. The duchess never apologized to anyone. Pushing herself out of her chair, she went on as if the entire exchange had not occurred at all. "Seeing as I cannot count on others to properly relay my instructions, I'm going to have to speak with Cook myself." She shot Miss Sparrow a disapproving scowl. "I want everything to be perfect for my son's intended and her mother."

"She is not my intended," Victor reminded his mother.

Predictably, she pretended not to hear him. He didn't know why he bothered. She didn't hear a word he said, not if it contradicted her own notions and certainly not when she was in this state.

Miss Sparrow glanced up and shrugged. To his mother, she simply said, "Very well, Your Grace. If that will make you feel better."

Victor rubbed his hand over his mouth. He envied her ability to dismiss his mother's insults. After the door closed behind the duchess with a snap, he removed his glasses and rubbed the bridge of his nose.

"How do you do it?" he asked.

"Do what?"

"Put up with…" Victor shook his head. He shouldn't have said anything; such a question wasn't just inappropriate, but utterly disloyal.

"The duchess?" Miss Sparrow knew what he was asking anyway and blinked in his direction. Her grin was far too pleased and smug—and it sent his temperature spiking.

"Well, yes…" He frowned.

Miss Sparrow withdrew a pendant that she had been wearing hidden beneath her gown and leaned forward. Victor squinted, unable to make out the ivory design from across the room, but also a little distracted by the stretched fabric of her bodice. She wasn't at all frail, and yet, she was still very… ladylike.

"What is it?" he asked.

She rose and strode toward him, lifting the chain over her head as she did so. In the process, the necklace caught on her cap, partially dislodging it and revealing a few curling strands of hair.

The color of a sunset.

A glorious sunset.

Stopping before him, she handed over the necklace. "Memento mori," she said.

Carved into the face of the pendant was a simple depiction of a skull and a flower in bloom, with the Latin phrase engraved along the border. Remember, you must die.

"A little morbid, isn't it?" It was a common lesson, taught by every art and history teacher worthy of the profession.

"Not at all." She was already tucking those flaming locks back into her cap, and Victor exhaled a sad sort of sigh. "It isn't about death, so much as it is about life—we only have one. Even dukes and duchesses," she said.

"And this helps you endure my mother?"

"It is a reminder that no matter what your mother says, this is my life. It's up to me to make the most of it."

Victor frowned. She was poor. She had little to no agency. Moreover, she was at his mother's beck and call twenty-four hours a day, excepting Sunday afternoons. Even during those times, he remembered his mother making demands of her.

"Good for you, I suppose." He pinched his mouth shut. Anyone who could find joy in such circumstances must be a little mad.

"You don't believe me, do you?" She cocked her head to one side, a half-smile dancing on that mouth of hers.

"I don't not believe you," he answered cautiously. "But my mother is...a demanding woman."

"But so am I." She winked. "I... find ways to enjoy my life. You ought to try it sometime."

He lifted his brows. "Oh really?"

Miss Sparrow hesitated, biting her lip as she examined him. "I'm not sure I should say..."

Victor waved away her concerns and after a moment, she exhaled.

"At least once a month, I make it a point to... escape."

Victor blinked. "Pardon?"

"I skip a day. You know," she said, sounding less hesitant now that she'd already committed. "I simply choose an appropriate time and invent some excuse to… breathe."

He raised his brows. "I'm not following."

A shrug. "I'm not sure I could stay on otherwise…"

Victor shook his head. Had she really just confessed to shirking her duties? And yet, he couldn't blame her… Hadn't he just been thinking how Miss Sparrow was often forced to work during her free time?

But, of course, he could never do the same… could he? "It's different for me. I've a dukedom to oversee." He straightened his shoulders. And yet, he couldn't help but imagine what it might be like to toss his responsibilities to the wind, even if it was only for a day.

"All those irritating little tasks, ultimately, are meaningless—in the grand scheme of life." Her lilting voice teased him, cajoling.

He had been right to think she was mad. Nonetheless, he found himself entertaining the suggestion. But no…

"Lady Lucinda and her mother are arriving today."

"Yes. But they'll be here tomorrow—and the next day. And the day after that."

She wasn't wrong. In fact, Lady Lucinda likely expected to become a permanent resident at Glenbrook Castle—as his duchess.

The thought weighed heavy in his gut. He shook his head, but his stare remained locked with Miss Sparrow's.

"You, of all people, deserve to duck out," she said.

Victor lost himself in the depths of the varying colors of green— several shades—perhaps hundreds dancing around in her iris. Along with browns, and golds, and even a little amber…

An itching sensation pricked the back of his neck. He was charmed. And intrigued. "What are you suggesting?"

God save him, her mouth stretched into a brilliant and inviting smile.

"Meet me in the foyer in twenty minutes, and I'll show you." She held out a hand, and for an instant, he thought she expected him to take it. But no, he was still holding her pendant.

What the devil was he doing?

"I cannot. You know I cannot," he said.

"That's what makes it so delicious." She plucked her pendant out of his palm and then backed away. "It's only one day, Your Grace. One day to remind you. Memento mori."

He had dozens of tasks requiring his attention, estate reports, ledgers to audit, letters to write.

Lady Lucinda.

He ought to have rejected Miss Sparrow's offer outright and reported her admission to his mother. She was far too cheeky, too outspoken.

Far too tempting.

"I cannot," he repeated. He was a duke. She was his mother's companion. And yet, his conviction was wavering, and he knew she could see it too.

"Twenty minutes," she sang back and then sashayed out the door.

CHAPTER TWO

EVALINA FELT HER insides buzzing. Not only had she confessed to defying his mother's wishes from time to time, but she'd also invited him to join her today.

Did she regret it? Not even a little.

Because the duke deserved some time to himself. No, he needed it—more than anyone she'd ever known. Whomever he chose to marry was not her business, but she hated how the duchess's constant pressure seemed to weigh him down.

He deserved to step away for one day.

He needed some perspective, and if she was the only one willing to ensure he got it, then she'd enthusiastically rise to the task.

But even as she tore off the mobcap, her hands were shaking.

He was a duke—a handsome and wealthy one at that.

Shoving a few pins into her coiffure, she leaned forward and studied her reflection closer than usual.

Her mouth was a little too full and wide, and her skin was the canvas for literally thousands of freckles—of which she was oddly proud.

Evalina tilted her head and sighed.

What did he see when he looked at her? Just another servant? A girl who could possibly be a friend?

A woman?

Her neck turned pink at the thought.

Of course he wouldn't join her. He was expecting guests. Evalina was foolish to imagine he'd take her up on her offer, even if it was only for one day—a few hours, really.

He wouldn't tell his mother. Of that, she was certain. She didn't know why it was so easy to trust him—with information that could get her sacked, no less. It was simply a feeling she had, something she'd seen in his eyes and, well…

She just knew.

Tucking the latest book she'd nicked from the library into her satchel, and with one last glance in her tiny looking glass, Eva dashed out of her attic room and down the stairs. Before reaching the foyer, however, she slowed her steps and tightened her lips into a more neutral expression. She couldn't be seen leaving the estate with a smile of anticipation.

"Miss Sparrow," Mr. Frye, the portly butler, greeted her. "I didn't think the duchess was going out today. Important guests are due to arrive, as you know."

"The duchess isn't going out, but I must." Eva twisted her mouth into a practiced angelic expression. "The duchess promised Mrs. Peterson that I would be on hand today to assist with the charity baskets."

Mr. Frye frowned, looking confused but not at all suspicious. "She hasn't mentioned any such plans. I would have thought she'd want you on hand—"

"It's been three weeks. She's likely forgotten." Eva removed her small notebook from the deep pocket in her skirt. "I have it written right here." She turned the book for the butler to read the note she'd made a few minutes before.

"I don't suppose you can cry off—not when it's for charity," he conceded reluctantly.

"I should think not." Eva raised her brows. "What would people think?"

Before he could answer, the duke himself came sauntering down the stairs behind her. "Are you ready?" he asked, lacking any of the subtlety required for their mission.

"But Your Grace…!" Mr. Frye's eyes bulged out and his face turned a cherry red.

"Yes, Frye?" The duke glanced at the man, not at all concerned. Why would he be? He was the duke.

"You aren't leaving as well, are you?" The butler was looking quite desperate now. "Your mother… The duchess… You are expecting guests. Has there been a change in plans of which I've not been informed?"

"Not at all," the duke answered. "Lady Lincoln and her daughter are still expected today, but I won't be meeting with them until this evening. I have... er—" The duke shot Eva a wincing glance.

"You forgot these, Your Grace," Mr. Sloan, the duke's valet, announced as he descended the steps, carrying a pair of black leather gloves. And, without missing a beat, he added, "For your meeting with the vicar."

"The vicar?" The duke's brows rose, but then he dipped his chin. "Ah, yes. The vicar wanted to speak with me..."

"To discuss the proposed renovation costs," Mr. Sloan finished for the duke. "Because the chapel roof has been... leaking."

Eva met the valet's eyes and nodded in approval, pleased to know that she and the valet were of the same mind—where the duke was concerned, anyhow.

"You are both going to the church, then?" Mr. Frye's frown was the most he could do to show his disapproval without arguing with his employer.

"Are we?" The duke turned to Eva, who would have rolled her eyes toward the ceiling if Mr. Frye wasn't watching her.

"That is what you said earlier." Eva spoke slowly, as though speaking to a toddler. "Since I am going to help with the charity food baskets, and you are meeting with the vicar at the same location, it only makes sense that we'd travel together." She smiled tightly, willing him to understand that, in order for this to work, deception was necessary.

He didn't answer immediately, instead turning to accept his gloves from the valet.

But when he turned back, his expression was perhaps more innocent than hers.

"My thanks, Sloan." He gestured toward the grand entrance. "Shall we, Miss Sparrow?"

Eva blinked. "Absolutely," she replied, and not bothering to wait for the butler to open the door, they stepped outside, leaving the cool darkness of the foyer behind. Her eyes watered in the light of day, and yet a giddiness swept through her.

To know, if only for a few hours, this sense of freedom.

It was odd, though. She wouldn't have thought that she could feel like this while accompanied by the duke.

With only the sounds of their footsteps crunching on the gravel, neither spoke until they were far enough from the manor that no one would hear them.

"You told Mr. Sloan?" Eva eventually asked. The valet was a favorite amongst the servants, if not with the duchess, who didn't pay much attention to any of the staff, really.

The duke shrugged. "I would trust him with my life," he said. "In fact, I have trusted him with my life."

"He was your batman, wasn't he, while you were in the army?"

"He was," the duke answered curtly. A sensitive subject, then. Eva supposed it made sense, when the duchess seemed to take every opportunity to berate him for having purchased a commission, for having risked his life fighting in France.

He had defied his mother's wishes back then. Why didn't he now?

But she wouldn't ask. No, this was a day for fun!

Furthermore, she noticed they were heading toward the stables. She'd intended to walk to the destination she had in mind and didn't want to be cooped up inside of a coach. "Must we take the coach?" she asked. "It's such a lovely day, I'd rather spend the time outside, wouldn't you?"

"We could take my curricle," he suggested, sliding her a quick glance. "Or walk, if you'd prefer."

The two options gave her pause. She'd seen the duke drive away atop his curricle on more than one occasion, and she wondered what it would feel like to fly across the countryside at such high speeds. The leather seat was at least five feet from the ground, the exterior was painted a royal blue, and the modern contraption was pulled by a rather magnificent pair of black mares.

"I think..." She touched her chin. "I would like to ride in the curricle, but I have a request."

"And what would that be?"

She bit her lip. In for a penny, in for a pound. "I want to go fast."

Sliding her an indulgent smirk, he chuckled. "Of course you do."

It was one of those special looks he'd sent her in the past. As though the two of them were in on a secret. It was why she trusted him. It was also why she found herself thinking about him, late at night, in ways that she shouldn't.

Touching herself...

With her heart fluttering, she met and held his gaze. "Well then?" She bit her bottom lip.

"The curricle it is, then."

CHAPTER THREE

"IS THIS FAST enough for you?" Victor had to raise his voice to be heard over the spinning wheels and thumping hooves. He should have known his mother's enigmatic companion would be so intrepid, that she'd be exhilarated rather than fearful to be flying across the countryside at breakneck speeds.

She wasn't afraid of his mother, after all. The thought had him biting back a chuckle.

"Can they go faster?"

Victor risked a sideways glance to see if she was serious, but when he did so, he found himself suddenly caught up in the most unexpected sensations... Like he'd been frozen for years and was suddenly seated near a warm fire.

The wind had caught her bonnet, causing it to dangle behind her. Or perhaps it wasn't the wind. Perhaps she'd done it intentionally.

Regardless, seeing her looking so free was... dizzying.

Her eyes sparkled emerald in the sunlight, her cheeks flushed a delicate pink, and dozens of spiraling curls had escaped her coiffure to tangle around her face and behind her.

Flaming red. Wild and untamed. By God, the color was even more brilliant than he'd imagined.

And he had imagined it more than once. He'd imagined touching it under wildly inappropriate circumstances.

Was it as silky as it looked? Would she protest if he tugged on it, or would she tilt her head back, exposing her neck...

Victor swallowed hard and forced his gaze back to the road in front of them. He didn't allow himself to look over again.

She trusted him to drive safely.

As they flew down the straight road, he absorbed the sound of her laughter. It was a rich, throaty sound that vibrated through his veins and was surprisingly infectious. By the time he drew the horses to a walk and turned around to head back toward the village, he felt an unfamiliar stiffness in his cheeks. When he frowned, he realized why.

How long had he been grinning like an idiot?

"Did you have a particular destination in mind?" he asked, his voice sounding a little strangled.

"I usually purchase a pasty from Mrs. Rooney's shop," she answered. "To eat later. Food always tastes better when eaten outside."

"And where would you like to picnic?" He sent her a sideways glance, or more of a glance really, reluctant to look away.

"If I told you now, this wouldn't be a proper adventure, now would it?" Her voice caught just a little.

Victor could have argued, but decided against it. It was oddly satisfying to allow Miss Sparrow to take control.

"Do you know how to drive?" he asked impulsively.

"I drove one of my father's carts a few times, but… Pokey was only a pony. I probably could have walked faster." She turned so that she was partially facing him, and out of concern for her safety, he wound his arm around her waist.

"Well then, if today is to be a true adventure…" Still supporting her, he offered her the reins. Of course, she took them.

Twenty minutes later, following a more harrowing ride than he'd expected, they rolled into the village. They'd never been in any real danger. Victor had been prepared to take control if necessary, and yet his heart was pounding like a drum.

"I don't know how you've stayed alive this long," he commented dryly, assisting her off the tall vehicle.

She smoothed her skirts and met his gaze. "What is life without a few risks?"

Victor contemplated her philosophy as they crossed the road to Mrs. Rooney's small shop. He'd lived three and thirty years in this world, overseeing multiple estates, participating in parliament, and following all the rules. He had a legacy to uphold. There wasn't room in his life for risk.

"It's different for me," he said.

She sent him a disapproving glance just as they entered the shop, but although Mrs. Rooney studied them curiously, she happily packed up a basket with four pasties and a bottle of wine.

"For the poor," Miss Sparrow informed the lively woman before bidding her good day.

As they exited the shop, Victor raised his eyebrows at her questioningly, and she explained, "It's best to account for as many possibilities as we can. What would happen if your mother came to this very shop and heard we purchased food for a picnic instead? Or if someone else overheard and it got back to her? I would be done for."

Victor was mildly flummoxed. Her reasoning made sense, and yet... "How do you think of such things?" And why did he appreciate her cunning?

"Experience, mostly," Miss Sparrow answered lightly. "I've not been caught yet, though there have been a few close calls. But enough about that—we've a picnic waiting for us." And so saying, she practically skipped back to the curricle with the basket of food swinging from her arm. When she reached the vehicle, she made a valiant effort to climb aboard herself before Victor all but lifted her back onto the bench.

"Have you always been... a little delinquent?" he asked while storing the basket on the floor by her feet. It struck him that, aside from knowing she'd been raised in a modest household three villages over, he knew very little about her past.

Victor got the curricle moving once more, this time at a more sedate pace.

This way he could look at her if the urge struck.

"Delinquent?" she said. "I wouldn't say I'm delinquent, per se..."

"What word would you prefer, then?"

Tapping her chin, she paused, but not for long. "An opportunist, who is also a realist."

Not the answer he'd expected, and he fought back another ridiculous grin. The unpredictability was refreshing and a little...

exciting. But though it was unexpected, he didn't think her response was inaccurate. Victor recalled how she'd handled Mr. Frye in the foyer and found himself nodding. She was also very good at reading people. She had known Mr. Frye wouldn't argue with her.

And she'd known she could confide in him—someone who could have sacked her in a heartbeat.

"Do your parents appreciate these…talents?"

"My father does, but my mum says they're going to lead to my ruin someday."

Her mum was not entirely wrong, and yet, having observed her handling of his mother these past months, Victor wouldn't change anything about this woman.

There wasn't much in this life that brought him pleasure… But Miss Evalina Sparrow did. It was as baffling as it was enticing.

They travelled in companionable silence for a few minutes, until they came upon an intersection in the road and Victor realized that he still had no idea where Miss Sparrow intended to take them.

"You still haven't told me where we're going."

"Drive straight for now, then take the second turn on the left."

Victor knew the road well. "We're going to the church?"

"Yes and no. We're going to picnic in the old cemetery behind it."

"Hmm…" A cemetery, he supposed, wasn't all that extraordinary a location for a picnic. He'd spent a fair amount of time at his own family's graveyard, especially in the months following his father's death. So he didn't argue. This was her adventure, after all.

He still wasn't entirely sure why he'd agreed to it.

He'd never been the sort to lose his senses when confronted with a beautiful woman—not the gentle ladies of the *ton*, and definitely not with any of his servants.

But something about her, the way she looked at him, the way she spoke now that she'd let some of her walls down, was strangely compelling. And the bench wasn't all that wide. With each bump and turn, his awareness of the feminine curves pressed along his side waged a silent war with his conscience.

A war his conscience was losing today.

He shook his head. Truth be told, he knew precisely why he'd come.

Evalina Sparrow.

This inner war had begun months before—and had been going on since the first time he'd met her. Perhaps a full day spent in her company would free her from his thoughts. She'd say something to reveal a lack in character, or she'd bore him somehow.

It was the best he could hope for, having already committed to the outing.

"Why is it different for you?" she asked. He didn't require her to expand on her meaning. She was taking up one of their previous conversations right where they'd left off.

"Because," he said, dismissing words such as 'responsibility' and 'legacy' while contemplating his answer. "I... I am Ferris." He was the duke, as was his father, and his grandfather, going back centuries. They had fought for and won their position. It was up to him to maintain it.

"Yes. But in the end, you are still just a man."

Her words slipped right through his armor, unleashing old but familiar doubts—ones he'd believed settled years before.

"I can't expect you to understand," he said.

Rather than argue, she placed her hand on his elbow, as though to comfort him. He shook his head. What the devil was wrong with him?

Conversation fell away for the remainder of the drive, both seemingly lost in their own thoughts. By the time they drove around the church to where centuries of villagers had been laid to rest, Victor conceded that as long as he'd already skipped out on his duties for the day, he might as well enjoy himself.

He relaxed his shoulders, but it was Miss Sparrow who broke the silence. "It's quiet today."

"Vicar Handley is in London this week, so the regular services have been postponed."

Miss Sparrow simply hummed in response.

Approaching the cemetery gates, Victor slowed the vehicle to a stop and then dismounted, turning to assist Miss Sparrow after him. Her dainty hand was dwarfed in his, but her grip was firm, her touch warm even through their gloves. The sun, although high in the sky, flickered through the tall trees and some drifting clouds.

"The weather's not usually so cooperative," he remarked as she turned to retrieve the supplies for their picnic from the footwell of the curricle.

"Lucky, isn't it," Miss Sparrow chimed brightly. "It would be a shame to waste a day like this toiling away indoors. What would you have been doing anyway, if you hadn't come out with me?"

Victor tugged the gate open and gestured for Miss Sparrow to precede him through it, tempted, but not allowing himself to set his hand on her back. After the gate closed behind them, they struck out along one of the narrow dirt paths that wove throughout the gravestones.

"Correspondence, mostly," he replied. "And there is still a decent amount of work to be done before Lady Lucinda's arrival."

"She's the one you're to marry, right? According to your mother, anyway."

Victor chuckled. "You're certainly blunt."

"Life's too short to dance around hedges."

Her ensuing silence had him contemplating an answer. Lady Lucinda had all the right connections. As the daughter of a wealthy earl, she'd been raised to manage estates like his.

She would be, as his mother had said on numerous occasions, the perfect duchess.

So why did the idea affect him like fingernails scraping a chalkboard?

His arm brushed Miss Sparrow's accidentally, but rather than move away, Victor flexed his hand. Her palm met his and without considering his intentions, he'd threaded their fingers together.

"I am expected to marry her, yes." The words tasted bitter in his mouth, and he fully expected Miss Sparrow to tug out of his grasp.

He felt a gentle squeeze instead.

"Do you always have to do what people expect of you?" she asked quietly.

His pulse thrummed in his neck, and he swallowed hard.

The question ought to be easy to answer. So why did he feel so conflicted?

And then, Miss Sparrow seemingly dismissed it. She dropped his hand and had turned to examine the massive tree that marked the border of the cemetery.

The trunk was thick, with twisting branches winding around and up, and in those gnarling shapes, one could almost make out faces and limbs.

Miss Sparrow sent him a mischievous glance.

"Let's climb it," she said in that matter-of-fact manner of hers, setting the basket on the ground.

She was so spontaneous, plucky.

Her lack of inhibitions energized him and for the first time in ages, he found himself feeling...

Excited.

Any other woman, and he'd decline the suggestion outright.

But she was not any other woman. No. She was Evalina Sparrow.

"As you wish." He settled his hand on her waist, offering support she probably didn't need as she stepped onto the lowest branch and pulled herself up.

But watching her well-worn half-boots disappear into the tree, exhilaration lifted his heart. And as he grasped the branch and pulled himself up, decades fell away.

"Do you do this often?" he asked, looking up before averting his eyes from ogling her legs.

And then just as quickly stole a second glance.

Trailing his gaze up the length of stocking-covered calves and thighs, he startled to realize she was staring down at him.

"Do I allow handsome dukes to look up my skirts? Not usually, no." She was laughing!

"I certainly hope not." Victor lifted his hand to the next branch but instead of gripping it, he wound his fingers around her ankle. "Evalina."

She stilled, as though torn.

Victor lazily circled her ankle bone with his thumb and then licked his lips.

CHAPTER FOUR

HEAT SPREAD FROM Evalina's ankle, up her calves and between her thighs, unleashing a flurry of butterflies low in her belly.

She'd been attracted to the duke for a very long time. And she'd suspected he was attracted to her. But even in her wildest dreams, she'd never imagined…

That he would touch her. That he would say her name.

Evalina.

They lived in the same castle, but in different worlds.

For the first time, it was she who was looking down on him.

Shadows painted the elegant planes of his cheeks and jaw, and his lashes looked thicker and longer from this angle. Searching his stormy gray eyes, she almost forgot to breathe.

Because those eyes looked oddly vulnerable. He was not humorless. He was not cold and emotionless. Was she the only one to see him this way?

Leaving the castle today, they'd had an unspoken agreement. One where they'd not been employer and employee, but not quite friends either.

For days, weeks, months, they'd been building to something else.

Her skin tingled beneath his touch. And oh, but she wanted…

More!

Before she could respond one way or another, he dipped his head and the warmth of his hand disappeared.

While working for his mother, she'd come to like this man—very much. She'd watched as he diligently ruled his household, balancing the needs of his demanding mother. Not once had she witnessed him lose his temper. No, he'd been honorable in all things.

But she'd also suspected there was a hint of sadness behind his façade.

She had come to *adore* him.

"Is it a family name?"

"Pardon?" Her voice cracked as she sought and found another branch to climb.

"Evalina. Is it a family name?" Leaves rustled and the bark cracked as he climbed the tree below her. She lifted her foot onto a higher branch, and knowing he could see the length of her legs, her thighs… if he chose to, she felt hot all over.

"My grandmother's. On my mother's side," she replied.

"It's lovely," he said.

"Thank you," Eva answered automatically.

"When my mother first mentioned that she was going to hire a Miss Sparrow to be her companion, I imagined a much older lady."

"Oh?" Taking another step, her skirts whipped around in the breeze, but she simply continued on upwards. She knew which branch she would stop at, having climbed this tree dozens of times on her own.

"But then I met you." His climbing abilities were better than hers, and she could feel him moving directly below her. "And I was… surprised."

"Most people are surprised when they meet me," she admitted. It was an easier admission without having to see his face.

"Because you are young?"

"Because of my hair and freckles. My brother once told me I have the uncanny ability of being loud without saying a single word." She secured her foot on one last branch, and then, trusting her strength, launched herself onto the one just above it.

This particular limb had been rubbed smooth, so she could edge away from the trunk leaving room for the duke, who managed to climb on with even more grace than she had.

"I rather like your hair and freckles." A lock of his silky hair fell over his face as he made himself comfortable beside her. It lent him a boyish air. Ironically, it also made him seem a little rakish.

"Haven't done this in ages."

"You need to get out more often," Eva said. He scoffed but didn't argue as the two of them simply stared out at the view quietly.

She'd always loved finding the tallest tree and climbing as high as she could. "From up here, everything looks small." She raised a hand and pointed to a familiar shape off in the distance. "Even Glenbrook Castle."

"Hmm," the duke answered, and Eva couldn't tell if he was agreeing or merely being polite.

"Sometimes," she ventured recklessly, "We get too caught up in the details of our day-to-day life, and in the grand scheme of the universe, they're rather insignificant, really."

"Are you implying I've lost sight of the forest for the trees?" he asked.

It was precisely what she meant, so she shrugged.

The branch bounced a little, and the duke snaked an arm around her back.

"You're too far out." He pulled her closer. "If I'd realized how high you would climb, I'm not sure I'd have allowed it."

Eva could only smile as she edged toward him. "I come here all the time." Her thigh pressed into his, which was as solid as the tree itself.

And warm.

She squeezed her thighs together. It wasn't the height that made her dizzy. It was him.

"Should I be worried?" His voice dropped, low and rumbling.

Eva turned to see his expression, and as she stared at his aristocratic profile, a shiver tracked down her spine.

Despite his chiseled jaw and firm chin, he didn't look half as austere as he did at the castle. She'd caught glimpses of this side of him before, but not like this.

"You don't have to worry about me." Eva allowed her feet to dangle, feeling breathless to be sitting here with…

Her duke.

Would he have come today if he knew how often she thought about him, if he knew that her insides quaked when he sent her one of those private glances?

She focused on the horizon.

And in the quiet, she felt the duke relax beside her.

"Why haven't you married?" He asked matter-of-fact like. As though his words didn't summon unfortunate memories. Guilty memories.

"Before your mother hired me, I was betrothed…" To a widowed farmer who lived one village over. "He was a pleasant enough fellow, but…" She'd suspected he could be cruel. "I rejected his proposal. He had six children from his first wife—all sons—and not that I don't like children, but they were…" Very much like their father. Eva would have had security, but for a price. She would have been trapped, cooking, cleaning, washing, not to mention tending the massive garden required to feed all those mouths… She winced a little. "My mother was not happy."

"Hmm," he said, and Evalina felt compelled to fill the silence.

"My father is a landed gentleman. He was willing to pay for me to have a season, if I really wanted one." She dropped her gaze to the distant ground. "But it would have been too expensive. And I'm not sure I would have made a good wife."

She didn't like talking about herself. Eva knew she was… different. Her mother would say she was selfish.

"Why not?"

"After taking care of my brothers, I didn't want…" She winced a little. "Working for your mother is a dream, comparatively." She shook her head. "I can't imagine never going anywhere… doing the same thing day after day—like my mother has done."

"Do you get on well with her?"

"I love her—with all my heart—but it's no secret that I'm her greatest disappointment."

"You're clever and smart. Not to mention beautiful. How could you be a disappointment?"

Eva's breath caught at the compliment. Was he only being kind?

"She wanted me to be just like her. And I… couldn't." It was a sore spot. "When I refused to marry Mr. Harrelson… She was not happy. Applying to act as a companion was my father's idea. He understands me better than my mother ever will."

"And are you happy? Acting as a companion?"

"Your mother is a challenge, but yes. And I find unexpected perks..." She smiled. "Particularly today." There was nothing she could do to stop the heat ebbing into her cheeks. Today was immeasurably enjoyable... because of him. In all the time she'd spent in the Ferris household, she had never dreamed of having him to herself.

Even if it was only for a few hours.

He withdrew his hand from her waist and Eva's heart sank. But then...

Very deliberately he tucked his arm along hers and, threading their fingers together, clasped her hand.

Sensations both warm and sharp shot up her arm. It was a simple gesture, something friends did on occasion. So why did it feel like more than that?

His hand wasn't limp and indifferent—no, he held hers firmly. And when he ran his thumb along her skin, Eva parted her lips, unable to speak, barely able to breathe.

When he met her gaze, his grey eyes darkened, and she knew...

He felt it too.

This feeling of connection—this feeling that made no sense at all—and yet made perfect sense.

He'd said she was beautiful.

Normally she would have searched for something clever to break this improper silence, and yet she didn't want to break it. She wanted it to go on forever.

She wanted him to kiss her.

"You are beautiful, you know." His voice was low and gruff, stoking the fires inside her.

How long had she ached for this?

If he turned her bones to jelly by simply holding her hand, how would... other things feel? She imagined his mouth on her lips, her neck...

"I'm not," she said.

"But you are." The same thrill of excitement lit his eyes.

Unfortunately, the branch they were sitting on moaned and cracked. Eva froze, but of course, the duke would never allow her to fall.

"I've got you." He managed to grip her and the solid trunk at the same time.

Locking her arms around his neck, she only dangled for a moment before finding a foothold on one of the lower, sturdier branches.

Eva clung to him, speechless, as she watched their old perch tear away from the tree, taking out two other branches before it landed on the ground.

"Oh dear," was all she could say. Because that very well could have been her—or both of them.

In the silence that followed, she lifted her lashes and stared into his eyes again. They were close enough that she could see every detail, every fleck of color. "Perhaps we ought to have our picnic on the ground."

And oh! How she wished she could read his mind. With her body pressed against his, clinging to him for life—quite literally—she could feel the thrill of some unnameable emotion thrumming from her head to her toes. And ironically, she was sure it had more to do with their sudden proximity than with the near miss.

Eva wondered if he felt it too, but stopped wondering when his gaze burned into hers.

Madness!

Anything between the two of them would be wildly inappropriate! They should not, could not. And if his mother learned of this little outing…

Eva refused to imagine how that scenario might play out.

Dear God, she should pull away, create some distance between them.

He tightened his grip, holding her even closer, and it was better than she'd imagined. The heady scent of leather and vetiver teased her nostrils and her head swam, inviting her to rest her face against his chest, which was broad and sturdy and dependable.

"Are you hurt?" he asked. Was the tremor she felt his or hers?

"No. I'm…" Her thoughts in turmoil, she struggled to find words. "No."

Neither moved to climb down and her heart skipped a beat

when he brushed his mouth along her cheek. "Promise me you won't climb trees alone anymore. I can't imagine what I'd do if…"

"If?" she asked.

"I can't imagine what I'd do if I lost you."

CHAPTER FIVE

ONCE VICTOR HAD her in his arms, he couldn't let go—to keep her from falling, of course.

Or so he told himself as he steadied his feet on the lower branch.

"I cannot promise you anything..." she whispered. Her lashes fluttered and she met his stare.

He was a duke, for God's sake, and yet he couldn't promise anything either.

With her hands around his neck, her ample breasts pressed against his chest. Only the two of them existed—holding tight to a tree trunk nearly thirty feet off the ground.

Nestled on top of the world, anything was possible.

"Memento mori..." he whispered. It felt like an endearment.

"Umm hmm..." He felt her little nod.

Having watched her cope with his mother's demands for nearly a year, he respected this woman's strength and her will. But she was also clever, a little rebellious, and adorably fetching.

All of which had been slowly chipping away at his reservations.

"I... I am afraid of falling."

"If you fall, so do I," he said.

She licked her lips. "It might be too late." Her smile was a little sad and a little apologetic.

But then the clouds in his future shifted, revealing an alternate path—one he'd not allowed himself to truly contemplate.

She was a companion—his mother's companion.

But her lips were the perfect shade of pink, and shining, and she did nothing to hide her thoughts.

Falling. She was afraid of falling.

For him.

Victor grazed his chin along the side of her face, bound by himself, but also oddly free. "So sweet." So perfect. How long had he longed for her?

"Your Grace," she whispered.

"Miss Sparrow," he returned. *Evalina.*

Had he known all along it would come to this?

He grazed the tip of his tongue along her jaw, her tender flesh like that of a ripe peach. Finding the edge of her mouth, his breath mingled with hers.

"Are you going to kiss me?" she asked. Blast and damn, her voice made him feel more powerful than his title ever could.

How scandalous could a kiss be, hanging in a tree? He succumbed.

Surrender had never been so satisfying.

It was his last thought as his soul left his body, making room for hers.

Evalina's lips parted on a sigh, sweeter than honey, new and exciting, but also...

Like coming home.

His world tilted and he tightened his arm around her waist, but still she wasn't close enough. "Evalina," he murmured against her mouth.

He explored behind her teeth, savoring velvet heat, and her tongue sparred with his.

It was everything, and yet he wanted more. When he would have explored her curves, tested the weight of her breasts, touched tender skin, he was thwarted. Because his hands were occupied, one around the tree, the other around her.

Their lips made a soft kissing sound when she pulled away. "Your Grace." Her voice was a little strained, her eyes clouded with desire.

"Victor," he said.

"Victor. Today." Of course, she knew the ways of the world. It was she who'd invited him on this adventure, and yet, he spied a hint of vulnerability in her eyes. "Only today," she said.

She was right, wasn't she? Reluctant to dwell on that truth, he sought her mouth again. Having denied himself for so long, he wasn't prepared for this to end. Hell, it had barely begun.

He needed to taste her again, drink her essence, explore. Claim.

It was innocent enough.

Until it wasn't.

He was hard and throbbing, and if they were anywhere else…

He wasn't accustomed to indulging himself. He was a man who walked a straight line—a man who not only followed the rules, but enforced them. With everyone except for…

This woman.

But indulge he did. And when she needed a breath, he trailed his mouth to her jaw, dragging his teeth and tongue over her skin. This was a moment out of time. This wasn't real. It shouldn't be real.

But it was, and if he had any doubt, his obvious desire cleared that right up.

"I'm sorry," he practically hissed—frustrated.

"I didn't plan this." She ducked her head, her hair soft beneath his chin.

"I know," he reassured her.

His answer had her looking up at him again. "How do you know?"

She wasn't afraid of him. She didn't treat him like a duke. She treated him like an equal. Just a man.

He would give her an honest answer. "I've been watching you for three hundred and seven days. I…" Victor shook his head, amazed by what he was saying. "I know you."

She didn't even blink, but tilted her head to the side, so he continued.

"The day you arrived at Glenbrook Castle, you were wearing a mint gown, cotton, I believe, with little vines embroidered along the hem. And the sleeves were short and puffy." He grimaced to himself. "If I remember correctly."

"Oh." Her throat moved. "It's my favorite."

"You curtsied, rather gracefully, in fact." Victor smiled, remembering. "Too gracefully." Because the right side of her mouth had quirked up just enough so he could tell she was… playing.

"You could have sent me away." She touched her fingertips to the side of his face.

"Never," he answered.

"I thought you were the most handsome man alive."

Before he could respond, a drop of water landed on her cheek, and then another. The weather, which had been so wonderfully cooperative earlier, had turned.

Her expression reflected his own disappointment.

Lightning flashed followed by rolling thunder. It was time to return to earth.

"Come on now, we can have our picnic in the chapel."

"But the vicar—?"

"Is in London this week." Acting on impulse, Victor winked. "We'll have it to ourselves." He would behave himself inside a chapel.

And as the drops of rain grew larger and more plentiful, he maneuvered them both onto a different branch, still gripping her hip.

"I can do it myself, you know."

"I know," he answered.

"Very well." He'd learned to recognize laughter in her voice.

Something had shifted between them, and whenever presented with the opportunity, she touched him, brushing his shoulder or one of his arms. And he did the same.

Securing her foot on a branch by grasping her ankle... longer than strictly necessary.

A hand on the back of her thigh, over her gown, normally quite inappropriate.

And when she landed on the grassy floor, he grasped her waist, steadying her at the same time the storm unleashed.

Victor scooped up their picnic basket and, with no one but the ghosts buried in the graveyard to witness their mad dash, they scurried to take shelter in the nearby chapel.

By the time they burst into the dark and quiet sanctuary, both of them were soaked. Breathless.

And laughing.

Her voice rivaled any church bells, hearty, happy, and utterly uninhibited.

Such a simple moment, but Victor couldn't help but believe it could change his life forever. The decision to embrace a new direction was his and his alone.

But could he? And if he did, would she have him?

He tore off his jacket, which had afforded him some protection, and draped it around her shoulders. Rainwater dripped from her hair onto her face, trailing along her smooth brow and cheeks in sparkling miniature streams. One drop gathered at the tip of her nose. Even shivering, she was smiling and she was beautiful.

Raw. Extraordinarily natural.

Not in the made-up manner ladies of his ilk strived for, but from within—a beauty that would never fade.

A gravitational pull existed between them, and before he could second guess himself, he walked her backwards until she was pressed against the wall.

With his palms flat against the old stones, breathing heavily, he touched his forehead to hers.

"Thank you." The words were anemic, but he wasn't sure how else to express what he was feeling.

"Don't thank me." Her chest heaved from running, and she was flushed, a pleasant rosy color infusing her cheeks. "Just kiss me again."

She needn't ask twice.

Moving closer, pressing his body along hers, Victor crushed their mouths together.

They both stood on solid ground—a stone floor, actually.

And this time, the kiss could go on and on and on… This time, they could fall together.

CHAPTER SIX

H<small>E HAD THANKED</small> her!

Thunder rumbled, shaking the stained glass even as the sound of rain pummeling the roof echoed around the empty chamber. Evalina clung to him…

Victor.

A hunger like she'd never known had her pulling him closer, running her hands over his shoulders, around his neck—tugging at his hair. And still, she wanted more. She wanted him to tear her clothes off. She wanted his hands everywhere! Wicked and luxurious fantasies came to life. What would it be like to give all of herself? To surrender with no expectations?

"Evalina." His voice strained as he trailed against her neck. How could a kiss be tender and violent at the same time?

She couldn't get close enough. Her thighs trembled and wet heat throbbed in her center. Was this the beginning, or was this the end?

It couldn't be forever. Even now, the woman who expected to become his duchess might be waiting back at the castle for him.

She swatted the thought away.

Eva wanted to give herself—all of herself—freely. She wanted all the pleasure even knowing pain would follow.

How could she go back to being invisible after this? Dear God, she wanted to mark him, and when he gripped her buttocks and squeezed, she scratched her fingernails down his back and would have torn his waistcoat off if she could.

He moaned, his face buried between her breasts. When he hitched her leg around his waist, she instinctively welcomed the hardness that pressed... right there.

Yes. Oh, yes.

"Evalina." He made her name sound like music and with the flash of lightning, sparks set flame to her blood. He dipped his head lower, pushing her bodice out of the way, and Eva arched her back.

Consume me.

Fill me.

Take me.

"You taste like heaven." His words felt as hot as her blood. Evalina mumbled something, she didn't know what, lost, savoring the friction between them. The whiskers on his jaw scraped her skin. The planes of his body made her feel soft and pliant. This wasn't a dream.

This couldn't be a dream. It was her life.

And yet... reality hovered like a demon ghost.

Despite the longing to be a part of him in every way, despite believing she might die if she couldn't have him now, he wasn't truly hers.

Another woman was coming to claim him. He belonged to another world.

A squeezing in her chest had her gasping for air, and she turned her head. "No. Victor."

He stilled.

Eva's heart broke at the sight of this man bent low, his cheek resting on her bosom, his hair disheveled from her fingers.

At some point she'd untied his cravat.

What was she doing? Surely a memory was better than nothing at all!

"I—" She wasn't sure what to say. She wanted him. But she wanted all of him.

His breaths matched to hers, equally ragged and pained as he lifted his head and rose to his full height. "I know," he said. "I know."

Evalina closed her eyes and, unwilling to let him go, burrowed her face into his chest.

But then, shuffling sounds shattered their privacy. From the altar, a man cleared his throat to announce his presence. The interruption was so unexpected that neither she nor the duke moved. In fact, his arms clasped her more tightly, locking her in their embrace rather than doing anything to conceal their indiscretion.

"Your Grace?"

"Sloan?" The duke finally turned to stare at the man, blinking in confusion. "What the devil are you doing here? And why are you dressed like a vicar?"

"Your mother, your Grace! She is coming here, and she's bringing Lady Lincoln"—his astute gaze shifted to Evalina—"and her daughter. She suggested they join the ladies' guild to offer their assistance with the charity baskets."

Startled into reality, Evalina straightened her spine and, with her back quite literally pressed against the wall, she shoved the duke away, sadly putting a few feet of distance between them.

"But there are no charity baskets!" *Obviously.*

"I know that." Mr. Sloan rolled his eyes towards the steepled ceiling and then stared at her pointedly. "You've already delivered them."

Evalina hadn't delivered anything, of course, and the valet must surely be aware of that... Which meant he must know more, possibly all the details of her and the duke's impromptu outing. And Mr. Sloan appeared to be aiding them—or attempting to, anyway.

The duke narrowed his eyes. "But why the cleric's collar?"

The valet maintained his patience, even as he glanced around a little anxiously.

"Because you are supposed to be meeting with him—with me—to discuss church renovations—but he is in London. Not to worry, however." Mr. Sloan, always quick on his feet, had apparently devised a ruse. He fingered the starched white collar around his neck. "I will play the part of the vicar."

Evalina felt grateful, even as her heart shattered.

She doubted she could ever piece it back together. It was over. Before it had even begun.

Lady Lucinda was here, and she would be wanting to insert herself into the community, helping to serve the poor. Drat! If his future intended wished to help out today, she mustn't be the villain Evalina had pictured in her mind.

She was a lady. And a decent one at that.

Tragically, however, she was going to claim the duke for her own and there was nothing Eva could do about it.

CHAPTER SEVEN

"M Y MOTHER IS coming here?" Victor asked his trusted valet. "With her guests?"

"With *your* guests. Yes, Your Grace."

"And you are—"

"The visiting vicar," Mr. Sloan provided.

Eva could mourn later. For now, she needed to work with the duke's clever valet. "Of course, because the duchess—"

"—doesn't know me from Adam." Mr. Sloan twisted his mouth into a crooked smile and then shuffled uncomfortably. "My apologies, Your Grace. But time is short and Miss Sparrow needs to either leave or hide. As soon as the duchess ordered the coach, I dashed over here. Which means they aren't far behind me."

Evalina ought to be embarrassed—scandalized, in fact. Because the valet had no doubt witnessed that kiss.

A kiss. Such a soft little word to describe an event that had given unfathomable meaning to her life.

She would not regret it! Perhaps, if nothing else, she'd reminded Victor that there was more to life than duty and tradition.

But when the duchess arrived, Evalina would once again be just a companion.

The thought was immediately followed by a tightening in her chest, and she looked up at her duke.

At Victor. Because she could not. Of course she could not!

Tears stung the backs of her eyes. She would submit her resignation tomorrow, return home, and assist her mother.

They'd have questions, of course. She'd simply explain that she'd become… homesick.

Her father wouldn't believe her, but her mother would be grateful for an extra pair of hands.

"I'll walk back." Eva gave a weak smile, picked up his jacket off the floor, and held it out for Victor to take. He grasped her wrist instead.

"No." He was shaking his head. "I brought you here. You'll return with me."

A sweet sentiment, but one that would cause more harm than good at this point. "It's all right." She met and held his gaze, conveying more than her willingness to walk through the rain. He had kissed her, awakening the passion they'd both kept in check.

It was something she'd wanted for months. She'd not been wrong in thinking he wanted it too. But allowing these feelings to run their natural course would only lead to disappointment.

"It isn't." His brows furrowed and he tightened his hold.

An approaching carriage, however, carried his guests, but also the urgency of their present circumstances.

"Miss Sparrow." Mr. Sloan gestured toward the door behind him. "You can hide in the sacristy until they leave."

"No," her duke declared. "She needn't hide."

Eva tugged, but he persisted in holding onto her.

"Victor…" she pleaded, and then clamped her mouth shut.

This was impossible, and although she ought to regret luring him away from the castle, she couldn't.

Because she'd lived better—loved better—in one afternoon than she had in her entire life. She would press the memory in her heart like a flower in a book.

She didn't know exactly when she'd fallen in love with him, but there was no denying it. And now she would leave. She wasn't a martyr. She would not remain at Glenbrook Castle while he betrothed himself to another woman. There would be a wedding. There would be children…

While all these thoughts raced through her mind, Victor continued holding her wrist, stroking his thumb over her pulse.

"I don't want to hide you." His eyes locked with hers. "Ever."

There was a plea in those stormy depths. What did it mean?

The thump of a carriage door closing nearby, followed by muffled women's conversation, signaled impending doom. Evalina's heart raced upon hearing the duchess's voice accompanied by two others.

Lady Lucinda and her mother.

It was too late to hide. Too late to run.

Eva stood at Victor's side and watched as the duchess entered the chapel followed by two elegant ladies.

All three women made up the picture of elegance, and their presence immediately transformed the peaceful chapel into something else.

Was this what a soldier felt before charging the enemy on the battlefield?

The duchess, wearing a heavily pleated, tailored chocolate-brown day dress, ignored Evalina to address her son.

"Fairchild." She spoke in a bright tone—a falsely bright tone.

"Mother." Victor could have blamed their appearance on the rain. Or moved away from Evalina. Instead, he placed his hand on the small of Evalina's back.

The duchess did not miss the motion and her throat moved before she folded her hands together over her middle.

Evalina had never, in the literally thousands of hours she'd spent with her employer, seen her looking disconcerted.

The woman's glare shot between Evalina and her son, and then briefly landed on Mr. Sloan.

Evalina had worked with the duchess long enough to know that, despite appearances, she was searching for the best way to take control of this situation.

"Mister...ah, Vicar. I trust you've completed your business with His Grace?" The duchess did not deign it necessary to present either the imposter vicar or Evalina to the two women standing behind her.

"Indeed! We'll be ordering new pews and a shiny new altar." Mr. Sloan did an excellent impression of the vicar's northern accent. "Eh, Your Grace?"

The duke met his valet's stare with an exasperated one. "Why don't we purchase a new bell while we're at it?"

"Oh, that isn't necessary, is it, darling?" The duchess's brows furrowed.

"The bell is sounding a bit off key these days," Evalina added, pinching her mouth together, hysterical giggles rising in her throat.

Oh, but this was bad.

Because, really, being caught alone with the duke was no grinning matter.

"The bell isn't the only thing that is...off." The duchess turned to face Evalina. "I understand you were to join the ladies' guild to deliver baskets to the poor today."

"Yes, Your Grace."

The older woman narrowed her eyes. "But the guild is absent, Miss Sparrow. I was confused when Mr. Frye informed me of your obligation, seeing as Mrs. Markwell said they were planning the fundraiser for the foundling hospital today."

Evalina blinked. Of course! How had she made such a grave miscalculation?

"I... Er..."

"Has the rain stopped?" Mr. Sloan practically flew down the aisle, placing himself between Lady Lincoln and her daughter and the imminent drama about to play out.

"It has, yes," the younger woman answered.

"I find myself in need of some fresh air, what with praying for everyone's sins and whatnot. Lady Lincoln, Lady Lucinda, will you allow me to show you the gardens around back? There is nothing like bluebells to bring one closer to God, wouldn't you agree?" He miraculously managed to steer them back outside, which was a relief, but only for a moment.

The duchess would have her say now.

"Your Grace." Evalina braced herself, knowing what was coming.

"I am not a fool." The duchess stared right through Eva. "Indiscretions will happen. And although you've proven adequate as a companion, you are a smart enough young woman to know your actions are cause for termination. You'll pack your belongings and be gone before nightfall."

"Of course—"

"No," Victor said.

Evalina had witnessed delicate confrontations between the two of them on several different occasions. Usually, he complied out of respect, for reasons she didn't always understand. He'd only ever argued with his mother over important matters. Like when the duchess wanted to turn out three tenant families so she could expand her gardens, and when she'd wanted to sack two servants who'd wanted to marry.

But in most instances, to keep the peace, and so as not to cause a scene, he tolerated his mother's requests.

And yet...

In that moment Evalina was reminded of all those times when he'd defended her to his mother, when he'd oh, so subtly reprimanded the duchess for speaking to her in harsh tones.

How he had held her gaze in shared amusement. Sometimes, she'd imagined it to be affection. He stepped forward, essentially placing himself between Evalina and his mother.

"Miss Sparrow isn't going anywhere."

"But Lady Lucinda—"

"Is a lovely lady, and presently, your guest. Nothing more." Standing beside but slightly behind him, Evalina admired the set of his chin. Even disheveled, he managed to look stern and aristocratic.

His mother's cheeks flushed an even darker shade of red. "But..." She blinked her eyes, summoning tears, a ploy Evalina had witnessed on more than one occasion. "They are your guests too, darling. We discussed this. Lady Lucinda is expecting—"

"She is a guest, Mother. Nothing more." And then he reached behind him, pulling Evalina forward. "I'm going to marry Miss Sparrow."

CHAPTER EIGHT

V ICTOR INHALED A deep breath.

This was not the way he'd intended to propose to his dear, sweet Miss Sparrow—*Evalina*. He'd never allowed himself to dream.

Before.

But now…

He'd allowed his mother to direct the course of his life for too long.

"Don't be ridiculous," his mother snapped.

"I've never been more serious."

The duchess forced a smile. "You have always done the honorable thing, and I'm sure you imagine you have some duty to…In some misguided sense of honor." She barely flicked a glance to Evalina, but for less than a second. "She is a lowly companion, darling. You have much greater duties to fulfill, duties that will require a woman of status, of breeding. A woman who is your equal—"

"Miss Sparrow is more than my equal." More importantly, "I love her."

Again, not the way he'd envisioned admitting this.

"Love is for simpletons. Come now. Why don't you find our guests and I'll deal with… her."

Victor knew precisely what she meant to do. Pay her off and send her away.

For this budding relationship to stand a chance, it was up to Victor to put his mother in her place.

"I've made my decision." He felt Evalina tense beside him, and turned so he could see her expression. "If she'll have me."

"Your father is no doubt rolling in his grave. You have responsibilities, Ferris. You have a legacy to uphold."

His mother got to the heart of the matter—the very reason he'd followed her guidance for so long.

But he was no longer the vulnerable young man he'd been when his father died, anxious to console his mother but also preserve the dukedom handed down for eight generations.

"I am Ferris," he said. "But I am not my father, and I will go forward making my own decisions. If you persist in opposing my decisions, I'll have you removed from Glenbrook Castle." He had tried, on numerous occasions, to convey his wishes but his mother refused to hear them.

"You are making a mistake." His mother appeared smaller somehow and his former self would have reached out to comfort her—to assure her of his loyalty and love.

But everything had changed. "I suggest you find your guests and return to the castle. I can have the dowager house readied if you are willing to accept my decision—and apologize to Miss Sparrow. Otherwise, we've other estates where you will be more than comfortable."

"But darling…" she made one last attempt but Victor only raised one brow.

"Think long and hard, Mother. You have twenty-four hours to make your decision." He squeezed Evalina's hand. "Please leave us now. I believe I have some groveling to do."

If not now, when?

Hoping he hadn't been ridiculously presumptuous, he ignored his mother as she exited the chapel to give Evalina the attention she deserved.

"I'm sorry," he breathed.

Her cheeks were a little pale, but she was not fuming. Tears swam in her eyes, turning the forest green an almost emerald color.

"You were… magnificent." It wasn't what he'd expected. But of course, Evalina wasn't like other women.

"Will you?" He leaned closer. "I know this isn't the proper way, but I've waited too long already and I can't go another day without asking. Will you marry me, Evalina? Will you make every day as magical as today?"

She blinked and then nodded. "Yes." But she shot a wary glance toward the door which had just closed behind his mother and leaned forward to whisper, "I'm not really duchess material, though."

Victor couldn't contain a chuckle. "You possess the only thing truly necessary to be my duchess."

"I do?" She tilted her head.

"My heart." She wasn't only the rainbow in a storm, she quenched his thirst. "I love you. It's as though I've waited my whole life for you."

By jove, his heart had come to life that fateful day his mother presented her new companion. Perhaps someday he would thank her.

Hearing the carriage drive off, Evalina grimaced. "She's going to hate me," she said.

"I won't allow it." But Victor was finished discussing his mother. He had been watching Evalina's mouth and, having tasted perfection, leaned in to claim more.

And more.

And more.

He only paused when a ray of sunlight slanted through one of the windows, casting a rainbow of refracted light upon her face. Evalina reached up to cradle his cheek.

"You are my duke, aren't you?"

"I have been all along." He turned serious, searching her gaze. "And you are mine."

"And I am yours. I do love you, Victor. I have since the first day I saw you, looking all serious and somber."

"I'm not sure I can bear a long engagement." His heart filled his chest and he could only recognize this sensation as joy.

"I thought today was just a dream. But it is real, isn't it?"

In answer, Victor lifted her off the ground, spinning them around in a circle.

He'd needed this day off to see everything he'd been missing. And thanks to this woman, he could embrace life and love in the only way that mattered.

"This might feel like a dream, but this is our life now. Don't ever let me forget it."

Evalina kissed his neck. "Memento mori, Victor."

"And so, for now, we will live!"

The End

Sign up for Annabelle Ander's newsletter and keep up with all her latest releases and sales!
www.annabelleanders.com

THE MOONSTONE MERMAID

by Meara Platt

CHAPTER ONE

Moonstone Landing
Cornwall, England
July 1832

J AMES PENNINGTON, NINTH Duke of Ashford, painstakingly made his way to the naturally formed pool along the river that flowed behind Stoningham Manor, home of his friend Daire and Daire's wife, Brenna, the Duke and Duchess of Claymore. Daire had taken his entire family on holiday and left the manor house to James for the next two weeks, insisting this place was where he needed to be in order to heal. "Bloody stupid idea," he muttered to himself, already tiring from the walk. "I should have gone to Bath instead."

However, the idea of taking the waters at any of the crowded pump rooms held little appeal for him. Anyone who was *anyone* went there to see and be seen, not necessarily to drink the mineral waters or soak in them. The marriage-minded mamas prowled those pump rooms and assembly halls and would hunt him down as diligently in Bath as they had in London.

Daily teas and nightly balls were out of the question for him. He was injured and seriously needed time to recover.

He trudged along the uneven ground, past the manor's garden and across a small meadow and its sweep of red poppies. The meadow sloped upward toward a copse of trees, and the pool, he had been told, was hidden just behind those trees. He eyed their pale-green leaves shimmering silver in the early morning light. A warm breeze rustled through the tree branches with a gentle *whoosh* and birdsong filled the air. He glanced down, noting the grass still held a crystal coating of dew, a remnant of the nightly mist that fell from the nearby sea.

All right, he had to admit this was a beautiful place.

However, that uneven climb was going to do him in.

"Thank the Graces," he muttered, taking a moment to rest now that he had reached the copse and heard the soft rush of the river flowing beyond it. He walked behind some tall shrubs, propping his cane against a fallen tree and then settling himself on it to remove his boots. He had just taken off one when he heard a splash.

Perhaps a bird had dropped a pebble into the water.

Thinking nothing of it, he tugged off his other boot.

Another soft splash.

He paused a moment, then shook his head and tossed off his shirt. A squirrel, no doubt, or a bird knocking something off a branch into the water. He was about to undo the falls of his trousers when he heard an unmistakably feminine trill of laughter and then more light splashes.

Bollocks.

Had someone usurped his pool?

He moved closer to peer through the shrubbery, almost falling backward as he caught sight of a perfectly rounded bottom, pale and glistening, poking out of the water. It was immediately followed by a pair of heavenly legs that also poked out for a moment before disappearing beneath the water.

A mermaid?

No, she had legs.

He felt a sudden yearning to see the rest of the young woman's body.

He did not have long to wait before she suddenly reemerged, breaking through the water with a dolphin-like grace, her long, dark hair whipping in the air and her pert, round breasts fully exposed to his view.

He turned away, his mind in a scramble and his heart about to burst through his chest as he debated what to do next. Leaving this spot seemed the most sensible thing, but it had taken him too much effort to get up here in the first place, and he really needed that dip in the pool.

"You are going to hell, James," he muttered, turning back to watch the lovely vision as she continued her mermaid dance, unaware of his presence while diving under and then coming up for air with hardly a ripple in the water.

He should go.

But for the life of him, he could not move.

One would think he had never seen a naked woman before.

In truth, he had seen more than his share. However, he could not recall ever responding so forcefully to a single one, not even those celebrated beauties considered *ton* diamonds. What made this little mermaid so special?

For one daft moment, he considered jumping in to join her. After all, women constantly invited him into their boudoirs. Did this pool not count as a mermaid's boudoir? And was he not considered England's most desirable catch? Nobody cared that he had a damaged leg. The Marriage Mart frenzy continued despite his accident because he was a duke and the young ladies all wanted to snare his title.

However, something stopped him from approaching her.

Gentlemanly good manners? A conscience?

Well, he would never be mistaken for a gentleman because he was still staring at the young woman and could not seem to stop. "Turn this way," he whispered, hoping to get a better look at her face. He had seen her body and deemed it spectacular, but it was her face that intrigued him most.

As though hearing him—which he knew was not possible—she turned, her gaze suddenly fixed on the shrubbery that sheltered him. Big eyes, the vivid green of a Highlands faerie glen, met his gaze. Lips the soft pink of rose petals now pursed slightly. Her slender, aquiline nose twitched. She took a hesitant step toward him, then abruptly changed her mind and hurried out of the water.

Blessed saints!

Was he dreaming?

He watched her dress, her movements lithe and sensual as she hastily donned her shift and then her gown, which would be damp because she hadn't stopped to properly dry herself off. She hurriedly tucked her feet into walking boots, laced them up, and ran off.

Wait!

He wanted to call out to her, but knew it was folly. What could he possibly say to make things right? The words "I did not mean to see you naked" would not work. "No, definitely not a proper introduction."

But with his mermaid gone, he could now have his swim.

Still lost in thoughts of her, James stripped off the last of his clothes. He meant to ease his way into the pool but slipped and lost his footing because of his lame leg. Flailing like an ungainly whale, he tumbled into the water with an enormous splash.

He came back up angry with himself, cursing and sputtering. His leg had twisted awkwardly and was now in spasms. "Bollocks. *Bollocks.*" He grabbed his leg and began to knead it along the scar tissue in the hope of making the excruciating pain stop. One particularly bad spasm tore through him and wrung another cry out of him. *"Bollocks."*

"Serves you right," a young woman said, staring down at him from her perch on a flat rock beside the pool.

He raked a hand through his hair to brush it off his face, and blinked to clear the water from his eyes. The vision in green muslin was his mermaid. Her hair was still unbound, the wet tresses spilling over her shoulders and curling about her hips.

"I thought you'd run off," he said through clenched teeth as another spasm gripped him. She was a beauty with her clothes off, but just as stunning with them on.

"I heard your cries and thought I had better return to help you on the chance you were drowning. I would not wish that on my conscience, even though your spying on me was reprehensible. Are you in terrible pain?"

"Yes," he muttered. "But it will pass eventually. It usually does. I did not mean to spy on you. Completely accidental, I assure you. I had no idea anyone else would be here. In fact, I was told no one *would* be here. My only intention was to take a morning swim to strengthen this leg."

"Your dive was quite graceful," she said with a note of teasing. "I mistook you for a fish."

"Very funny," he muttered. "I thought you came to help me."

"I did. I'm sorry. What can I do for you?"

All manner of ideas crossed his mind, none of them appropriate.

"Nothing for the moment. Just make sure I don't lose consciousness and sink beneath the water."

"Is the pain that bad? Have you passed out before?"

"No, but it is sometimes a close thing."

She continued to eye him warily. "How much of me did you see?"

His silent stare told her everything she needed to know.

A blush stained her cheeks and she groaned lightly. "If you breathe a word of this to anyone, I shall hold you under the water and drown you myself."

"I assure you, Miss... Er, what is your name?"

Up close, she looked soft and innocent. He knew she was never going to do anything to hurt him. However, she was profoundly embarrassed knowing that he had seen her in the altogether.

An innocent.

Now he felt truly depraved for watching her.

The fact she was taking in an eyeful of him did not really settle their score. He did not care that she was staring at him. As far as he was concerned, she was welcome to look her fill.

"I have no intention of telling you who I am," she said, pursing her lips in a way that made him want to kiss her. "Who are *you*? And what are you doing on the Claymore property?"

"I might ask you the same question. In fact, I did just ask it. But for the sake of calling a truce to this awkward situation, I am James Pennington." He revealed no more, not quite ready to let on that he was a duke. "Claymore is one of my good friends. He invited me to stay here while he and his family are on holiday. What's your excuse?"

"I do not owe you an explanation."

"You owe me your name, at least." The water was crystal clear and he was in it only up to his waist. How much of him could she see beneath the water? Not that he was particularly bashful, but the water was quite cool at this hour and his nether region was feeling it. No one was going to mistake him for a magnificent stallion at this moment.

"I am not giving you my name."

"Very well, I shall call you my mermaid."

"Do what you like. We won't ever see each other after today."

"Why? Are you going away?"

"No." Her eyes narrowed as she watched him still kneading his leg. "But I will have to avoid this pool, since I cannot risk meeting you here again."

"You needn't. Let's work out a schedule for the next two weeks. Do you always swim at this early hour?"

She nodded. "Yes. Is this how long you will be staying? Two weeks?"

He nodded. "That's right. Then I will head to Bath or return to London; I haven't decided which yet. But about our schedule... What if I come an hour later? Will that give you enough time to finish your swim and return to your mermaid cove? Then I shall have my turn. Workable plan?"

She knelt on the rock, and her expression gentled as she mulled over his proposal. "Do I have your solemn oath you will not spy on me again?"

"Yes. I never meant to look the first time. Have you seen enough of me yet? Or would you like a closer examination?" he said in jest.

"I am fine right here." Her mouth tipped up at the corners in the hint of a smile. "Is it feeling any better? Your leg?"

He sighed. "Not really. My efforts to ease the cramping have been a failure so far."

She leaned forward. "Perhaps you shouldn't massage it so hard. Let it go and try stretching your body instead. Like this." She rose and then began to arch her own body, gracefully dipping one way and then the other, like a sapling gently swaying in the wind. "Make sure you bend far enough forward and then back so that you feel the tug of the leg muscle in each direction. Hold it to the count of five, then put your weight on the injured leg. Try this every morning when you get out of bed."

"I've already tried exercises," he muttered. "They haven't helped so far."

"Because you are probably doing them wrong. Have you tried the one I just showed you? It is remarkably simple." She nibbled her lip. "We have an excellent army hospital in Moonstone Landing.

Our local doctor, Dr. Hewitt, volunteers his time there often. You ought to speak to him as well as the army commander, Major Brennan. There may be something they can offer to ease the pain."

"Some miracle treatment the finest doctors in London could not come up with? I've tried enough of them, and they don't work." He did not mean to sound surly or dismissive, but he had been dealing with this problem for months now with no relief from the unrelenting agony.

"They are city doctors. It is not at all the same thing. Even I could do better than them."

"Is that so?" He studied her, surprised by how difficult it was to stop looking at her lovely face. There was intelligence behind her eyes, and a softness in the curve of her lips. *Lord, those lips.* They dipped at the ends in a sensual pout. "What would you suggest I do?"

"Apply warmth to the injured area, a hot, moist cloth several times a day. Stretching the injured limb will help, as I mentioned. Massaging it as you are doing now should also help, but softer. You are rubbing too hard and bruising your leg."

"Any other helpful hints?" She was not telling him anything he had not heard a hundred times before from his team of doctors.

"Lavender oils will help," she said, overlooking his surliness. "Chamomile or yarrow oils also work, but they don't smell as nice. Mr. Bedwell's mercantile serves as our local apothecary. You'll find whatever you need there. But I would also recommend eating plenty of apples and dried fruit, especially apricots and raisins. Cherries are excellent, too. Best before they fully ripen so they are still a bit tart. Drinking brine or cider will help. My preference is cider. Brine will only make you gag. Stop consuming wine or scotch, or any other spirits, for that matter."

He had never heard of these suggestions about food and drink before, and now wondered whether she was making up these country remedies to make a fool of him. But there was an earnestness about her that made him trust her. "Are you suggesting food will heal me?"

"They will help reduce the inflammation that is the cause of your pain, Mr. Pennington. Just ask anyone in town. Better yet, ask

Dr. Hewitt. He will confirm every word."

Who was this girl?

He needed to see more of her... No, not in the sense of taking her clothes off. Well, that too. But he wanted to get to know her better. She seemed educated and her voice was refined. Not snooty or pinched, as often heard among the Upper Crust. Her gown was well made, but he would not call it fashionable.

She had no fear of being caught trespassing, he noted. Her only concern had been about his seeing her without her clothes on. Otherwise, she seemed quite comfortable here. Did she know Claymore and his wife socially? She was no one's servant, that much was clear. Her gaze was too direct when she studied him.

"Will you meet me at the mercantile later this morning and assist me in selecting those oils?" he asked.

She laughed and shook her head. "No. But I shall write out my instructions and leave them on this rock for you tomorrow. Remember, I swim first. This is our deal."

"I gave you my oath and I will keep to it."

"Well, then. There is nothing more to say to each other. Good morning, Mr. Pennington."

She flitted off before he could ask for her name again.

No matter—the village was not very large. He would find her. He simply had to. It was a rare event to encounter a mermaid, even one with legs. He had no intention of losing her.

Would he find her here tomorrow?

CHAPTER TWO

*O*H, *LORD! OH, Lord!* He'd seen her naked.

Who was this stranger who called himself James Pennington? Could she trust him?

Verity Angel hurried back to Moonstone Landing, her heart still pounding and her cheeks aflame. She hoped no one else had spied her at Stoningham Manor, for the accidental encounter with that man was humiliating enough.

How was she to avoid him for the next two weeks?

Perhaps it would not be too difficult. If he had come here to recover from a severe leg injury, then it was possible he would remain holed up at the manor house for the duration and never come into the village.

Yes, this was her fervent hope.

"Stay right where you are, Mr. Pennington, and we shall get along quite nicely," she murmured, hurrying down the high street toward her home. She passed the bustling fish market along the dockside and waved to the fishermen's wives. They were hard at work preparing their fish for sale.

"Ye're out early, Verity," one commented, returning her cheerful greeting.

She nodded. "I thought I would take a walk before it got too hot."

With another wave, she walked on toward her house, which happened to be the grandest among a charming row of them, all of them with unobstructed views of the harbor and the sea beyond. Locals referred to these quaint homes as the seaside cottages, although most were quite a bit larger than simple cottages.

She sneaked in through the garden, relieved to find the kitchen door open. This was how her father always started his day, unlatching the back door in order to walk to their chicken coop and fetch the morning's batch of eggs. He would then help her mother light the hearth fire before he went off to work.

Verity waited for him to pass, then quietly made her way through the kitchen and up the back stairs to her bedchamber. Her siblings shared their bedchambers, but this one was hers alone. After all, she was a grown woman of twenty and needed her privacy, especially now that her body had filled out.

That wretched Mr. Pennington had noticed, too.

"Nothing to do about it now," she chided herself, sitting down to brush out her hair that was almost dry. She styled it in a simple chignon, then returned downstairs as though to start her day.

"Verity, dear," her mother called out, "would you run to the butcher's and pick up some meat for tonight? Make sure he gives you the finest cuts."

"Yes, Mama." Verity listened patiently as her mother added a few more items to her list. This was their normal routine, her running errands while her mother got her brothers and sisters up and ready for the day. Verity did not mind, since she enjoyed the relative quiet of the morning. The earlier, the better. Anyway, everyone knew the best cuts of meat and freshest vegetables were always to be had at the start of the day.

She sauntered through town, picking up the items on her mother's list and thinking more about Mr. Pennington. She felt some remorse for not helping him more than she had. Well, she would gather up some useful items for him later.

Upon returning home, she dropped her purchases in the kitchen, and then went into the music room to practice the pieces she had selected for tomorrow night's harp recital. She rarely played in public, but Vicar Trask had begged her for this one concert to raise funds for several new church projects, and she did not have the heart to turn him down.

The entire village council had thought the recital a good idea for purposes of what they termed *cultural improvement*. They wanted to show the visiting London elite that their local residents were just as refined as anyone else.

Satisfied with her rehearsal, she went off to browse the local bookshop for something interesting to read. The day was spectacular, and she now had the entire afternoon free. And what a glorious day it was. The sky was a vivid blue, marred only by a few soft white clouds floating along on a gentle breeze.

The water was calm, too. The vessels in the harbor were hardly bobbing or straining their moorings as the tide rolled in. The air was a bit warm, but a stop later at Mrs. Halsey's tea shop for an ice or a tall glass of lemonade would remedy that. She decided to include a stop at Mr. Bedwell's mercantile and ask him to set aside some aromatic oils.

"Are ye feeling achy, Verity?" Mr. Bedwell remarked when she entered his shop and ordered several bottles of lavender oil. "Carrying that big harp around is sure to strain your muscles, and you being such a dainty thing and all."

She had been toting her instrument around for years without a problem. Yes, it was large and a bit unwieldy, but she was used to it. "It isn't for me, Mr. Bedwell."

He arched a bushy eyebrow. "Yer mother, then?"

"No." She licked her lips, stalling until she came up with an innocent explanation. "Um, Brenna's husband invited an injured friend to stay at Stoningham Manor while they were on holiday. Brenna asked if I might gather some medicinal supplies for the gentleman."

"Gentleman? Oh, you must mean the Duke of Ashford. I heard he was coming to stay. Brenna... I mean... Gad, I've known ye all since ye were little tykes in leading strings. Hard to think of Brenna as the Duchess of Claymore now. Well, the surprising turns life takes. Who would have ever guessed? She mentioned their friend was badly injured in a carriage accident. Leg crushed."

"Yes, terrible shame." Verity also had a hard time thinking of her cousin as a duchess. Not just Brenna had married well—two other cousins had done the same. Cara had married the Duke of Strathmore and Felicity had married the Earl of Bradford.

Good fortune came in threes, and her three cousins had used up all the available goodwill. What were her chances of marrying a duke?

A big, fat "no chance at all."

Not that she cared. Her duke, who had merely introduced himself as James Pennington, was infuriating.

"Have you seen the Duke of Ashford?" Verity asked the mercantile owner.

"No, I don't think anyone's seen him yet besides the staff at the manor house. I heard he rode in late last night. Perhaps yer father knows. He's the town constable and up on all that is going on in the village."

Her father was the last man she would ever ask. First of all, he did not know she was sneaking out of the house to swim each morning. Nor did she ever want him to find out. That alone was bad enough, but for him to learn she had encountered a naked stranger, who had seen her naked as well?

The volcanic explosion would be heard from here to China. A Hun invasion would seem tame compared to the wrathful vengeance he would unleash on the man.

This was saying a lot, because her father was the most composed, calm, rational man she had ever met. However, he was very protective of his children. She was the eldest and the apple of his eye.

Yes, best if she and the duke, alias Mr. Pennington, avoided each other for the next two weeks. A man that handsome would have women after him by the droves.

He was probably a debauched rake, too. He certainly had alluring eyes and an inviting smile capable of making women swoon.

The cad.

Although she hadn't actually seen him leer at her. But neither had he beaten his chest in remorse…just issued a polite apology, the sort one might give after accidentally stepping on another's foot.

Nor had he cared enough to cover himself up. Obviously, he was used to walking around naked in front of women. She would not be surprised if he took a different conquest to his bed on any given night of the week.

Well, she was not going to be one of them.

Not that she had been a paragon of good behavior herself, discreetly gawking at him, even glancing at his backside and privates whenever he wasn't looking because he was quite nicely formed and she was curious.

Did he realize how clear the water was? Or that she saw *everything* down to the silt at the bottom of the riverbed?

She wasn't trying to study those parts of him that lay beneath the water. She wasn't…much. The upper part of him was fascinating enough. Big, broad chest, powerfully muscled shoulders, and a flat stomach so taut, it rippled. Above those powerful shoulders was a handsome face capped with a thick head of golden hair. His eyes were the color of mahogany, dark and rich.

She left the mercantile and stopped in at Mrs. Halsey's tea shop. "Good afternoon, Mrs. Halsey. Could you put together a basket of dried fruits for me? Apples, apricots, and raisins, if you please. And a jug of apple cider, too."

"What do you want with all those dried fruits and cider, Verity?"

"Um…Brenna asked me to help out their guest, who is staying at Stoningham Manor while she and her husband are on holiday. He's hurt his leg badly, and I thought these might help relieve some of the inflammation. Um…put it on the Claymore account." She would settle up with Brenna upon her return to Moonstone Landing.

"I assume the gentleman you mean is the Duke of Ashford," Mrs. Halsey said, now scribbling in her account book.

"Yes. Have you met him?"

"No, Verity. Have you?"

Verity cleared her throat. "Not that I am aware. I was curious what he looked like."

The kindly proprietress shrugged. "I hear he is quite handsome. You ought to be careful or he just may steal your heart."

"Oh."

Mrs. Halsey was teasing her, but it was not far from the truth. He was sinfully gorgeous.

"Is there anything else I can do for you, dear? I'll have your order ready within the hour."

Verity shook her head. "That is everything for now. Thank you, Mrs. Halsey."

She walked out of the tea shop and ran straight into her father, who was patrolling the high street. "Verity, love," he called to her when she tried to walk straight past him and the big, handsome man who was limping alongside him.

Oh, dear heaven.

No.

No.

"Ah, Papa. I did not see you there." She stifled a groan as he introduced her to the Duke of Ashford, her very own Mr. Pennington.

She saw the flicker of surprise in the duke's eyes, but his surprise was quickly replaced by amusement. Smiling rakishly, he took her hand and bowed over it. "A pleasure to meet you, Miss Angel," he said, all innocence and politeness. "The constable mentioned his daughter plays the harp. He has been raving about your talent. I'm sure you are quite accomplished."

She wanted to appear equally casual, but could not manage it. Heat shot into her cheeks. "He exaggerates, of course. I am nothing special."

To her surprise, he frowned at the remark. "I do not believe that for a moment. I look forward to your recital. It is tomorrow evening, is it not?"

Her stomach sank. She did not want him showing up. "You must not feel obliged to attend, Your Grace. In fact, I urge you to stay home."

Her father cast her a warning glance, a *what in blazes are you doing, Verity?* scowl. "My daughter is shy, Your Grace. The concert is rather daunting for her. You mustn't pay attention to anything she says."

"Oh, yes," Verity added, trying to slip her hand out of the duke's. "You must ignore me. It really is for the best."

He grinned, refusing to let go of her yet. "I shall keep it in mind."

Her father now pointed to the elegant Kestrel Inn that was across the street. "If the weather holds, Verity's recital will take place in the inn's formal garden. Otherwise, it will be moved indoors to one of the elegant salons."

"Rest assured, Constable Angel, I do not intend to miss your daughter's performance, rain or shine." Although the duke had addressed her father, his gaze remained firmly fixed on her.

Verity finally managed to slip her hand out of his. "Well, I ought to be going now."

She did not have anything to do other than get away from this man who was making her senses reel.

Before she could escape, Mr. Bedwell called to her and lumbered over. "Glad I caught you, Verity. Did you want me to deliver the lavender oils to His Grace, or was he going to send someone to pick it up?"

Verity blushed as she glanced at the duke. "You may ask him yourself, Mr. Bedwell. Here is the man in question."

Mr. Bedwell bowed and fussed while her father made the quick introduction.

Once again, the duke was politeness itself. "I'll take the lavender oils with me now, if you have them ready."

"Indeed, Your Grace. I'll fetch the bottles right away."

Mr. Bedwell shuffled off at the same time the mail coach rumbled down the high street and drew up in front of the inn. "Your Grace, please forgive me," Verity's father said. "May I leave you in my daughter's care for a moment? I make it a point to see who gets on and off these daily passenger coaches."

"Go to it, Mr. Angel. I'm sure your daughter will keep me entertained."

"Gad, you are insufferable," Verity muttered when her father was safely out of earshot.

The duke cast her another of his smugly satisfied grins. "What have I said? You are the one tossing out remarks."

"You might have mentioned you were a duke," she grumbled.

"When? Earlier? As we stood nakedly staring at each other?"

She closed her eyes and groaned. "You promised never to speak of that incident."

"I won't. But now I understand why you were so desperate to have my promise." He chuckled. "Who knew my mermaid was the constable's daughter? No wonder you were afraid to give me your name."

"I wasn't afraid," she retorted, sticking her chin into the air. "I simply saw no point to it."

"Verity, I give you my oath that I am never going to tell anyone, especially not your father. I do not have a death wish. So you may as well cease your worry. Your secret is safe with me. Must I assure you again? Upon my oath, I will never do anything to harm you."

"Thank you," she said, letting out a breath. Could she trust him? He sounded quite sincere. "Why did you come into town, Your Grace? You should have stayed resting at the manor."

"First of all, I am not a hermit. I fully intend to avail myself of all that Moonstone Landing has to offer."

"Well, do not think to avail yourself of me," she warned. "I am not on offer."

That remark earned her another of his insufferably charming grins. "Not available? Does this mean you are betrothed?"

"No." She felt her cheeks turn hot again.

"Married?"

"No."

He arched an eyebrow. "Interesting."

"It is not interesting at all. We ought to have nothing more to do with each other."

"I don't think that is possible. After all, I saw you. You saw me. My little mermaid, you were devouring me with your eyes."

She gasped. "I was not."

"You were. Do you realize your nose twitches whenever you lie to me? Or are you merely lying to yourself? You thought you were being discreet while ogling me, but trust me when I say that you were not."

"I wasn't...and you were just standing there in all that clear water. You were hurting. I wanted to do something to help, but did not know what."

He surprised her by giving her cheek a light caress. It felt affectionate more than wolfish. "You look pretty when you blush. Thank you for ordering the lavender oils for me. I'll try rubbing some on my leg tonight."

She nodded. "Put some on a hot, moist cloth and then apply the cloth to your skin. Let it absorb into the damaged muscle. Mrs. Halsey is preparing a basket of dried fruits for you, too."

"At your request?"

She nodded. "She ought to have it ready shortly. Mr. Halsey will drop it off at the manor when he makes his final round of deliveries for the day."

"That is very thoughtful of you, Verity." He leaned on his cane, a sign that his leg was tiring, but she doubted he was going to admit it to her. "Truly, most thoughtful."

She shrugged. "These country remedies do work. I promise to write them all out for you and leave them on the rock tomorrow morning."

"Why don't you write them out now? I have nowhere else to be. Do you? I'm sure the innkeeper will allow us to borrow some stationery. Is there a library at the inn? Or a quiet room where we can work?"

She nodded.

They waited another minute for Mr. Bedwell to return with the bottles of lavender oil, then walked to the inn. Her father was deep in conversation with her cousin Thaddius, who was the innkeeper, and another gentleman who appeared to be one of the new arrivals.

Since the discussion appeared serious, she did not wish to disturb them. The inn was familiar to her and she knew where Thaddius kept all the writing implements and supplies for the accommodation of his guests.

She led the duke into the inn's library. "Make yourself comfortable, Your Grace." She motioned toward a leather wing chair that had a matching ottoman. "Let me help you put your leg up," she said, attending to the task before he could refuse the offer. He was obviously struggling with that leg and needed to get the blood flowing through it before it began to spasm again.

After making certain he was comfortable, she went to the large desk situated in the center of the room and began to rummage through the drawers. It did not take her long to find what she needed. Paper, sharpened quill pens, ink pot. Blotting paper. Sand shaker.

"You seem to know your way around the inn, Verity."

She nodded. "The proprietor is my cousin, Thaddius. He's an Angel, too. So is the bank manager, by the way. And did you know that the Duchess of Claymore also happens to be a cousin of mine?"

He laughed. "Brenna?

"Yes, Angel is her maiden name."

"I did not realize. Nor am I all that surprised. You seemed quite at home on their property."

"My other cousin, Cara, is Duchess of Strathmore."

One golden eyebrow shot up again. "Any more surprises?"

"My cousin, Felicity, is married to the Earl of Bradford."

He now stretched both legs languidly before him. "Is this your subtle way of telling me that I should marry you?"

She almost spilled the ink on herself. "No! I just... You have such a smug way of looking at me that I wanted to take you down a peg or two."

"Is that how you think I am looking at you?" He appeared surprised, and his voice was soft and husky as he asked the question.

"I don't know. Yes. Maybe. I just don't want you looking at me."

"Why? Are my glances too heated? Do I warm your insides?"

She set down her quill pen. "No, you curdle them. Now be quiet and let me write your list."

He burst out laughing. "You are awfully rude for a mermaid. Women usually fawn over me."

She snorted. "Are you always this full of yourself?"

"It is a fact, Verity. Just watch and see. This inn is a very elegant establishment. I'm sure it is filled with well-heeled guests who have daughters or nieces of marriageable age. These ladies are like bloodhounds and will catch on to my scent within minutes."

She rolled her eyes. "Oh, I see. The scent of a duke is potent?"

Well, he *did* smell nice. Musky and male.

"Yes, in fact it is. Do you not feel giddy in my presence?" he remarked with a chuckle.

She laughed softly. "Exceedingly full of yourself."

"Care to place a wager? Not a money wager."

"Then what?"

"If I win the wager, you must kiss me."

She snorted. "And if I win?"

He grinned. "Then I must kiss you."

She laughed again. "I knew you were a naughty fellow. No, if I win, then you must buy me anything I wish from Mrs. Halsey's tea shop."

He nodded. "Fine. I'll buy you the tea shop itself if you wish. You are not going to win the wager. I assure you, I will have a dozen women around me before you finish writing out your list."

"Giggling peahens, no doubt," she muttered. "Fine. Twelve women before I finish writing my list."

He paused a beat, then two. "You don't believe me, but you will soon see. Wager is on, starting now."

She straightened the sheaf of paper before her and dipped her quill into the ink pot.

In turn, he picked up a newspaper and began to read quietly. "Just watch what happens."

Verity tried to ignore him.

But he simply could not be ignored.

To her surprise, ladies started to gather in the doorway. Verity heard their giggled whispers as they peeked in. One. Two. Three. Four. Ugh, she still had three-quarters of her list to write, and there was now a fifth lady peering at him from the threshold. "Do they have nothing better to do?" Verity muttered.

"Getting worried, are you?" The duke winked at her.

She frowned at him.

When several more gathered, the first ones became emboldened and began to saunter in. At first, they pretended to peruse the bookshelves. One approached him to ask what book he would recommend for her, and then they all did the same. Six, seven, eight...nine. *Drat.*

He set down his newspaper, smiled at them all, and then rose to select a book of romantic poetry. The wretch began to read aloud, his voice deep and resonant, his smile rakish as he spouted those rhyming words of love.

I adore you.
No one afore you.
What utter drivel.

One could not concentrate with all the women sighing and swooning around him. She had a few choice rhyming words for him, too. *I abhor you. Deplore you. Ignore you. No more you.*

Verity's heart sank as number ten and eleven scurried in.

She did not think any of these women had ever picked up a book in their lives, but this was the excuse they all now made for coming into the library...and what a surprise to find the handsomest duke in all of England seated right there, reciting a poem and making each feel as though he were spouting those insipid verses to her alone.

Verity did not know why she should care. After all, he was so far out of her reach that it was laughable.

By the time she finished her list of instructions, he had more than a dozen ladies seated in a circle around him as he held court. Verity wanted to hand him the list and leave, but she could not approach him without tripping over someone's feet or someone's hem. Politely asking any of these ladies to move was never going to work. Not one of them would ever give way to accommodate a mere constable's daughter.

Since he appeared to be in his glory, Verity decided to keep to their original plan and leave this paper for him by the pool tomorrow morning. She walked out quietly, never thinking he would notice. But she had barely made it out of the inn before she heard him calling out to her. "Verity! Miss Angel!"

She was about to cross the high street on her way to Mrs. Halsey's tea shop, but stopped and waited for him to catch up. Her heart tugged as she watched him hobbling toward her.

"Why did you run away from me?"

Verity looked at him, surprised he cared. "You were busy with those other ladies. Dear heaven, you are good at this seduction business."

He grunted. "I told you they would flock to me. They always do. Doesn't mean I welcome their attention. I only played it up because of our bet."

"You seemed quite comfortable around them. Well, you handily won. I concede."

He nodded. "There is a lesson in this for you. Never bet against me. I do not wager unless I am certain I will win. However, since this is hardly the time or place to claim my reward, how about joining me for tea and cakes instead? I noticed you were heading in the direction of the tea shop."

She shook her head when he pointed to Mrs. Halsey's establishment. "I was, but only to ensure she had filled my order. I cannot take tea with you today. My mother is expecting me home. I usually help make our supper."

He said nothing for the longest moment, then gave a curt nod. "All right. Let me walk you home."

She watched him leaning heavily on his cane. "No, Your Grace. It is too far for you to walk, and you really need to rest your leg."

"Are you ashamed for me to see your home?"

"No, it is a lovely cottage amid a row of beautiful cottages near the harbor. The view of the sea is spectacular from most of the rooms in our house. We have a splendid garden, too. Our home is the largest in the row."

"Sounds lovely."

"It is," she said. "Perhaps tomorrow, all right? But only to stop in to have you meet my mother and siblings. I won't invite you for a meal tomorrow because it is the night of my concert, and my stomach will be in a roil throughout the day."

"That's right. Your concert. I do not want to interfere with that," he said with genuine concern. "How about we leave everything to the day after your concert? Spend the entire day with me then, Verity. Show me around your village. If the weather cooperates, I'll have the Claymore housekeeper pack us a picnic basket and we'll dine on the water. I noticed there were boats offering cruises along the coastline."

She nibbled her lip. "I shouldn't."

"Why not? Bring along a chaperone, if you wish. Whatever makes you comfortable. I would like for us to talk and get to know each other better."

No.

No.

Too dangerous.

"All right, Your Grace. But why?"

He cast her a wry smile. "I've never met a mermaid before, and I am curious."

She shook her head and chuckled. "Do be serious."

He shifted uncomfortably, leaning too heavily once more on his cane. "All right, let's be serious for a moment. You offered to help me heal, Verity. You made sensible suggestions and went out of your way to put them into effect. No one has done this for me before."

"No one?" Her eyes widened in surprise. "But your family... Surely they wanted the best for you."

"My closest relation is a maiden aunt who is mostly interested in the social position afforded to her because of our relation. Other than that, she has no interest in me. We nod politely if ever we happen to see each other. I give her a generous allowance and she rarely bothers me for more. I have no other family. They are all dead."

She gasped and reached for his hand, then realized how forward the gesture was and quickly drew it away. "Your Grace, I'm so sorry."

He laughed mirthlessly. "So am I. I never expected my adulthood to be like this."

"Alone...too much on your own. Is your maiden aunt able to travel? Perhaps if you warmed up to her and included her more in your life, then things might change between you. Would she join you here? We would make her feel quite welcome."

"No, Verity. She is comfortably settled in Bath. And I have become used to being on my own. It isn't so bad. I am showered with attention and pampered everywhere I turn. A privilege of being a duke."

"Your Grace, in truth, this sounds awful."

He shrugged. "It is not ideal, but this is what it is. Verity, this seems to overset you more than it does me."

"I cannot help it. You deserve better."

He eyed her affectionately. "You are an odd little thing. Do you think any of those peahens in the inn's library gave a care about me beyond my title? Do you think even one of them spared a thought for my leg? Or my pain?"

"Or your loneliness?"

He shook his head. "I am not lonely. I usually prefer my own company to the sycophants and toadies who surround me."

"Like those ladies in the library? Do not be too hard on them. You were jovial and charming to them," she said. "They might have asked about your injury if they realized just how deeply you were suffering. Speaking of which, you really need to get off your leg now."

"I know." He nodded. "And you need to get home. I'll not delay you."

She watched him as he limped away.

This proud, confident man who appeared to have it all was actually feeling quite lost, she realized. The pain was not only in his leg. His heart had been wounded, too. She considered going after him, but changed her mind.

She would wait for him by the pool tomorrow and they could talk.

Still, she felt quite bad about dismissing him just now. Why had she told him she had to make supper? Yes, she often helped her mother and would do so tonight. But it was not a requirement, and no one was going to punish her if she avoided the task.

But she knew why she had done it. There was something about this man that frightened her.

Not in a scary way. In a consuming, I-could-fall-in-love-with-you way.

She had never been in love before and never realized the feeling came with so many aches. She ached watching him struggle to walk down the street. She ached knowing he had no family to love or that loved him in return. She ached because he was an unhappy soul, and probably did not realize that he was because he had never experienced true joy.

What could she do about this? Nothing, she supposed. He would be gone in two weeks. Besides, she dared not get too close to him.

He was a hot flame and she would get burned.

Was this the beginning of love? Or was she careening down the path to heartbreak?

CHAPTER THREE

JAMES WALKED ACROSS the meadow to the copse and its hidden pool just as the distant church bells chimed the eight o'clock hour. He was looking forward to his swim, hopefully this time without wrenching his leg and tumbling headlong into the water.

Verity had promised to leave her list for him.

Instead, he was pleasantly surprised to find her waiting for him beside the pool. There was just something about her big eyes and earnest regard that made him smile. This was quite something, because he had not smiled in a very long time. "Good morning, little mermaid. Did you have your morning swim?"

She nodded. "Yes, Your Grace."

He felt a swell of pleasure, for this meant she had purposely remained to see him. Her luscious mane, still wet from the recent swim, was tied back in a simple bow at her nape. But this simplicity accentuated her beautiful features.

She handed over a parchment that contained her instructions all neatly set out in columns of dos and don'ts. "I refined the list last night. I thought it would be helpful to clearly outline the things you must do to heal your leg and those you must avoid. The water's lovely, by the way. You'll find it most refreshing."

"Thank you for this." He gave the parchment a quick perusal before carefully rolling it up and putting it in the pouch he had brought along with him. "Verity, this formality between us is unnecessary. I would like you to call me James whenever we are not in company."

"Is that really your name?"

"Yes, my given name is James. Pennington is the family name. I go by Ashford because it is my title, although my friends simply call me Ash."

She pursed her lips. "Then why ask me to call you James if no one else does? I don't think it is a good idea."

He was going to kiss her if she kept up that alluring pucker. "Because you are not like anyone else. You are as unique as the circumstances of our first meeting, that's all I meant. My point is, you and I share a secret bond."

She gave a groaning laugh. "We share a *secret*, that's for certain. A ruinous one that I hope will never be found out."

"I think we shared more than our bodies in that moment."

"Dear heaven," she muttered.

"We shared a deep understanding of each other," he insisted. "Perhaps it is only in my mind, but there is a connection between us. Do you not feel it, Verity?"

"I'm not sure."

"As for me, it feels right that I should allow you to call me by a name that I have not allowed anyone else to use. I hope this makes sense to you. Or am I merely rambling?"

"It makes sense, I suppose. But I am not sure it is wise. I am honored, although I do not understand why you feel this deep connection to me. What makes me so special? You must have seen *naked* ladies before." She spoke the word "naked" in a whisper, that shyness making him like her all the more.

"Your body is delightful, but this is not really why I find you special. How can I explain this when I am still struggling to understand the reason myself? There is something genuine about you. Compassionate. Honest and trustworthy. You haven't asked anything of me or tried to manipulate me into giving you anything."

Her eyes rounded. "I never would!"

"Yes, this is exactly what I mean. You are the one who has been generous and considerate to me. So, it is settled. You are to call me James."

She sighed. "Very well. I still think it is a big mistake."

"It isn't." He glanced at the pouch where he had neatly stowed the paper she had given him. "Well, I now have your list and I am about to take my swim. But there is one other matter of business for us to discuss. You still owe me a kiss from yesterday's wager."

He noticed her smile falter and hurried to finish his thought before she grew skittish and ran off. "What I mean is, I will understand if you are not ready to kiss me. Verity, would you rather we put it off?"

She let out a breath and nodded. "Yes, please. My stomach is already unsettled because of tonight's concert."

"Then so be it. I do not want to interfere with your important evening." He sat on the fallen log because standing in one place too long always caused his leg to seize and begin to spasm.

To his delight, she sat beside him. "Thank you, that is most appreciated. I am a little scared about it."

"About my kiss? I would be gentle, Verity."

She emitted a trill of laughter. "I was talking about the concert."

He chuckled. "My mistake."

"But kissing you would also scare me," she admitted. "It isn't because you are a duke. Lips are lips. Some are nicer than others, I expect. Besides, my father is the village constable and I do not think even you would dare step out of line and earn his ire."

"I will admit my heart stopped in that moment he introduced you as his daughter. It took me quite by surprise. I like him. He seems a good man, and certainly takes his responsibilities seriously. I see where you get your honorable qualities. But I suppose your mother is also a very decent person."

"She is. Although raising five children has taken a bit of a toll on her. I help her out as much as I can now that I am back home. But—"

"Back? Were you away?" Sitting on the fallen log was not very comfortable for him, but he would sit here all day if Verity remained beside him. He liked her and wanted to learn as much as he could about her.

She nodded. "I was in London for almost a year studying music with one of the masters at the Royal Conservatory. Women are not permitted to take classes at the conservatory, so I was never a student there. I resided with a cousin of my father's, a solicitor of some renown in London. I gave his children music lessons, and in turn I took my own private lessons with the master."

"That is quite impressive, Verity. How did he find you? What made him agree to take you on?"

"He passed through Moonstone Landing one summer, heard me play, and insisted my father allow me to train with him in London. I think I reminded him of his daughter who had passed away a few years earlier and would have been about my age had she survived. He told me she was quite talented, and hearing me play brought her back to life for him. Knowing this, each lesson was bittersweet for me. I worked so hard because I did not want to disappoint him. But I could see the sorrow in his eyes as well as the joy."

"His daughter lived on through your music. That must have been quite a burden for you," James said, for he had his own burdens and understood how such a thing could weigh on her heart. "When did you return to Moonstone Landing?"

"Several months ago. I had gone as far as I could with my lessons. What was the point when I would never be permitted a career? Anyway, I missed my family and wanted to come home. It was a fascinating experience that I do not regret, but it had run its course. At the same time, the master decided to return to his home and family in Florence. He was very kind to me and said I had helped him get past his grief. I was glad for him because I did not want him to suffer. It was a good point to end my musical dream."

"I'm sorry it had to end for you." He never understood Society's strict rules that would prohibit a female from performing in the great concert halls of England or around the world. "With all your training, tonight's concert should be simple for you."

"I'm sure you are right. Still, I feel so on edge. I've played at plenty of parties and fancy affairs before. But I have never been the featured performer. Usually, I am merely incidental. A harpist hidden behind a few ferns or off in a corner plucking out a tune while everyone mingles with the other guests. They might enjoy the music, but I am never noticed."

"But tonight, all eyes will be on you."

She nodded. "More to the point, eyes that may not want to like me or ever admit I might be as talented as the finest London musicians. There are always a few detractors in any crowd, don't you think?"

"Yes, but that is their failing, not yours. It sounds as though you are going to delight the rest of the audience. What is it you think you lack?"

"Experience, I suppose." She cast him a heartwarming smile. "But it is mostly that I am shy by nature. However, I believe in myself and know that I am very good."

"Then get up there and show yourself off," he said with a jovial laugh. "Command that stage. I shall be there with a bouquet of roses in hand to celebrate your triumph. Is there a flower market nearby? I've only noticed the fish market."

"Oh, you needn't. Please don't. It would only get tongues wagging, especially among the elite guests staying at the inn who will be in attendance. They are in your social circle. Flowers from you will only mean one thing."

"That I hope to make you my mistress?" He gave an incredulous laugh. "I never would. I hope you know that."

"I wasn't certain. Thank you for assuring me."

She sought to rise, but he held her back a moment. "Don't leave yet, Verity. Give me a few more minutes of your time."

She glanced around and then sat back down, wrapping her arms around her knees as she waited for him to speak. "All right. But I really cannot stay much longer."

"I know."

"Is there something else you wish to discuss, Your Grace?"

"James."

"Yes, James. Do you wish to review the exercises? The foods I've suggested for you?"

"No. Just sit with me," he said. "You may find this odd, but I feel at peace when I am with you. It is not something I have felt in years."

She seemed pleased by the remark. "Does this mean your leg feels better?"

"No, Verity. I still feel the pain, although listening to you as you spoke of your time in London made it easier to ignore. As for our kiss—"

"I know I owe you one," she said hastily, "but you agreed it would not be today."

"Nor any other day, if you do not wish it. I will never force you, even though I won the bet. It was a silly thing and neither of us needs to take it seriously."

She stared down at her hands that were still wrapped around her knees. "James, I would not mind that kiss. That isn't what I meant."

He did not know why the comment made him feel ridiculously elated.

Having kissed his share of women, adding another to the list should not have set his heart aflame. But it did. Not only did he wish to kiss Verity, he *ached* to kiss her. In fact, he did not think he would ever know peace in his life if he did not kiss her. "Well, you just let me know when you are ready and I will be happy to oblige."

She looked up, her green eyes wide as she stared at him. "Will you make it something special for me? Not just any kiss and then done."

Blessed saints.

"Of course, my pride will not allow me to give you anything less than my best."

She smiled. "I was peeved yesterday when you were proved right. Those ladies flitted to you like so many happy moths to a flame. But I am glad I lost the bet. Your kiss shall be a fond memory to hold in my dreams. *Chicks,* I shall tell my grandchildren, *have I told you about the handsome duke who kissed me?*"

Laughing softly, she rose and this time insisted she must leave. "Everyone on the Claymore staff must be up by now. I dare not risk one of them coming to look for you and finding me here. Don't get up. I'll see you tonight. And don't forget to read what I have written down for you."

He watched her run off.

She stayed on his mind as he swam lazily circles in this naturally formed pool. He thought about what Verity had told him, about her studies with a Royal Conservatory master. She had mentioned yesterday that three of her cousins had made matches with peers of the realm. Two dukes and an earl, to be precise.

This no longer surprised him.

Whatever was in the waters around Moonstone Landing ought to be bottled and sold as a miracle elixir.

Upon finishing his swim, he returned to the manor house, tried the recommended exercises, and then ate some of the dried fruits packed in the basket she had ordered for him. He also thought of her when applying the lavender oil and a warm, damp cloth to his scarred leg. Surprisingly, it did help ease the relentless pain.

Feeling invigorated, he went for a ride around the countryside. The riding paths took him past meadows dotted with vibrant red poppies, red stone cliffs, and spectacular views of the sea in all its vibrant colors. Varying shades of green swirled and clashed with deep blues, while white-crested waves broke upon the rocks along the shore.

Birds hovered over the water, and more of them nested in the many crags and niches in the cliffs. He rode his big gray along an isolated stretch of sandy beach and breathed in the salty air that surrounded him.

He noticed several elegant manor houses in the distance, and recalled what Daire had told him about this area. Several peers had settled here, finding a peace that had eluded them anywhere else in England.

They had found love, as well.

It was plain to see how deeply Daire loved his Brenna. No doubt this was the real reason Daire, that scoundrel, had urged James to recover here. It wasn't about fixing a busted leg. It was about finding love for himself.

Rather than return to the manor, James rode to Moonstone Landing. He did not expect to see Verity, but hoped he might. Seemed he could not get enough of her company. He looked forward to spending an entire day with her tomorrow.

But today, he would be mostly on his own.

He had just left his horse in the care of the Kestrel Inn's head groom, a chatty fellow by the name of Matchett, when he saw Verity's father on the high street. "You look well today, Your Grace," Malcolm Angel remarked, greeting him with a jovial smile.

"I do feel much better," James replied. "The sea air is refreshing, and your quieter pace of life seems to agree with me. I thought I would take a walk around the charming village and better acquaint myself with it. How did it come by its name? What exactly is a moonstone and how is it significant to this village?"

"Can you walk down to the harbor with me?"

James nodded. "Yes, walking is not the problem as long as it is at a leisurely pace. Standing too long in one place is what usually sets off the pain."

"I am sorry for that," Constable Angel said with obvious sincerity. "Then if you do not mind walking with me, I shall tell you about our magical moonstones."

They ambled down the street toward the harbor and its bustling fish market, although fish were not the only goods sold here today. "Farmers bring their crops to market, too," Verity's father said. "Wheat, corn, vegetables. Fruit freshly picked off the trees. Fish market is every day, but Wednesdays and Saturdays are the full market days. As for how the village got its name, that is a story in itself."

"Since you've brought me down to the water, I assume the sea has something to do with it."

"Aye, Your Grace. The moonstones lie beneath the water, quiet as any other stone. But on the night of a full moon, they come to life and shine for those who experience true love. It is quite a sight to see. Their glow transforms the water, turning it to shades of pinks and golds, silver and emerald. Rainbow colors. But this only happens if true love is present."

"Have you ever seen them shine, Mr. Angel?"

"Oh, yes. So have many others, including your friend, the Duke of Claymore. Those moonstones are never wrong, either. If you kiss a lass under a full moon and those moonstones burst into brilliant light, then you know you have found your true love."

"I see."

The constable laughed. "You don't believe me. Well, I only hope you will experience it for yourself someday."

"It would be nice, but I shall not hold my breath waiting for it to happen. I only came here to allow my leg to heal."

"Perhaps there is more of you that needs to heal than you realize." The constable was quiet as they walked on toward the fort that loomed over the harbor. "Viscount Brennan is in command of Fort Arundel and the army hospital beside it. The viscount prefers to be addressed by his rank and not that title. So we call him Major

Brennan. He is an army man and proud of it. The hospital is well run, and you'll find several doctors there who might give your leg a proper look."

"Your daughter has already chided me about it," James admitted. "I've been examined by the top London doctors, but Verity was not impressed. She insisted I speak to one of your local men, a Dr. Hewitt."

"Yes," the constable said with a burst of laughter, "you ought to pay attention to what Verity says. Although I apologize on her behalf if she was too forward to suggest this. One will always get an honest opinion from her, whether or not one cares to hear it."

"I always prefer honesty," James agreed, giving a moment's thought to her name. Verity Angel. *Truthful Angel.*

His angel of truth.

As they strolled back toward the inn, the constable stopped beside a memorial on the village green. "Let me show you this, Your Grace. It will help you understand why the people here are so special."

James listened as Verity's father related the tale of a sea captain who had died saving the village children from drowning when the boat they were on began to sink in a storm. "My nieces, Cara, Felicity, and Brenna, were on that vessel," he said, his voice trembling with emotion. "My nephew William, too. They were all so little at the time, barely old enough to be in school. The captain saved our precious wee ones. However, he did not survive. We all learned quite a lesson that day about valor and sacrifice. The children took it to heart, as well. Each child vowed to make something of themselves so that the captain's death would not be in vain. Verity, influenced by her cousins, took this same vow. I never saw a child work harder or ever be so eager to please."

He paused and wiped a tear from his eye. "Neither the terror of that incident, nor the relief when it was over and all the children were saved, ever leaves you. Verity was too young to be on that boat, but there are times I wonder what might have been if she had been out there and I had lost her. It is just a fatherly foolishness, I suppose. She is quite special to me. I should not play favorites with my children, but you might understand one day when you are a father. Sometimes, one just glows with a special magic. I cannot explain it."

"I think I understand, Mr. Angel." Despite being his father's heir and striving hard to please him, James's younger brother had always been the favorite. Seemed his entire family felt this way, adoring the lazy little cheat. James had never understood it, but perhaps there was a fault in himself that he had not discovered but others saw.

He would ask Verity in the hope she would tell him the truth. Odd, how ready he was to trust her when he did not know her at all. They had only met yesterday and done more gawking at each other than talking.

He bade the constable a good day soon after. "I shall see you tonight, Mr. Angel."

"Yes, Your Grace. Until then," Constable Angel said, hurrying off to continue his patrol of the village.

James returned to the Kestrel Inn for a bite to eat. He was immediately seated in a quiet corner overlooking the inn's garden. Several men were in the garden preparing a makeshift stage and bringing out chairs for the audience for tonight's performance. To his surprise, Verity was there, too.

He smiled watching her give orders. No doubt she wanted everything to be perfect and was overthinking every detail. Perhaps she needed the distraction from thinking about the recital itself.

She waved to him and smiled upon noticing him peer out the window.

He smiled back. She was a pretty thing.

He turned away a moment to place his order, but by the time he returned his gaze to the garden, Verity was gone. Stifling his disappointment, he took a sip of the cider just delivered to his table. Verity would be pleased he had decided to try out her suggestions instead of imbibing the wine or ale he would ordinarily have had with his meal.

A few moments later, he heard a rap on the window and turned to find her grinning at him from the other side of the pane. "Splendid," she said, pointing with delight at his glass of cider.

Come join me, he mouthed, motioning to the empty chair opposite his.

She smiled and nodded.

Her smile stole his breath away.

She disappeared and then reappeared a moment later beside his table. "Are you sure you do not mind my joining you?"

He rose as politeness dictated. "I would not have invited you otherwise. Have a seat. I am glad for the company."

She sat and immediately glanced out the window. "Thaddius's workers will be relieved not to have me telling them what to do at every turn. May I have a chamomile tea?"

He resumed his seat. "Yes, order anything you like."

"Just the tea." She smiled at the girl who came over to take her order. "Thank you, Mabel."

"My pleasure, Miss Verity. My family's coming to hear you tonight. We are all so thrilled."

She groaned once Mabel left their side. "This is why I am so on edge. Everyone in the village will be here tonight. I do not want to disappoint them."

"You won't, Verity. Don't think too hard about it. Those songs are etched into your soul. You will play them as easily as you take in the air you breathe."

"Harp music usually puts everyone to sleep. I'm not sure how to keep it vibrant. My father will be the first one closing his eyes and snoring like a honking goose throughout."

James laughed. "I'm sure your mother will elbow him if he does. Will your siblings be there?"

"No, they are too little and cannot be trusted to behave. There's quite a gap between me and my siblings. My mother is actually my stepmother. She is a lovely woman who has made a good home for all of us. She always made me feel loved, something I needed after losing my own mother at a young age."

"You are fortunate to have a caring family. Claymore feels the same about his stepmother. Not all of them are cold and vindictive. I expect many are kind and nurturing." His own mother never was, but his parents were not a love match and did not really care much for each other. His mother had dutifully delivered an heir and a spare to ensure continuation of the Ashford bloodline. His father was pleased, and then moved on to enjoy his life as he wished, sparing very little time for James. Nor had his mother bothered much with him.

But somehow, they all had time for the wastrel spare, Arthur. With his corn-gold hair, bright-blue eyes, and angelic face, he had been the adored one. Always needy. Always in trouble.

Always outspending his allowance.

"James," Verity whispered, "what is the matter? Your expression has suddenly turned sad."

He shook off those unpleasant thoughts. "I am fine, Verity. Your father showed me a little around town today."

"He did? Oh, I am glad. But I hope he did not show you everything. I would love to be your guide. I hope you will enjoy seeing Moonstone Landing through my eyes."

"I will. I am sure of it." She would add her very own sparkle to every historical detail. "Your father told me about the moonstone lore."

She inhaled lightly. "Oh, drat. I wanted to tell you about it. Is it not the most romantic thing you have ever heard?"

He arched an eyebrow, trying not to appear too cynical.

"Oh, I know love matches are not how things are done among those in the *ton*. But can you imagine anything more beautiful than those moonstones glowing on the night of a full moon just for you and the person who has stolen your heart? Is there anything more fulfilling than two people in love and knowing their love is real?"

"A love that will last forever?"

"Yes, and it will because they have found the one person to share their hopes and dreams, and their heart. The one person they can always trust. The one who will understand them and support them as they walk through life together. Stop giving me that cynical stare, James. I wish this for *you*, with all my heart. I wish you true love."

He smiled. "And I wish the same for you, Verity."

"Thank you. This is the next thing I hope to accomplish."

He arched an eyebrow. "Finding yourself a husband?"

She nodded. "But I will only marry for love. I don't know when it will happen for me, or if it will ever happen. I would be terribly sad if I never saw those moonstones glowing."

"You must have a dozen young men ready and willing to court you."

"Yes, there are several who have shown interest, but I feel nothing for them."

He took a sip of his cider and then set the glass down on the elegant table linen. "Perhaps a stranger will come along and steal your heart."

"Maybe." She took a sip of her tea that had just been delivered to the table, steam floating upward from the delicate porcelain teacup. "James, do you think it is possible for true love to be so quick and sure? Do you believe in love at first sight?"

CHAPTER FOUR

"A MAN IN my position can never leap into something so important as marriage on a mere whim," James replied to Verity's question about true love. "So, I suppose my answer is no. I do not believe in love at first sight."

However, he gave the question a lot more consideration after they parted ways.

Love at first sight. Had he not felt this when first spying Verity in the water?

Well, it was probably lust at first sight and nothing more. But he did look forward to spending time with her. He had enjoyed his meal this afternoon at the Kestrel Inn because of her charming presence.

His thoughts were on her now that he was back at the manor and exercising his leg. When he finished, he rubbed lavender oil into the scarred tissue before wrapping his leg in a warm, damp cloth, and then relaxed in bed while reading through a pile of Ashford estate documents concerning matters that needed to be addressed immediately.

His thoughts remained on Verity as he walked into the Kestrel Inn garden that evening with a noticeably less pronounced limp. The lavender oil was helping. He was led to a chair in the front row. Several couples took seats beside him, obviously *ton* members of the highest standing. He was introduced to the Duke of Malvern and his wife, Hen—short for Henley, it was quickly explained to him. "But she does cluck at me at times," Malvern teased his wife, a pretty woman he obviously adored.

The Marquess of Burness and his wife, Phoebe, took seats on the other side of James. "Has Claymore told you much about this place?" Burness asked him.

"Only that it was the right spot for me to heal." James pointed to his injured leg and the cane he'd tucked beside his chair.

Burness pointed to his own missing arm. "I'll never fully come to terms with losing it. But being here, having Phoebe by my side, makes it bearable. That's really why Claymore invited you here, I expect. It isn't about your leg. More about your anger and frustration, or whatever else unhealthy you are feeling. You'll begin to understand as you settle in. It is a matter of healing the heart, not a damaged leg or missing arm."

They said no more, since Verity's performance was about to get underway.

James held his breath as she walked onto the stage that already had her harp set upon it. Torches were lit all around the stage to illuminate her. He thought she looked like an angel in dark red silk. Well, she was an Angel by name, was she not?

Her hair was drawn back in a simple chignon, the style accentuating her natural beauty. She required no adornment, and he noted she had no jewelry save for sparkling earrings. Even those were simple ruby studs affixed to each earlobe.

He eased back in his chair as she began to play.

Any doubts he held about her abilities melted away. In truth, he hadn't any. His concern was more for her own confidence. He quickly realized she was in her element when at her harp, playing flawlessly and with vibrance.

Lord, she was good.

He was a wretchedly cynical man who quickly lost patience over the smallest things. But Verity's music transported him and held his rapt attention. He did not think the sound of a harp could touch his soul, but it did. Those gentle strains moved him and carried him off to a tranquil place, a place where wrongs could be forgiven and second chances allowed.

James found himself smiling at her, although he did not think she could see him or would notice even if she could. He thought of the moonstone lore and the possibility of true love.

Was this why he was here? To fall in love with Verity?

The moon shone bright and silver against the ink-dark sky above them. Not nearly a full moon yet. That would not happen for another ten days or so. Just in time for his departure. But he would never leave without kissing Verity under the silver glow of a full moon.

He wanted to believe in the moonstone lore.

Obviously, this was the entire point of Daire's invitation. The Marquess of Burness had cut straight to the heart of the matter. It was not his leg that needed healing but his heart.

When the concert ended, everyone swarmed around Verity to congratulate her. James stayed away, for his leg was not steady enough to withstand jostling and he did not want to make an ass of himself by falling. He was content to watch her from a distance until the first rush of admirers passed. The crowd around her soon began to thin, and most of the guests ambled toward the dining room, where light refreshments were offered.

He now made his way forward.

She had a special smile for him that touched his heart. "What did you think, Your Grace?"

"Best concert I have ever attended, Miss Angel. Well done."

"Thank you."

He held out his arm to her. "May I escort you inside? I assume that is where the vicar will start his donation campaign. How much is he hoping to raise, and for what purpose?"

She placed her hand on his arm and they walked indoors. She was as graceful as a swan, and he hobbled beside her. "It is a daunting task before us," she said, subtly slowing her steps to accommodate him. "The vicar would like to raise a thousand pounds for general repairs, supplies for families in need, shoes for the schoolchildren whose families cannot afford them. Coats and blankets for the winter. Food for the hungry. There is always a need for everything."

She left his side to give her short speech, then stayed beside the vicar and other village officials while they made their plea to the mixed crowd of locals and affluent Londoners.

James felt his leg begin to strain because he was standing in one place too long, so he moved a little further back and leaned against a decorative pillar to ease the weight off him. Several ladies and gentlemen he recognized from various London affairs he had attended over the course of the Season now approached him. "Lovely creature," several gentlemen remarked, ogling Verity. "What do you think, Ashford?" one of them already in his cups asked. "Is she mistress potential?"

"No."

"What? You prefer them blonde? Or perhaps a fiery redhead?"

He ignored the sot.

"She puts on airs. Thinks she is one of us," Lady Rothwell intoned. "What a pretentious little snip. Her talent is passable, at best."

Lady Rothwell's daughter, a *ton* diamond who had made her debut earlier in the year and was thought to be a contender as his next duchess, echoed her mother's opinions. "Quite a common girl," she said, turning to him with a smug smile. "What is your opinion, Your Grace?"

He detested being drawn into these petty conversations, so he ignored the question and turned his attention to the progress of the donations. As an incentive, several local businessmen had prepared baskets to be sold to the highest bidder. He noticed mostly the locals were bidding on those.

As always happened at every affair, the ladies all found reasons to approach him. Since he was not doing much talking, they began to pass comments among themselves, complimenting each other on their fashionable attire and mocking Verity's gown. They somehow believed their snide remarks were earning his favor.

He waited for one of them to disagree with the others and pass a kind remark, but none of them did.

Since his height gave him some advantage, he was able to see over most heads and keep his eyes on Verity, who was still standing up front. Her expression was earnest, but he noticed the worry in her eyes. She was placing the blame on herself because the vicar had not yet reached his donation goal. Frankly, one thousand pounds was a lofty target, and not one likely to be achieved in a month of trying.

"And will you look at her gown? Two years out of fashion, if not more," another young lady said, snickering.

Gad, were they *still* brutally gossiping?

A few gentlemen passed crude comments about what they would do with Verity if she were their mistress.

James had heard enough.

He made his way to the front and addressed the vicar. "How much more do you need to meet your goal?"

The vicar gave an acknowledging nod to the Duke of Malvern and his wife, as well as the Marquess of Burness and his wife. They had contributed a hundred pounds each. Same for Viscount Brennan and his wife, Chloe. The vicar introduced them to him and mentioned the wives of these three men were sisters and longtime residents of Moonstone Landing.

James did not see a great resemblance among the three women, although they stood together like a close-knit family and seemed very much at ease with each other.

"Are you the same Brennan who is fort commander?" he asked the dark-haired man who stood beside Lady Chloe and held a military stance.

"Yes," the man responded, glancing at the elite crowd in the back still smirking at Verity. "Do you know those louts?"

"Unfortunately, I do."

"We are quite fond of Moonstone Landing and its inhabitants," the viscount said, now frowning at said louts who were noisy and generally disrespectful. "Verity is someone very special to us, although those no-talent halfwits will never look beyond their noses to acknowledge her abilities. The gentlemen are probably passing crude comments because she is beautiful. The ladies are probably commenting on her gown and its supposed lack of style. They are so predictable, believing themselves superior. But all they are is callow and petty. This is why Chloe and I are happily settled here. Same for Malvern and Burness. We don't have to endure that endless nonsense."

He paused a moment and studied James. "Well, I've run off at the mouth, haven't I? I apologize if I have insulted your friends."

James shook his head. "They are not my friends. In fact, I walked up here because I intend to make them pay. Rest assured, they will make up the vicar's shortfall in donations and more. My greatest pleasure will be in wiping those smug grins off their faces."

He excused himself and addressed the vicar. "When factoring in the other smaller donations, does this leave you about five hundred pounds short?"

"Yes, Your Grace." The vicar glanced at Verity, who was standing close by, and lowered his voice. "I've run many events to raise funds for special projects. Baked goods sales, puppet shows, dances. Begging seems to be a major part of my job. But Verity has never done this before. She is taking it very hard, believing she has somehow failed me. I've told her this night's contributions are excellent, but she does not believe me."

"Well," James said, "let's see if we can make her smile. Put me down for five hundred pounds."

"Your Grace!" The vicar was genuinely delighted, but James was more interested in Verity's response.

The vicar quickly made a victory speech. "Thank you all, especially Miss Angel and her brilliant performance! And three cheers to His Grace, the Duke of Ashford, whose generous contribution has put us at our goal!"

A cheer rang through the crowd, but James had his eyes on Verity and saw the moment her face lit up like a little beacon in the night. Gad, she was beautiful. Her eyes sparkled as she ran up to him. He knew she wanted to throw her arms around him, but held herself back. "Your Grace..."

He took her hand and bowed over it. "Your performance was the best I have ever heard. Truly impressive. You ought to be very proud of yourself." He had complimented her earlier, but now repeated it for the benefit of the crowd. "My friends in the back quite agree." He pierced them with his angry glower. "Come up and pledge your donations. You do not wish to be mocked in London as skinflints and paupers, do you?"

"But the goal is reached," Lady Rothwell intoned.

"And now I expect your help in exceeding it," James shot back. "Open those purse strings to help a child in need."

"Why are you making such a fuss, Your Grace?" the sot who had made the unpleasant remark earlier about Verity called out. "Who will care?"

"I will care. And I assure you, the gossip rags will run wild with the story of your heartlessness that I shall give them."

They rushed forward, obviously furious but afraid to say a word against him. Those with daughters of marriageable age came up first, Lady Rothwell in the lead, because they knew James would dismiss their daughters from contention if they refused him. Well, they should have known he had already dismissed them.

His disappointment was profound, for not a single one of them had shown any decency toward Verity, whether to acknowledge her talent or the fact she did look beautiful in her gown.

Verity greeted the elegant group graciously and thanked each for their pledge. James took pleasure in standing behind her, guarding her like a gargoyle to make certain no one slipped her an unkind remark outside of his hearing. He felt good about doing this. In fact, he enjoyed this moment more than he had enjoyed anything the entire year.

Burness grinned at him. So did Malvern and Brennan.

Once Verity had taken donation pledges from the unpleasant lot and they had moved on to drink themselves silly, James relaxed his stance and stepped to Verity's side.

Malvern approached him and gave him a friendly pat on the back. "Claymore said we would like you. He was right. We hold an annual tea at St. Austell Grange, and it is next week. You are most welcome to join us. Verity will be there as well. It has become a tradition that she plays her harp while the guests arrive and walk about the grounds. But she will be free after the first hour to enjoy the tea. She is as much a guest as anyone else. The orchestra takes over afterward, and then the dancing starts."

Malvern's wife joined them. "You do not want to miss our affair. Mrs. Halsey bakes for days and days. Her cakes and sweet treats are not to be missed."

James acknowledged their invitation. "I shall be delighted to join you."

"Excellent," the duchess said, and hurried past him to hug Verity. "You were amazing! We are so proud of you, and quite daunted by your talent. Of course, we always knew you were good, but to hear you in concert was a revelation."

"Thank you, Hen." Verity hugged her back.

James watched the exchange with a swell of pride. Duchess Hen's sisters Phoebe and Chloe also gave the girl a hug. More important, Verity called them by their given names, a surprising familiarity that would be considered scandalous among the *ton*. But these three sisters accepted this informality as though it were something natural, which meant they accepted Verity as a friend. Well, she had that way about her. Did he not insist on the very same thing when asking her to call him James?

He had never cared a whit for the social rules, and he quickly realized those of the Upper Crust who settled in Moonstone Landing felt this same disdain.

There were only a handful of people left now, all friendly faces to Verity. The innkeeper ran up to her as the last of them were bidding her farewell. "You were magnificent, Verity!" He scooped her up in his arms and twirled her around.

She gave a merry shriek. "Thaddius, you clot! Put me down."

"You showed them all!" He finally set her down, but they both remained laughing and tossed teasing jibes at each other. James supposed happy families did this with each other.

He had never once seen this happen in his family. What a miserable lot they had been.

He meant to leave quietly, but had just made it out of the dining hall when he heard soft footsteps behind him. He turned and was almost knocked off his feet when Verity threw her arms around his waist and hugged him fiercely. "Thank you, from the bottom of my heart. What you did for all of us was remarkably kind and generous." She drew away and ran back into the dining room.

He watched her as she returned to her family.

She had to know he had done this for her. Only her.

His mermaid.

Dear heaven, what was happening to him?

CHAPTER FIVE

JAMES ARRIVED AT the copse while the church bells chimed the eight o'clock hour. He was eager to see Verity and give her the gift he had purchased on impulse yesterday afternoon, something he knew she would like.

The gift had been burning a hole in his pocket since last night. He had meant to give it to her then, but she was constantly surrounded by well-wishers, and he was not particularly keen on having an audience when he presented it to her.

No matter—he would take care of it today.

He felt acute disappointment when finding himself alone at the pool. The little mermaid was not waiting for him there. "Blast," he muttered, shedding his clothes and losing all excitement for his morning swim. He missed seeing her smiling face.

However, he could not fault her. She must have been drained from last night's performance and probably overslept.

He took a halfhearted swim, then got out of the pool to dry himself off and don his clothes. As he limped to his pile of clothes, he saw Verity grinning at him and holding out his drying cloth. "Here, wrap this around you for the sake of propriety."

He laughed. "You must be joking. Close your eyes, you little imp. Stop gawking at me."

"There, is this suitably proper?" She sealed her eyes shut tight, which caused her nose to scrunch. "Forgive me. I know that was unpardonably brazen of me. But I have also given thought to what you said yesterday about a bond between us. Oh, I do not wish to make too much of it, but I must agree. I feel as though we have been friends for ages. I hope I am not being a goose to trust you and feel so comfortable around you as I do."

"You are not a goose at all. This is the same I think about you. I'm glad you are here, Verity. Did you have your morning swim?"

"No, I lazed in bed the extra hour. But I have our day planned out and wanted to catch you before you rode off elsewhere."

He stepped behind the shrubbery to dry himself off and dress. "I wasn't going anywhere else. This day is reserved entirely for you."

She gave her back to him while he put on his trousers and buttoned his falls. "Would you mind if we saved the boat outing for tomorrow? I've brought two of my brothers along as chaperones today, but I think they are the ones who need closer looking after. I would not put it past them to jump into the water to swim with dolphins if we spot any. My father insisted on their coming with us, so I think we must stay on dry land. Do you mind?"

"Not at all. Frankly, I am surprised he did not insist on your entire family coming along. The rules are certainly different here. Young boys would never be considered proper chaperones in London."

"We are much more practical here. My father knows their antics will keep us fully occupied." She turned back to him with open eyes as he stepped out from behind the shrubs. "I thought we could have our picnic by one of our prettier beaches. There are pirate caves near it, but we won't go in the caves beyond the entrance because it turns frighteningly dark after only a few steps in."

"I'm sure Claymore has several lanterns we can borrow."

"No, best not. It will only encourage my brothers to explore, and then they will get lost. We'll have the devil of a time trying to find them. Just a picnic and a walk along the beach will do. I'll let the boys swim if they get too much out of line."

"Are your brothers already here?"

She nodded. "Having a bite in the kitchen with my aunt. She is the Claymore housekeeper."

"Of course. Why am I not surprised? You Angels are everywhere." He gave his locks a quick brush by raking his fingers through them. "You have the oddest family."

"I know. Duchesses and housekeepers. A countess and a constable. We are all over the place."

"I can see why a duke would offer for an Angel. Are your cousins as remarkable as you? Claymore is wild for your cousin Brenna. He told me she taught at an elite girls' school in Oxford."

"Yes, she is the smartest among us." She picked up his cane and handed it to him, then walked beside him as he slowly made his way toward the manor house. Climbing the slight rise was difficult, but coming down was just as hard and probably more damaging if he fell. "Cara and Felicity are smart, too," she added. "But Brenna stood out."

"You are also a standout, Verity. Introduce me to your brothers." He guided her toward the kitchen entrance, since it was closest and the boys were already in there. "How old are they?"

"Gabriel is twelve and Michael is ten. My parents named them after the archangels. I have a fifteen-year-old brother, Elmer, and two younger sisters as well. All of them are ginger-haired and freckled like my stepmother. I am the only one who takes after my father."

He grinned. "You are a lot prettier than your father."

She laughed. "So I have been told a time or two."

She led the way into the kitchen and called out to the Claymore housekeeper. "Auntie, don't give them too much food or they'll end up with bellyaches."

Two ginger heads looked up. The boys had been digging into a batch of freshly baked scones and emitted howls when the housekeeper took the plate away. "We hardly ate anything for breakfast," the eldest boy complained.

"We are growing boys, and Mum says we need our sustenance or else we'll wither," the younger one insisted.

"Mama packed plenty of food for our picnic," Verity reminded them, then playfully grabbed two scones and handed one to James. She took a bite of hers. "Mmm, delicious, Auntie."

Her aunt turned to respond and realized James was standing behind Verity. She became somewhat flustered and immediately fell into a respectful curtsy. "Your Grace."

When she realized her nephews had remained seated, she gave each boy a light smack on the head and told them to get up and greet him properly. They scrambled to their feet and gave polite bows.

"A pleasure to meet you boys. You must be Gabriel. And you are Michael." They both had Verity's green eyes.

"Yes, Your Grace," the older one answered.

"Please forgive the shocking informality, Your Grace," Verity's aunt said, not yet over the embarrassment of being caught feeding her nephews. Perhaps she was also embarrassed to find him in the kitchen. Dukes were not in the habit of walking into the servants' domain.

But James liked this informality. Yes, it would probably hasten the downfall of all barriers between the classes, but he had felt nothing but shame in the way his peers had treated Verity last night. Let every blasted barricade fall, as far as he was concerned.

Verity shuffled the lads outside and waited with them by the rattletrap of a rig that had brought them here. In the meantime, he went upstairs to change into proper attire for a country picnic and perhaps a little cave exploring, although Verity had ruled it out. A plain work shirt, light neckcloth, and dark trousers of a sturdy weave would do. He brought along a jacket but did not bother to put it on. He would don it if they encountered company, which he hoped they would not. He retained the boots he had put on this morning. The soft leather was worn in and quite comfortable. Those would be especially suitable if they were to undertake a day of walking.

Well, Verity was aware of his limitations. She would be careful not to let him strain his leg.

"All right, Angels," he said, stepping out the front door. "Let's get underway."

The boys had been running circles around the rig while waiting for him to appear, but they now scampered into the back seat and immediately began to push and poke each other. Verity hopped into the driver's seat and took up the reins.

James climbed up last, feeling a bit helpless for requiring the assistance of a footman. But he easily settled on the driver's bench beside Verity and stretched his leg in front of him. "Miss Angel, you are in charge today. Where are you taking us?"

"Brigand's Beach, Your Grace, and a picnic afterward...or perhaps beforehand, depending on the tides." Since she handled the worn conveyance and the horse drawing it with ease, he relaxed and enjoyed the ride. Her brothers continued to poke and prod each other. Verity, obviously dismayed they were behaving like little heathens, kept turning her head to frown at them. "I am not stopping this carriage, so you had better quit fighting and trying to push each other out."

"Yes!" Michael immediately tried to push Gabriel out now that Verity had unwittingly given him the idea.

"Quit it!" Gabriel gave his brother a hefty push back.

"You might rethink that strategy, Verity," James said with a grin, reaching back to put his arm between the boys before they succeeded in sending each other flying onto the roadway. "First one who moves," he said in his most commanding voice of authority, "shall muck out my horse's stall for a week."

"Verity! Can he make us do that?" Gabriel asked, looking so innocently outraged that James had to bite the inside of his cheek to stem his laughter.

She nodded. "He's a powerful duke. He can do anything he wants. You had better listen to him or he'll have you cleaning out his bedpans, too."

"No!" they shouted in unison, but the threat appeared to work and they quieted down. It helped that James engaged them in conversation, asking them questions about the area, their favorite spots in Moonstone Landing, and their favorite activities. Once he got them talking, they were little chatterboxes.

He did not mind this either, for having them chew his ear off was a healthy way for boys to be. Well, he thought so. This was so much better than enforced silence or wallops to the head that followed a hiss to keep silent. The few times he and his father rode together in the ducal carriage, the old man wanted nothing to do with him, and made his displeasure quite clear. James had learned at an early age to keep his feelings to himself.

As a consequence, he could count on one hand the number of people he would consider friends. Perhaps Claymore was his closest and only true friend. As for the ladies, none had ever gotten close to him.

His fault, most likely. They all blended into each other, all of them beautiful and mercenary, all of them knowing every detail of his family's long and exalted history but knowing nothing of *him*.

"Is this not the prettiest countryside?" Verity commented, drawing him out of his thoughts.

"Yes, quite beautiful." They rode past many places he had seen when riding his gray yesterday, but it helped to know the who, how, where, and why of each meadow, pasture, and cove they passed.

Verity pointed to her left to a particularly scenic vista of red stone cliffs that plunged down to swirling azure waters and crashing waves. "This road traverses the Earl of Woodley's property," she explained. "To the right is his manor house, and to the left are caves considered the area's authentic pirate caves because they were once used for smuggling by real pirates who plundered the Irish Sea."

"Ooh! Can we explore them, Verity? Pleeeease?" Michael asked, clasping his hands together as though in prayer.

"Not these caves, nor any others today," she replied. "We're going to have a picnic on Brigand's Beach and then take a walk, but that is all."

"There are caves at Brigand's Beach," Michael insisted.

"Yes." Verity sighed. "But we cannot go inside, Michael. Remember, I warned you how dark and slippery these caves can get. We haven't the supplies to explore them safely."

"The duke can't walk anyway," Gabriel advised his brother. "He'll fall on the rocks and crack his skull open. Have you always needed a cane to walk, Your Grace?"

"Gabriel!" Verity said. "That is not polite."

"It's all right. It is a good question," James said, wishing adults could be as guileless as children. "No, I used to have no trouble walking until a few months ago. Then I was in a carriage accident."

"What happened?" Gabriel asked, his sincere expression of concern similar to the one on Verity's face.

"I was on my way to one of the Ashford estates along the Yorkshire moors when the weather suddenly turned foul. My driver and I headed for the nearest inn, but it was still miles away. That area is rather barren, and we were on the open road and fully exposed to the storm. A flash of lightning struck close and spooked my horses. The driver could not control them. He was thrown off, fortunately surviving the fall by landing on soft marsh grass. I tried to climb out through the window to get onto the roof and then the driver's seat. I had just managed to get onto the roof when the team darted off the road onto quicksand. The wheels got stuck, which made the horses even more skittish than they already were. They broke loose and kept galloping off."

The boys had their eyes wide, big green orbs staring at him.

"I tried to jump clear of the carriage as it began to roll over, but I did not quite make it, and it crushed my leg."

He noted Verity's expressive face and could see every caring feeling that passed across her lovely features. "How long was it before anyone found you?"

"Out there? It took hours. I lay there overnight and wasn't found until the next morning. By that time, the rain had stopped and I had managed to dig my leg out from under the carriage. However, I could not walk on it because it was so badly mangled. A gentleman on the way to Scarborough saw my driver and was kind enough to stop and help him search for me. That unpleasant adventure was several months ago, as I mentioned earlier. I have been trying to strengthen the leg ever since."

"That must have been scary," Gabriel said, the young lad fully appreciating the seriousness of the accident.

Michael, on the other hand, was bouncing in his seat. "Were you hit by lightning?"

"While I lay out there in the rain? No, but it was a close thing. Lightning travels along the ground for a short distance after striking. I felt the ground sizzle around me a time or two. Fortunately, I was far enough away that I only felt strong tingles but did not get burned."

"I fell out of a tree and broke my arm once," Gabriel volunteered. "It hurt like blazes. But Dr. Hewitt treated it and I'm good now."

Michael was still bouncing in his seat. "I haven't broken anything yet."

"That's a surprise," James muttered with a chuckle. "Let's hope you don't. It is not pleasant. Sometimes, the bone may heal but you will still feel pain forever afterward. You want to be careful and try to avoid injury."

They reached a sandy beach where the approach was along a relatively flat stretch of land that James could manage. At the other end of the beach were carved-out openings at the base of a cliff. Those were the caves Michael must have wanted to explore.

Verity was adamant. "We will take a walk to them, but not go in, Michael. Do not whine about it."

"All right," the boy muttered.

The two lads then ran to a shady spot on the beach to set out a blanket and their picnic basket.

Verity watched them a moment and then turned to James. "I know you cannot walk the entire distance, so I will take the boys on my own after our picnic. Just to the mouth of the caves and back. As I've repeatedly told Michael, we are not going in. I'll distract them by having them collect seashells and dip their feet in the water, if need be."

"Are you sure it will be all right?"

"Yes, Gabriel and I will keep close watch on Michael. I won't be gone long. Stretch out on the blanket and enjoy the sunshine while you wait for us. The sun is good for your bones."

They settled on the large blanket and enjoyed a surprisingly generous array of food. Cold chicken, cheeses, apples, and freshly baked bread were only a small part of what her mother had packed. There was plentiful cider as well as two ginger cakes and a lemon cake neatly wrapped in checkered cloths. "We'll save the cakes for later," Verity said before kicking off her walking boots and telling her brothers to take off theirs. "The sand is warm and you'll enjoy burrowing your toes in it."

The boys eagerly obeyed.

James watched them walk along the beach. They scooped up shells, and the boys rolled up the legs of their breeches to their thighs in order to frolic among the waves that swept to shore. For the first time in his life, he could see himself as a family man, a father and husband. Yes, he could be that to someone like Verity.

He was in the midst of his reveries about his idyllic future and his idyllic family when he heard Verity suddenly cry out. "Bollocks," he muttered, immediately picking up his cane and getting to his feet when he saw Michael running off toward the caves. Verity and Gabriel gave chase, but Michael was a quick little devil.

James hobbled as fast as he could toward them. In truth, he felt useless, and his leg would be in spasms soon from the effort of running in soft sand. But instinct warned he had to do it. Perhaps it was merely wishful thinking on his part that he might be needed.

It struck him in that moment that no one really needed him. They wanted his title. His maiden aunt depended on his benevolence to keep her in comfort but otherwise cared nothing for him. Not a soul in the world would miss *him*.

Michael was now climbing the rocks at a spot where the gentle waves turned rough and swirling as they were caught in a small, canyon-like pathway carved out by the relentless pounding of water against those rocks over thousands of years. James heard deep rumbles inside the caves as those waves broke with force inside the hollow rock.

He saw Verity warn Gabriel to stay on the sand while she scampered up those rocks to chase Michael. Then he heard her scream as Michael slipped and fell into the water. His heart surged into his throat when he saw Verity jump in after him.

Gabriel, using some sense, carefully made his way up those rocks and then sank flat onto his stomach in order to try to reach a hand to either of them.

James had just reached the boy when he saw him haul Michael out of the water. Verity had managed to shove the boy upward into Gabriel's arms. But the swirling water now had her in its grip and suddenly pushed her under and out to sea. At least, James hoped it was pushing her away from those treacherous rocks. Still, there was extreme danger, since the current now seemed to be holding her under.

You're a mermaid.

Swim out of this, Verity.

But he dared not wait for her to come up for air. What if she could not?

James dove in after her, hoping to find her before it was too late. Could he pull either of them up even if he did find her?

It did not matter. He was going to save her or die trying.

The salt water burned his eyes, but he quickly adjusted to it.

Harder to deal with was the sand and silt that swirled around him, roiling and clouding the water. *Verity.* He was growing desperate to find her.

His lungs were starting to ache. Hers had to be ready to burst.

Please, no.

Please.

Where are you, Verity?

As though in answer to his prayer, he suddenly saw her in a circle of light, her dark hair unbound and floating upward, her green eyes open, and her expression desperate.

The sun's rays had struck the water in such a way as to create a prism of light around her. Whether plain luck or divine providence, he did not know or care. He had found Verity and would never let her go.

He reached out, grabbed her hand, and tugged her to him with all his might. Then, with all the strength within his soul, he swam them both upward. She gasped and inhaled deeply as soon as they broke the surface of the water. He did the same, taking in great gulps of air, but did not pause to rest because they still had to swim clear of that treacherous current.

Verity was too weak to manage it on her own, so he held on to her.

Not that he had any intention of ever letting her go.

She did not resist or make any attempt to push away. He kept his arm around her, quietly rejoicing every time she coughed or took a deep breath because it meant she was alive.

He carried her out of the water and onto dry sand, but had taken no more than a few steps before his leg gave out. He collapsed awkwardly, landing atop her.

"Bollocks," he muttered, and quickly rolled off her onto his back. But that momentary feel of her breasts against his chest, and her wrapped in his arms, shot heat through him. For whatever reason, exhaustion or delirium, the fantasy of making love to Verity took hold and gave him wild thoughts.

It was ridiculous. He had yet to catch his breath. He had yet to let go of her hand, which he would not do until he was certain she had recovered.

But those wild thoughts stayed with him even as her brothers reached them and asked if they were alive. "Yes," he said, now sitting up and turning to Verity, who had been caught underwater longer than he had been. She had yet to move or open her eyes. "Verity..."

He placed a hand over her heart to make certain it was still beating. He knew only elation when he felt its strong, steady rhythm beneath his palm.

"Yes," she said weakly, "give me a moment."

"Take all the time you need." James reluctantly removed his hand from the soft mound of her breast, for it did not need to linger there. She was alive and breathing. Her gown was pasted to her body, revealing every appealing curve and every blessed detail of her lovely bosom.

Gad, he should not be having wild thoughts. But he ached to taste her, to trail his lips and tongue along her skin. She would taste so sweet. Her breasts. The intimate mound between her legs. It was not only lust he was feeling but permanence as well. She was the one he wanted writhing beneath him and clutching his shoulders as he brought her to pleasure.

He had never shared anything with anyone. And yet he wanted to share the rest of his life with Verity.

He would speak to her later in private. Perhaps the present he meant to give her would serve as a bridal token instead.

No.

What was he thinking?

He had only known Verity a handful of days. Had Claymore, Bradford, and Strathmore acted as rashly toward the Angels they had married? How long did it take for them to know?

He set the thought aside as Verity slowly sat up. Michael immediately burst into tears and hugged her. "I'm so sorry, Verity!"

She embraced him fiercely. "Hush, Michael. I'm just glad none of us were hurt."

Gabriel was not about to let his brother get off so lightly. "He almost killed you! Michael, what were you thinking? His Grace and Verity warned us of the danger, and you just ran off like a spiteful brat. You have to tell Papa what you did."

Now Gabriel was crying and hugging Verity.

Michael, who was still weeping and kneeling beside Verity and Gabriel, kept whispering, "I'm sorry. I'm sorry."

James could see how torn up the boys were over almost losing their sister. *This.* This is what mattered and what no one had ever felt about him. He could pass from this earth and no one would shed a tear. Perhaps Claymore might, but it would be regret more than inconsolable sadness.

Michael looked so helpless and hurt, just standing there watching Gabriel and Verity hug.

James sighed. "Michael, come here."

The boy threw himself into James's arms and gave him a hug so intense and pure of feeling, he felt it in his soul. "You saved her," the lad whispered. "You saved her."

And James felt bloody good about it.

"Does this mean you will always listen to us from now on?" he said in a stern but affectionate tone.

Michael nodded against his chest. "Yes. Always."

Since they were all soaked to the skin, they packed up their picnic wares and climbed back into the rickety rig. "I'll take the reins, Verity," he said, knowing she was still unsettled from her near drowning. His leg was strained and starting to spasm, but he overlooked the pain by sheer force of will. Taking care of these wet Angels was a priority. He would have all night to toss a vat of lavender oil on the scarred limb.

Verity was trembling, so he drew her close and kept his arm around her. James knew the moment she began to return more or less to herself when she took out the two ginger cakes and the lemon cake from their picnic basket at her feet. She handed a ginger cake to each brother and kept the lemon cake for herself to share with him. "You do realize you've given each brother an entire cake to themselves," he said.

She smiled at him and nodded. "Yes, it will keep them occupied on the ride home. This one's for us. I hope you like lemon cake."

"I do."

"Good. Do you have an appetite?"

For her as well as the cake. "Ravenous."

It seemed every inhabitant of Moonstone Landing was on the

high street and staring at the bedraggled lot of them as their rig passed by. Verity guided him toward her home, which turned out to be a beautiful cottage overlooking the water. It was large and well maintained. The boys hopped down as soon as they came to a stop, and ran inside calling for their mother.

Verity remained beside him. "Would you like to come in for a few minutes? I'll introduce you to my mother, and then I'll run up to change out of this wet gown before I drive you back to Stoningham Manor. Do not even think of walking. Your leg must be hurting like blazes."

"It's all right."

"I'm sure it is not," she said with a sigh, but cast him a charming smile. She hopped down, then came to his side to assist him. She made no fuss about helping him. He was pleased by how smoothly she handled it without making him feel helpless.

They had just walked into the house when her father caught up to them. He looked at James and then his children, all of them soaked and exhausted.

Michael immediately burst into tears. "Verity almost drowned and it's all my fault, Papa. I went onto the rocks by the caves when she told me not to, and then I fell in. She jumped in after me and pushed me to Gabriel, who got me out of the water. But she couldn't get out, so the duke jumped in after her. And then those lights shone in the water and—"

"What lights?" Verity asked.

"Those colored lights. It looked like a rainbow on the water. Gabriel saw them, too. Didn't you, Gabriel?"

The boy nodded. "And then there was a final rainbow burst of light and the duke swam to the surface clutching Verity in his arms."

"I am ready to take my punishment, Papa," Michael said, his chin raised high as though he were ready to face the consequences like a man of honor.

"The duke said he would make us muck out his horse's stall if we misbehaved," Gabriel suggested.

"And clean out the bedpans, too," Michael added, now turning to James. "I am ready to do all of it."

"Me too," Gabriel said, placing a protective arm around his

brother.

But Michael insisted on taking the punishment all by himself. "It was my mistake. You can watch me, Gabriel. I won't mind the company. But I must do it all on my own."

Their father cast him a questioning gaze. "Is this amenable to you, Your Grace?"

James nodded. "You have good lads, Mr. Angel. Perhaps a bit out of hand, but I suppose this is how most boys are at that age." His only experiences were in boarding school, and there were always instances of foolish pranks and sometimes serious misbehavior. The masters were strict, but he still preferred them to being with his parents. His mother was indifferent to him and his father beat him for the slightest transgression.

Often, James had no idea what he did wrong. His father was just a bitter, angry man.

His heart tightened as he watched Malcolm Angel with his children. The man never raised a hand to them. Instead he took them aside to talk to them. This was perhaps worse for the boys, who obviously adored their father. Michael especially. He had disappointed this kind man he worshipped and admired.

Verity's stepmother was a pretty woman who obviously felt overwhelmed by the presence of a duke in her home. She had two little girls clinging to her side. "Mrs. Angel, you'll forgive me if I do not stay," James said, pointing to his soggy attire.

The only thing dry was his jacket, which he'd left in the rig during their picnic. Verity's gift happened to be safely tucked in its breast pocket.

Should he give it to her now? Had Michael been telling the truth about those lights?

James thought of the moonstone lore.

Everyone else was thinking of it, too. Verity's expressive face showed everything. Her hope, doubt, confusion. Ultimately, her acceptance and love.

She believed in those moonstones.

Did she love him?

The more problematic question was, did he love her?

CHAPTER SIX

VERITY WAS CRUSHED.

She watched as friends and family walked past her while she played the harp in a corner of the parlor at St. Austell Grange, home of the Duke and Duchess of Malvern. It was their annual tea party, and the entire village had been invited.

Her hour was almost up and she had yet to see James.

In fact, she had not seen him since the day of their disastrous picnic. Her near drowning had shaken her quite profoundly. She had yet to work up the courage to go near water again. Not even the harmless pool in the copse where she had first met James felt safe yet.

Had he gone for his daily swim? Had he waited for her? Did he miss her?

Henley came to her side. "Verity, put away your instrument and come join us. The weather is perfect for an outdoor stroll."

"I don't mind playing a little longer."

"But I mind," Henley insisted. "Come outdoors and sit with me and my sisters. It is completely selfish on our part. We want to know what happened between you and the Duke of Ashford. Is it true? Did those moonstones shine for you?"

Verity shook her head, hoping to hold off tears. "I don't think so. Michael must have been mistaken. Oh, Hen! I haven't seen him since that day. Not that I blame him for running away. My brothers were awful. Noisy. Disobedient. Stuffing their faces as though they hadn't eaten in a month. Trying to push each other out of the carriage."

"Oh dear."

Verity nodded. "The duke was polite about it, of course. A thorough gentleman, not to mention we both almost drowned while he was trying to save me. I would not blame him if he never spoke to me again. I don't even know if he is still in Moonstone Landing. Has anyone seen him at all this week?"

"Come with me." Hen led Verity to her sisters, who were seated at a table on the terrace. "Sit down." She poured Verity a cup of tea and then turned to her sisters. "Phoebe, Chloe, what have you heard about Ashford?"

"My husband told me," Chloe said, her gaze now on Verity, "that Ashford left for Bath the morning after your almost-drowning incident. But I'm sure he said Ashford was coming back."

"Truly?" Phoebe asked. "Let's hope so. He was only supposed to stay here for two weeks, and those are almost up. But if he said he would return, then he will. Verity, I know he liked you."

Hen and Chloe nodded in agreement.

"Perhaps I was a passing fancy, but nothing more." Verity could not bear to talk about him. "Please excuse me."

So this was it. She would never see James again. Never give him the kiss he had won from her in the silly bet they had made that day at the Kestrel Inn library.

He must have forgotten about it, shoved it from his memory now that he was consorting with the fashionable set in Bath.

She walked to the gazebo overlooking St. Austell's beautiful cove, glad to be away from the crowd. A light breeze floated around her, carrying the sounds of the orchestra tuning their instruments. The dancing would soon begin. Guests began to wander toward the dance floor.

Verity was relieved, because she did not want company. Everyone had heard about her near drowning and those moonstones supposedly glowing.

What did they think James was going to do? Propose to her?

This was not going to happen.

Michael had gone to the Stoningham Manor stable every day to muck out the stalls, even though the big gray James rode was not there. Nor were there any bedpans to be emptied in the bedchambers, since neither James nor Claymore and his family were home.

"Are you going to mope all afternoon?" her father said, coming to stand beside her as she gazed out over the scenic cove and its blue waters. "There's a young man who is eager to speak to you."

"Oh, Papa. Not today."

"Are you certain?"

Why was her father so insistent when he knew she just wanted to be left alone? "Yes, Papa. Kindly leave me to my misery."

"Very well, love. But I really think you ought to greet this young man. In fact, he's standing by the gazebo, hoping for permission to approach you."

"What?" She wasn't paying attention to her father because the water was suddenly glistening and beginning to turn colors.

She blinked.

It could not be the moonstones, because everyone knew the lore and this was not possible. Moonstones only glowed on the night of a full moon. It was the middle of the afternoon and the sun was brightly shining. A full moon was a requirement, was it not?

"Will you look at that," her father said, sounding annoyingly jovial. "Moonstones." He strode off.

Had he seen them, too?

"Wait, Papa! I—"

The breath caught in her throat as James stepped into the gazebo. "So, you do not care to see me?"

Verity rushed to him and hugged him fiercely. "I thought you were never coming back. Oh, James! You will make me cry. Those moonstones are shining again. Do you see them?"

He closed his arms around her. "Yes, love. They are bright as starlight. Was there a doubt?"

"Yes! Doubts galore. I was sure my brothers had scared you off. Why did you run away?"

"I wasn't running away. I was making marriage plans."

She gasped. "Who is the lucky bride?"

"You, if you will have me. You are my mermaid and always meant to be mine. How could I lose you to the water? How could I ever lose you to anyone or anything? I rode to Bath to fetch my aunt because I wanted one bloody member of my family to share this day with me."

"Is she here?"

He groaned lightly. "No. She claimed it was too much of an effort to make the trip."

"James, I'm so sorry." She meant it sincerely, and ached for him because she knew how hurt he was by this.

"Don't be. I was a fool to think anything had changed. I haven't even asked you to marry me yet. I should have done at least that before running off like a heedless dolt."

"Those moonstones shone because we love each other," Verity said, feeling as though she was walking in a dream. "Is there a doubt what my answer will be?"

"I've spoken to your father, and he has consented to our marriage. He and I will obtain the license tomorrow."

Verity's heart soared, but she gave a hearty laugh. "Aren't you forgetting something?"

His smile melted her heart. "Asking you to marry me? Yes, that is an important detail that I hope to rectify immediately." He reached into the breast pocket of his jacket and withdrew a small box. "I have been carrying this around since the day of your harp recital. I wanted to give it to you then as a gift in celebration of your recital. But now, it is a bride token. A rather plain one for a future duchess, but I shall buy you something more spectacular tomorrow."

She took a moment to open her gift and cried out softly. "James, this is beautiful! It's perfect. I don't need anything else. I cannot think of a single thing I would love more." He had given her a cameo brooch with a young lady playing a harp etched in it. Probably one of the Muses because of the style of her long, curly locks and the flowing robe she was wearing. "It is exquisite."

"So are you, Verity. I'm going to kiss you in a moment, but there is a little more I need to say to you."

"Wait, James. It is up to me to kiss you, because I lost the bet."

He smiled again and tweaked her chin. "Ah, yes. My grand prize. I am eager to collect it. Do you have any idea how to kiss a man?"

Heat ran up her cheeks. "No. Is there an art to it?"

"Yes, in fact, there is. Do you mind if I show you how it is done? After which, I intend to officially ask you to marry me. I wish to be clear on this point because I am going to kiss you long and hard. I am going to kiss you until your legs turn to water and cannot hold you up. And I think we are going to gather quite an audience for that performance."

"Then may I give you advance warning that I am going to accept your offer of marriage because I love you with all my heart? My legs have already turned to water and I cannot think of anything I would like better than to have you kiss me. Should I hold on to your shoulders? They feel divine. Your arms, too. There is something quite appealing about your muscles. You have the most beautifully formed body I have ever seen on a man."

"Seen many men, have you?"

She blushed again. "No, I... You know what I mean. Clothed you look divine, and no one has ever looked better."

"And unclothed?"

"Well, I have only you to judge about that. But I am fairly certain no one can surpass you. You, however, have seen other women without a stitch. Dare I ask how I would compare?"

"None of them were mermaids, and none can ever come close to your splendor. I knew you were meant to be mine the moment I saw your rounded bottom and gorgeous legs poking out of the water that first day at the pool."

"Oh, heavens. My bottom?"

"And exquisite legs. Close your eyes, love. It is time for me to kiss you." His mouth closed over hers, and with that gentle crush of his lips against the softness of her own, he pledged his heart and soul.

He pledged to protect her and love her.

He pledged to always be faithful.

He pledged to give her happiness and a houseful of unruly children who would adore her, and hopefully adore him. He meant to make theirs a true family home.

His lips pressed down on hers with a hungry need, that of a man who had grown up without love and was now famished for it.

As predicted, a crowd had gathered around them by the time he ended the kiss. Verity's smile was incandescent as she looked out among her friends and family.

Her father now stepped forward.

"Papa, he loves me."

"I know, my dearest." He was tearful with joy. "I'm sure all of Moonstone Landing knows by now. Those moonstones are blinding in their brilliance."

She turned to James. "Oh, I did not realize everyone can see them."

He took hold of her hand. "Does it matter? They shone for us, and this is what counts."

She cast him an impish grin. "In broad daylight, no less."

"Because I love you that much, Verity," he said in all seriousness. "Will you marry me, my moonstone mermaid?"

The End

Additional Dragonblade books by Author Meara Platt

The Moonstone Landing Series
Moonstone Landing (Novella)
Moonstone Angel (Novella)
The Moonstone Duke
The Moonstone Marquess
The Moonstone Major
The Moonstone Governess
The Moonstone Hero
The Moonstone Pirate

The Book of Love Series
The Look of Love
The Touch of Love
The Taste of Love
The Song of Love
The Scent of Love
The Kiss of Love
The Chance of Love
The Gift of Love
The Heart of Love
The Hope of Love (Novella)
The Promise of Love
The Wonder of Love
The Journey of Love
The Dream of Love (Novella)
The Treasure of Love
The Dance of Love
The Miracle of Love
The Remembrance of Love (Novella)

Dark Gardens Series

Garden of Shadows
Garden of Light
Garden of Dragons
Garden of Destiny
Garden of Angels

The Farthingale Series
If You Wished For Me (Novella)

The Lyon's Den Series
Kiss of the Lyon
The Lyon's Surprise
Lyon in the Rough

Pirates of Britannia Series
Pearls of Fire

De Wolfe Pack: The Series
Nobody's Angel
Kiss an Angel
Bhrodi's Angel

Also from Meara Platt
Aislin
All I Want for Christmas

About Meara Platt

Meara Platt is a USA Today bestselling author and an award winning, Amazon UK All-star. Her favorite place in all the world is England's Lake District, which may not come as a surprise, since many of her stories are set in that idyllic landscape, including her award-winning fantasy romance Dark Gardens series. If you'd like to learn more about the ancient Fae prophecy that is about to unfold in the Dark Gardens series, as well as Meara's lighthearted, bestselling Regency romances in the Farthingale series and Book of Love series, or her more emotional Moonstone Landing series and Braydens series, please visit Meara's website at www.mearaplatt.com.

SAY ANYTHING, DUKE

by Kathleen Ayers

CHAPTER ONE

"P ARTHENA, HURRY ALONG." Mama gave a frustrated wave. "We are the last guests to arrive."

Miss Parthena Holm dutifully lifted her skirts and trudged forward, pausing only to take in the splendor of Lady Baldwin's estate rising majestically out of the perfectly manicured lawn. Her ladyship must employ an entire herd of gardeners. A line of carriages stood in the drive, the Holm carriage being the last. No surprise there. They would need to trudge to the front door deftly avoiding the footmen hauling baggage about.

"Fedelia!" Mama said shrilly. "Stop gawking. You've been here before."

"Yes, but not as the entertainment," Parthena said under her breath. Mrs. Holm in all her wisdom, had convinced the austere Lady Baldwin to allow Parthena and Fidelia to perform during this impromptu house party, showcasing their talents in the hopes some gentleman would be struck speechless and offer to wed them. A valiant effort on Mama's part.

Parthena was only passable on the violin. Fidelia not much better on the pianoforte. Any gentleman whose attention they drew would likely be half-deaf.

"I worked tirelessly to have Lady Baldwin grant us this honor," Mama intoned. "One day you will appreciate my efforts on your behalf."

"An honor," Parthena muttered, as Fidelia took her arm. "Mama probably begged Lady Baldwin to put us on display. As if we are horses for sale at Tattersalls."

"Oh, far worse than that," Fidelia said with a mysterious air.

"Worse than trying to entice a suitor with our poor playing? I suppose Mama has tried everything else."

Mrs. Holm's pursuit of decent matches for her daughters was no great secret in Hampshire. The entire county knew of the dreadfully named Holm children. In addition to Parthena and Fidelia, there was also Leta, and a brother, Ovid.

Mr. and Mrs. Holm assumed, for some odd reason, that such names would give their children notability. Which they did. Only not in the way Parthena's parents hoped. She despaired of her name, which made her sound like architecture, not a young lady. Also, the literal meaning of Parthena in Greek was *perpetual virgin,* which did not give her hopes for the future.

"Stop dragging your feet," Mama urged. "I prevailed upon Lady Baldwin for this privilege, a difficult task, and we *must* make the most of it." She shot a pointed glance at Parthena.

"So you've said," Fidelia said.

"I've apologized profusely, Mama," Parthena added. "It isn't as if I planned the events which took place on our previous visit. Indeed, I did not enjoy the attention it brought me."

"Humph." Mama raised a brow.

"I did not." Parthena possessed the unfailing ability to attract bad luck in the form of tripping, speaking out of turn, catching clothing on capons and an assortment of other—well, Mama referred to them as *tragedies.* Thus her lack of suitors. What gentleman in his right mind would want to saddle himself with a wife who was given to such catastrophe?

Her mother's exact words.

"The expectation is that you restrain yourself." Mama strolled ahead of her and Fidelia.

Parthena wanted to state, rather emphatically in her own defense, that naming her *Parthena* did not help matters.

"I do not want a repeat of the *incident,* Parthena," she said over her shoulder.

"You will not be disappointed. I swear."

"Splendid. Now, you and Fidelia are to accompany Lady Belinda tomorrow evening." Her mother paused. "Fidelia on the pianoforte, you on the violin."

"We are *accompanying* Lady Belinda?" Belinda was Lady Baldwin's all too perfect niece. She was pleasant enough, if one admired willowy, demure young ladies of good breeding. "As if we are common musicians for hire?"

"Don't flatter yourself," Fidelia whispered. "We aren't at all that good."

"But I thought the entire point of this visit was for *us* to perform for Lady Baldwin's guests," Parthena said.

Her mother made an exasperated sound. She did that often in Parthena's presence. "You will be performing. Think of yourselves as a foil, if you will, to highlight Lady Belinda's lovely soprano. There is a match in the making at the house party. A duke. As a foil, you are helping to facilitate such a match. Lady Baldwin will be most grateful."

"A foil?" And a duke present, though that was the least of her worries. More concerning that Lady Belinda's voice sounded like a wounded cow and was an assault to the ears.

"Yes." Her mother turned, pinching her fingers together, admonishing Parthena to not speak another word. "Do keep your limbs close to your body, Parthena, so as not to cause anyone bodily harm. No verbal sparring in which your opinion is the only one that matters, which is rarely the case. And play the violin to the best of your ability. Possibly invite the admiration of a gentleman." Mama looked skeptical. "That is all I ask."

"But Lady Belinda—"

"Or I will entertain the suit of Captain Percival Rogers." Her mother gave her firm look. "Do I make myself clear."

"Abundantly." Captain Rogers was two years older than Parthena's father, deaf in one ear and ate only soft foods as he lacked most of his teeth. He'd offered for her at least three times and while she liked Captain Rogers, the idea of kissing him was repulsive. Besides, what did it matter if Parthena's only reason for being at the house party was to help Lady Belinda land a duke? She didn't care. It was only Lady Baldwin's assumption that her niece would shine far brighter with the Holm daughters at her side that Parthena objected to.

Rather insulting.

They hurried inside, ignored by most of the footmen and servants rushing about, searching for any sign of Corman, Lady Baldwin's butler, or Lady Baldwin herself. But their hostess was not in evidence, which meant she was already entertaining her more important guests out on the terrace. Not waiting for her poor relations to arrive.

Lady Baldwin and Mama were cousins, once removed. An association Mrs. Holm touted frequently but their hostess did not. Still, Lady Baldwin did welcome Mama over for tea several times a year. When Lady Belinda's birthday was celebrated with fireworks and a picnic, the Holm family had come to enjoy the festivities. The Holms had even been invited to dine once, but after *the incident*, no longer.

Parthena searched about the foyer for her violin case, almost hoping that the instrument had been misplaced to save them all a great deal of misery. No such luck. She saw the case clearly sitting at the bottom of the stairs. Making her way over to retrieve the instrument, Parthena halted at the sound of trunks colliding and falling to the ground. She whipped about, clasping a hand to her throat.

Good grief. I've only just arrived.

Corman, stiff-lipped and annoyed, strode forth, glaring at the footmen who had all come to a standstill. "What has happened—*oh.*" He swung his gaze in the direction of Parthena who had frozen in place, staring at the mass of clothing, underthings and a pair of slippers spilling out across the floor from her battered trunk, mixing unpleasantly with the contents of a larger, much finer trunk.

"Oh, no," Mama whispered, pressing a palm to her lips.

Parthena's well-used trunk, one purchased secondhand, had a lock which hadn't worked well in some time, though she'd latched it tight. Her trunk had been dropped on the larger, breaking the lock and opening the latch on its own.

Corman turned red. "That is the duke's trunk."

Well, of course, it had to be, given Parthena's luck. Fine, black leather. Crest stenciled across the edge in gold.

Her underthings. Hose. Slippers. All had all fallen to mix somewhat intimately with the duke's personal items. And she still didn't know which duke, exactly. Which was off-putting, not knowing whose shirts your petticoat was splayed over.

Parthena thought she might swoon. Or expire of mortification. And in doing so would have to be carried out, causing her family further embarrassment.

"Wexham," Mama said under her breath, eyeing the crest on the trunk answering Parthena's earlier question of which duke was in attendance.

"Mrs. Holm." Corman raised a brow. "Shall I assume these belong to Miss Holm?" He sent a pointed look in Parthena's direction. Lady Baldwin's butler had never cared for Parthena, much less so after the *incident*.

Her mother nodded. "I regret to say it is."

His lips rippled with dislike. "I'll have to inform Lady Baldwin. And the duke. His trunk has been damaged. The lock broken by that of Miss Holm. This entire affair," he gestured towards the pile of clothing. "Is most alarming."

Parthena eyed Corman. It wasn't as if she'd tossed her bloody trunk at the duke's. And the sight of her underthings was far more alarming to her than Lady Baldwin's butler or her herd of footmen. But perhaps this Wexham was a bit of a prig. Didn't care to have his things mingle with that of a young lady so far beneath him. The duke might find the fact that her petticoats had touched his—she looked to his trunk—shaving kit to be offensive.

"There's no need for that, Corman." A gentleman came forward dressed in a coat the color of toast. Amusement had the corners of his bright blue eyes crinkle as he took in the foyer. "I'll inform His Grace." Corman looked as if he might argue but the gentleman held up one hand. "Find Laraby. I believe he's having tea in the kitchen. He'll put things to right."

"Very good, Mr. Shore." Corman spun on his heel and moved in the opposite direction.

Mama let out a visible sigh of relief.

"Allow me to introduce myself, the gentleman stepped forward. Mr. Duncan Shore, ornithologist." He laughed at her mother's blank look. "A fancy way to say I study birds."

"Oh." Mama smiled. "I am Mrs. Holm, and these are my daughters. Miss Fidelia Holm and Miss Parthena Holm."

He smiled politely at Parthena before sliding his gaze to Fidelia, eyes alight with interest.

A blush rose on her sister's cheeks.

"Don't worry about Wexham, madam. Corman is far more distressed than the duke will be. Laraby will put things to rights. He's the duke's valet."

Mama nodded. "Thank you, Mr. Shore."

"Mrs. Holm." He bowed. "Miss Holm. Miss Holm." Striding off he headed in the direction of the terrace.

Fidelia let out a long, drawn-out breath, gaze fixed on the departing Mr. Shore. "What a lovely gentleman."

"Indeed. And educated. A scholar. You could do worse, Fidelia." Mama said, as she began shoving Parthena's clothing back into the trunk, careful to avoid the duke's things. "I begged you for *one* instance in which you did not embarrass the entire family, Parthena. We haven't even been here an hour. Must I lock you upstairs, only allowing you out for Lady Belinda's performance?"

"How is this my fault?" Parthena whispered back, conscious of the servants watching. "The trunk is as ancient as the duke likely is."

A throat cleared. "May I be of assistance?" A short, dapper man stood to the side. "I am Laraby, His Grace's valet. If you wish to join the other guests, I can wait for your maid, Mrs. Holm."

The Holm ladies did not have a maid, but there wasn't any need to announce the fact. "That won't be necessary," Mama nodded. "But I thank you, Mr. Laraby."

"Stop gawking." Laraby clapped his hands at the footmen who were all still standing about. "Take Mrs. Holm's trunks upstairs. The two rooms at the end of the hall."

Their usual rooms no matter the number of guests Lady Baldwin would invite. Two small bedchambers with a connecting door that overlooked the side of the driveway.

Within moments the entire affair had been rectified, the duke's trunk once more shut tight and Parthena's, well, she hoped that hers stayed closed until it found its way to the rooms assigned them. If Lady Baldwin was feeling charitable, she might even send up one of her own maids to help them unpack.

Mama bustled up the stairs, behind two footmen carrying their things. "Let us freshen up before making our appearance. Hopefully, Lady Baldwin won't have Corman escort us out the moment we step outside."

"I didn't drop my trunk, the footman did." Parthena fumed. "I am the offended party. What about *my* dignity?"

"Enough Parthena," her mother smiled, seeing a plump maid appear with a bow. "Let us unpack."

CHAPTER TWO

A SHORT TIME later, Parthena stood beside her mother and Fidelia looking out through the glass of the terrace doors at Lady Baldwin and the rest of her little party. Upon arriving to their assigned rooms, a stout little maid appeared who proceeded to unpack their things with ruthless efficiency. There had been no time to rest. Mama insisted they join the other guests immediately, as there were several unattached gentlemen in attendance.

Parthena had no doubt the news of her latest misstep was already making the rounds. She doubted her barely adequate violin playing would sway any man in her direction.

"I wonder which one of these gentlemen is the Duke of Wexham," her mother stopped at the entry to the terrace, surveying those gathered. "Lady Baldwin tells me his estate is only an hour's ride from here. He rarely leaves, not to visit London or even Wickham."

"Truthfully, Mama there is nothing of interest in Wickham." Parthena spoke of the nearest village with no small amount of affection. "But I share the duke's opinion of London. I don't care for town either." Even if she did, the finances of the Holm family would prohibit travel to London.

"Likely that one," Fidelia pointed to a portly, elderly gentleman. "He looks to have gout which makes travel difficult and is appropriately anciently ducal."

"Fidelia," Mama chastised. But she kept her eyes on the rounded gentleman dressed smartly with a neatly trimmed beard.

Parthena peeked at the other guests whom she was reluctant to join for obvious reasons. "Perhaps Wexham is disfigured."

Mama pinched the bridge of her nose as if praying for patience. "Why would you say such a thing, Parthena?"

"Well, if he isn't ancient or gout-ridden, the obvious reason for his reclusive nature would be a disfigurement of some sort which makes his appearance unappealing. In any case, I don't care to make his acquaintance. I should like to return to our room. I'm in need of a respite given earlier events."

"You will not. An apology must be made to Lady Baldwin for causing such an uproar earlier. The duke is likely upset no matter the intervention of Mr. Shore. His things were spilled across the foyer for all to see. You do not wish to offend a duke."

"You want me to apologize for my underthings? Mama, you must be joking." Would there be no end to her humiliation? "The footman dropped my trunk. And it isn't my fault the latch doesn't work correctly."

"Parthena." Mama hissed. "His Grace might have found your— things mingling to be an affront to his senses. Think of Lady Baldwin and the position you have put her in."

An affront to his senses. Wexham was not only a disfigured recluse but a prig as well. "I suppose I can't have my slippers insulting a duke."

Mama nodded, missing the sarcasm of Parthena's remark entirely.

Fidelia tugged her forward and whispered, "Thena, you're only making it worse."

She discreetly kicked her sister in the shin. "Let go this instant. I do not need to be led about."

They swatted discreetly at each other for several moments, Parthena's feet sliding along the floor as Fidelia started to drag her forward, oblivious to the scene they presented to the others on the terrace. Finally stumbling into the sunlight, Parthena looked up to see a dozen pairs of eyes turned in their direction.

Lady Baldwin took a deep breath, resigned to the presence of the Holm women.

Mama hurried to Lady Baldwin, her niece, Lady Belinda, by her side. Greetings were made before her mother profusely thanked their hostess for the privilege of allowing Parthena and Fidelia to accompany Lady Belinda. "I believe Parthena has something she wishes to say to you, my lady."

Lady Baldwin lifted her chin, gazing at Parthena through narrowed eyes. Waiting.

Fidelia pinched her arm. "Go on. Mama won't be satisfied until you do."

Parthena made her way forward, conscious of the sudden silence as she greeted Lady Baldwin and Belinda politely. Clearing her throat she said, "I apologize, my lady, for the accident which took place upon our arrival and the impolite behavior of my trunk."

"Unfortunate indeed, Miss Holm. Be forewarned that during your stay," her voice lowered. "I will not tolerate a repeat of *the incident*. The Duke of Wexham is an honored guest, one who rarely leaves his estate. That he has done so for this gathering"—she shot an adoring look at Belinda—"is of great importance. Against my better judgement I agreed to allow you and your sister to accompany Lady Belinda tomorrow evening, but your mother prevailed upon me to do so. Do not make me regret my kindness."

"Yes, my lady." Parthena lowered her eyes.

"Come, Mrs. Holm." Lady Baldwin took Mama's arm with a smile, one that did not reach her eyes. "I wish to introduce you to Lady Hanson." She dismissed Parthena without another look. "Fidelia, you may join us."

Lady Belinda regarded Parthena with her lovely eyes the color of bluebells. Everything about Belinda was rather perfect. Proper. She never spoke out of turn, nor did disaster follow her about. Aside from her singing voice, Belinda was the epitome of English womanhood.

"I understand you are to accompany me tomorrow night." Belinda's lips pursed into a rosette. "I don't like it any more than you, Miss Holm. Nor was it my suggestion. Let us make the best of it." And with a polite nod, Lady Belinda turned to engage the young lady behind her in conversation, leaving Parthena standing in a sea of Lady Baldwin's guests.

"Right." Hands clasped before her, Parthena strode towards the opposite side of the terrace which faced a tall hedge and nothing else notable. She would pretend great interest in the myrtles before her while she gathered her thoughts.

Snatching a glass of lemonade from a passing servant, Parthena settled herself on a chair set just around the corner of the terrace. Confident she was hidden by the curve of the house, she lifted her feet and placed them on the balustrade and sipped her lemonade. Hopefully, she wouldn't be forced to apologize to the Duke of Wexham, likely a disfigured, priggish fop who would display nothing but horror at the thought of her chemise touching his breeches.

She looked about for somewhere to set the half-full glass of lemonade and decided the balustrade would work. No one was around to chastise her for doing so.

Thus far Lady Baldwin's little gathering was proving to be a mortifying experience. She vowed to keep herself contained for the duration or Mama might really send her off to wed Captain Rogers. She would spend the rest of her days married to a man who could only comfortably enjoy porridge at every meal.

Crossing her legs, Parthena cursed when the toe of her slipper nudged the lemonade just enough so that that the glass went tumbling over the balustrade and into the row of hedges below. Parthena sat back, eyes roaming left and right, relieved to see that she was far enough away, it was unlikely anyone had seen.

A growl sounded from below her, followed by a curse.

Apparently, this end of the terrace wasn't as deserted as Parthena had first thought. She fixed her gaze on the pond in the distance, squinting at the folly she could just make out on the other side.

A gentleman stepped out from the hedge, wiping off the shoulder of his coat. He bent and picked up the now empty glass before looking up at her.

"Does this belong to you?"

Parthena kept her focus on the folly and pretended she didn't see him. Out of the corner of her eye, she caught sight of a head of coal-black curls and a magnificent pair of cheekbones, all atop an expensively dressed pair of broad shoulders.

I've ruined his coat to be sure.

She continued her perusal of the pond and folly and did not acknowledge him. Perhaps he wouldn't press further and just…wander off.

"Stop behaving as if you can't see me." He brushed another drop of lemonade from his coat. "I know that you can." He vanished from sight, which had Parthena's shoulders slump in relief.

Thank goodness he'd moved on.

"I'm still speaking to you." His lean form jogged up a set of stairs barely glimpsed from where she sat.

There was no help for it. She'd caused yet another incident. Parthena could only hope to convince this—she looked over at him—*alarmingly handsome gentleman*—not to report her to Lady Baldwin.

"Goodness, where did you come from, my lord? You startled me." Parthena placed a hand to her throat as if shocked by his abrupt appearance.

"Really?" He didn't sound convinced. "You didn't see me jumping about as you doused me with lemonade?" The glass was set down beside her.

"I—" she cast up her hands in surrender. "Very well. I inadvertently pushed my glass of lemonade off into the hedges. Accidentally. I suppose I've ruined your coat which looks incredibly expensive and fits you perfectly."

A dark brow raised at her.

"I won't be able to replace your coat. Your outrage will be wasted on me for I fear it won't be nearly as bad as that of the duke's whose trunk was attacked by mine earlier. I've only just arrived and two such incidents in such a short time guarantees I'll be asked to leave this gathering by Lady Baldwin and thus will not act as a foil tomorrow evening."

A half-smile crossed his lips as he regarded her from eyes the color of amber. A curious hue. Parthena's heart made an odd waffle in her chest.

"It was your trunk which attacked that of the duke's?"

"So you've heard of me."

"What do you think the other guests are whispering about, Miss Holm?"

She frowned at the use of her name. Unsettling to know it was being bandied around the terrace.

"Rather unkind of you to mention it. But a clumsy footman is the true villain here. I've expressed my regrets to Lady Baldwin, who insists I apologize to the duke for the entanglement of my *things* touching his. As if my slippers were begging for ruination by throwing themselves at Wexham's shirt." Parthena halted. "Excuse me. It is rude to speak so, but I find the entire insistence that I must apologize to be ridiculous in the extreme."

Sunlight turned his eyes to gold. "You do?"

Goodness. They resembled the honey Parthena had drizzled over her toast that morning.

"Well, yes. Wexham must be a terrible prig for Lady Baldwin to insist he would be insulted over such a minor thing. But he is a recluse."

"Is he?" He cupped his chin in one hand, leaning against the balustrade to watch her.

"Possibly there might also be something horrifying in his trunk that he wouldn't want others to see. Which would account for Lady Baldwin insisting he'd be offended. Gout medicine." Parthena tilted her head at him. "All dukes have gout. Spectacles, but those aren't so bad. Possibly a peg leg."

"A peg leg?" A burst of laughter filled the air around them, low and delicious, settling inside Parthena like the vibration of a cello.

"I am only theorizing." He was quite delightful, this gentleman. Not at all put off by her opinions. A rarity.

"You think the Duke of Wexham is a pirate?" He laughed again. "Because he does not venture out?"

"Or horribly disfigured. Why else would he hide at Wexham Park? He never ventures to London." She tapped her chin. "Protruding teeth, perhaps."

"Or a skin condition," he offered. "Possibly crossed eyes. Or only one eye. There may have been an eye-patch in the trunk."

"An excellent point." She smiled up at him. "I hadn't considered any of those." Good lord, but he was breathtaking, especially when a dimple appeared in his cheek. And clever. He also smelled of bergamot, which Parthena adored.

"Your logic is rather sound, Miss Holm." But he didn't answer whether he knew Wexham or not. "But you've not considered that the duke might not care for society. Or London. Perhaps he prefers the country."

"Are you acquainted with Wexham?" She hesitated. "My lord?" He hadn't introduced himself, so Parthena wasn't sure how to address him. Given his crisp accent and clothing, she assumed him to be a lord of some sort.

Footsteps sounded behind Parthena along with the rustle of silk skirts. She turned to see their hostess marching towards them with military precision. "Lady Baldwin must have seen me spill the lemonade. You should flee while you have the chance so as not to witness my chastisement."

Another small laugh came from him as that honeyed gaze trailed over Parthena. "You are most delightful, Miss Holm."

Warmth crept up her chest. No one ever declared her delightful. "An opinion not shared by others, my—"

"Your Grace," Lady Baldwin came to a stop, displeasure pulling at her lips, all of it directed at Parthena. "I see you've made the acquaintance of Miss Holm. What a happy coincidence. Have you apologized Miss Holm, for your earlier display?"

Parthena's stomach made an unsteady pitch. *This* was Wexham? Good Lord, she'd just spent the last several minutes insulting him. Not a sign of gout nor remotely ancient. "I—"

"A splendid apology, madam," Wexham answered smoothly. "But an unnecessary one. I assured Miss Holm that it was of no consequence. It wasn't as if a peg leg came tumbling out of my trunk." He tilted his chin in Parthena's direction, eyes twinkling in the sun as if made of gold.

She coughed, earning another scathing look from her hostess.

Parthena rose and fell into a clumsy curtsey. "Your Grace, it was a pleasure to make your acquaintance."

"Miss Holm," Wexham took her hand, the edge of his thumb trailing over her palm. The light touch sent a roar over Parthena's skin, so unexpected her breath caught. "The pleasure was mine."

She kept her chin lowered even after Wexham released her hand, not daring to raise her eyes. Her pulse was still fluttering as the last bit of bergamot floated to her nostrils, and Wexham disappeared with Lady Baldwin.

CHAPTER THREE

ATTICUS GOSLING, DUKE of Wexham inclined his head politely as Lady Baldwin led him away from the most interesting person he'd met thus far at this house party, and that included Lady Belinda who he was expected to offer for at some point. Not that there was anything wrong with Belinda, just the opposite. She was perfectly suitable. But the little time they'd spent in each other's company was enough for Atticus to know that while she would make an excellent duchess, he felt little for her. No spark. There was no sense of intoxication at her presence.

Unlike Miss Holm. She made his head buzzy, as if Atticus had swallowed an entire snifter of brandy.

"I do apologize, Your Grace," Lady Baldwin intoned. "Had I known you'd been subjected to Miss Parthena Holm I would have rescued you sooner. The girl has the unfailing ability to cause unpleasantness whenever she appears." She gave a drawn-out sigh. "But Mrs. Holm is a distant relation of mine, and she despairs of finding appropriate matches for her daughters. I do everything in my power to help her. Fidelia," she inclined her head towards a lovely brunette, "will do well. But Parthena is another matter."

Atticus made a sound in his throat, which his hostess took as agreement. Lady Baldwin was an ambitious, social climbing matron who desired nothing more than a connection to a duke. She'd once been a friend of Atticus's mother and when he'd made the decision to wed, he'd called upon her for assistance. He had no female relatives to turn to. Conveniently, Lady Baldwin had a niece of marriageable age. Seemed simple enough.

"I hope I did not make a mistake in offering to have the Miss

Holms accompany Belinda tomorrow. But Fidelia plays the pianoforte exceptionally well."

"And the other Miss Holm, what is her talent?" Parthena's earlier comment about being a foil now made a great deal more sense.

"The violin." Lady Baldwin made a dismissive sound. "Adequate at best. But, I promised Mrs. Holm that both would perform with Belinda. My niece sings like a songbird, Your Grace."

"I look forward to hearing her."

A smile spread across Lady Baldwin's features. "Ah, there you are, Belinda." She led Atticus to her niece. "Excuse me for a moment while I check with Corman on the refreshments."

Lady Baldwin wasn't trying very hard to hide her motives.

"Your Grace." Lady Belinda blushed prettily. She had delicate features with wide blue eyes and a trim figure. Daughter of a marquess, she was well-bred with a large dowry and a multitude of connections. Belinda would perform her duties in the marital bed and outside of it.

But nothing stirred when Atticus looked at her. Not his heart or his cock.

Still, Belinda was an adequate choice. A good decision.

Atticus listened with one ear as Belinda chattered away about a ball she'd attended in London and assumed he gave a fig about who'd been present. His eyes kept drifting to a spot over Belinda's shoulder, to Parthena Holm.

A SHADOW CAME to stand over Parthena as she waited for the inevitable. Either Mama or Lady Baldwin would return to inform her that Wexham had raised a fuss. She'd insulted a duke and must be escorted out.

"Have you been sitting here the entire time?"

Every so often, Parthena would tilt her chin, enough to see him standing beside Lady Belinda. They made a splendid couple, both richly dressed and absurdly attractive. Pity he had to be Wexham. Before Lady Baldwin arrived, Parthena had been considering his lips and what kissing him might feel like. She'd acted on such an urge only one other time, with one of the village lads.

Fidelia came to stand before her, a glass of punch in one hand. "Staring out at that folly across the pond. Talking to dukes." She wiggled her brows. "Ensuring the anger of Lady Baldwin."

"She is particularly wrathful, isn't she? As it happens, Fidelia, I didn't realize he was Wexham until after I insulted him with the insinuation that the duke might be ancient, gout ridden and possibly have a peg leg."

Fidelia looked towards the heavens. "You didn't. Please tell me you're joking."

"I am not," Parthena assured her. "Wexham wasn't the least offended. He laughed at my wild imagination."

"Really? Usually a gentleman flees from you as if his coat was on fire."

Parthena gritted her teeth. "There isn't any need to remind me."

"Wexham is not at all what I expected. Quite handsome. Just look at those curls."

Sneaking another look at the duke, Parthena tried not to sigh. "Lovely. Black like a raven's wing. Wait until you catch a glimpse of his eyes. An unusual light brown, they appear gold."

"And he's a duke. No wonder Lady Baldwin is so filled with determination. Mama tells me that Wexham is expected to offer for Belinda. I hope he does so after our musicale since we leave the following day. Bad enough we'll miss the celebration which is bound to include fireworks, such as we had on Belinda's birthday."

Fidelia adored fireworks.

"I suppose." The idea of watching Wexham prance Belinda about left Parthena with an uneasy sensation in her mid-section, as if she'd had one too many servings of treacle. She turned away from Fidelia to take in Wexham. She'd never really wanted to be anyone other than herself, but just then, watching Belinda place her slender fingers on Wexham's arm, Parthena desired nothing more than to be a young lady who might catch a duke's fancy.

Wexham bowed to Lady Belinda and moved away from her, a half-smile tugging at his mouth. He deliberately paused, looked directly at Parthena and...*winked*. As if they shared a secret known only to the two of them. Then he strolled off in the direction of Mr.

Shore.

A pleased sound erupted from her. Perhaps she didn't need to be Belinda.

"Parthena? Are you well?"

"Exceptionally, Fidelia. I was merely contemplating Mr. Shore who studies not only birds, but you, it seems."

A blush stole across her sister's cheeks. "The duke is Mr. Shore's patron. I spoke to him for some time after we came out to the terrace. He and Wexham grew up together and are close friends."

"You don't care for scholars or birds, Fidelia." But Parthena was smiling.

"Most scholars do not resemble Mr. Shore." Her sister laughed. "And I will learn to like birds."

CHAPTER FOUR

ATTICUS HAD A difficult time keeping his attention on Belinda, his intended bride, because he was far too enthralled with watching Miss Holm. The entire house party was dining al fresco at a half dozen circular tables set out on the terrace. He could just make out Miss Holm, her sister, and mother sitting at a table some distance from him. Purposefully, he assumed. Any further from the main table where Atticus sat, and their small group would be situated in the gardens.

He replayed their all too brief interaction earlier that day. The shock when Miss Holm realized he was Wexham. The soft flutter of her lashes when she blushed after Atticus winked at her. Miss Holm was a most curious creature.

Every so often Lady Baldwin would glance at Miss Holm, lip curling with disapproval.

Duncan, being of no importance to their hostess, had switched seats and placed himself directly across from Fidelia Holm. What would Lady Baldwin do, he wondered, were he to stand and take a seat with the Holm ladies and Duncan?

"Are you enjoying the duck, Your Grace?"

"Delicious," he said to Lady Baldwin, barely tasting anything on his plate.

Parthena was speaking, demanding his attention as well as those seated around her. Hands fluttering about in the air as she told her tale, features expressive and not the least composed. So unlike another other young lady at this house party. The light of the lamps glinted off the dark brown ringlets framing her face, bouncing off her cheeks as she spoke. She took a deep breath, pausing, and looked in his direction.

A breathless sensation struck Atticus. Desire for Parthena. Not all of it physical.

"Your Grace," Lady Baldwin addressed him, the ghost of a frown on her lips as if guessing where his interest lay. "Is there something about the roasted potatoes which distresses you?"

"Not at all, madam. I fear I was lost in thought, contemplating something Mr. Shore related to me yesterday concerning a business matter."

"I thought Mr. Shore's expertise was with birds."

"Oh, it is," he assured her, schooling his features. "But Mr. Shore is also well-versed in land management."

Parthena stood, still immersed in whatever story she related, gesturing wildly. Her left hand struck out, smacking the footman behind her, in the nose.

The serving dish the footman held went up in the air as he grabbed his wounded nose, which was now bleeding. The serving dish had been filled with peas. The tiny pellets rained down on the unsuspecting Lady Hanson, seated at the next table.

Lady Hanson shrieked.

Atticus could only press his lips together to keep from laughing.

Lady Baldwin set down her fork with an irritated sound. "I only hope," she said under her breath to Belinda, "she does not stab you with the bow of her violin tomorrow evening. If you'll excuse me, Your Grace." Lady Baldwin came to her feet with a grimace. "I must see to Lady Hanson."

"Of course," Atticus demurred, struggling to keep his features bland.

"I warned my aunt against inviting Mrs. Holm and her daughters. But—" Belinda looked towards Lady Baldwin who was motioning for her butler, Corman. "Mrs. Holm pleaded and assured her there would not be a repeat of *the incident*. I suppose she underestimated Parthena."

"The incident?"

Belinda colored. "I really shouldn't speak of it, Your Grace."

Parthena, meanwhile, had taken a step back from the table, a stricken look on her features as she took in the peas littering the floor, the bleeding footman, and Lady Hanson. Duncan's shoulders shook with silent laughter while Fidelia merely gave her sister a patient look.

The long-suffering Mrs. Holm stiffened and took a deep breath as she observed her daughter, tipping up her glass of wine.

"My aunt and Mrs. Holm are distantly related. Very distantly," Belinda started. "Cousins, I believe."

"Lady Baldwin related as much to me."

"And as such, she feels duty-bound to assist Mrs. Holm in any way she can, given their situation. Mr. Holm has been ill for some time. The circumstances of the Holm family are greatly reduced."

Parthena's family was not wealthy. Not of note. He'd assumed as much given where they were seated.

"My aunt hosted a dinner last year, a small gathering of local gentry, and invited Mrs. Holm and her daughters. There is no secret she's trying to find husbands for them. The eldest is the only one to have succeeded thus far. Leta." Belinda gave an elegant roll of her shoulders. "They are all oddly named. At any rate, stuffed capons were on the menu. Somehow Parthena," she nodded in Parthena's direction. "Managed to," Belinda cleared her throat, "trap her hand in the cavity of one of the birds."

Atticus blinked. "The cavity? Her hand became stuck inside a capon? How is that possible?"

"I'm not sure how it happened, Your Grace. Capons are rather small in size. She mentioned something about currants. Regardless, her hand became stuck."

Atticus looked towards Parthena who now resembled more a deflated souffle than a young lady. She was looking anywhere but at Lady Baldwin.

"In attempting to dislodge the capon from her hand, Miss Holm spilled the contents of her glass. The glass rolled across the table, along with the wine within and onto the lap of Mr. Odam, who pushed back his chair abruptly from the table." Belinda bit her lip. "Mr. Odam and his chair tipped over and into Corman," she discreetly tilted her head in the direction of Lady Baldwin's butler. "Corman went spinning across the length of the dining room and into the gravy boat held aloft by one of the other servants. Quite a mess."

Atticus stared at Belinda. "You must be exaggerating. I cannot fathom—"

"I am not, Your Grace. Miss Parthena Holm is the terror of hostesses everywhere. There is good reason why Mrs. Holm despairs of her ever finding a match. I doubt there is a gentleman courageous enough. So you see, by extending an invitation and allowing Parthena and Fidelia to accompany me tomorrow evening, my aunt bestowed a great kindness. Which I'm sure she now deeply regrets."

WELL THIS WAS *utterly* horrifying.

Parthena had spent most of the meal observing the Duke of Wexham, absorbed with the shape of his mouth when he spoke to Lady Belinda and the graceful movement of his hands as he speared a sliver of duck.

Mooning over Wexham. A duke. One intended for Lady Belinda.

Yes, but he winked at me.

Parthena launched into an amusing story about a visit to the cheesemonger and a wheel of cheddar to distract herself from the sight of Wexham seated beside Belinda. In the process of describing how the cheddar rolled off the counter and headed out the door— Mr. Somerset, the cheesemonger, who still wouldn't allow her back in his establishment—Parthena unintentionally smacked a passing footman with her hand. In the nose. Rather hard. There seemed to be a bit of blood. The poor footman lost his grip on the serving bowl of peas he carried, which in turn, spilled over Lady Hanson.

"Dear God," Fidelia murmured. "The Misadventures of Parthena Holm continue."

Everyone enjoying the evening meal among the flickering lamps and the aromas wafting from Lady Baldwin's garden stopped speaking immediately. Jaws dropped. Lady Hanson jumped about and shrieked as if a hive of bees attacked.

Parthena cleared her throat. Apologized to the footman, though he was too busy trying to stop the blood streaming from his nose to accept, and stepped back, pretending complete absorption in her skirts. This wasn't nearly as bad as a capon attached to her hand and tossing Corman into a gravy boat, but nearly.

Lady Baldwin surged forward to comfort Lady Hanson, all the while her scathing glare remaining on Parthena.

Mama swallowed her entire glass of wine and pinched the bridge of her nose. "Parthena," she said in exasperation. "You are a magnet for misfortune."

Entirely true.

"I'll just." Parthena waved her hand, careful to keep it close to her side and not hit anyone else. "Take a walk about the gardens, shall I? Let my meal settle a bit before venturing back inside for this evening's entertainment. Charades, perhaps."

"A splendid suggestion, Parthena," Mother intoned. "Walk about the gardens at least twice. Pray do not trip into the fountain. I think after your stroll, you might consider retiring for the evening. Tomorrow will be another day."

Mother's way of informing Parthena that it might be in everyone's best interests if she did not join the other guests in the drawing room. At the sight of her, Lady Baldwin might insist the Holm ladies return home immediately.

"Yes, Mama."

She slid away, daring a look in Wexham's direction. The duke was likely as horrified as everyone else by Parthena.

But Wexham had that same half-smile from earlier on his lips, the amber of his eyes drawing over Parthena in a way that had the heat flying up to sear her cheeks.

Perhaps the duke didn't mind a disaster now and again.

CHAPTER FIVE

PARTHENA HAD BEEN sitting on this bench for the better part of an hour, watching the other guests through the large drawing room window overlooking the gardens. Laughter filtered through the night air. A game of charades was in process, which Parthena dearly loved but unfortunately, wasn't very good at. No one ever guessed at her clues correctly. Fidelia said the other players were all put off by Parthena's gyrations.

"Gyrations." She made a piffing sound. "I am not a spinning top."

The crunch of a boot on gravel had Parthena turning in the darkness, where a much larger shadow loomed on the path before her.

"Lady Hanson and her gown would disagree," the low tenor brushed her skin sending tiny goosebumps up her arms. "You'll be relieved to know I checked on the footman, whose name is Perse. Nose not broken. He forgives you."

Parthena came to her feet. "Your Grace." The bench was beneath a small tree and in standing, one of the branches above her head became stuck in her coiffure, tugging at the pins in her hair.

Wexham gave a small chuckle. "Stay still, Miss Holm. I will come to your rescue." A moment later, the light touch of his fingers moved along the strands of her hair.

"I—sometimes get into trouble. Unintentionally, Your Grace." She winced at the tug on her hair.

"Lady Baldwin claims you to be a menace." Wexham brought with him that delicious scent of bergamot along with a hint of smoke from a cheroot.

"Not entirely untrue."

"I've been looking for you, but you made my search somewhat difficult," Wexham murmured. "All the trees are still standing. The fountain is in good working order. Nor have you tripped and rolled downhill." His breath followed the curve of her ear while Wexham worked to get her free from the branch. He was so close; the buttons of his coat were pressed into her breasts. If her chin tipped up, just an inch—

The light caress of his fingers disappeared, and the branch snapped back. She clasped her hands, instructing the trembling along her skin to stop. "Thank you, Your Grace."

"I am only teasing, Miss Holm. Though your propensity for catastrophe is exceptional. Lady Belinda related the tale of the capon to me. I'm still trying to work out how it happened."

"Currants, Your Grace. I am overly fond, and the capon was stuffed with them."

"Ah. I will note you adore currants."

The way he said the words had the most delicious sensation wafting across her chest.

"I wanted to show you something." He took off his glove and held up one broad hand. The pinky was twisted at an angle. Crooked. Imperfect. "You weren't completely mistaken in assuming I was disfigured. I broke my finger when I was ten. Never healed correctly. I fear I will never play the violin. Not even adequately."

Parthena gave a small snort. "That makes two of us, Your Grace. I only hope to not embarrass myself." She nodded at his hand. "I do not believe that counts as a deformity. I was hoping you had a peg leg."

Wexham laughed softly. "Or an eye-patch."

"Stay within an arm's length of me for any given amount of time and you might need one," she said ruefully. "Oh, I didn't mean—"

"Please sit, Miss Holm."

She did and Wexham sat beside her on the bench, filling the air around her with the scent of warm bergamot and something deliciously male. There was just enough moonlight to make his eyes glow in the darkness.

"You have lovely eyes, Your Grace," she said without thinking.

"Rather like a cat. Or possibly a hawk." Parthena cleared her throat. "That was slightly improper—"

The slide of his forefinger along the top of her hand halted the rest of her words.

"Thank you, Miss Holm. That is a lovely compliment."

The silence lengthened and grew between them while Parthena's heart hammered away in her chest. Wexham was too close. Too delicious. He'd touched her hand. Even now, his palm was splayed, fingers nearly touching her own.

"So," she cleared her throat. "Given your lack of deformity—"

Wexham smiled and wiggled his crooked pinky finger. "Why do I hide in the country?"

Good lord he was handsome.

"It really isn't any of my affair," Parthena stated, realizing how forward she was in asking a duke, one she was barely acquainted with, such a personal question.

"I don't mind telling you, Miss Holm. Society has never been something I've cared about. Balls hold little appeal, which is a pity since I dance quite well. Cards are of little interest, though I play at times. But the air in London is too thick to see the stars," he gestured to the sky. "I realized a long time ago that I am not made for the amusements of town like so many others. I'm also not fond of house parties, but Lady Baldwin is most persistent."

"I think you and Lady Belinda will make a lovely couple, Your Grace."

"Do you?" The tip of his forefinger touched hers.

"So it is only you, moldering about your estate?" She frowned. "No one to keep you company?"

Wexham and she were leaning towards each other, shoulders almost touching as they conversed. There was a curl dangling just near his cheek. Parthena's fingers itched with the need to touch that dark tendril.

"I'm often alone, but rarely lonely, Miss Holm. A duke has many responsibilities, most of which I handle myself rather than delegate to a secretary. I have hobbies. The stars being one. There is Mr. Shore to entertain me," he said. "And his birds."

"My sister tells me you are Mr. Shore's patron. Do you also have an interest in birds?" Wexham was exactly the opposite from what Parthena had imagined a duke to be. Which made him far more appealing.

"Shore and I have been friends for many years. He's always been partial to robins and wrens. Things that nest. When I was only a lad, he coaxed me to rise early in the morning and listen to the chorus at my disposal. Another thing I cannot hear in London. That lovely symphony taking place outside my bedroom window every morning. Such a wonder should not be taken for granted."

The finger trailed down the edge of her own.

Parthena did not pull away. "What a whimsical, unduke like thing to say, Your Grace."

"Can I not be whimsical and a duke?" he asked, observing her with those lovely, amber eyes.

Another raucous burst of laughter sounded from the drawing room, reminding Parthena she should go inside. It was lovely to believe for a time that Wexham was here for her and not Belinda, but it wasn't the case and Parthena needed to remember that. Difficult when he was so close and his scent swirled around her.

What would he do if I kissed him?

"I should go in, Your Grace," she said, stifling the urge. The duke was not the baker's son whom she'd had a schoolgirl crush on.

Wexham nodded. "Yes, of course."

Parthena stood only to find that by some unimaginable poor luck—the only sort she ever seemed to have—that her foot landed upon a pebble, rolling her ankle. She wobbled, reaching out to take hold of the bench but found herself grabbing at the Duke of Wexham instead.

Wexham's arm went immediately around Parthena's waist to steady her.

"Thank you, Your Grace."

He did not release her, but instead took the opportunity to pull Parthena more fully against him. He took a deep breath, the motion forcing the tips of her breasts into his chest.

Parthena's fingers curled into the lapels of his coat, tugging him closer. She stood on tiptoe.

Good lord. What am I doing?

Her mouth collided with Wexham's in the most explosive, marvelous way. This kiss was the sort Parthena only read about in the lurid romantic novels she'd kept hidden beneath her mattress so Mama wouldn't find them. The duke, no matter his solitary existence, was vastly more experienced than her. His mouth was gentle but insistent, moving with practiced seduction until she sagged, knees buckling, clinging desperately to his larger form.

Wexham's hand moved down her waist hovering just above her bottom, pushing their hips together.

Oh.

Parthena's mind went blank at the pleasurable sensation of those wonderful ducal hands on her. A whimper escaped her as Wexham's teeth nipped softly at her bottom lip.

They slowly, reluctantly, pulled away from each other.

Good grief. What was that?

"Miss Holm," he whispered against her mouth, but his hand stayed on her bottom. "I apologize."

Wexham did not appear apologetic. Not in the least.

"Your Grace." Parthena stumbled back, unsure how to proceed in this instance. Usually at this point, she'd broken something, toppled a cake, or set something on fire.

Well, that is partially the case. I do feel as if I've been set aflame.

"Parthena."

She nearly swooned at the sound of her name on his lips, which didn't sound all like a Greek column when Wexham said it. Her entire body tingled and ached in places Parthena had never been aware of, and she had to resist the urge to kiss him again.

"I'm—" What does one say after being made senseless by a pair of lips? "I should retire for the evening." Taking a step back, she promptly hit the back of her knees on the bench, winced, and then ungracefully tripped away. "Good night, Your Grace."

"Try to make your way inside without assaulting any more of Lady Baldwin's staff, Miss Holm," he said softly into the moonlight.

"I shall endeavor to do so."

ATTICUS STAYED STILL as Parthena half stumbled and half strolled back into the house as if she were foxed. The feeling was not unknown to him. A hurricane had wrapped itself around Atticus as he kissed Parthena, with the force of a wind strong enough to rip the strongest tree from its roots.

Attraction, yes. But something more, which if given time, would—

As the Duke of Wexham, an ancient and much lauded title, Atticus's duty was to wed an appropriate, well-bred young lady whose lineage equaled his own. Property. Status. Wealth. A marriage meant to strengthen both families.

Parthena Holm met none of those requirements.

Her family was of such little note as to be nonexistent. No wealth to speak of or connections save Lady Baldwin. He doubted Parthena could pour tea without some sort of calamity befalling her and whoever was unfortunate enough to call upon her. After all, Parthena had once gotten her hand stuck in a *capon*.

A *bloody* capon.

A sound of amusement escaped him, shattering the silence of the garden.

If Parthena had not had the sense to run back to the safety of the house, there was every chance that the explosive attraction between them might have resulted in ruination among Lady Baldwin's gardens. Mrs. Holm was sure to never be invited back after that.

Atticus finally straightened and looked up at the sky, thinking of how dazzling he found Parthena. Another burst of laughter bubbled out.

And if she were a star, she'd fall from the sky and land directly on Wexham Park.

He walked slowly back to the house, Lady Belinda, and the rest of the house party, uncertain whether he could wed Lady Belinda after all.

CHAPTER SIX

PARTHENA VENTURED DOWN the stairs, searching the hall for any sign of the Duke of Wexham.

It wasn't as if she were avoiding the duke, necessarily, but given the events of last night, she wasn't ready to face Wexham just yet. Or see his disapproval at her blatantly bold behavior, though he had kissed her back.

She rubbed a hand along her backside.

And took her in hand, so to speak.

Fidelia waited for her at the bottom of the stairs, a shawl draped across her shoulders. Her sister had suggested a walk around the pond that shone in the distance. There was a folly on the other side, one Parthena had taken note of yesterday. She wanted to do a bit of exploring, which also aided her in avoidance.

Parthena also did not want to see Lady Belinda or Lady Baldwin. The former due to guilt, the latter because after last night, if she so much as twitched, their hostess was likely to throw the Holm family out.

Fidelia took her arm, and they walked out into the sunlight. The day was glorious, but dark clouds hung at the edge of the horizon, a warning that a storm was on its way. Keeping to one side of the house to avoid the other guests who were once more splayed across the terrace, she and Fidelia started down the path, weaving through the trees and around the pond.

"How is Mama this morning?" Parthena asked. Honestly, Fidelia was the only person she wasn't avoiding today.

"Last night wasn't nearly as bad as the capon incident, but still, quite terrible." Fidelia bit her lip. "I don't think we'll be invited back again. Which is perfectly fine." She squeezed Parthena. "Lady Baldwin is insufferable. I don't care for the way she treats Mama like some beggar coming to her door. Lady Hanson was absolutely horrified, but after, in the drawing room, she shared a glass of ratafia with Mama. A great deal of merriment ensued. You are partially forgiven."

Somewhat of a relief. "I did write Lady Hanson a note expressing how sorry I am."

"I'm sure it was well received. Just manage to...not be yourself until we leave, Thena." Fidelia winked at her. "Keep your arms close to your side. Don't make any bold statements. Play your violin." She lowered lips to Parthena's ear. "Don't make eyes at the Duke of Wexham."

Parthena nodded. "I will do my best."

"Miss Holm." The shrubs along the path rustled and Mr. Shore appeared, brushing off his coat, a sketchpad tucked under one arm. "Miss Holm." He bowed again to Parthena, though he was merely being polite. His eyes never left Fidelia.

"Good day, Mr. Shore. Have you been out sketching?"

"Indeed I have. I'd like to show them to you, if I may, Miss Holm." He glanced at Parthena. "And you as well, Miss Holm. Perhaps over tea?" He nodded in the direction of the terrace.

Fidelia was enamored of the ornithologist and he of her. Her sister deserved to find happiness even if Parthena couldn't possibly fathom that traipsing about to draw birds would be fun.

"No thank you, Mr. Shore." Parthena wouldn't dare intrude. "I'm going to walk to the folly and watch the ducks floating about the pond for a bit." She held up a hand as Fidelia tried to protest. "You can see me clearly from the terrace. Relatively. Besides," she looked towards the folly. "Looks solid enough. I can't possibly cause it to collapse."

"Try to come back before the rain starts," Fidelia cautioned, as thunder sounded in the distance. "The sky is darkening. We are in for a storm."

Being stuck in the folly during a thunderstorm was vastly preferable to having to endure the censure of Lady Baldwin.

"I will." Parthena watched as they strolled down the path back to the house. She could just make out the Duke of Wexham, hands on the balustrade, with Lady Belinda beside him. Lady Baldwin was likely hovering about somewhere. She couldn't make out the duke's features, though he was looking in the direction of the folly. Parthena touched a fingertip to her lips, still feeling the press of Wexham there.

Which made the sight of Lady Belinda dangling from his arm that much more annoying. Parthena was a hopeful romantic, but she had no illusions that Wexham would suddenly declare his affection for her and discard Lady Belinda. That was an *impossibility*. No matter the amount of attraction swirling about between them. So sudden and unexpected. The force of it had taken her completely by surprise.

Wexham must feel it too or he wouldn't have kissed her. Or grabbed her bottom.

She reached the folly and skipped up the steps, a dangerous proposition, and entered the folly. A bench rounded the inside though it didn't look as if it had been used for some time. Brushing aside the leaves littered about, Parthena sat and listened to the wind pick up and the thunder increase.

The first drops of rain splattered the roof. Parthena looked up to see Mama, pacing across the terrace, wringing her hands and waved.

Mama did not wave back.

Another roll of thunder. A streak of lightening shot across the sky. The rain started with a vengeance.

Parthena cupped her hands. "I'm perfectly well," she shouted, the last word screaming out of her as a sheet of rain, a wave of pure water, struck her so hard she nearly fell over. Sputtering, she waved again and saw Wexham beside her mother, urging her inside. There was an area on the other side of the folly, hidden behind a large shrub which would offer more shelter. Another sheet of water slammed into her, the wind so strong the rain was streaming across the folly sideways. The water caught Parthena full in the face, drenching her gown and pulling the pins from her hair.

Well, of course it did.

Thank goodness she was far enough away from the house that no one would witness her wandering about like a drowned rat.

Crawling over the bench partially sheltered by the bush, Parthena was relieved to see the rain didn't reach this far.

A thump sounded on the steps, along with another crack of lightning. Had a tree fallen? She couldn't see clearly as the sky had gone completely dark. Suddenly a large figure appeared, looming in the small confines of the folly.

Parthena held back a scream.

Until he lifted his head, black curls dripping water, as was the rest of him.

"Your Grace?" Parthena blinked in surprise. "What are you doing here?"

"You—you fell against the wall." He wiped back a large wave of wet curls. "I've come to rescue you, Miss Holm. I am worried for your safety."

Wexham had left the terrace and run to the folly because he thought she might be injured.

Parthena's heart swelled inside her chest, until she realized the other guests must have seen him. "I'm perfectly well, Your Grace. But you shouldn't have—"

He ripped off his coat, now nothing more than wet wool to reveal his shirt, clinging to every bit of muscle Parthena felt beneath her fingertips last night.

The amber gaze dropped to her bosom and then trailed down the length of her body.

Parthena recalled what she was wearing. One of her oldest dresses, well, frankly, they were all old, but—the cream muslin with tiny red flowers was particularly thin in places. Her breasts strained against her bodice, pulling at the wet fabric. Nearly transparent.

"Perhaps you could lend me your coat," she whispered.

"I would prefer not. It is wet." Wexham took two steps towards her, slightly feral looking with his wet clothing and hair. That spark between them flared sharply, winding itself around Parthena's mid-section with alarming sensuality.

"Your boots are ruined." Parthena's nipples, to her surprise, grew taut beneath her clothing, whether from his perusal or the chill in the air she wasn't entirely sure.

"Entirely worth it." Wexham made an odd humming sound in

the back of his throat. A growl, possibly. It sent streaks of sensation down her back. "*You* are worth it. Parthena."

"My terrible name sounds so much better when you say it. Did you know the translation is Perpetual Maiden?" She was babbling, undone by the way Wexham was looking at her.

Reaching out, Wexham's hand, the one with the crooked pinky finger, traced a pattern over her cheek, his thumb brushing along the seam of her lips.

She nipped the edge, instinct forcing her to immediately draw her tongue over the spot to soothe the sting.

Wexham's eyes widened, so gold and glowing, all Parthena could think of was being trapped by a large cat.

Her gaze lowered for a moment, gathering courage, then Parthena leapt at him, curling her body around his.

A groan came from him, a low delicious sound that warmed Parthena from the inside out. This was certain to end in catastrophe, as nearly everything did for her.

He picked her up, carrying Parthena to the bench and sat her on his lap, his hands roaming along the lines of her wet dress. She felt the press of something thick and hard beneath her and Parthena twisted a bit, placing herself directly on top.

"You have no idea—"

"I do, actually, Your Grace. My eldest sister is already wed, and I did grow up in the country."

"Dear God. Please don't tell me any more. I'm about to forget every bit of manners instilled in me." He pressed a kiss just beneath Parthena's ear, shifting her so that when she moved, a tingle burst up between her thighs, through the wet folds of her dress. Lifting her hem, she fluttered out her skirts and pressed down once more. Parthena bit her lip at the ache stretching down between her legs. The more she pushed down on the hardness pulsing between his thighs, the more her pleasure increased.

"I'm not ruining you in this bloody folly," his voice was rough. "But I certainly wish to." Wexham kissed her then, ravenously, as if he would never have enough of Parthena Holm.

She rocked back and forth across that ridge, reveling in the sensations coursing through her body. Watching the play of emotions on his handsome features, Parthena threaded her fingers through the thick locks of his hair.

Wexham's fingers dug into her hips, sliding her back and forth, his gaze intent. "This isn't at all how I meant this to be." The words were rough. "For one thing, you should be naked beneath me."

A small cry left her, thinking of their bodies sliding into each other. "Yes." Her movements became ragged as she chased the pleasurable sensation building up inside her.

Wexham pulled her down against him, slowing the movement as she took hold of his shoulders, staring down into that beautiful amber gaze. A low moan came from her as his lips found hers once more.

Pure, unadulterated bliss shot through her. Parthena's legs twitched, her hold on his shoulders slipped, fingers curling into his shirt.

Wexham buried his face in her neck. Whispered her name. The swelling beneath her pulsed and jerked. Neither said a word, their ragged breathing mixing with the sound of the storm outside. Parthena bent and laid her head on his shoulder, awestruck by what had erupted so quickly between them. They hadn't even discarded their clothing. Nor touched each other. Was she ruined?

Parthena's cheeks were hot. *Completion.* That's what Leta called this blinding, nearly painful bliss, usually the culmination of physical relations. Immensely pleasurable. Though she'd ground herself against Wexham like some doxy, which was vastly improper. "What you must think of me."

Wexham gently moved her off his lap but kept her close. "What *you* must think of me, Parthena."

"I think you wonderful," she whispered. "But that isn't normal. What we did."

"More usual than you might imagine. But stripping away your clothing," he nibbled at her neck, "is not an option. Not at present." His tongue flicked around her ear. "You aren't ruined." He shrugged. "Well, I suppose a little. And if anyone should be embarrassed, it should be me. I behaved like some green lad." A gentle kiss brushed her mouth.

"I behaved most improperly."

"We both did." He tucked a bit of Parthena's hair behind her ear. "I look forward to hearing your adequate violin playing this evening."

Parthena pressed her forehead to his. "Why? I am merely a bookend. A foil." She hesitated, not knowing how to continue. How to ask about Belinda. Would this mean he would still wed her? The thought sent a pain through her heart.

"You are neither of those things." Atticus's mouth met hers, interrupting her thoughts. "Never a bookend. Or a foil. Your choice of music, for instance, is bound to be interesting."

Warmth bloomed inside her. "Everyone in the room will be watching me, waiting for the bow to fly out of my hand and blind one of the servants. And as to what I will perform, I suppose it will be whatever Lady Baldwin wishes."

"But what would you play, had you the choice?" He nuzzled into her neck. "If I was the only one listening?"

Parthena thought for a moment. "There is a tune my father used to sing for my mother," her fingers trailed over the edge of his jaw, the feeling for him stuck in her throat. It was much too soon. "A love song."

Wexham sighed, lips trailing over hers. "Then play it for me tonight, Parthena." He took her hand and placed it over his heart. "And only me. Because you are all I will see tonight."

The rain pattered away, an excuse to not leave the intimacy of the folly, so they did not. They spoke of nothing, yet everything. Atticus loved the stars and constellations. Families. Dreams. Their shared love of the country and mutual dislike of London.

Mostly though, Wexham held her close to his heart.

When the rain finally stopped, he put his still damp coat over her shoulders, pressed a kiss to her palm and whispered he could not wed Belinda.

Because Parthena was the most dazzling star in his sky.

CHAPTER SEVEN

PARTHENA STARED AT herself in the mirror. She wore her best gown. Her hair done in a lovely, though uncomplicated style with just a few curls left to dangle at her temples. There wasn't anything special about her slightly plump form or the oval of her face. None of the beauty of Lady Belinda.

Nothing that would indicate she would attract the attention of a duke.

Wexham had led them both out of the folly and towards the house, careful to keep a respectful distance, though his coat covered her shoulders. Parthena had been surprised to find that while it seemed like hours, she and Wexham had only been trapped in the folly for a short time. He'd assured Parthena he would make the necessary explanation to Lady Baldwin. She was not to worry.

"You look glorious." Fidelia appeared from Mama's room, connected to theirs. "What exactly happened with Wexham in the folly?"

"Not a thing," Parthena assured her as Mama came into the room and smoothed her skirts. "We spoke of the stars. Constellations and such. He gave me his coat." She rolled her shoulders. "The folly was in plain sight of the terrace," she smiled at Fidelia. "Goodness, you could see us."

"Not entirely," Fidelia pressed a kiss to her cheek.

Knuckles rapped sharply on the door. "Come," Mama said, stepping back a pace as Lady Baldwin sauntered into the room.

"There has been a change of plans for tonight's performance. Your...presence," she gave a toothy smile and a lift of her chin. "Is no longer required."

Mama's own smile faltered. "But—"

"I'm having the carriage brought around. Mary," she waved to the young girl who'd assisted them earlier, "will pack your things."

"My lady," Mama looked askance at Fidelia and Parthena. "What has happened? My girls are ready to perform with Lady Belinda."

"Yes, I saw enough of Parthena's performance earlier today," she snapped.

Parthena's stomach pitched unpleasantly.

"I believe it would suit all of us better if you and your daughters departed as soon as possible," Lady Baldwin said. "I've found another young lady to accompany Belinda. I'm not sure what you hoped to accomplish earlier today, Parthena." Displeasure colored her features. "Except to create a spectacle as you are wont to do on nearly every occasion. I find I can no longer tolerate your lack of decorum. Not when it may cost my niece her future."

The beat of her pulse became unsteady. Wexham promised he would smooth things over with Lady Baldwin.

"I expect you all to be gone within the hour." Lady Baldwin walked towards the door before turning once more. "There will be no more invitations, Mrs. Holm. We are family, but our connection is now far more distant. Do not call upon me." She shot another look of dislike at Parthena.

"You are overreacting, Priscilla." Mama said quietly. "Nothing untoward occurred today. It isn't as if Parthena went into the folly and enticed Wexham. He merely rendered her aid, as any gentleman would. The storm was severe."

"Your daughter," Lady Baldwin's words seethed with unbridled anger, "aspires far above her station. She behaved inappropriately with the duke. Throwing herself at him like some—" Lady Baldwin clamped her lips shut. "Wexham told me himself. He is most appalled at her boldness."

Parthena inhaled sharply. Wexham said he would *explain* the situation to Lady Baldwin. Perhaps she'd mistaken his meaning. Heat seared her cheeks. She had thrown herself at Wexham. Grinded her hips against his...*anatomy.*

"I didn't want to tell you, Mrs. Holm. But you've forced the issue. I realize how disappointed you must be, indeed we all are. Now, I will send Mary up to help pack your things. My niece's performance will begin in an hour, and I want you well on your way by then."

Mama's face crumpled in disappointment as she took in the blush stealing across Parthena's skin. "I apologize for any embarrassment my daughter has caused. Please give my congratulations to Lady Belinda on her engagement. We will leave as you wish."

Nodding stiffly, Lady Baldwin sailed through door, not bothering to close it behind her.

"It isn't true, Mama," Parthena stuttered. "Not a word of it."

"The Duke of Wexham paid you a crumb of polite attention and you launched yourself at him? Because he is a gentleman and sought to help you?" Mama's voice raised an octave. "That I should have a daughter behaving so shamefully. Even for you, Parthena, this is too much. Your reputation will be destroyed once word of this gets out. And it will. What on earth made you think the Duke of Wexham had any interest in you?"

Parthena opened her mouth, wanting to say Wexham found her *dazzling*. That he wasn't going to wed Belinda. That when he kissed her the entire world fell silent except for the two of them.

"Not another word." Mama made a snapping motion with her fingers. "When we return home, you will accept the courtship of Captain Rogers lest you become a pariah."

Mary, the maid, came to the door with a polite nod, and set about packing their things, efficiently ending the conversation that had broken Parthena's heart.

CHAPTER EIGHT

A SHORT TIME later, Parthena hugged the violin case to her chest while their trunks were loaded atop the carriage. Not even Corman bothered to see the disgraced Holm women out. Like everyone else, he was in the drawing room as Belinda sang off-key to the Duke of Wexham.

She hugged the violin tighter. Confused and saddened. Could she have misunderstood Wexham's intentions towards her?

No. Impossible. Wexham felt as she did.

"Then why am I standing here?" she whispered under her breath.

Fidelia took her arm and led her forward. "Well, at least we won't have to act as bookends for that performance." She nodded in the direction of the drawing room. "I'm sure Wexham is wishing he were deaf right about now. I didn't even get to bid Mr. Shore goodbye."

"I didn't throw myself at Wexham." Parthena's brow wrinkled. "That is to say I may have kissed him first, but—"

"Shush, Thena." Fidelia lowered her voice. "Mama will hear you. She is already beside herself if she is threatening you with marriage to Captain Rogers. Perhaps you misinterpreted his manner towards you."

"I did not," she stubbornly asserted.

"He is a *duke*, Parthena," Fidelia hissed. "Lady Belinda is the daughter of a marquess. They are the *same*. We are daughters of an impoverished country squire. Related to no one of consequence especially now that Lady Baldwin has discarded us."

"Just because a pair of slippers are more than I can afford and made for another young lady does not mean they won't fit me perfectly."

"A duke is not a pair of slippers." Fidelia stopped. "Whatever you are thinking, Parthena, do not embarrass yourself or your family any further."

She could still hear Belinda singing. The musicale wasn't over yet. The doors to the drawing room would be open. Wexham did not want her gone. She refused to believe it. But Lady Baldwin did.

"Lady Baldwin wouldn't have asked me to leave unless she worried I had garnered the duke's affection."

"Thena."

"I am not wrong." Parthena felt the truth inside her bones. "But if I am, Wexham will at least know what is in my heart. Considering Mama wishes to marry me off to Captain Rogers, I am willing to take the risk." She broke away from her sister, violin case stuck beneath her arm and ran around the side of Lady Baldwin's home. The windows would be open. She would stand outside.

"Parthena!" Mama cried from the carriage. "Come back this instant."

Deftly avoiding a cluster of shrubs, because that would be very bad if she caught herself in their branches, Parthena skidded to a halt on the lawn, the light from the drawing room spilling out over the grass. The windows, just as she expected, were open wide to let in the cooler air. A bold, grand gesture was required on her part, so that there could be no further doubt on the state of her affections. Whether accepted or not.

Wexham sat one row back, on the side Parthena would have stood. A frown pulled at his beautiful mouth.

Play for me Parthena. Only me.

So she did.

CHAPTER NINE

ATTICUS SAT IN his seat, gaze focused on the empty spot where Parthena *should* have been and was not. According to his hostess, who imparted the information as Atticus and the other guests made their way into the drawing room, Parthena, Fidelia and their mother had returned home unexpectedly. When he expressed concern that he hoped all was well, Lady Baldwin casually made mention their return was at the request of Captain Rogers. The gentleman to whom Parthena would soon be wed.

Parthena was *not* marrying another man. She wouldn't. Not after…

Unless she loved this Captain Rogers.

That was the thought that had Atticus frowning as he considered the possibility.

Duncan slid quietly into the seat beside him as Belinda mercifully finished the song. Handing Atticus a glass of brandy he said, "You look like you could use this. Lady Belinda is quite lovely, but she can't sing to save her life." His friend looked at him. "Fidelia was supposed to accompany her, but Corman tells me the Holm ladies have departed. Did Mr. Holm fall ill?"

The strains of a violin interrupted Atticus's response, the sound coming from outside the drawing room windows.

Lady Baldwin stood next to Belinda as the other guests offered their polite applause, waiting impatiently for Atticus to come forward. Her smile froze at the melody coming from outside, eyes widening. She clapped her hands at Corman, urging him to shut the windows in a furious whisper.

Atticus came to his feet, eyes shutting for only a moment as he listened to the violin outside.

Parthena. And she was more than just adequate on the instrument.

The melancholy notes plucked at his skin. His heart. He doubted she'd ever played for the mysterious Captain Rogers.

"Your Grace," Lady Baldwin hurried to him, dragging along Belinda, nostrils flaring as she glanced outside. "Might I have a word?"

Atticus bowed. "I am sorry, my lady. But my earlier decision stands. I fear it will not be changed."

Lady Baldwin reddened. "You cannot be serious, Your Grace. Miss Holm—"

"Dazzles me." He cut her off and turned to Belinda. "Our tentative courtship is at an end, my lady. I hope you can understand, but I don't believe we suit."

Belinda nodded slowly. "We do not, Your Grace."

Atticus ignored the curious looks of the rest of Lady Baldwin's guests, including Duncan, and marched over to the open window, his only thought to get to Parthena as quickly as possible.

Parthena had her eyes closed as she played with the moon rising behind her, hair unraveling from the pins trying to hold it back. The melancholy notes of the love song soared over Lady Baldwin's lawn.

She was playing for him and only him.

"I'm coming, Parthena," he said through the window. Then, pushing it open further, Atticus wedged himself through the opening and climbed out. Easier than going around, especially when all he could think of was her.

A lone tear ran down her cheek as he approached, her violin falling silent. "Wexham." She pointed the bow at him. "You cannot wed Lady Belinda."

"I cannot," he agreed. "We have decided we do not suit. Put the bow down so I do not lose an eye. While you have visions of me becoming a pirate, I would rather stay a duke."

"Oh," she sniffed. "Well, I don't suppose you'd look good with an eye patch." Parthena bit her lip. "I must know, Your Grace. What is this?" She placed a hand on his chest, swatting his chin accidentally with the bow. "Between us?"

"The seed of a great love," Atticus whispered. "One that has already taken root." He took the bow from her hand, kissing her fingers. "Never doubt it again, Miss Holm."

He took Parthena firmly around the waist, kissing her soundly in full view of every guest staring at them out of Lady Baldwin's window. So there could be no mistaking his intentions.

The End

Additional Dragonblade books by Author Kathleen Ayers

The Five Deadly Sins Series
Sinfully Wed (Book 1)
Sinfully Tempted (Book 2)
Sinfully Mine (Book 3)
Sinfully Yours (Book 4)
Sinfully Wanton (Book 5)

The Arrogant Earls Series
Forgetting the Earl (Book 1)
Chasing the Earl (Book 2)
Enticing the Earl (Book 3)
The Haunting of Rose Abbey (Novella)

About Kathleen Ayers

Kathleen Ayers is the bestselling author of steamy Regency and Victorian romance. She's been a hopeful romantic and romance reader since buying Sweet Savage Love at a garage sale when she was fourteen while her mother was busy looking at antique animal planters. She has a weakness for tortured, witty alpha males who can't help falling for intelligent, sassy heroines.

A Texas transplant (from Pennsylvania) Kathleen spends most of her summers attempting to grow tomatoes (a wasted effort) and floating in her backyard pool with her two dogs, husband and son. When not writing she likes to visit her "happy place" (Newport, RI.), wine bars, make homemade pizza on the grill, and perfect her charcuterie board skills. Visit her at www.kathleenayers.com.

I Know This Much Is True

by Chasity Bowlin

PROLOGUE

June 7th, 1827—London

"YOU DO NOT have to go."

Caroline Davies looked up from the soothing task of folding her meager clothing items into a trunk. "Effie, you know that I must. She is family."

"I am your family," Miss Euphemia Darrow retorted. "Mrs. Wheaton is your family. The other girls here are your family. Lady Stanhope is the sister of the man who fathered you, then abandoned both you and your mother. She is *his* family."

Caroline sighed. "I don't like it any better than you do. I am seventeen years old and have not been able to find a position. You send me for interviews, and I freeze like a startled fawn, unable to answer the simplest of questions. I fear I am your greatest failure."

"That's only nerves," Effie insisted. "It will get better over time!"

"How much time?" Caroline asked softly. "Because the school is overcrowded already. In some cases, the girls are sleeping three to a bed because you haven't the heart to turn away any child in need. I'm taking up space that could be better served in helping some poor girl who does not have a family member willing to take them on . . . or one who will be able to eventually move on and be employable. This is a good opportunity for me and for others."

"As a servant. She is your aunt by blood, but she is offering you a home as her servant! Companion to her daughter, indeed."

"Which is more than she is required to do," Caroline pointed out calmly. "But I might have a chance to finally know something of my father . . . to understand why he did not marry my mother before I was born."

Effie crossed her arms over her chest in annoyance. "Your home is here. No matter how far you may travel from it. If the situation becomes unbearable, you will return here, and I do not care what your aunt has to say about it." Effie then pulled a small box from the pocket of her skirt. "Happy birthday, Caroline."

Caroline looked down at the small proffered box and smiled. Effie always marked her birthday. Every girl's, in fact. And if their birthdate was not known, one was chosen for them. And always, the day brought some little gift or treat to make it special.

Opening the box carefully, she was stunned by what lay inside it. The simple gold locket was familiar to her. It had been her mother's and bore small portraits of both her parents inside it. But the chain on which it rested, of fine, delicate links, that was new. New and terribly dear. "Oh, Effie. You should not have gone to such expense, but it's so beautiful and so very treasured."

Effie lifted the necklace from the box and draped it about Caroline's throat. "This is a tangible reminder of where you came from, but also where you can return. You will always have a home here."

CHAPTER ONE

June 5th, 1829

A VERFORD COURT WAS buzzing with activity and with people. There was to be a wedding, and not an insignificant one. Lady Jane Bancroft, the half sister of the Duke of Avingden, was set to marry Harris Stanhope, Viscount Warrington, in what was said to be a great love match.

The Duke in question, Antony Bancroft, had his doubts. Stanhope was a boorish sort, loud and somewhat obnoxious. But Jane didn't seem to mind him, and so there they all were, gathered at the family seat for a summer wedding, surrounded by family, friends, and a number of people who fit neither category. And Antony was close to banging his head on the nearest hard surface just to escape it all. In particular, he wished to escape the woman who was currently speaking to him. *At length.*

He was looking for an escape, or he might have never seen the surreptitious exchange between the two young ladies perched on a bench in his grandmother's garden. For the first time, perhaps since the entire debacle had begun, he felt some stirring of interest. A little spark of intrigue that might, if he was lucky, sustain his sanity through the remainder of the summer.

Over the last few days, he'd developed a singular habit: to preserve his sanity, he'd taken to looking past Isabella when she spoke. Isabella, the woman he was likely going to marry—the woman whom everyone expected him to marry, certainly—and the sound of her voice were both torturous to him. Oh, the tone of it was dulcet enough. In truth, her voice was not displeasing at all. It was the cacophony of drivel that spewed from it.

He'd tried. God above, Antony thought, he had tried. But Isabella could rattle on about dresses and town gossip until it was a wonder her lungs didn't simply deflate and wither in her chest, as it appeared she never paused to draw breath. It had been a truly remarkable discovery to realize that if he stared at a point just past her shoulder, the appearance of attentive listening could be maintained while his mind was free to focus on other things altogether.

That the thing he seemed to focus on more often than not was the companion of the prospective groom's younger sister, Miss Caroline Davies, was a perturbing coincidence. She was a lovely girl, really. Too lovely to be in service, that was a certainty. She was a poor relation to the Stanhope family, though the exact nature of that kinship remained quite muddy. Of course, the lack of close connection could only be a bonus.

In fact, the very idea of her being in the Stanhope household when the whole family seemed lacking in manners and couth was simply intolerable. The notion that she might be forced to endure the unwanted advances in that home that so many young women in her position did was positively infuriating to him. He found himself feeling unaccountably protective of the young woman who, to his understanding, had no one else to look after her. It was only natural that he, as a gentleman, should feel some sense of obligation regarding her welfare, he reasoned. Of course, that sense of obligation did not quite extend to the degree with which she often occupied his thoughts. Or that his thoughts were very often of a carnal nature. But his thoughts were his own, he reasoned, and so long as he never acted upon them, then surely it was of little consequence.

That particular day, Isabella was droning on far longer than normal. No mean feat to be sure. And he had been watching Miss Davies in the company of her charge, Miss Ruby Stanhope, with more interest than two young ladies sketching in a garden likely deserved. But then he noted the way they bent their heads together and giggled. He noted the way that, occasionally, Miss Davies' gaze would drift toward him and then she would look away, almost guiltily as she scribbled on the page before her. It sparked no small amount of curiosity in him. And curiosity when it came to Miss Davies was surely a terrible affliction.

"What do you think, Your Grace? . . . Your Grace?"

The repeated address was lacking enough in patience to pierce even his greatest efforts to practice willful deafness. Glancing more directly at Isabella, he said, "Forgive me. I was distracted for a moment."

"Distracted by what . . . or is it a whom?" Isabella demanded, all but stamping her foot in annoyance.

"I'm not quite certain. How do you classify Caesar?" He'd seized upon his grandmother's bulldog who did everything possible not to live up to his noble moniker as a convenient excuse. And indeed, the unfortunately dim-witted animal was roaming the garden.

Isabella's lips twisted in an expression of complete hatred. For most, the dog was an annoyance. He was lovable, but stupid, and therefore often underfoot or in the way. But this was much more than simple irritation; she truly detested the beast. "That animal," she said, "is a menace. Do you know that he drooled all over my new satin dancing slippers? Not simply on them, Antony, but in them. *In them.*"

As he knew that Isabella had a habit of tossing her belongings about in her room as though she were trying to replicate the destruction of a typhoon, it was hardly a surprise. The dog would have had no trouble accessing them. "You cannot leave things lying about for him, Isabella. While it was terrible of him to do so, he is possessed of such limited intellect that we must assume the responsibility of ensuring that he does not do injury to himself or to our property . . . but what was your earlier question?"

"I asked if you thought it more romantic for people to wed by special license or to have banns posted and wait that wretchedly long three weeks?"

"I have no opinion one way or another. Has someone proposed to you, Isabella?" He certainly hadn't. Even as he thought it, he saw Miss Davies get up from her seat and make for the house. A moment after her, Miss Stanhope did as well. But when Miss Stanhope rose, the sewing basket she picked up tipped over slightly, and the item that Miss Davies had hidden in it fell to the ground, missed entirely by everyone except Caesar, who trotted over and scooped it up with his shovel-like, protruding lower jaw.

"Oh, no! I was simply speaking in generalities. Special licenses do carry a certain amount of cachet, do they not?"

"I rather think they are indicative of inappropriate choices," he replied. And then realized that she'd managed to back him into a conversation about matrimony—a subject he'd been attempting to avoid with her for some time. "Pardon me, Isabella. I believe Caesar is about to consume a plant that would not be the thing for him."

Making a hasty exit, he headed directly for the dog and the purloined item. All the while, he was thinking that he would either have to break with Isabella entirely or marry her, but the limbo they were currently in could not continue indefinitely.

»»»«««

"YOU MUST HAVE it! I put it in your sewing basket!" Caroline hissed. Her heart was racing with a kind of fear she had never known. "Ruby, please, tell me you have it!"

Ruby Stanhope, her cousin and her dearest friend, shook her head. "No, Caroline. I've checked the basket twice, and it's simply not in there. Are you certain that's where you put it?"

Caroline blinked in surprise at what was surely a stupid question. "Where else would I have put a sketch that you dared me to create?"

Ruby's eyes widened slightly as understanding dawned on her. "It was *that* sketch?"

"Yes. It was *that* sketch!" Caroline wanted to drop her head into her hands and weep. What a disaster it all was! "Why would I have needed to surreptitiously pass you any other drawing? Ruby, if that falls into the wrong hands, I'll be ruined. You will be ruined. Your mother will send me straight back to the Darrow School, and Effie will be so terribly disappointed in me."

"Perhaps whoever finds it will fail to recognize him?"

No. That wasn't even a possibility, Caroline thought, reflecting on the damning sketch in question. On the one hand, she was quite proud of her work. In terms of her sketching, it was one of the most detailed and well-executed pieces she had ever completed. On the other hand, sections of the drawing were painfully incomplete due to her own ignorance. But there would be little doubt for anyone viewing it that the subject of the sketch was none other than the Duke of Avingden.

He was a remarkably handsome man. From their first meeting days earlier, she'd been all aflutter at the very sight of him. Not that it mattered in the least. He was the Duke of Avingden, and she was the illegitimate poor relation of the man his half sister was set to marry. But even poor women could dream, and in her dreams, none of that mattered. He would look at her, fall instantly and hopelessly in love with her, and sweep her away from everything.

So when she'd set out to sketch him, she'd captured his masculine beauty perfectly. From the chiseled planes and angles of his face, to the sweep of his dark hair as it waved away from his forehead, it looked exactly like him. But that was the only part of the sketch that looked exactly like him, as the rest of him, at least without the well-tailored and elegant clothing he favored, was a complete mystery to her. The shoulders and chest hadn't been so difficult. What she'd seen of classical art had filled in most of the blanks in regards to that portion of the male anatomy. The rest of it, however—well, she had no notion really. Well, perhaps she had *some* notion. But to say that she lacked detail was to put it mildly.

Ruby, knowing her secret tendre for the duke, had challenged her to draw him in a manner that reflected her feelings for him. And now, since everyone in the house knew of her love of sketching, the discovery of the drawing would reveal her infatuation to everyone. It was bad enough that the sketch was a very incomplete nude, but for the entire household to know that she had such great curiosity about how the duke would look beneath his fine clothes—it was an unmitigated disaster.

"I should just start packing now. It's only a matter of time before they toss me out."

Ruby had no great words of wisdom to offer, nor did she have the ability to offer any real comfort. Instead, her cousin simply took her hand and gave Caroline a gentle pat. "It surely won't come to that."

Caroline chewed her lower lip nervously as they made their way into the large drawing room where other guests were gathered for the afternoon's games. It would come to it. She was certain of it. And the weight of everyone's disappointment in her weighed upon her like a physical burden, as though she were hauling heavy stones about, balanced precariously on her shoulders. The slightest wrong move, and it would be naught but chaos and destruction.

"Miss Davies!"

Caroline's blood chilled. Being called out by the duke or the dowager were not her only concerns. There was also him: Sir Percival Heatherton. The single most irritating and willfully obtuse man to have ever graced society.

Turning her head, she acknowledged, "Sir Percival."

"Come partner with me in whist! I know you'd be crack at it."

She was, in fact. But he didn't know that. Not really. "I'm afraid I am otherwise engaged, sir, but I do thank you for the invitation."

"Ah, well. I've no real wish to play whist anyway. What are your plans? Perhaps I might join you?"

Caroline looked at Ruby in desperation. And Ruby, God bless her, complied. Her cousin placed her hand to her forehead and swooned dramatically, falling against Caroline with enough force that they both stumbled.

"Oh, dear. I was outside for far too long. The sun has taken quite a toll," Ruby bemoaned dramatically.

"Forgive me, Sir Percival. I must see my cousin upstairs."

"Of course," he said. "And once she's settled, you can come back and enjoy a game with me!"

"Do not wait for me, sir. Find yourself another partner. I fear I will not be able to leave Ruby's side until I am certain she is well."

Sir Percival appeared quite taken aback. "Surely a servant can sit with her!"

Caroline's temper spiked. "Sir Percival, my cousin needs me, and I intend to be there for her. Good afternoon, sir."

Walking away, with Ruby still leaning heavily on her, though purely for show, Caroline muttered. "The man is insufferable."

"He would offer for you. In a heartbeat. If you want a husband—"

Caroline shuddered. "Spinsterhood looks infinitely more appealing than marriage to him. Now, let's go hide in your room for the remainder of this dreadful day."

"I have a box of chocolates!" Ruby whispered. "I smuggled them in so Mama would not lecture me about my figure."

"Then we shall make a strategic retreat and enjoy your chocolates well away from any prying eyes." And far, far from Sir Percival, who gave her no peace at all.

CHAPTER TWO

A NTONY WAS ON a mission—a mission spurred by the highly imaginative bit of artwork he'd discovered in the garden. The folded-up bit of paper that Miss Davies had intended for her cousin, which had not reached its intended destination at all, was now tucked into the pocket of his waistcoat.

At last, after an exhaustive search of the house, beset by near misses and unfortunately unavoidable polite conversations with individuals he had no real desire to speak with at all, Antony found his cousin, Theo, in the blessedly empty billiard room. It was only a short while before dinner, and he hoped it would be enough time to convince him to aid in his newly formed quest.

It was a wonder to many that the two of them were so close, as they could not have been more different. Slight and fair, Theo was the antithesis of Antony in every way. Yet, despite their obvious differences, they had developed a surprisingly close bond that was more akin to that of siblings than merely cousins. It was for precisely that reason that Theo was the only one he could trust in his current situation.

"What do you think of Miss Davies?" he asked without preamble.

Theo frowned. "I do not think of Miss Davies. Not in the least. Why would I?"

"Well, she is a young woman visiting for the summer . . . a family connection to the Stanhopes, who will now be forever linked to us. One would think you would have at least some opinion of her," Antony pointed out, being intentionally vague.

Theo simply shrugged as he circled the billiard table, examining every angle before deciding on his next shot. "She's little more than a servant, has no dowry, no connections, and nothing to recommend her. That is all I need to know about her. A better question, cousin, would be why you are thinking of her. Especially given that you have the lovely Miss Isabella Parker to occupy your thoughts. Indeed, I should wonder that you have a spare thought for anyone given the extent of Miss Parker's charms."

Antony frowned. "You seem quite taken with Isabella."

Theo tensed. "There is not a gentleman alive who has encountered Miss Parker who is not taken with her. I would never presume to importune her—or you—with my admiration."

It was an opportunity. Theo was quite the catch on the marriage mart, despite his lesser title. Handsome, if not precisely robust, he was charming and possessed of a respectable title and quite extensive fortune. And he was the answer to Antony's prayers. "Cousin, I must confess something to you."

Theo walked idly around the table, examining the position of each ball very carefully. "Very well. Confess."

"I cannot marry Miss Parker." The moment he uttered the words, Antony felt as though a great burden had been lifted from him. He exhaled fully and felt positively freed by it. "I thought I could. I thought that perhaps my feelings for her would grow with greater acquaintance, hence inviting her family to spend the summer here with us in anticipation of this wedding. But I have been proven wrong. The more time I spend with her, the less time I desire to spend with her."

Theo's shot went wide, the cue striking the felt and the ball skittering off the table entirely. "Have you taken complete leave of your senses? She's beautiful. She's more than beautiful. I would dare you to find a more perfect example of feminine beauty in all of the *ton!*"

"Isabella is beautiful," Antony conceded. "But that's all she is. I need more, Theo. That simply isn't enough to base a marriage on."

Theo shook his head as if astounded by his cousin's idiocy. "What is it you would have me do?"

"Just dance attendance on Isabella while I figure out . . . while I figure things out." He could not, under any circumstances, let it be known that Miss Davies had been sketching him in the altogether, or as much of the altogether as she was familiar with. That sketch, the mysterious paper he'd managed to rescue in the garden before Caesar had a chance to scoop it up in his gaping and unfortunate maw, had been—to say the least—a revelation. The drawing had been well executed, although in many regards he thought perhaps the artist had flattered him unnecessarily. *Or perhaps that was how she perceived him.* For his part, he had no small degree of appreciation for the prettiness of Miss Davies, with her sparkling eyes and sweetly curved smile.

"Figure things out . . . with Miss Davies?" Theo asked pointedly.

"Just so," Antony admitted. "I cannot help but feel there is something there, a connection, that must be explored."

Theo shook his head. "Are you certain? If you do this, there will be no going back regardless. This ephemeral connection you speak of may be nothing more than fancy, but Isabella Parker will not simply be idle while you pursue another woman right under her nose!"

"I will not marry Miss Parker. That fact remains independently of whatever comes of my interest in Miss Davies," he stated firmly.

"Fine. I shall lavish my attentions upon your almost-betrothed who is a diamond of the first water while you play chasey-chasey with a girl who is little better than hired help," Theo conceded. "And I shall think you mad the entire time. Incidentally, cousin, what if Miss Parker decides she prefers a lowly lord to an exalted duke?"

"Then I shall wish you felicitations and toast you at your wedding breakfast."

With that, Antony left the billiard room and his sputtering cousin. He needed to find a way to speak to Miss Davies alone. That could well be a Herculean task, given how his grandmother had structured events for the house party and wedding. So perhaps he needed to enlist the aid of someone else in his endeavors. But that was a last resort, of course. The fewer people who knew what was happening, the safer it would be for Miss Davies all around.

But there was one person he could trust. His valet, Thompson, could make inquiries about her discreetly and help him to arrange opportunities for their paths to cross. It was the perfect plan.

Smiling to himself, Antony made for his rooms. The sooner he could instruct Thompson on what he required, the sooner he could begin wooing Miss Davies in earnest.

CAROLINE WAS POSITIVELY on tenterhooks. Since their afternoon in the garden, when she had put pencil to paper to create that salacious drawing of her wildest imaginings of the duke, fear had been her constant companion. Had he found it? Had someone else found it and apprised him of her improper behavior? Or, heaven forbid, had someone found it and given it to her aunt?

Maneuvering through the crowded drawing room, trying desperately to avoid Sir Percival, she maintained her nonchalant act as if nothing untoward was afoot. She smiled politely, and later would no doubt be asked to read aloud or play the pianoforte to humiliate herself in the fashion determined by her aunt. And she was supposed to do all of these things with just enough skill to not draw undue attention to herself and away from Ruby. It had been made quite clear to her from the moment her aunt had taken her on that her position was tenuous at best and that she was only to ever show Ruby to her best advantage. Creating nude drawings of a wealthy, powerful, and very well-connected gentleman would certainly result in the type of "undue attention" her aunt frowned upon.

Now, gathered in the drawing room prior to the dinner hour, she waited to be called out. Branded as some sort of morally deficient strumpet in front of everyone, they likely would not even wait for morning to toss her out on her ear. It was all she could do not to ring her hands in distress. The only thing preventing her from making such a display was a single shred of hope that perhaps Caesar had found the offending bit of artwork and salivated over it until its contents were to remain forever a mystery to whoever was unlucky enough to find his soggy treasure.

"Caroline, have you had any indication that Mama or the duchess are displeased with you?" The whispered inquiry was from Ruby, who had sidled up next to her.

"Nothing . . . not yet, at any rate," Caroline said. "Perhaps it hasn't been found?"

Ruby's expression shifted to one of alarm. "Or perhaps they have yet to determine precisely what they mean to do with you?"

Caroline's stomach knotted at the thought. "Ruby, could you endeavor to be slightly less honest? Occasionally, a bit of unwavering optimism, no matter how poorly grounded in reality it is, would be quite welcome!"

"Well, you did make a fairly realistic likeness of the duke wearing . . . well, nothing. In all fairness, Caroline, I cannot imagine that there will not be dire consequences for it."

Knowing that Ruby was correct did not help her nerves at all. "I only drew it because you told me to!"

"I didn't tell you to draw him nude! That was entirely your idea," Ruby fired back in a heated whisper.

Caroline's eyes widened in outrage. "You dared me to draw him as I longed to see him. How else should I like to see him, Ruby?"

"Picking flowers for you, riding his horse while dressed in gleaming armor . . . not nude, Caroline. Good heavens!"

And at that very moment, the object of Caroline's curiosity entered the drawing room. As always, he took her breath away. He was so unbearably handsome. With dark, shortly cropped hair and lean, chiseled features, he was simply beautiful. But it was his eyes which always drew her. Deep brown, fringed with thick lashes and topped with slashing dark brows, they were kind and warm in a way that one typically did not see with gentlemen.

"Good evening, Miss Stanhope . . . Miss Davies."

Had he paused? He had paused! Why? What could that possibly mean? Caroline was in such a state that she couldn't even reply. She simply stood there, blinking owlishly while panic suffused her.

"Good evening, Your Grace," Ruby said and then shifted so that her elbow connected sharply with Caroline's ribs.

Spurred to action, Caroline dipped her head in acknowledgement. "Your Grace."

"You are well, Miss Davies? My grandmother's abundantly scheduled entertainments have not left you exhausted?"

"The dowager duchess is a remarkable hostess," Caroline managed to say, speaking around the lump in her throat. Or perhaps she was suffering some fatal heart seizure brought on solely by panic. "Everything at Averford is just as it should be, Your Grace, and no doubt that is largely the dowager's doing." Had she sounded sharp? Oh, she had. Now he thought her a shrew. If he had seen the sketch, he'd think her a strumpet and a shrew. Good heavens.

The duke smiled, though his expression was quite curious. "I see, Miss Davies. That is excellent to hear. I shall leave you to it then. . . . Oh, but I nearly forgot. You are quite the artist, are you not, Miss Davies?"

Beside her, Ruby let out a squeak of alarm. It was Caroline's turn to land a strategically placed elbow. "I dabble, Your Grace. I merely dabble."

"Well, Averford offers many inspiring sights. A ruined abbey on the far edges of the property boasts charming vistas of the valley to one side and the sea to the other. I imagine even for one who only dabbles at artistic endeavors, it would be a wellspring of inspiration. Perhaps we shall get up a party and picnic at the site."

"It's a lovely idea, Your Grace, but I fear your grandmother's schedule may not afford such lassitude. She has planned an endless array of entertainments, after all."

He merely smiled. "We shall see, Miss Davies."

CHAPTER THREE

FROM HER VANTAGE point across the room, the Dowager Duchess of Avingden watched her grandson making his advances toward the young Miss Davies, companion to Miss Stanhope. It was about time, she thought. Half the eligible debs of the *ton* had been paraded before Antony with no interest at all on his part. And perhaps Miss Davies was not quite the thing, but she was well raised, genteel, lovely enough to counteract the lack of a dowry, and not the least bit objectionable in any way. The dowager was beyond caring whom he married and was focusing solely on the hope that he *would* marry!

Her grandnephew, Theo, was present as well. In truth, all the town beauties she had invited had been more for his benefit than Antony's. She had long known that Antony would never be content with a society wife. Duke or no, he was a man with very different interests. Theo, however, adored society and all that it had to offer.

Beckoning to the younger man, she sat imperiously, tapping her silver-tipped cane against the floor as he approached.

"Good evening, Your Grace," he said, sketching an overly exaggerated bow before her.

"Oh, stop your nonsense, Theo. None of us have time for it," she snapped. There was no heat in it. Truthfully, she adored him as much as Antony, but she also recognized that he frequently needed a firm hand. "Why has my grandson begun to pay such particular attention to Miss Davies?"

"I've no notion what you mean, Aunt," he denied far too quickly.

The dowager tapped the ottoman at her feet with the tip of her cane. "Sit."

He did so, clearly not liking it. But she wasn't overly concerned about bruising his vanity—not when he had such an abundance of it. "Does he have an attraction to the girl?"

"I cannot say."

"You will not say," she corrected. "You forget, Theo, that I can smell the lie on you from a mile away. There's some plan afoot between the two of you, and I will know what it is!"

Theo sighed. "He likes her. Though I daresay the Stanhope clan will not care for it. They may well turn her out if they get wind of it, and he will never forgive either of us!"

"Good heavens, you are duller than weathered rock at times! Turn her out, indeed. I have but to whisper a single sentence to the girl's aunt, and her station would be elevated from poor relation to adopted daughter in the blink of an eye! But there is some scandal there, I think. She was brought up in the Darrow School, and we all know why young ladies wind up there!"

Theo frowned in confusion. "Why do they wind up there?"

The dowager shook her head in annoyance. "My dear boy, how you get on in the world is a mystery to me at times. She's a by-blow. Illegitimate. That's why she was at the Darrow School. Though, I daresay it speaks well of Lady Stanhope that she took on such a burden—whether the girl is her blood or her husband's. I had a feeling about her the first time I met her."

"Lady Stanhope?"

The dowager whacked his arm with her fan in a gesture of pure annoyance. It landed with enough force to make him wince.

"No, you dolt. Miss Davies, of course. I knew Antony would find her compelling."

Theo shook his head in confusion. "If you knew that, then why invite Miss Parker and all these other young ladies? It seems unnecessarily risky when you want him angling for her alone."

"Because a diamond is always beautiful, Theo, but its true sparkle is only seen when it is shown against the right background. These lovely, shallow, society-obsessed young ladies are the foil needed to illustrate what makes Miss Davies so very special . . . and so very perfect for Antony. What is it that the two of you have planned?"

"He's asked me to keep Miss Parker occupied while he pursues Miss Davies."

"I will see to it that you are seated near one another at dinner," she determined with a sharp nod. "Of all those gathered, she is the one I most worry about."

"Because you think he could have feelings for her?"

"No. Because she's very used to getting what she wants, and she wants Antony . . . or rather, she wants what Antony represents. Her aim is to be a duchess. Do whatever you must to keep her from interfering between them."

Theo rose from the ottoman. "I do not understand why you couldn't just introduce Miss Davies to him and tell him she'd make an excellent wife!"

"Of course, you do not! You're the manageable sort, Theo. Antony, to my dismay, is the defiant sort. Always has been. The notion that his pursuit of Miss Davies might be forbidden or frowned upon will only make him more determined. Trust me and do as you are told."

Theo shrugged. "I'll do what I must. If that means dancing attendance on the lovely Miss Parker, then I certainly shall endeavor to persevere."

The dowager watched him walk away, heading in the direction of Miss Parker. Scanning the room, she noted Miss Davies' exceptionally high color. Something was afoot, she thought, and she would find out what.

Sir Percival approached Miss Davies, and the dowager noted the way the girl's eyes scanned the room for an avenue of escape. Not that she blamed her. He was an odious little man. He was only ever invited to her parties because he lived too close by to snub without some sort of recompense. And he was of low enough rank that he never sat near her at dinner. Thank heavens for that. But he would be sitting next to Miss Davies.

A glance at Antony, and she smiled smugly to herself. He was watching Sir Percival with the intensity of a hawk, clearly unhappy to have the man trying to poach the lady who held his interest. Oh, yes. Even though she had a moment of sympathy for Miss Davies, she'd put Sir Percival directly beside her and let Antony's jealousy do a good portion of her work for her.

IT HADN'T GONE as well as Antony had hoped. Perhaps Miss Davies' drawing had simply been an artistic endeavor and had little or nothing to do with any particular feelings she might have for him. The more he considered it, the more Antony believed that to be the case. After all, she'd looked at him almost as if he were an annoyance rather than a welcomed partner in conversation. If she was that reluctant to even speak with him, surely the notion that she might harbor a secret attraction for him was utterly pointless.

It was possible that her affections were otherwise engaged. Sir Percival had been paying particular attention to her. While she did not seem to welcome the little toad's advances any more than she had welcomed his, Sir Percival, courtesy of his rank, was in a better position to be close to Miss Davies. He was seated beside her at dinner and made multiple attempts to engage her in conversation. Attempts, Antony reasoned, that were rebuffed as politely as possible, given their setting.

Course after course, all through dinner, those thoughts plagued him. So much so that he was an entirely wretched dinner companion to everyone around him. And yet, when he looked up, he had a clear line of sight to Miss Davies and to Sir Percival beside her. He could watch her to his heart's content, but it seemed a pointless exercise if her feelings for him were so terribly and, in all honesty, dishearteningly indifferent.

And yet, there were moments when he would catch her looking at him. It was not indifference he saw in her gaze then. There was interest there, or perhaps she simply found it curious that he kept staring at her. But the moment their eyes locked with one another, she would look away, as any demure young lady should. But would a demure young lady draw scandalous images of eligible bachelors? He was no closer to discerning the truth about how she might feel for him than before. But it did at least let him cling to the belief that not all hope was lost. He had to get her alone, he reasoned. And he had to confront her about the drawing. It was the only way to learn the truth—whether his hopes might be realized or whether they were to be dashed forever.

CHAPTER FOUR

June 6th

"**H**E'S STARING AT you again."

Notching her arrow into the bow that had been provided for the day's archery competition, Caroline turned her head, but only slightly—just enough that she could glance from the corner of her eye to where the duke stood. Indeed, he was staring at her. He smiled at her, clearly having caught her looking. Immediately, Caroline turned her face forward once more. "Oh, do not tell me he's looking, Ruby! You tell me, then I feel compelled to look as well, then it becomes an endless cycle of humiliation. He must think me positively mad at this point!"

"If he does, he's quite brave to still be standing close by while you have a weapon," Ruby pointed out.

The tinkling laughter, clear and bell-like, rang out across the field. Miss Isabella Parker was struggling with her bow while no less than four gentlemen battled for the privilege of helping her.

"I loathe her," Ruby said quietly. "I shouldn't, I know, but I can't help it. Why she is just so . . . so . . ."

"Perfect?" Caroline supplied as her cousin struggled for the words.

"Yes. Exactly. Precisely. Who can possibly be *that* perfect? There must be something wrong with her."

Caroline eyed the young woman in question with no small degree of envy. "If there is, it certainly isn't physical. She's so lovely it almost hurts to look at her. And by all accounts, she is nice. Nice to everyone. And it's no secret that the Duke of Avingden has been courting her for some time. They are well matched." *Much to my eternal disappointment,* she thought.

"He was courting her, but she appears to be quite taken with his cousin, Lord Theo. They were laughing and talking all through dinner last night, and I saw them walking in the garden earlier . . . standing very, very close to one another."

Caroline shook her head. "I cannot imagine any woman choosing Lord Theo over the duke."

"Because he is a duke," Ruby surmised.

"No. Because he is *the duke.* There is a distinct difference," Caroline pointed out. It had nothing whatsoever to do with his title. It was simply about him. He was, in a word, perfect. Or as close to perfect as any man might be. "But I can't focus my attentions on him . . . not when he's as far out of my grasp as the moon. Let's talk about something else. *Anything* else."

"Have you considered which gown you might wear to the ball tomorrow night in honor of Lady Jane's nuptials to my worthless dolt of a brother?"

He wasn't worthless. He simply had very little to recommend him aside from his title. His neck was thicker than his head, and since every person who had any dealings with him at all referred to him as thickheaded, that was actually quite impressive. "My pink gown, I think. It's fetching, but not too fetching. Still perfectly suitable for my role as poor relation-come-companion."

Ruby shook her head sadly. "I do not understand why Mother thinks you must dim your light in order for me to shine. Why can't we both shine?"

"Because that, my dear cousin, is not the way the world works. I know my place in it, but I do adore you for your ability to forget that I am . . . not your social equal," Caroline finished rather lamely. *Bastard* was an ugly word, one she detested and one that had all too often been applied to her by others with unkind hearts.

"You are. And anyone who says differently is beneath us both."

ANTONY WATCHED UNTIL he saw Miss Davies make for the house. Then, as discreetly as possible, he followed. There was no nefarious intent on his part, but he was aware that if anyone observed them, what his intentions were would simply not matter. Despite the risks, he had to find a way to speak to her alone.

He could hear voices drifting along the corridor toward the morning room. Staying back as far as he dared, he waited until he heard the soft sound of goodbyes. Miss Stanhope was going to lie down, and Miss Davies intended to return to the garden. Hurrying forward, he ducked into an alcove and waited as Miss Stanhope passed him on her way to the main staircase. Upon entering the morning room, he found Miss Davies seated at a small writing desk, her head bent low as she focused on the correspondence in front of her.

He cleared his throat lightly, and her head came up as she swiveled in her chair to look at him. Immediately, her expression went from startled to shocked to utterly horrified.

"Good afternoon, Miss Davies. Might I have a word?"

She appeared positively panic-stricken. Her eyes went wide even as her face paled perceptibly. Her lips parted on a soft exclamation of either surprise or dismay. He was too distracted by the sight of those parted lips to be able to decipher the reason for them.

And then, the spell was simply broken. A loud crash sounded from somewhere in the house, and he turned back to the door, torn between the need to stay just where he was and to go investigate. Another opportunity to speak with her privately might not come his way. That was the linchpin in his decision. Whirling on his heel, he turned back, only to discover that the morning room was now empty. The half-written letter lay abandoned on the desk, while the only other entrance to the room, via the terrace, revealed the sight of Miss Davies darting across the lawn to where the other guests were gathered.

"She ran," he muttered. "She bloody ran from me. Am I an ogre? Does she despise me so much? If so, why draw what she drew?"

Befuddled by the vagaries of the feminine sex and by one member of that group specifically, he was still shaking his head as he exited the morning room. There he found himself face to face with Theo. Isabella was not with him.

"Where is Miss Parker?"

"Oh, now you're interested in her," Theo replied dramatically.

"No, I am not. But your agreement to dance attendance upon her begs the question of how you aim to do so without being at her side!"

Theo laughed. "My, dear cousin, you have no notion how the feminine mind works. If Miss Isabella Parker is to value my courtship of her—and I am courting her outright, to be clear—she must not feel it is an absolute certainty. It is to my benefit for her to wonder just how much of my affection she holds."

Antony was utterly exhausted by all of it. "Why would Miss Davies run away?"

"You're a duke. She's, quite frankly, no one of any particular import. Why wouldn't she run from you?"

"I'm not evil. I'm not some licentious animal on the hunt for her," Antony protested. "I'm a perfectly honorable man with perfectly honorable intentions!"

"To propose?"

"To court her with a proposal potentially forthcoming," Antony responded. "But how can I court her if she flees the room upon my entrance?"

"Maybe you're attempting to court the wrong member of the family. If you express to the girl's aunt, Lady Stanhope, that you wish to spend time with her—no, she'd never permit it. Not when she's trying to marry off her own whey-faced daughter."

Antony drew back at that. "Cousin, you are very unkind. Miss Stanhope is not unattractive."

"Not unattractive does not mean she is beautiful," Theo answered pragmatically. "But she does have a marriage-minded mama. If you've no qualms about disappointing Miss Stanhope, then you must seek to be close to her to ensure that you have the option of being close to Miss Davies!"

Or he could enlist the aid of Miss Stanhope. Secretly, of course. "Good day, cousin."

Turning on his heel, Antony returned to the morning room and picked up the discarded letter that Miss Davies had been writing.

My dearest Effie,

I have been unbearably bold and have courted scandal quite reck-

lessly. If only it weren't for that infernal drawing—

The missive stopped abruptly, likely because of his interruption. Shuffling the paper aside, he withdrew a clean sheet of foolscap and began scribbling his own letter. This time, he wrote to Miss Ruby Stanhope and begged her aid in secretly courting her cousin and companion.

CAROLINE RAN BLINDLY—UNTIL her lungs were on fire and her slippered feet ached from continuously slapping against the ground with each stride. When she stopped, she was deep in the garden maze and far away from any place she recognized. How far had she gone from the house and the other gathered guests? And how in heaven's name would she find her way back? She detested mazes. They left her feeling panicked and unreasonably fearful. If there was any testament to just how much the duke unnerved her, that she'd run headlong into the center of one was proof enough.

"Miss Davies? Miss Davies, are you well?"

It was all Caroline could do to bite back the groan that welled up within her. Sir Percival. Of all the people at this infernal house party to see her mad dash from the duke's side, it had to be Sir Percival. Unfortunately, there was no place to hide, and she could hear his footsteps on the gravel path as he came closer.

"I am well, Sir Percival. Just seeking some time alone for quiet reflection," she called out, praying he would take the hint. Of course, he hadn't taken any other hint that he'd been given, or even outright refusals, for that matter. The likelihood that he would suddenly develop a clue was slim to none.

No sooner had the thought occurred than he appeared, creeping around a corner of the maze. "Ah, there you are! I say, Miss Davies, you are quite the runner. You bolted like a shot!"

"And typically, Sir Percival, when a lady bolts from company, more company is the last thing she wants," Caroline pointed out.

"Ah, but I am not company. We are friends, are we not?" he said with a cheerfulness that certainly did not match the tone she was attempting to set.

"We are acquaintances at best, sir. And it is really quite improper for us to be here alone. I think perhaps I should return to the house." She was far less concerned about being ruined than being bored to death.

"It would be just as improper to leave you unescorted, Miss Davies! What sort of gentleman would I be to leave you alone in the elements?"

"It's a garden, sir. And despite its circuitous nature, I daresay I can navigate it well enough to return safely. You need not exert yourself so on my behalf."

He kept walking forward until he was just an arm's length from her. "My dear Miss Davies—Caroline, if I may?"

"No, you may not," she said.

"Caroline," he continued, as if she had not spoken at all. "It is most fortuitous that I have found you here. I have been hoping for a chance to speak with you privately from the very first moment I saw you here. Every time we have encountered one another throughout the season, I have been struck by your beauty. Regardless of the circumstances of your birth and your lack of fortune, I am quite enamored with you."

"I am flattered, Sir Percival, but I—"

"I have been wanting to present an offer to you . . . a proposition, if you will."

Caroline's eyebrows lifted in shock even as her jaw tightened with anger. There was a wealth of difference between a proposition and a proposal. "I can assure you, Sir Percival, that my answer will be unequivocally no. You need not embarrass either of us further by continuing."

He smiled at her in such a way that it could not have been more patronizing had he patted her on her head. Of course, he'd have needed to stand on a chair to reach the top of her head. "Miss Davies, you must understand that I will be very generous with you. You need not be a poor relation in your aunt's house. I would provide you with a home, servants of your own, a sizable allowance. It is a very generous offer."

"To be your mistress," she said. "Tell me, Sir Percival, what price should I ask for my self-respect? You lack the fortune, sir. Not for every sovereign in all of England."

"Now, Caroline, you understand how the world works. You are not the sort a man marries . . . but you are the sort of woman a man desires. And I do desire you. Greatly."

"Then I would advise you, sir, to grow accustomed to disappointment." With that, Caroline swept past him. Perhaps anger had heightened her instincts, or there was some sort of divine guidance leading her. Regardless, she found her way unerringly out of the maze and back into the garden. And once more, squarely face to face with the duke.

"Miss Davies, is aught amiss?" he asked.

Anger chased away her nerves and granted her the ability to speak, though she'd never admit to the humiliation she'd just endured at the hands of a wretch like Sir Percival. "No, Your Grace. Nothing. Merely a pesky insect that had to be squashed. Pardon me, sir."

CHAPTER FIVE

THE BALL WAS in full swing. Couples twirled and swayed about the dance floor. It wasn't simply those in attendance for the grand house party. Others had come from neighboring estates and even from London to attend. The number of eligible gentlemen abounded, surely a relief for all the young marriage-minded ladies in attendance. For herself, all Caroline wanted was to disappear. The way she'd run from the duke that afternoon—the humiliation of it was not something she would ever recover from. He must have thought her some sort of lunatic. That it had been immediately followed by Sir Percival's dishonorable proposition only added insult to injury.

"Smile, Caroline! Good heavens, you look more like you're attending a funeral than a ball," her aunt scolded. "Whatever is the matter with you?"

"Just a slight headache, Aunt. Perhaps I should retire for the evening."

Her aunt recoiled in horror. "Absolutely not. Ruby will need you here. And I need your eyes on Ruby because I cannot imagine what sort of trouble she'd get into without the both of us watching her. Naturally, the duchess has invited a high caliber of people, but men will be men—even gentlemen."

Of that, Caroline was completely certain. Across the ballroom, she caught sight of a shock of jet-black hair, nearly a head above everyone else. The duke. "Of course, Aunt. You are quite right. But I will go to the ladies' withdrawing room for a few moments. Perhaps a bit of quiet will help."

"Take Ruby with you. Ten minutes, Caroline, and no more.

Ruby will hardly find a husband if she's closeted in a room where men are not even permitted," she snapped.

Caroline held her tongue, and the sharp retort that had immediately sprung to her lips was contained, but only barely. It left a bitter taste. The whole exchange was a familiar one. Every party, rout, ball, or assembly—they were all opportunities for Ruby to find a suitable husband. And not for the first time, Caroline wondered what her own fate would be should Ruby do just that. When her aunt had no need of her to serve as companion to her daughter, and if Ruby's as-yet unknown husband had no desire to have his wife's poor relations in the home, what would become of her?

Arm in arm, she and Ruby left the ballroom and headed to the ladies' withdrawing room. There were greater things to worry about than a naughty drawing or even Sir Percival's ham-fisted efforts to lure her to be his mistress. Her entire future was hanging in the balance. It had been for some time. She could simply no longer ignore it.

ANTONY SCANNED THE ballroom once more, and finally, his gaze landed on his quarry. For once, it was not Miss Davies. No. It was Sir Percival. Antony had been following Miss Davies back to the house after encountering her near the maze when he'd glanced behind him to see Sir Percival exiting it—and looking quite perturbed.

His moment of indecision had rendered his quandary moot. The desire to continue in pursuit of Miss Davies and the desire to question Sir Percival had left him torn. In the end, he'd elected to follow Sir Percival, as he suspected the man to be the pest Miss Davies had spoken of. By the time he'd caught him to him, he'd been back in the company of the other guests on the south lawn, enjoying archery and other activities. Discussing Miss Davies with him in that setting would have been a disaster. Bandying her name about where it might be easily overheard would have drawn the wrong sort of attention to her.

So now, he found himself once more following behind Sir Perci-

CHASITY BOWLIN

val to question him about what had transpired. That the man was so terribly short should have made it easier to catch up to him. But what he lacked in height was well compensated in pace. He was near the terrace doors before he finally caught up to him.

"Sir Percival, might I have a word with you in private? It's a rather sensitive matter," Antony explained.

The other man paled instantly. "Certainly, Your Grace."

Antony gestured toward the terrace. "Outside, if you please." He then stepped through the door, and Sir Percival followed. He didn't stop until they reached the far corner of the terrace, a spot where no one could lurk about to eavesdrop.

"Your Grace, what is it I can do for you?" the man asked.

"What transpired in the maze today with you and Miss Davies?"

Sir Percival's lips opened and closed rather like a landed fish as he sputtered. "I . . . well, it was not what . . . what did Miss Davies tell you?"

Antony recognized guilt when he saw it. "Miss Davies has said nothing about you. She did indicate that whatever had happened in the maze had been an irritation or annoyance. A nuisance, if you will. Did you make a nuisance of yourself, Sir Percival?"

The smaller man sighed heavily. Then he withdrew a cheroot from a silver case concealed inside his coat. "Would you care for one?"

"No, thank you. I only want an answer," Antony insisted.

"I did, Your Grace. I meant no harm to the lady. I offered her a . . . situation. A generous one. And she declined. I might have been too persistent in my offer upon her initial refusal."

"You asked her to be your mistress? A young, respectable, un-married, and quite innocent young woman who is currently a guest under my roof—and you felt that was a prime opportunity to make your indecent proposal?"

"You need not take me to task, Your Grace. Miss Davies has put me quite firmly in my place for it. How did you know? You said Miss Davies had not told you!"

"I was attempting to have a private word with Miss Davies my-self."

Sir Percival's eyes widened. "Oh. So you mean to proposition her yourself, then. I was poaching!"

"No, Sir Percival. I mean to propose. Not proposition. They are very different things, I assure you. One is the highest honor, while the other is only a degradation!"

"Propose? Your Grace, she's penniless!"

"I have no need of anyone else's wealth, I assure you." Antony was truly beginning to detest the little man. "Do not importune her again, Sir Percival, or you will face my wrath. Now, I must go and find her in order to demonstrate to her that not all men are of your . . . ilk."

CHAPTER SIX

I T WASN'T ENOUGH to be just a wallflower. Caroline was striving for actual invisibility, to the point of hiding behind potted palms and ducking behind columns. She was desperate to avoid further encounters with Sir Percival, and given the danger inherent in having further dealings with the duke, it was to her benefit to stay hidden.

Unfortunately, her aunt was not being at all cooperative. She kept dragging Ruby forward to present her to one eligible, if the term was used loosely, gentleman after another. Each time, Caroline would be hauled over to play chaperone to Ruby and the prospective suitors. One could not be an invisible chaperone, as that negated the very purpose of the position.

"What is wrong with you?" her aunt hissed.

"I'm trying to avoid Sir Percival," she answered with the half-truth.

"You could do worse. He's got a tidy fortune and a knighthood! What possible objection could you have to him proposing?"

"He didn't propose. And he will not propose," Caroline answered. "He has . . . other ideas where I am concerned. Improper ones that I want no part of."

Her aunt's eyes narrowed into midnight colored slits. "Did he . . . make you some sort of offer?"

"He did."

"And you turned him down?"

Caroline nodded. "Of course I did!"

"Caroline, I would never encourage you to sacrifice your honor, but you must realize that there are very few gentlemen who would be willing to overlook the sort of . . . flaws that are attached to your name. Bad enough to be penniless with no marriage portion, but to be illegitimate, as well? Perhaps you should consider his offer. Naturally, if you accepted we would have to part company entirely, but I would never begrudge you an opportunity to secure your future."

Caroline felt the blood rush to her face. "That is a degradation I will not suffer. I will return to the Darrow School and work as a governess or paid companion before I would—well, I am not that sort."

"Your mother made that choice and, until she and my brother were taken ill with fever, was quite content with her lot. I would never force you to do such a thing, but do not dismiss it out of hand. Pride and honor will not fill your belly or put a roof over your head."

Her aunt walked away, and Caroline felt as if her entire world had just been upended. The question of whether or not she'd still have a home if Ruby married first had just been unequivocally answered. Her aunt would toss her into the street at the first moment she could. The purpose of bringing her into their home had only been to provide companionship for Ruby and to help Ruby overcome some of her shyness in social settings. There had never been any feeling for her. Not in the least.

Dashing away a tear that she could not contain, Caroline quickly made her way out of the ballroom. She didn't care where she went so long as it was quiet and dark and no one would remind her of all the many reasons she would never be quite good enough.

When she was far enough away from the ballroom and any prying eyes, she let her tears fall. Not many of them. Only a few trailed unchecked down her cheeks as she leaned back against the wall and tried to fathom how she could ever have been so blind about her aunt's motives.

"Is everything alright?"

Caroline's head came up, and she found herself looking directly into the lovely face of Miss Isabella Parker. She might not have been the most beautiful woman in the world, but she was certainly the most beautiful woman at Averford Hall.

"Fine. Just a bit of a megrim," Caroline lied, forcing a smile. "The heat of the ballroom has worsened it."

"There's a maid in the ladies' withdrawing room who will fetch you a draught for the pain. I'll go and get her," Miss Parker offered.

"No. That's quite all right. I am on my way there now. Thank you. You've been most kind."

Miss Parker's angelic countenance was etched with concern. "You're certain? I hate to leave you alone when you are ill."

"I'll be quite all right, I assure you. No doubt Miss Stanhope will come in search of me soon enough."

Miss Parker smiled warmly. "The two of you are quite thick as thieves. I envy that. I do not have close friends in that way. Women do not seem to care for my company, and men . . . well, if they are in my company, there is always some underlying purpose, isn't there?"

Caroline didn't want to feel sympathy for the young woman before her. From a distance, everything about her life seemed as though it was quite perfect. And yet, she was now forced to admit the grass truly was always greener on the other side. "You are not without friends, Miss Parker. Your kindness will not be forgotten. Thank you again."

Miss Parker nodded. "Good evening, Miss Davies. I do hope it improves for you."

After the other young woman had walked away and Caroline was once more alone, she moved toward an alcove that would afford some concealment. There, she slid down the wall, lowering herself until she was resting on the floor. In the distance, a clock struck the midnight hour. It was her birthday. And her entire world was falling apart.

ANTONY HAD LOST sight of Miss Davies. Indeed, she'd vanished from the ballroom, and he had no notion of her direction. So he followed up on the missive he'd sent earlier.

"Miss Stanhope, may I have this dance?"

Ruby Stanhope's eyes widened in shock, but that shock was

quickly replaced with the brightness of conspiratorial glee. "Indeed, Your Grace, I am most gratified by the invitation."

Antony offered her his arm and led her to the dance floor. It was a country dance which would allow for a significant amount of time to converse, thankfully. Taking their position on the dance floor, he waited until the first chord was struck before speaking. "Where has Miss Davies escaped to?"

Miss Stanhope shook her head slightly. "I cannot say for certain. I know that she had words with Mother earlier. Mother is . . . well, she has no intention of continuing to provide for Caroline if I wed."

Antony digested that bit of information. "I see. And is that why you are discouraging suitors, Miss Stanhope?"

"Well, there haven't been any suitors I cared to encourage, Your Grace. I would only ever consent to courtship or marriage to a man who would be willing to provide support to Caroline, as well."

"Or perhaps, you could focus your efforts on aiding Miss Davies in making an acceptable match first. Tell me, did you receive my letter?" he asked.

"Only just before the ball. I read it but hadn't had a chance to respond—do you mean to ask for Caroline's hand?" she asked.

He gave a jerky nod. "Indeed. That is my intent, but first I must locate her."

"She will have gone as far from the ballroom as possible. Some-place quiet. Mother upset her terribly," Miss Stanhope stated. "You should find her at once."

"As soon as our dance—"

Abruptly, and without warning, Miss Stanhope swooned. Antony caught her before she collapsed to the floor. But what shocked him more than her swoon was the fact that as she lay there limp in his arms while the crowd gathered about them, she gave him a wink.

"Clever," he whispered, just before he was shooed out of the way by several concerned matrons, each one offering up some vinaigrette or other to rouse the young woman. And in that crowd, Antony simply sank back, further and further, until he could escape the ballroom. Then his search began in earnest. One room after another, he made his way through the lower floors of the house.

He was nearly ready to go upstairs, thinking perhaps she'd re-treated to her chamber, when a flash of white in an otherwise darkened alcove under the stairs caught his eye. It was a bit of fabric—the train of her ballgown, he realized. He'd found his quarry.

"It makes me sound like an ogre to say so, but I am quite glad to find you, Miss Davies, when you have nowhere to run."

CHAPTER SEVEN

T HAT VOICE WAS painfully familiar. Caroline looked up to see the duke looming over her, handsome and dashing as ever. And so painfully beyond her reach that she wanted nothing more than to give in to her tears. But then the strangest thing happened. He stepped into the alcove with her and settled himself on the floor against the opposite wall, apparently quite content to simply remain in her company.

"You're a very talented artist, Miss Davies. But I fear you have not had the time to devote to your craft that you should have. Having seen your work, I must say your skills are impressive."

He'd seen her work. The blasted sketch that had caused her such stress had been in his possession all along. For a while, that particular worry had been pushed from her mind by the ugly exchange with her aunt. That the woman would push her to accept a dishonorable offer had stung. She certainly hadn't assumed that her aunt had any fondness for her, but had some degree of family loyalty really been too much to hope for?

"If your desire was to humiliate me, then you have succeeded, Your Grace. There is no need for you to continue suffering my company," she replied softly.

"I do not suffer your company, Miss Davies. I seek it. I sought it this afternoon . . . and you ran from me. Am I really so frightening?"

Yes. Yes, he was. The idea that she might humiliate herself in front of him when her regard for him was so very high was intolerable. "Why do you seek my company?"

"Because you are lovely. Because you are not silly and obsessed with society and dresses and all the nonsense that the *ton* seems to focus on. Because when you look at me, Miss Davies, I cannot tell if you love me or hate me. But I know that you are not indifferent to me, regardless of how you may try to appear so. Most importantly, Miss Davies, I think your reactions and your feelings toward me are for me and me alone . . . independent of my title."

"I cannot withstand the disgrace of another improper offer in the span of a day, Your Grace. I beg you not to," she whispered.

"And if I mean to make you a proper offer, Miss Davies?"

Caroline's head came up and she stared at him in shock. "A proper offer?"

"Yes. I'd like very much, Miss Caroline Davies, to ask you to be my duchess."

ANTONY WATCHED HER closely. Even in the dimly lit alcove, her expression of incredulity was impossible to mistake. It pained him to think that her life had been such that a man offering for her seemed so shocking. "Do not leave me in suspense, Miss Davies. Will you marry me?"

"Why?"

Antony considered his answer carefully. "I can offer you security. You will never again be treated as a poor relation, relegated to the position of little better than a servant. You will never again have to tolerate the absurd arrogance of Sir Percival."

"You mistake me, Your Grace. I wasn't asking why I should marry you, but rather why you would ever wish to marry me."

He laughed softly, his lips remaining curved in a smile as he answered her. "For the only reason a man ever ought to ask a woman to marry him—because I love you, Miss Caroline Davies. And if you'll have me, I will spend a lifetime proving that to you."

"It's my birthday," she said. "And I have nothing left to wish for because you have just given me everything I have ever wanted."

He leaned forward, pushing himself up with the palms of his hands flat against the floor until his face was only inches from hers. Then he hesitated for just a second, long enough for her to protest if she wished to. But that was the very last thing Caroline wanted. So she pressed her own hands against the floor and pushed herself forward until their lips brushed—softly at first, and then the contact became more insistent. It was infused with so many things: longing, desire, tenderness and also hope ... hope for a long and happy future together.

EPILOGUE

One Month Later

CAROLINE LAY IN bed staring up at the ceiling. It wasn't insomnia keeping her awake. It was gratitude. She had so many things in her life to be thankful for, things she had never imagined would be hers. A husband who adored her, a home of her own, a title—for heaven's sake. Who would have ever thought such a thing was possible!

"Have I not exhausted you sufficiently, wife?" Antony murmured sleepily against her shoulder.

Caroline grinned. "I am quite wide awake. Happiness does that to me."

His eyes opened, and he fixed his gaze on hers. "And are you happy, Caroline?"

She scooted down in the bed so that she was lying fully in the circle of his arms and they were nose to nose. "I never dreamed such happiness was possible. There is only one thing that might make it better."

"Name it and you will have it. I still owe you a birthday present," he said.

"I want my sketch back . . . so that I can complete it."

He laughed. "The sketch is mine forever. My most treasured possession, as it was the first inkling I had that you held me in any regard at all. But I will pose for a new sketch. Naked as a newly born babe, if that's your wish."

"In art, it's called nudity. Not nakedness. Nakedness implies hedonism."

He turned them over then so that he was on his back and she

was straddling the firm muscles of his thighs. "Then by all means, let us indulge our hedonistic impulses."

Caroline leaned forward and kissed him. "You are my birthday present," she whispered against his lips. "What more could I ever want than to be your wife?"

"To be the mother of my children?" His suggestion was accompanied by the sweep of his hand over the curve of her hip until he could reach the hem of her nightrail and tug it upward.

And for the remainder of that night, their wedding night, they indulged in the hedonistic delights that might well bring that wish to fruition.

The End

Additional Dragonblade books by Author Chasity Bowlin

The Hellion Club Series
A Rogue to Remember (Book 1)
Barefoot in Hyde Park (Book 2)
What Happens in Piccadilly (Book 3)
Sleepless in Southampton (Book 4)
When an Earl Loves a Governess (Book 5)
The Duke's Magnificent Obsession (Book 6)
The Governess Diaries (Book 7)
A Dangerous Passion (Book 8)
Making Spirits Bright (Novella)
All I Want for Christmas (Novella)
The Boys of Summer (Novella)
When The Night Closes In (Novella)

The Lost Lords Series
The Lost Lord of Castle Black (Book 1)
The Vanishing of Lord Vale (Book 2)
The Missing Marquess of Althorn (Book 3)
The Resurrection of Lady Ramsleigh (Book 4)
The Mystery of Miss Mason (Book 5)
The Awakening of Lord Ambrose (Book 6)
Hyacinth (Book 7)
A Midnight Clear (Novella)

The Lyon's Den Series
Fall of the Lyon
Tamed by the Lyon
Lady Luck and the Lyon
The Lyon, the Liar and the Scandalous Wardrobe

Pirates of Britannia Series
The Pirate's Bluestocking

Also from Chasity Bowlin
Into the Night (Novella)

About Chasity Bowlin

Chasity Bowlin lives in central Kentucky with her husband and their menagerie of animals. She loves writing, loves traveling and enjoys incorporating tidbits of her actual vacations into her books. She is an avid Anglophile, loving all things British, but specifically all things Regency.

Growing up in Tennessee, spending as much time as possible with her doting grandparents, soap operas were a part of her daily existence, followed by back to back episodes of Scooby Doo. Her path to becoming a romance novelist was set when, rather than simply have her Barbie dolls cruise around in a pink convertible, they time traveled, hosted lavish dinner parties and one even had an evil twin locked in the attic.

Website: www.chasitybowlin.com

LOVE IS THE DUKE'S BEST REMEDY

by Sara Adrien

CHAPTER ONE

Cockspur Street, London, 1819

DESPITE THE HIGH cost of land, London surpassed Edmund's hometown in Northumberland with its abundance of squares and spacious streets. The view had remained unchanged for his entire two-and-twenty years of life, just as busy, just as noisy, and just as hot. Cockspur Street, like the Haymarket it led to, was so broad at least four carriages could—and did—traverse it simultaneously. Hence, the noise.

Edmund Brandon, the Duke of Northumberland and proprietor of the stately house at the corner of the bustling avenue flinched at the bright sunlight when he pulled shut the carved walnut door of his four-story townhouse. How could people walk with such energetic sprints while he had no energy? He cast his gaze upon the majestic façade of his residence and sniffed at the Grecian embellishments that adorned it. The architecture had an air of grandeur that was hard to ignore and impossible to live up to.

The sun cast a spotlight on him and the grandest estate on this side of Pall Mall. He was on stage, all eyes on him. He'd had nowhere to hide since his parents had died in a carriage accident just after he graduated from Oxford.

Speaking of evil eyes, his solicitor approached for his daily visit—Warren Brewster, short and stout, like a far too cheerful teapot with a balding spot where hair made room for the knob on the lid.

"Good morning, Brewster." Edmund pulled on his hat and turned right toward Hopkins Street.

"Where're you off to on this beautiful, sunny day?" Brewster asked.

"Apothecary."

"You didn't sleep?" Brewster balked as if it were abhorrent not to sleep well and wake refreshed, ready to enjoy the scorching morning rays. He stopped like a dog pulled by a leash in a direction he wasn't willing to go. "Piccadilly is this way. As is Regent Street."

"I know." Edmund strode in the opposite direction, hoping he'd give up and leave him alone.

Brewster struggled to keep up. "Why can't you take a stroll along the boulevards that give you—" he drew a circle in the air as if he'd just conceived of the backdrop for a Shakespeare play— "exposure."

"Exposure." Edmund rubbed his eyes. Parvenus, like Brewster, had attached to his heel like barnacles on a schooner.

"This way, Your Grace." Brewster grabbed his elbow and tugged at him. "We must parade you to the matrons shopping for suitable homes for their daughters' large dowries. Go on."

Enough! He wasn't just a home for a dowry, nor would he be paraded along Pall Mall as part of a buffet for debutantes. Edmund tore his arm from Brewster's grasp.

"You'll be at the opera alone!" Brewster shouted. "All eyes on you in a box for a duke without as much as a mistress!"

"Once and for all, Brewster, I don't care if all eyes are on me. They've always been. I have plenty to show for my title. I am the duke, not you."

"B-but I've always been there."

"Like a leech. I never asked for your advice. You follow me around in the House of Lords, picking up what I don't need."

Brewster opened his mouth and closed it like a fish gasping for water.

"I will not be trapped into a marriage of convenience or for diplomatic connections, to give you better business prospects."

"W-why else would you marry?" Brewster asked as if Edmund were making no sense.

Edmund folded his arm indignantly. "Love. Family."

"That's what mistresses can give. You can't think of only yourself when you choose a bride."

"Who says I want to choose? Perhaps Fate will send her to me. I won't parade myself like a show dog. Love doesn't go where ambition blocks the path to the heart."

"Nobody will grant your request for that futuristic environmental restoration plan if they hear you speak like that in Parliament. You'll have no credibility."

"And how do you intend to improve my credibility, Brewster? Hm?"

"By drafting a proper plan for your presentation to the Lord Chancellor Marlowe."

"Nonsense! He'll hear me out."

"He won't listen if you don't show him that you have your personal affairs in order."

"Says who?" Edmund grimaced at the absurdity of it all. Brewster exerted more pressure on him than even his mother would if she were in Town for the season.

"Says Marlowe! 'If a man can't control his home, he won't be able to manage his estate.'"

"He said that?"

"Yes."

"To you?"

"At the races."

"How grand for Marlowe to question my personal life while he's gambling his fortune on a horse."

Brewster shrugged. "He has sway in the House. He makes the rules."

"The laws are the rules, and he does not make them."

"He can prevent them from passing, just like the permits for your restoration plan." Brewster curled his lower lip, exposing his lower incisors, which were just as dull as his worldviews.

Edmund exhaled deeply. The sun was burning, and his black top hat was like a magnet for the heat.

"Look, if you showed off a pretty woman on opening night, he'd see you're at least courting someone respectable. It might be enough."

"I'm not going to the opera tonight, and I'm not bringing a woman."

CHAPTER TWO

L OLA RIFLED THROUGH the stack of recently delivered letters but found not a single one from her brother. His words were her lifeline, her solace. But now, two interminable months had crawled by, each void of his familiar script. And with each passing day, the weight of that silence became heavier. She brushed some hairs out of her face, tugged at her white apron—an unfashionable but effective way to hide the holes she'd mended in the only dress she had left—and stepped outside.

Lola had been working as hard as she could to save money to buy back their parents' old cottage. It was just her and her brother these days, so she wasn't merely lonely—she felt deserted. This was not what they'd planned when he'd purchased a commission to enlist. Neither had they planned to run out of funds. Or for him to be injured. Or for him to be gone past Lola's twentieth birthday—but he had, and she was alone.

Luckily, the landlady, Mrs. Kitty, only cared about Lola's rent for the room in the attic and not for her use of the flat roof in the back of the house facing the Wimpole Mews where Lola had planted her medicinal herbs and flowering teas. She understood plants. Even Green Park and Pall Mall were full of lush elder berries for cough syrups, red clover for rashes, St. John's Wort for a general remedy for unease, and wild chamomile. One just had to know where to search—preferably before sunrise. Summer was the best time to harvest because the plants were more potent, and Lola could carry them to the apothecary before the sun's heat wilted them.

If not for the generous apothecary, Mister Alfie Collins, Lola wouldn't have a livelihood, the cot in Mrs. Kitty's attic, or an address where her brother could send letters. She sighed, switched her basket to the other side, rested it on her hip, and entered the foyer at 87 Harley Street, a building occupied by the apothecary and his doctor friends. Lovely people. Good customers.

>>><<<

EDMUND BURST INTO the apothecary. "I need something stronger."

Collins looked up from grinding a beige-yellow powder with his mortar and pestle. He'd already set up the parchment to transfer the mixture and the vial to preserve it.

"Good morning, Your Grace." The wall behind him was lined with many tiny drawers, a grid of at least ten by ten. He could reach for any of them and pick the right herb or powder to create his concoctions, but Edmund's case was challenging even to him, the most talented apothecary in the British Empire.

Edmund took his top hat off and rubbed his head. Lack of sleep had tensed his scalp.

"What can I do for you, Your Grace?" Collins scooped the powder he'd ground onto a square piece of paper and set it on his delicate brass scale. He made a note, then curled the paper, forming a funnel, and the powder drizzled into the glass vial sitting on the counter next to the scale like sand falling in a glass timer.

"The tea didn't help." Edmund sighed. "I tried the lavender oil on the pulse points, the valerian root in the tea, the chamomile baths. Give me something stronger, please. Anything!"

The apothecary squared his shoulders and eyed Edmund with an intelligent gaze. He paid attention to the man behind the name, something most people didn't. At the House of Lords, he was just his title; at the club, he was his father's heir; and at Almack's, he was an appetizing piece of man meat. Only Collins saw Edmund for the exhausted person he truly was.

"Your eyes are bloodshot. Have you been up reading?" Collins asked.

"Of sorts, yes. Balancing the accounts."

"And did you have a light meal before bedtime, as I recommended?"

Edmund nodded. "Dinner is at one o'clock now. I just had an apple and walnuts at eight."

"What about walking?"

"I walk everywhere. Came here from Cockspur Street on foot."

"You walked to Harley Street? It's a mile and a half at almost eighty-six degrees!"

"I know how hot it is, Collins." Edmund placed his hat on the counter and unbuttoned his coat.

"You don't need my medicines, Your Grace. There's nothing physically wrong with you."

"There is! I told you my symptoms. I don't sleep. I can't breathe. And I feel hollow." He tugged at his cravat and piled it on the counter, relieved to be just in his linen shirt. The apothecary was like a doctor, so Edmund thought it all right to relieve himself of a few layers.

Collins produced a brass funnel from a drawer and stepped around the counter to listen to his chest. Just as Edmund unbuttoned his shirt and pulled the fabric aside, the door sprang open.

A waft of summer blossoms reached Edmund's nose before he lifted his gaze to the beauty holding a curved wicker basket loaded with an array of blooms. Fiery red and gold petals, layered like a thousand sunsets, nestled against star-shaped buds of delicate lilac with tiny sun-kissed centers. Feather-like leaves cradled clusters of stark white flowers, their sharp, green scent crisp like a newly mown meadow.

Edmund reached for the bunch of sunny yellow marigolds, which splashed cheer into the bouquet like a hearty child's laugh. Lacy umbels of tiny snowflakes lent a touch of elegance, their earthy sweetness mingling with headier fragrances. Astonished that he could breathe deeply, he caught the musky, balsamic scent while frothy clusters of tiny yellow flowers enveloped him in a sweet, hay-like aroma. Closing his eyes, Edmund inhaled again, the basket's contents a testament to nature's bounty, an intoxicating essence of summer captured within each bloom.

At a clang of metal on wood, he opened his eyes, to see Collins had set aside the stethoscope and hoisted the basket of blooms onto his counter.

"Thank you so much, Miss Viola." Collins separated the different bouquets and with a knife he produced from a drawer, slit the coarse hay she'd used to tie them together.

"It was a pleasure, as always. Two shillings, please."

Edmund reverted to his tedious task in accounting. "Two shillings for flowers?"

"These are the finest medicinal plants in bloom this side of the equator, mister." Her gaze took him in, from the top of his hair to his boots. Edmund could have sworn she lingered on his exposed chest as if her gaze could see the truth in his heart.

"Edmund Brandon, the Duke of Northumberland." He reached for her hand, but she hesitated. How absolutely adorable. Women usually accepted his hand and expected his kiss on their knuckles in return, yet she wasn't prepared to accept it at all.

Intriguing.

EDMUND BRANDON, THE *Duke of Northumberland.*

Lola sucked in her upper lip and stared at the fine specimen of manhood before her. She'd seen her share of well-built men working in the fields, carrying logs, swinging axes in the sun, but never had she seen such harmony of a sculpted chest and chiseled stomach. His breeches rode low on his hips, and she saw the ridges above his hip bones.

Her eyes trailed back up, past his navel to his pectorals. His Adam's apple gave a slight bob when he swallowed, and he licked his lips. She blinked her stupor away aware; she probably seemed like a dimwit, batting her lashes for the duke.

He reached for her hand.

Heat rose to her cheeks as she laid her palm on his index finger. He secured her fingers with his thumb and lifted them to his mouth. His lips touched her skin, unleashing a jolt of tingles in her stomach like a spray of magnolia blossoms blowing in the wind.

When he released her hand, a heartbeat later than she'd expected, his deep gray-green eyes met hers and his forehead furrowed. His shock of deliciously disheveled dark chestnut waves bristled as if he'd been a stallion sprinting through the forest up north. How could such a young man have such wise eyes, and be so unkempt, yet ooze refinement?

Lola's thoughts scattered. She could not think of anything to say, especially to a duke. Especially to this duke. She'd never met one, but she had a feeling that he—with his bared chest and deep dark eyes—was different than most.

The apothecary handed her the money. "Thank you. See you on Wednesday."

Oh yes, the flowers. Every bit of coin would help her brother recover once he'd returned. Lola turned to the door toward the foyer.

"As I said, Your Grace. It's not the valerian, lavender, or chamomile that will aid your insomnia. You have to find out what's keeping you awake."

"Collins, just give me something to put me to sleep, a sedative." She paused to listen, even though she knew it was rude to eavesdrop. She couldn't help herself. The duke's balmy voice had a hint of arrogance and a pinch of determination that warmed Lola's insides. He knew what he wanted and gave clear orders. Not many aristocrats had a reputation for steadfastness. So she stood just inside the door and pretended to fiddle with something in the basket.

"You're restless, but it's not medicine you need."

The duke took his black top hat from the counter and put it on, then hooked his fingers into the collar of his coat and swung it over his shoulder. With his other hand, he reached into his pocket, and Lola noticed how the fabric stretched over the length of his crotch.

She blinked.

She shouldn't stare.

Having a brother approximately the duke's age, she knew exactly what she was looking at.

Another peek?

"I have to be at the House of Lords in twenty minutes," the duke said.

"That's more than an hour's walk, Your Grace," the apothecary protested. "If you continue to put yourself in such stressful situations, your body will never come to rest."

"My body will rest when I'm dead. It's sleep I need. For now, I need to make it to Parliament on time. Good day!" The duke headed for the door, passing close by her elbow.

Lola cleared her throat. "Forgive me, Your Grace, for overhearing, but I could take you there in under a quarter of an hour." She couldn't believe she'd dared to offer a duke a ride in her brother's carriage.

He cocked his head. "On a broomstick?"

She followed him through the foyer and down the white steps. Outside, where the bright white Marylebone houses with their black wrought iron fences all looked the same, he towered in all his glory. He tilted his head to hold the coat with his chin as he buttoned his shirt and pushed it back into those stretched breeches. As he did so, the coat got loose and began to slide toward the ground. Lola caught it.

She laid it over her arm like the servant she was and offered it to him. "I don't have a broomstick, Your Grace."

"That's not what I meant. You're so pretty you'd likely float to a crystal palace in nothing but sparkles atop a cloud, but I need to leave now unless the dandy who owns this phaeton will let me borrow it."

So he'd seen it. Her brother's prized possession, a black lacquered phaeton with a lightly sprung body atop four large wheels. Mrs. Kitty's mare with her long white tail neighed an invitation for a ride.

The duke stood agog, eyes darting from the phaeton to her and back again.

Lola moved to place her basket on the seat, then climbed into the driver's seat and untied the reins. "Are you coming?"

CHAPTER THREE

E DMUND MADE IT to Parliament in under a quarter of an hour and asked Lola to wait. Flower girl turned coachman—or was there such a thing as a coachwoman? No matter, she needed the money and was ready to do any honest work. And he'd needed a ride. The idea occurred to her that he might have other places to go. Perhaps this was an opportunity for her.

When he returned, the duke heaved himself back into the carriage and checked his pocket watch. "It's only ten o'clock."

"Now what?" Lola asked, ready to drive him wherever he had in mind.

His eyes skimmed her skin as if he was touching her with his fingertips and it sent gooseflesh down her arms. "I don't have anywhere to be until seven o'clock tonight."

"What's at seven, Your Grace?" she asked before she could stop herself. She was being rude. Lola bit her lip.

"The opera."

In for a penny, in for a pound. She'd already been too bold, so what difference did it make if she offended him now? "How wonderful! With costumes and an orchestra? Oh, please tell me you have a box and opera glasses!"

He squinted. "I *do* have a box. *And* opera glasses."

Lola clapped in glee, forgetting the reins. The mare tossed her head and took off at a trot, heading toward a patch of green grass she could see just down the street.

The carriage swerved, and Lola lost her balance.

A firm but gentle hand gripped her waist. "I have you." Heat radiated from where the duke's fingers pressed against her through the layers of her gown, sending a shiver of awareness down her spine that seemed to whisper, *this man is danger and salvation.*

The duke took control of the reins and slowed the horse to a reluctant walk.

"Where are you taking me?" she asked.

"To Regent Street. You'll need a gown if you're attending the opera tonight."

Lola wasn't sure she heard him correctly. "I beg your pardon?"

"I'm sorry. I didn't mean to assume, but you seemed rather smitten with the prospect of the opera. It occurs to me that at least one of us should enjoy the performance."

Smitten with the opera? No. Perhaps with something else entirely. A girl like her had no prospects. But how did the saying go—one shan't look a gift horse in the mouth?

They arrived at a department store on the corner of Oxford Street. Lola read the sign over the doors:

Debenlope, Freeworth & McKentin

The duke hopped off the carriage with athletic ease, reached up, and helped Lola off.

"Pick any gown you like. I'll buy it for you in a few minutes."

"I mustn't let a stranger purchase a gown I'll only wear one night."

"Then buy another for the night after."

"Your Grace, I live in an attic. I use woolen coats and knitted stockings."

"Then buy those, too."

She stepped back and quirked a brow. "Why?"

"You did me a great favor by driving me to Parliament today. I nearly missed an important deadline. Consider it a thank you."

"Your words are thanks enough, Your Grace." Lola curtsied and turned, ready to climb back onto the phaeton. "Good day—"

"Wait!" The duke reached for her, but he only caught her lower arm. An unsettling jolt shot fire bolts through her veins, springing her heart into a hasty gallop.

Lola froze, her breath catching as she turned back to face him. The duke's eyes were ablaze, reflecting the heat of emotions she couldn't yet decipher.

"Please," he murmured, his grip gentle but insistent, "Don't go just yet."

For a moment, the world around them dissolved—no bustling streets, no distant chatter, only the charged space between them. Her resolve wavered, and despite every sensible thought urging her to retreat, she found herself anchored by his earnest gaze.

In that heartbeat, Lola realized that he'd brought a heat to her heart she would not easily put out.

>>><<<

EDMUND SENT A messenger to announce he would attend opening night. Too bad he couldn't see Brewster's face when he received the note.

When he arrived at the dressmaker's, ready to purchase some nice things for the girl he'd all but hired for the night, he floundered. The flower girl stood outside one of the most elegant stores in London, face buried in her hands, shoulders drooping. She sobbed uncontrollably.

"Miss Viola?" Edmund touched her shoulder, but she didn't turn to face him. "What happened?"

"Nothing. I'm just Lola." She heaved, and a sweet sniffling emerged from behind her hands, a slight sound with a girlish vulnerability that tugged at Edmund's heartstrings.

"Something must have occurred to make you cry. Pray tell."

"Nothing happened. That's the thing," she cried.

"Where's the dress?"

"They didn't let me in. The servant's door is around the corner, they said."

Edmund pinched the bridge of his nose with his thumb and index finger. "Those stupid idiots."

Lola blinked and licked a tear off her cupid's bow. "You're a duke. You curse?"

"Oh, this one can do much worse!"

She beamed at him, still blotchy from crying, lashes adorably fanned out and stuck together with tears.

Edmund brought both hands to her cheeks. "Listen to me. You are a rare beauty, and as with a rough gem, it takes a connoisseur to see the glimmer within."

She sniffled and pouted.

"Let's show them all you're a diamond of the first water, shall we?"

She nodded and took his arm. Her hand fit perfectly as if she'd belonged there all along and just didn't know it—until this moment.

CHAPTER FOUR

O H, THIS GIRL was adorable. Even sniffling and red-eyed, she had more fire and composure than any of the eligible debutantes Brewster was so fond of promoting.

Edmund knew what she needed. Not a gown with ruffles and a feather stole. She had class and beauty and needed something simple to frame her beauty.

And he knew just where to find it.

The simple gesture of offering his arm to her had been thrilling. Correction: It wasn't the gesture, it was her touch.

Within minutes, they reached the corner building facing Piccadilly.

35 Regent Street

Klonimus and Sons

Jewelers

A bell rang as he pushed the door open, and Raphi Klonimus, the second-eldest son in a family of Jewish jewelers, welcomed him with a bright, friendly smile.

"Edmund, what a pleasant surprise! Have you brought any difficult sheet music for us to work out?"

"Hello Raphi, it's good to see you. I haven't had time to play recently." Edmund unbuttoned his coat. "Can you believe the heat this month?"

"Don't you start with it, too. This is nothing compared to the summers in Italy."

Edmund smiled and inclined his head toward the young woman on his arm. "Raphi is an old friend one of the Crown Jewelers. He has a degree in mathematics and another from the conservatory in Milan, Miss Viola."

"My friends call me Lola." She curtsied, and Raphi gave a gentle smile.

"Welcome, Lola. What is the occasion for your visit today?"

Edmund intercepted Raphi's knowing stare. *No, not an engagement ring. Stop looking at me like that.* "The opening of the opera tonight."

"Don't tell me you have tickets for Rossini's new opera!" Raphi seemed awed.

"It's just *Cinderella*."

"J-just?" Raphi asked. "Since Rossini moved to Naples—" he turned to Lola for a moment to explain—"that's the operatic capital of Europe—as director of music for the royal theatres, he's had more success than any other contemporary composer."

"You've met Rossini?" Lola asked.

"Yes, in Milan. I saw *Cinderella* in *La Scala* when it first came out two years ago."

Lola's eyes grew wide.

"I know exactly what you need for tonight." With the elan of an excited musician, Raphi stepped behind the polished counter and produced a wooden box. He retrieved a key from his waist pocket and opened the box with a click. Then he handed it to Edmund. "I have another piece from this collection. Please take a look, and I shall be back in a moment." Raphi left through a door at the back of the store.

Edmund took the book-sized box and turned it toward Lola. She stepped forward and crossed her arms, hugging herself. Edmund opened it and she leaned in to see inside. On a pillow of white velvet lay a yellow-gold necklace. Richly facetted oval rubies reflected the light in a blaze of crimson. Yellow gold bezel settings encircled each one like a halo of tiny diamonds, sending a spectrum of rainbow sparkles back to the rubies.

Lola held her breath, and Edmund thought her expression fanned the full spectrum light could offer.

"Do you like it?" Raphi asked.

Edmund nodded. "Can I borrow it for the night?"

"Certainly."

MINUTES LATER, IN his carriage, Lola asked, "How is it possible that the Crown Jewelers let you borrow such an exquisite necklace?"

"I'm an old friend of Raphi's, but I don't get out much."

She had no doubt.

Especially when they arrived at his home, a veritable gilded cage.

His servants drew her bath, brought fresh pink roses to a chamber they designated as hers, and to her astonishment, a lady's maid arrived with a raspberry-colored dress, plainly cut, with a train that bustled in the back. Another maid—who was, apparently, a skilled seamstress—took it in some places and let it out in others so that by the time the clock struck six, Lola had transformed into a fairytale princess.

She knew she was one when the duke, Edmund arrived like her prince, just outside her room to escort her.

CHAPTER FIVE

EDMUND SLEPT FOR the first time in what felt like years. Not just dozed off, but slept. More energy raged through him than he ever remembered. So he was more than ready that morning after the opera to suffer another visit from Brewster.

He wondered if his newfound sleep was because of Lola. That created a problem. Of course, he found her beautiful, and he desired her as he'd never desired any woman ever before, but to desire her because he thought she helped him to sleep was a new level of want altogether.

He wasn't sure how to proceed.

As a royal duke, albeit only a distant cousin to the Prince Regent's mother, Edmund held the highest rank among the British peerage, below the members of the royal family. His actions reflected on the nation, and he couldn't risk fathering a bastard and muddling his bloodline. He'd grown up doubting peoples' intentions toward him, so he'd never joined the raucous parties at pubs with his peers at Oxford.

Edmund bit his lip, worried about the flower girl who he'd convinced to remain at his house, chaperoned by his staff, of course, because it had gotten late and, frankly, he didn't want her to go. And *that* had been before he'd discovered her presence in his home helped him to get the rest he so sorely needed.

"Of course, Marlowe doesn't want to sell the land. It's been in his family for generations. But I need direct access to the sea," Edmund said, facing Brewster in the foyer.

"He wants to meet you face-to-face," Brewster said. "I wouldn't do it."

"Do it anyhow. Tonight. Dinner. Set it up."

"Don't see him alone. He's a feisty old man. If we say the wrong thing, we could lose everything."

"*We* wouldn't lose everything, *I* would." Edmund nudged Brewster out the door and slammed it shut with a bang.

"Hullo." Lola appeared bag in hand, back in her patched dress from the previous morning.

Please don't go. "Are you hungry? Why don't you sit and have something to eat?"

She let him take the bag from her and set it on a stool. "Mrs. Kitty is surely waiting for me. I should go back and water the flowers."

"It's supposed to rain."

She raised her eyebrows at the clear blue sky out the window.

"I'll take you back personally after breakfast."

"I have the phaeton and should return it to Mrs. Kitty."

"Then I will accompany you." He led her toward the dining room. "I didn't know what you liked, so I had the cook prepare one of everything."

With a wistful smile, she picked a slice of toast, the most modest piece of food next to coddled eggs, bread pudding, a fruit platter, and sausages. Instead of sitting, however, she picked a piece off the corner of the toast and stuffed it in her mouth, taking a grand tour of the room.

He smiled. She was clueless about how to behave in the presence of a duke. So sweet, natural, and honest, something most people lacked around him because they wanted something from him.

Refreshing. No, better. Mesmerizing.

"Did you sleep?" she asked.

Oh, right, she knew about his insomnia; they'd met at his apothecary. "I fell asleep at my desk for a moment."

Her eyes trailed over the table and landed on his clean plate. "You don't sleep, you don't eat, and you don't go to the opera often. What does a duke do, Edmund?"

"I buy land, employ people, and make money."

"What do you use the land and people for?"

"Wood, mostly. We harvest the wood in Northumberland and then sell it."

She crinkled her nose. "That must make you a lot of money."

He shrugged. "The land I want to buy tonight has lots of old oaks."

"Why don't you use your land instead of letting it go barren?"

"I intend to convert it to farmland, but I need an environmental restoration plan. That, in turn, needs approval by the majority vote in the House of Lords. And to ensure that, I need to show them that … never mind."

"So you just want the trees, then you'll get rid of the land."

"I'll sell it in pieces for development. Roads, villages, ports."

She tilted her head back in understanding, but the way her eyes narrowed, he could tell she didn't like what she'd heard.

Barnie, the butler, appeared. "Your Grace, Mr. Brewster is here."

"Again? What does he want?" Edmund rose and strode to the foyer.

"I set up the dinner with Marlowe but you're making a big mistake going there alone." Brewster puffed from exertion as he entered, sweat rolling down his temples like a hot kettle overboiling. "You should bring a woman, a serious one, to show that you are serious about starting a family and so forth."

"I don't need to be in his good graces; I just need his business."

"And you'll get it if you're in his good graces. Listen, Edmund, I know a lot of good girls from reputable families. And some not so reputable, but he doesn't have to know that."

"No, you don't. And you never think of love." Edmund looked over his shoulder and heard a rustling from the dining room. "Besides, I already have someone in mind."

Brewster stilled as Lola peeked through the door into the foyer. "Who's that?"

"The woman I'll bring to dinner with Marlowe."

THE SHORT MAN gave Lola a once-over that instantly made her feel dirty. She didn't want anyone to know that she'd slept at Edmund's house ... if her brother came back and her reputation was in shreds, what would he say? He hadn't survived the war to come back to a ruined woman. All of her work would have been in vain.

But the short man left soon enough and she retrieved her bag, ready to go home.

"Thank you for your hospitality, Your Grace." She curtsied.

"Lola, I have a business proposition for you," Edmund said.

That didn't sound good—for her reputation, at least. But she did need money. And Edmund had said he employed people, so perhaps his proposition was above board. At the very least, she could hear him out. "What do you want?"

"I'm going to be in Town until Sunday and I'd like to hire you to be by my side."

Oh, dear. That sounded *very* bad for her reputation. "I am not for hire," she told him and made to push past him and out the door. "Thank you, Your Grace. The opera was wonderful. I truly appreciate the opportunity. It was the chance of a lifetime and for that, I am grateful."

He stopped her with a hand to her forearm. Little tingles traveled up over her shoulder and to her heart. "I don't mean like *that*. I need a woman who can pretend to be my fiancée and who can attend a series of boring events with me."

"You want to fool the Ton that you have a fiancée?"

He inclined his head. "There are certain people who believe that without a future wife, I don't appear serious about managing my private life *and* business. I'll pay you."

Lola shrugged. She didn't pretend to understand the workings of the Ton or its members, so what he said could be true. And, at least, he wasn't asking her to pretend to be his wife.

"How much?"

His eyes sparkled. "As much as you ask."

Even so, it wasn't in her nature to be deceitful. Besides that, she was out of her depth of understanding. She wasn't an aristocrat by any means. As much as she needed the money, it was best that she refuse him. She'd make an outrageous offer, and he'd back up. She could go home and forget she'd ever stepped into his fairytale of a life. "My brother's commission. And my parent's old cottage. Plus, furnishings and warm clothes for the winter."

He nodded.

"And two years' worth of firewood. Cut into sections and stacked."

He nodded again.

"And all the sacks of flowering seeds from a catalog of my choice."

He furrowed his brow. "Only until midnight on Sunday?"

"Deal."

CHAPTER SIX

L OLA WAS STUPEFIED. Nobody would pay an officer's commission, buy back a cottage, stock it with firewood, and add pounds and pounds of flowering seeds on top. Certainly not for her. She was just a flower girl.

"You could get any of the elegant ladies from the Ton. Why me?" she asked.

"Because I need someone honest, smart, and beautiful. Most women have one of these qualities, rarely all three."

She swallowed hard. "Edmund, I would have stayed for free if you'd asked me."

"I would have added a fortune and the ruby necklace, too. I'll be gone most of the day but please be ready for dinner at seven." He turned and started off, but then paused and turned back to her. "I'll have some gowns sent to you."

THE DAY PASSED quickly enough while Lola explored the house, spoke to the staff, and prepared for dinner. A black dress with intricate lace from the collar down to the cleft between her breasts had been delivered, and to her astonishment, it fit perfectly.

The lady's maid swept up her hair and teased a few curls loose that fell in ringlets. She rubbed pomade that smelled like jasmine on Lola's lips and smeared her cheeks with a pearlescent paste. Lola thought she looked like a polished piece of furniture, ready for the market.

Downstairs, the silver cutlery gleamed under the flickering chandelier light, each piece laid out with precision. The design on the fine porcelain plates mirrored the vibrant yellow, orange, and pink roses arranged in the center of the table, and crystal glasses stood ready, on the crisp white tablecloth with matching starched fabric napkins. Elegant candlesticks completed the setting. In the corner of the room, next to an elegant sideboard adorned with crystal decanters and sparkling stemware, Lola caught a glimpse of the dashing duke in formal evening attire. Even though his black velvet coat was cut to fit him perfectly, his tight bottom in the tight breeches caught her eye.

He turned to her and blinked. Lola remained in the doorway, taking in the perfection before her with hidden glee—and it wasn't the dining room she'd admired. Again, he blinked as if he hadn't seen her well, then he blinked again. His arms fell limp to his sides and he opened his mouth but no sound came out.

Lola folded her hands primly in front of her and cast him a shy smile. "You're half an hour late," she said.

He smiled and came closer. "You're radiant."

She laughed, willing her blush to cool lest he see how she felt. He only wanted her for a few days. She'd take even a few hours with him. Any minute with the dashing duke would give her enough to feast on for a lifetime.

Dinner was a feast. Lord Chancellor Marlowe, as Edmund had called him, turned out to have a gentle demeanor. He'd brought his grandson, James.

The first course arrived: four triangular open-faced sandwiches with watercress.

"What is this?" Lola whispered to Edmund.

"*Paté de foie gras.* Goose liver."

Lola wrinkled her nose but made every effort to eat anyhow. "Is there going to be soup and then salad?"

"Brewster sent a menu late this afternoon to change the meal according to our guests' preferences."

"It sometimes feels like a jest when they give us more spoons and forks than food on the plates," Marlowe said in a conspiratorial tone. He picked up one of the triangles and ate it like a finger sandwich.

Lola smiled and followed suit. It didn't taste as bad as it sounded.

The next course puzzled Lola further—three hard ovals in a

dish.

"It's crab. An imported delicacy from Portugal. Try it." Edmund turned back to James in a heated debate about a restoration plan.

"Your Grace, if you were to get control of our land, which you may or may not, what would you do with our estate?" James asked.

Edmund used the long prongs of the salad fork then held the shell down with his knife and nudged the white crab meat out, then *plop*, the fork was loaded. He popped it into his mouth.

"I'm not pleased with your restoration plan," Marlowe said. "You're taking fourteen generations of stewardship to turn a fast profit. If you didn't deforest the land, you wouldn't have to restore it. Why don't you think of the future?"

Lola tried to stabilize the slippery shell, but it was coated in melted butter, and she had to be careful not to splatter her dress. Finally, she managed to use her knife to hold the crab in place.

"If I sell the wood from your land and give you a portion of it, you'll be a very rich man," Edmund told Marlowe.

Lola inserted the fork and heard a *squelch* and a *crunch*. There, now she just had to get the right angle to nudge the meat out.

"I'm rich enough," Marlowe said. "I want to preserve the legacy of my ancestors for the generations to come."

Swish! The entire crab, buttery sauce and shell included, flew through the air. *Oh no!*

Barnie, the butler, caught it and stuck it in his pocket. His expression didn't change.

Edmund gave Lola a deadpan stare.

James bit his lips.

Marlowe was too intent on the conversation to be distracted. "Leave my estate alone."

"I can't do that. I need egress to the sea and your land has direct access and an established port. It would be a shame not to use it."

"It is being used," James snarled. "By the people who live and work there."

"It's not. The permits have been frozen until the port is repurposed as a trading post for environmental restoration."

Marlowe threw his napkin on the table. "How did you make that happen behind my back? Who did you persuade at the House of

Lords?"

"You bastard!" James rose and set his wine glass down with force.

Lola flinched as the crystal stemware clanged.

Marlowe waved to the footman for his hat. "Remember this, it's better to preserve than restore."

CHAPTER SEVEN

LONDON SWELTERED UNDER a dome of heat, the air thick with the unfulfilled promise of rain. The city's denizens moved as if through a miasma, collars wilted, brows beaded with sweat, yearning for the relief of a rain shower that lingered, teasingly, just beyond reach. How odd for Londoners to crave rain when they usually complained they had too much of it.

Edmund regretted that the evening hadn't gone as planned. He hadn't impressed Lola with the dinner, an unfamiliar experience because people usually feigned delight just by the virtue of dining with him.

Lola hugged herself. "You didn't need to accompany me. It's my phaeton."

"Certainly, I did."

They passed the apothecary's building at 87 Harley Street and pulled into a small alley between the buildings.

His mind chewed over what Marlowe had said: *better to preserve than to restore.* How could this work in a world where one had to produce, sell, and be faster and more efficient than one's competition? And why? Could Brewster be wrong?

Edmund's head spun with so many questions that he didn't pay much heed to the rusty hinges of the crooked back door Lola had led him to. After he followed her up a winding staircase to a door that was more of a hatch, he waited while she lit a lantern, and he found himself in a tiny room with the basics of a functioning household: a cot with a clean pillow and a small escritoire with an ink well and a quill that had seen better days, a small table with a washbasin, a fogged mirror hanging above it. There was a low door that reminded him of one for a chicken coop on the wall across from the entry; he doubted it led to another room. This was it, all she had. Edmund's heart clenched. She deserved better than this.

"Do you live here alone?"

"Yes, we sold our cottage when my parents died. It was just... too..." She gasped for air as if choking back sobs.

Edmund could understand. He'd done so many times, at least when he was younger and the death of his parents was still new. "Painful. Everything reminded you of them."

"Yes. You must know how stepping into your father's shoes as the duke feels?"

"I can never get away." Edmund still couldn't hide the grief, nor did he wish to. Not from her.

Lola dusted off her new dress as she hung it on a hook he hadn't noticed at first. Then she dropped the shawl on the bed with a proprietorial air and turned to that chicken coop door. Was it a closet of a sort? But no. Ducking through the opening, he followed her into the dark, muggy summer air he so hated in London. In the dim light, he saw they were in a flower garden on a rooftop.

Lola lit a lantern and handed it to him. "This is my business." She lit another and hung it on a thin wire hook on the side of the building.

The whole roof came alive, a lush summer paradise with a view of London. Cultivated beds of color glowed in the orange flicker of the lantern.

Edmund walked through the corridor between the raised beds. "You did this?"

Lola spread apart some bushy greens with yellow tips on their buds. "Look. This is *Hypericum*, St. John's Wort. Once the yellow flowers show tiny black dots, I'll harvest them. The little leaves have tiny holes, which are actually glands." She picked a leaf and handed it to him. "St. John's Wort is good for the nerves, rashes, and burns. Mr. Collins makes cold compresses with it, or sometimes mixes it into oils."

She pivoted to the raised garden bed behind them. "There's not much left in this bed because I harvested the crocus in March, the dahlias in July, and the foxglove was late this year, but I had a good harvest in May."

"You grew all that here?"

"Yes. I rent the room, and Mrs. Kitty lets me do what I want with this space. She wouldn't use it otherwise. I built this to pay for everything."

"You built the raised beds?" Edmund walked to the edge of the one that had been harvested and searched for the mark. There it was, in the corner, a burn mark with his crest. "These are planks from Northumberland." *His wood.*

"Yes, they were used for a box to transport a piano. I got the planks for free and built this." She smiled, pride mixed with a *je ne sais quoi* that made his breath hitch.

"How many of the shipping crates did you need to build all this?"

"Ten. Twelve perhaps. I collected wood whenever I could."

She'd put his wood to better use than he ever had. "And the soil?"

"Carried it."

Edmund swallowed hard. She'd created a rotating crop system out of nothing. Nothing that she'd had to purchase, anyway, except perhaps seeds. But the point was that even after months of drafting the environmental restoration plan for Marlowe's land, he hadn't produced a coherent approach like this. His eyes fell on a few little coniferous trees at the end of one of the raised beds. "Will you sell those in the winter?"

"No, this is rosemary." Lola bent down, tore a few needles off, rubbed them between her hands, and held them out for him to smell.

A potent blend of pine and mint carried a freshness to his nostrils that invigorated his senses, and something woody let him forget how hot the night was. "How can something smell cool?" The question spilled out of his head before he'd finished forming it.

"It has camphoraceous undertones and a lemony sweetness, see?" Lola took one of the crinkled needles and brought it to his mouth. "You can eat it."

LOLA PLACED TWO wrinkled rosemary needles in Edmund's mouth, and he chewed them, suddenly able to take a deep, cooling breath. He gently grasped her wrists, lifting her hands with the remaining dark green needles to his face, and dipped his face into her palms.

At first, she thought he'd smell them, but with the softness of down whisking through the air, Edmund placed a kiss on her left palm. Then her right.

Lola's heart dropped to her knees and her hands relaxed.

"People rarely surprise me." His voice became muffled as he cupped her hands with his, pulling them toward him. He kissed her wrist.

Lola reached and touched his hair, just above the temples where the tension bore testament to his sleepless nights. He let go of her hands and put both of his on her waist. She met his gaze, his deep gray-green eyes like the velvety surface of sage leaves.

When his attention fell to her mouth, her lips tingled in anticipation, and she parted her mouth.

"This was not part of our arrangement but may I—"

She didn't let him finish the question lest the mention of their reason for being there ruin the moment. For once, Lola wanted to feel seen by a handsome man like this duke, held in his strong arms and cocooned in the magic of the moment. She no longer wanted to be the girl who could merely supply the flowers for the backdrop of his dining room, she wanted to be the light in every room with him. It was presumptuous. Insolent even. But she didn't care. The summer heat, combined with the blood in her body that he'd set aflame with his tender touch, melted her resolve.

For a moment, Lola ceased to be the flower girl who planted and raised the most beautiful and fragrant blossoms, only to deliver them to someone else. This time, she'd reap what she'd sowed.

And it was glorious. As soon as her lips touched his, he inhaled sharply and opened his mouth.

She knew what to do, how to invade and explore. And his response nearly made her legs buckle. He hesitated at first, but then his soft lips melted onto hers. Could this be his first kiss?

The London heat was forgotten, replaced by a different kind of warmth that radiated from him, spreading through her like wildfire.

Every inch of her skin tuned into his touch as her body awoke, responding to the sweet pressure of his kiss. His mouth was tender like a rose petal's touch but firm and delicious at the same time.

He reached for the back of her head, pulling her closer. She felt the length of his hard body pressed against hers, yet longed for more, closer, deeper. When he broke their kiss and looked up at the dark sky, she longed to bring him back to her.

Something cold on her cheek pulled her out of her reverie—a raindrop. She looked up to see sparkling drops falling from the sky as if the summer was weeping for her, the stupid flower girl who'd fallen for a duke. But she ignored her conscience because she wanted him now. Never mind tomorrow, it would come soon enough.

Another raindrop fell, and another, until it wasn't just drops but sheets of water cascading down from the heavens, soaking them to the skin. The sudden chill was a stark contrast to the heat of their kiss, but it did nothing to dampen the magnetism between them.

Edmund raised his brows.

She shrugged, and they broke into laughter.

Without a word, he scooped her into his arms and carried her through the pouring rain back to her tiny attic room, where he gently laid her down on the bed.

His eyes were dark with desire. His hair was slicked back from the rain, droplets trickling down his forehead. He wiped them away with the back of his hand before turning his attention back to her.

CHAPTER EIGHT

HE KNEW HE shouldn't, but he was at sea with emotion.
"Lola"—he choked on his words like a green boy—"may I please kiss you again?"

A lazy smile spread across her face and the moonlight reflected from her perfect white teeth. "You already kissed me quite thoroughly."

"I was holding back."

"Really?" Her tinge of sarcasm held an undertone of fear.

"I promise I won't do anything you don't allow. But … I—" A million thoughts flooded his mind. Reasons not to do this. A duke and the flower girl. He fell to his knees and begged, "Please tell me to stop."

She sat on the bed, but instead of pushing him away, she plopped backward and arched her back.

Edmund's heart stopped. Or perhaps he just forgot to breathe.

Before him, like a delicacy on a platter, lay the most beautiful girl in black lace, soaked through so the fabric clung to her skin.

"Lola." Her name was a benediction, yet it paled in comparison to her touch when she reached for his head and drove her hands through his wet hair.

Like a trained puppy, he leaned in, longing for her touch and rasping for air. He didn't remember being so aroused, ever. She took the lead; he was the royal duke at her knees.

Her touch grew more urgent, and she pushed his head down. She sprawled on the bed, brought her hips to the edge of the bed, and pulled his head to her thighs.

Edmund's heart galloped like the horses at the race tracks in his chest. He peeled back the dark fabric of her gown, relishing in her response underneath. She lifted one leg, then the other, to give him access to remove the layers of black lace until there were only the stockings, translucent and wet, held up with the garters.

She still had her slippers on, elongating her long legs into paths of sinful pleasure. As he kissed his way up from her ankles to her knees and higher, she whimpered. Resting on his haunches, he realized it had taken a beauty like her to bring him to his knees. She was unapologetically fierce, strong, and sincere. He made himself comfortable there, nuzzling her thigh and preparing to explore her secret places.

He hesitated before he lay his hand on the apex of her legs.

"Don't stop."

"Lola, have you ever ... I mean ... do you know..."

"I haven't, but I do know. Please don't stop." She arched her back and lifted her hips toward him.

"Are you a virgin?"

"Yes. Oh yes, but please don't stop now."

Edmund swallowed hard. He shouldn't take advantage of the innocent flower girl, but she felt as though she was meant for him. Every kiss had an air of belonging right where he placed it. She was so right, but he was so lost.

"Edmund, please. I've heard and seen more than the sheltered debutantes."

"But you've never been with a man?"

She shook her head. "I've never ... *ahem* ... I haven't before."

She propped herself up to look into his eyes as if she could discern the truth as if she saw directly into his heart. "I'm with you now. You're a man."

That was his undoing. She saw him, Edmund, not the duke, the transaction, the management of the estate. He wasn't just a bag of coins to her or a ticket to St. James Palace. He was a man, and she was a woman. And he needed to be with her more than he needed the air he breathed.

He parted her folds using his thumbs with as much curiosity as ardor. First, nuzzling her thigh, then he pressed a chaste kiss on her mound and another on her swollen pearl.

She moaned and called his name.

He held her hips with both hands and nudged her into the position, propping her legs wide open. When he spread her to his view, she rewarded him with a drop of her essence and welcomed his kiss.

He inserted his middle finger slowly, just a prelude. But she surprised him when she met his thrust and clenched her insides. He nibbled her pearl and she let out a cry.

"Edmund!"

Yes, say my name.

He wanted to forget himself, thrust into her, and ride her so long and so hard they'd collapse from exhaustion, but she didn't give him a chance to think about it.

She pressed his head down, inviting him to deepen the kiss.

He slid another finger in and moved more vigorously, running his tongue over every petal of her dewy softness as she rode his hand. He traced her shape, the perfect pink flesh of her, with his tongue up one side and down the other.

"More!" she cried.

He withdrew.

"More, please!"

"Lola, 'more' means…"

"I know." She sat up and pulled him by the wet fabric of his shirt. She dug her hands under the layers, tugging at the fabric until the buttons went flying, and she found his skin.

He struggled to get out of his wet clothes, and there were hands everywhere, fighting the layers of fabric between them.

Until there wasn't.

A cool chill ran over Edmund's back as if the heat wave had broken and cooled his body from the outside. Or perhaps the burning desire for her outshone the heat … it didn't matter.

Nothing mattered anymore when he finally stood and stepped out of his breeches.

CHAPTER NINE

T HIS WAS A mistake. A grave, irrevocable, sinful mistake.
    And it was hers to make. Her secret to keep. Her pleasure to remember for a lifetime.

If her reputation was ruined by striking a deal with an aristocrat, by selling herself in a mere business transaction, then she was glad it was this handsome duke bestowing her with the most bone-melting kisses, keener than in her wildest imagination.

He stood naked before her. Chiseled perfection, sculpted to the last detail. Every muscle and sinew carved with precision. His broad shoulders tapered down to a narrow waist, his torso a harmonious blend of strength and grace. Each ripple of his abdomen was clearly defined, and yet, for all his strength, he had an elegance, a balance that spoke of careful control and measured power.

She gave him power over her heart.

But it was his face that truly captivated Lola—the strong jawline, high cheekbones, straight nose—every detail perfectly proportioned. His green eyes glowed with a palpable heat as if a fire had been lit within him, the flames dancing in his irises, reflecting his desire. She melted under his gaze, lost in the molten depths of his eyes.

And melt she did when he climbed atop her. He kissed a path upward from her thigh over her hip bone, her navel, and up to her ribs until his hands cupped her breasts.

"You're shivering," he whispered. "Are you cold?"

She nodded, for she broke out in goosebumps and had no other words for how she felt. Without him, she'd forever be cold, no matter how stifling the temperature.

He tugged at the hem of the black lace, then again. He tore the fabric right in the middle, unwrapping her impatiently like a present he'd waited for all his life.

His hands were hot on her cool skin. Raindrops chased each other down the windows of her little room in the attic, pattering against the glass and the thin roof shielding her from the heavens above.

But she was on top of the world, spiraling with pleasure she'd never felt before.

CHAPTER TEN

THE NEXT MORNING, Edmund woke with a startle. He was naked under a sheet in a shabby-looking attic. Then he remembered and looked down at the smooth, taut bottom against him. He tightened his embrace. *Lola. His Lola.*

Oh, how badly he wished this to be true, but he'd taken more than he should have. She'd never be his. Their bargain had been for her company, not her body, but in the process, he'd lost his heart.

He rolled her carefully off his arm, placed a tender kiss on her forehead, and rose.

His eyes trailed over the humble abode, and truth replaced the haze of last night's passion. He'd fallen for her. What he'd done to her was inexcusable, but it felt as though he'd unleashed a torment from his soul and tamed the demons of insomnia. He hadn't merely slept last night, but he'd rested.

He put on his still-damp breeches and looked out the window onto her rooftop garden. The leaves, now a deeper, lusher shade of green, glistened with droplets of rain, reflecting the early sun rays in a million tiny prisms. Birds sang their melodious tunes, their chirps amplified by the stillness, filling the air with joyful hope, while every blade of grass, every petal, seemed to pulse with new life under the gentle caress of the summer breeze. Gone was the scorching heat and weight of August.

Edmund felt invigorated. She'd done that. She'd given him rest, but she'd brought him back to life.

The covers rustled. "It's Sunday," she said sleepily.

Edmund turned and looked at her swollen lips. A little smear of blood on the covers confirmed that he'd truly taken more than he ought, and he didn't know what to give her in return to make up for his transgressions.

"Good morning."

She crawled toward him, holding the covers against her breasts to hide them. How adorable that she was embarrassed even though he'd ... well, it was a new morning.

"Isn't the race today?" she asked.

Edmund froze. "What time is it?"

She squinted and counted as the church bells rang somewhere in the distance. "Ten."

"We have to be there in an hour!" He hurried into his clothes, as did she, and they darted to her phaeton.

BACK ON COCKSPUR Street, Edmund quickly shaved with his valet's apt assistance and changed into his riding attire, a bottle green coat, and striped breeches. By ten-thirty, he sat at the breakfast table, unable to eat. One by one, he stacked the juice glasses.

"What's with you this week?" Brewster said when he waltzed in. "We're late for the race."

"I don't care about the race," Edmund said to the glasses, ignoring his solicitor's nervous pacing.

"Marlowe does. He's wagered his lands on a single horse. If he loses the land to someone else, we don't have any leverage for the restoration plan. No land from Marlowe, no plan, no money."

"Why exactly do we need money if we don't build anything?" Edmund stacked a fourth glass on the tower he'd built on the table. "You know, when I was little, I loved building with rocks, twigs, and anything else I could find. But now, I don't have anything to show for my work."

"You have money to show for it."

Edmund gave him a shrewd glare, fully aware that Brewster would get twenty percent of whatever he derived from Marlowe's estate. "First, I didn't agree to your scheme. Second, I'd have no less if the plan failed. So why does it matter so much?"

"Because, Edmund, you need to get bigger and better. Or else stop."

And stop Edmund did when Bernie, the butler, announced Lola, a vision in a gown of fine sprigged muslin over a dress of beige-brown silk with a darker beige sash sprinkled with white dots. Her hair was fashionably dressed in a loose, twisted braid under the white straw bonnet with a ribbon that matched the sash. She wore white kid gloves and cream-colored slippers and truly looked like ... Edmund tried to find words, but all he could do was respond to his body, recognizing the torrent of passion raging in his veins from the previous night.

As if pulled by magnetic force, he found her side, took her hand, and twirled her in a circle.

"Thank you for this beautiful gown." She beamed at him and his heart melted.

"Thank you for gracing me with your beauty." He bowed deeply and kissed her knuckles, then trailed a path of kisses upward to her elbow, reveling when she blushed and chuckled. He did that to her. Oh, and how much more he longed to do.

Brewster cleared his throat. "Time to go."

Edmund deflated. He made a mental note to hire another solicitor. Preferably, one with no interest in his private life.

CHAPTER ELEVEN

"WHAT IF SOMEBODY recognizes me as nothing but a flower girl?" Lola twitched uncomfortably when Edmund offered his arm and led her to the white tent alongside the green race track.

"The Ton don't procure their own flowers or herbs. You look like a lady, and nobody knows where you're from."

Somehow, Edmund's reassurance stung, but Lola smiled, ready for her last day by his side. The end of her fairy tale would soon come, and she'd revert to her old life. Edmund would remain nothing but a memory while she waited for her brother's return, or even remained alone forever.

In the tent, a buffet with refreshments, cold champagne in polished glass flutes, trays of petits fours, and cubed cheeses caught Lola's eye.

"It's a picnic," Edmund said, "help yourself."

For her, a picnic meant a basket of apples and sandwiches. She didn't recognize anyone except Brewster on the other side of the room speaking with a fair-skinned woman who eyed the other guests from her perch under a parasol that she twirled like a bayonet.

Edmund led Lola to a pair of two women, who looked a lot alike. "May I present Mrs. Cavendish and Lady Olson?"

"How nice to meet you, Lady Viola, is it?" the red-lipped one asked as she gave Lola a cool once-over.

"Just Miss," Lola said with a curtsy. She wasn't sure if this was what it took, but she wanted to be professional; that was the deal with Edmund. Feelings aside, what had happened last night could easily be chalked to a list of escapades. Hers only had this one entry. Perhaps he'd already forgotten that it was mere hours since … since… Lola flushed at the thought.

"Well, Miss Viola, Edmund here is the catch of the Ton and has eluded us for years."

"We just couldn't wait for him any longer," the other one said, batting her lashes at him.

"They are sisters, Lola, and you ought to know that they've quite mastered the art of favorable marriages. Good day, ladies." Edmund began to lead her away.

Just when Lola thought they could escape the fangs of these ladies, Brewster waved Edmund over.

"Would you please excuse me for a moment? I think he's found the Lord Chancellor, who could secure some sway for our restoration plan in Parliament."

And he was off.

Lola, at sea among the women in expensive gowns and accessories, tugged at her bonnet, stifled by the tight bow that kept it in place.

"It suits you," said someone behind her.

Lola turned to find James Marlowe, the grandson of the man whose estate Edmund was trying to annex. "I hear you have much set on the favorite horse," she said, unsure how to converse with Edmund's opponent even though he was no more than twenty and looked rather friendly.

"The horse is mine, and I'm the jockey," James said. "Would you like to meet her?"

⪼⪻

"SHE'S TALKING TO Marlowe," Brewster said when the Lord Chancellor had left.

Edmund, from afar, admired the beauty who'd captured his heart. "It's harmless. They're just talking."

"We only have the deal in Parliament if Marlowe retains his lands. Should he lose his estate in the race before the vote on Monday morning, all we've worked for is null."

"Then we find another way to expand." Edmund was only half listening, as Lola threw her head back and laughed heartily at something the young Marlowe said.

"How do you know she's not working for them?" Brewster asked.

"She's not."

"Nobody else knows this girl. Where did you even find her?"

Edmund crossed his arms. "That's none of your concern."

"It is as if she's risking the deal. So where? Tell me!"

"At the apothecary on Harley Street."

"As a patient?"

"As his supplier of fresh herbs and blooms."

Brewster elbowed Edmund in the arm. "Seriously? A flower girl?" He walked away, laughing. "A flower girl and a duke, it's too darn absurd."

Lola turned as Brewster approached her, crossed her arms, and turned back to the young Marlowe.

When Edmund returned to Lola's side, James Marlowe took his leave to prepare for the race.

"What did he tell you?" Edmund asked.

"Nothing in particular." Lola's smile didn't quite reach her eyes. Nor did she make eye contact with Edmund.

"But you laughed."

"So I did."

"About what?"

"A jest."

Edmund narrowed his eyes. "Lola, he's the enemy."

"Then why did you bring me here? To embarrass me if you don't trust that I can carry on a polite conversation without jeopardizing your precious deal to exploit Northumberland?"

"Lola." Edmund reached for her, but she jerked away.

"Miss Viola, please meet my wife." Brewster presented the skinny fair woman from earlier.

"I hear you can work wonders with blooms, darling. Perhaps you could come to my gardens sometime and advise the staff." His wife left, leaving a frigid hole in the atmosphere.

Lola blinked.

"And when you're done—" Brewster winked at her—"I'll show you my favorite spots in the bushes."

Lola ran. She didn't know where to go, she just ran away from the green and toward the cobblestone streets.

CHAPTER TWELVE

T HE DISTINGUISHED RACE crowd gathered around Edmund and Brewster as if watching a dogfight. A tent behind them offered little respite from the heat. The ice meant to cool the refreshments had surrendered in puddles of defeat.

"What got into you, Brewster?" Edmund shouted in plain sight of the Ton. Under the scorching sun, he couldn't breathe. He tugged at his cravat until it came loose and he threw it on the ground.

"She's not a suitable duchess, Edmund, she probably doesn't even have a dowry." Brewster laughed.

"You think I care about her dowry? Or where she's from?"

"See reason, Edmund. It's all right to tup a few flower girls, we've all done it, but you need a duchess by your side who can carry herself with poise, a partner in life, not just in bed."

Edmund seethed. The voices in the crowd merged into a single high-pitched murmur.

His hand stung. He'd hit something fleshy with a hard center.

Brewster wobbled backward, spat blood and something white like a pit—or a tooth—and yelled.

But Edmund was running after Lola. She was getting away.

He ran faster. "Lola!" Looking this way and that, he realized he'd lost her. She hadn't taken his carriage, and she was nowhere to be seen.

Edmund could barely catch his breath, but not from the exertion of running across the grass fields, feet swift against the earth as the sun beat down, cloaking him in its relentless heat.

Discouraged, he took the carriage home, where the butler announced a guest waiting for him in the parlor. Was it her? His heart soared but then he entered the room and saw his childhood friend sitting there waiting for him. As glad as he was to see him, Edmund couldn't disregard the bitterness he felt over Lola running away.

"Raphi!"

"What's happened? I've never seen you so rattled. And...are you? Edmund. You're drenched with sweat."

Edmund sank onto the settee by the wall, burying his face in both hands. "I mucked it up."

"The race? Did you bet on a horse?" Raphi came to his side and put a gentle hand on his shoulder. If only they'd allowed Jews at Eton and Oxford; Edmund would have preferred a kind friend like Raphi by his side to Brewster, the leech.

"Not the race. The deal probably. But Lola—" his breath caught, and he swallowed a lump at the back of his throat.

"Ah, the beauty with the collar?" Raphi had many brothers and was married to his childhood sweetheart. He understood matters of the heart.

Edmund dropped his hands and looked at his friend. "I hired her."

"Miss Viola?" Raphi arched a brow and crossed his arms. "She didn't strike me as—"

"She's not! She's a flower girl."

Raphi pressed his lips together and listened.

"I met her at the apothecary when she delivered medicinal herbs and blooms."

Raphi assumed an expression of respect. "It takes a lot of knowledge to recognize the right plants, as far as I know."

"She grows some of them herself and harvests them in the early morning hours."

"And the problem is..."

"The problem is that—"

The butler appeared. "Your Grace, Mr. Brewster is here."

"Edmund!" There was the chipped man-kettle, holding a blood-ied handkerchief to his mouth. "Marlowe's horse lost the race. There's no land. No deal!"

Edmund shrugged.

Raphi rose to greet Brewster but only received a cold, cursory glance. A Jew was of no interest to Brewster. Edmund simmered. He'd lost patience with Brewster's high-handed arrogance and narrow-minded worldview.

"You owe me, Edmund! I've been working for months to try to pass the deal. I wrote up the paperwork—" Brewster enumerated on his fingers—"scheduled the meetings, organized the—"

"You've clung to me for too long, Brewster! I didn't ask for your help, and I don't want your deal!" Edmund stood and walked to him. "And just so you know—"

"Just so *you* know, Your Grace, on that high horse of yours, money runs out. Credibility must be built. Flower girls may know how to tell fertile soil, but they won't annex the land for your estate."

"Get out!" Edmund roared.

Brewster planted his stubby legs firmly. "You haven't paid me for my service."

Edmund tightened his fists, ready to knock the last teeth out of his smug grin when he noticed how Brewster's eyes trailed to the jewelry box on the mantel. It was the one the ruby collar necklace was kept in; Raphi was here to take it back.

"The day still has—" Brewster fumbled in his pocket, producing a golden pocket watch. He pushed the lever, and it sprung open. "Nine hours before midnight. Have you dismissed the flower girl?"

"You're dismissed," Edmund growled. "Leave!"

"Suit yourself. Mourn the thieving lass, but mark my words, Edmund, your reputation has dissipated like the morning fog in the scorching heat." As Brewster slipped his watch back into his pocket, a flash of sparkling red peeking out of it caught Edmund's eye.

Edmund walked to the mantel, picked up the box, and handed it to Raphi. "Thank you for the loan. It's a beautiful piece."

Raphi took the box and hefted it as if testing its weight. He frowned and opened the box. "As I said, it's unlike you, Edmund. You're not usually a ruthless businessman." Raphi, two feet taller than Brewster, cast him a condescending look.

Instead of watching Raphi's expression, Edmund turned to Brewster, who stood in the doorway, as if undecided whether to pounce or flee.

"Edmund, it's empty," Raphi said.

Brewster sniffed. "As I told you. She's a conniving thief."

Edmund's heart thundered in his chest, and a tempest of fury coursed through his veins as he surged toward Brewster. The coarse fabric of Brewster's collar bunched under Edmund's clenched fists, as he pinned him against the wall with a force that echoed his inner turmoil. "What have you done?"

Brewster met his gaze, defiance in his eyes. "Nothing, Your Grace." He spat the words into the charged air between them.

Edmund reached into Brewster's pocket and found the watch.

Plus, something else.

CHAPTER THIRTEEN

L OLA CLIMBED TO her room in the attic and sank onto the bed.
"Hey, sis." A voice came from the shadows.

Lola wondered at the power of her imagination in her hour of need. Oh, when would her brother finally return? Sobbing into her pillow, she shook her feet, but the fine slippers fit so well that they didn't fall to the floor, as if the elegant didn't want to mingle with her humble flower girl surroundings.

Lola's fingers gripped the sheets as if to hold the shattered shards of her heart together. Each tear that soaked into the fabric seemed to carry a piece of her lost hope, blending sorrow with the linen. In her quiet room, she conjured her brother's comforting voice, a bittersweet symphony in her head.

"Darling sister, why are you crying?" he asked, tone laced with concern.

She knew it was foolish, this imaginary dialogue, yet she couldn't help but scold herself for indulging in such thoughts.

"Lola, a beauty dressed in such a lovely dress, surely has a reason for these tears," he said, as usual trying to coax a smile through her grief. It was her mind's trickery, nothing more.

As she wallowed in self-reproach, an unexpected warmth caressed her back, slicing through the lonely chill that had enveloped her.

"Lola?" His familiar voice sparked a surge of hope that she dared not believe.

Startled, she bolted upright, hastily wiping away the remnants of her tears as she blinked into the dimly lit room. "Leo?" Her heart hammered against her chest, fear and hope warring within her.

Could it truly be him, or was her grief-stricken mind playing the cruelest of tricks?

As her eyes adjusted and the figure before her became clearer, all doubts evaporated. There he stood, her brother Leo, alive and as real as the beating of her heart. His hair was shorter, his shoulders broader, and his face slightly sunburned, but it was him, her beloved brother.

Overwhelmed, Lola launched herself into his open arms, the familiar scent of him wrapping her in a cocoon of safety. As she clung to him, the floodgates opened anew, but these tears were different, they were tears of relief, of joy. After what felt like an eternity of despair, she finally allowed herself to believe in the possibility of happiness again, cradled in the arms of her brother, her protector, her confidant.

And confide she did.

They talked for what seemed like an eternity. He told her of his adventures on the Continent, and she told him about the flowers, her little business, and the duke.

"What if you're with child?" her brother asked when Lola hung her head, ashamed of her stupidity.

As her eyes cast down in a pool of shame, the distant clatter and murmurs outside her room slipped by unnoticed. It was only when the door burst open, ushering in a breathless Mrs. Kitty, face painted with exertion and a flicker of thrill, that Lola's world snapped back into focus. Clutching the doorframe for support, Mrs. Kitty managed between gasps, "He refused to wait."

The question, "Who?" had barely left Lola's lips, when her heart, already tightening, sensed the answer. She stood, movements shaky as she swept the remnants of tears from her cheeks, leaving trails of resolve in their wake.

Filling the doorway with his determined stance, Edmund declared, "Me!" His voice, a blend of hope and insistence, seemed to echo off the walls, circling Lola in an invisible embrace. He stood on the threshold, a testament to the persistence of love, or perhaps folly.

Lola's breath hitched, and her gaze locked with Edmund's as if the intensity of their eyes could rewrite the past. The air hung heavy with the weight of unspoken promises and regrets, the silence between them a canvas for a thousand possibilities.

Leo walked to Edmund.

Wham! He punched him in the stomach.

"Leo!" Lola came to Edmund's side as he bent over and coughed, reaching to the wall for support. "My brother ... oh, Your Grace!"

"I deserved that." Edmund coughed. "I'm an idiot."

He took a deep breath and fell to one knee.

Lola's heart stopped beating. She forgot to breathe.

"May I please make this right?" Edmund asked Leo.

While her eyes followed the goings-on, Lola's mind was unable to process that this was real.

Leo nodded, crossed his arms, and took a wide stance. "If you ever hurt my sister, I'll kill you. Royal duke or not, it's all the same to me."

Edmund pinched his lips and gave a nod.

Then he reached for Lola's hand. "Can you ever forgive me for being a stupid idiot who couldn't see the forest for all the trees in Northumberland?"

Tears pricked her eyes, and her voice failed her.

"I should have never proposed a business arrangement, Lola. If I'd recognized the symptoms, I should have ... I mean...I felt them, and I searched for a way to keep you close, and business was the only way I knew how."

"Which symptoms?" she asked.

Edmund blew through barely parted lips. "At first, I thought it was the summer heat, but it was you who brought my blood to boil with your beauty. Then I thought you'd exhausted me, and that's why I slept. For the first time since my parents died, I rested at night. But it wasn't the heat, Lola. Not the sun, not exhaustion, and not anything that the apothecary's teas could cure."

Lola wiped a tear with her free hand, interlacing the other with Edmund's fingers.

"But the rumor is true, you know. Miracles in medicine and matters of the heart happen at 87 Harley Street for that is where I found you, my love." Edmund reached into his pocket and produced something sparkling.

Somewhere in the distance, Mrs. Kitty gasped, and Leo cleared his throat.

But Lola only had eyes for Edmund.

"Please accept this token of my love," Edmund held the ruby necklace up. "And this is an apology bracelet to match." He produced more jewels from a different velvet-lined box he pulled from his pocket. It bore the address of the jewelry store. "This is a pair of earrings because I was so stupid, it takes more than one piece."

Then Edmund's eyes locked with hers. "And if you can find the strength in your heart to forgive me, it would be the greatest honor if you'd accept this engagement ring and agree to be my duchess."

EPILOGUE

Sent to:
Mister Alfie Collins, Apothecary
87 Harley Street, London

Dear Alfie,

I am delighted to inform you that we have safely arrived in Northumberland, a journey we completed in a third of the time originally estimated. It seems my new brother-in-law possesses an uncanny skill at handling the phaeton, surpassing even my bride's considerable love for speed. Amidst the whirlwind of our departure from London, my sole regret was the inability to extend an invitation to our nuptials to you.

I am also pleased to report that the issue of my restless nights has been thoroughly resolved. You were correct in your assessment—it was not a physical malady that plagued me, but rather a certain emptiness of the heart. Now, with my soul's counterpart by my side, sleep eludes me no longer. The exchange of love between us has proven to be both bountiful and healing.

Upon our return, we restored Lola's ancestral cottage, which now serves as a comfortable abode for her brother. The cottage is conveniently situated a mere two fields away from my estate, creating a pleasant sense of closeness between the new duchess and her brother.

She's a most unlikely duchess, and I love her more than I love life itself. With the assistance of my steward and the support of several villagers, she has transformed vast tracts of deforested land into flourishing gardens.

She struck an agreement with Lord Chancellor Marlowe to collaborate on widening the roads to gain access to the port, which has become a collaborative effort, approved by the environmental restoration plan that she has adapted to include an exhaustive list of domestic medicinal plants. She eagerly anticipates informing you that we can significantly increase this year's supply of calendula officinalis, chamomile, lemon verbena, and valerian. Lola assures me that she will communicate the specifics of this endeavor in a forthcoming letter.

I hope the news of our endeavors brings you joy and that we may continue to count on your promise to visit us soon.

Yours sincerely,
Edmund Brandon, Duke of Northumberland

The End

Author's Note

I hope you enjoyed my Regency story inspired by the movie *Pretty Woman*. It's one of my favorite movies because it's like *Cinderella* and *My Fair Lady* packaged in the elegant Hollywood feel of the late 1980s and early 1990s.

In the movie, the opera that moves Vivien, played by Julia Roberts, is *La Traviata* by the Italian composer Giuseppe Verdi. However, the opera didn't come out until 1853, which is more than half a century after my story takes place. The opera is based on a play by one of my favorite French authors, Alexandre Dumas, *La Dame aux Camélias*. As much as I would have liked it, I couldn't use this in my story set in 1819. I also couldn't have my heroine sing along to a Walkman playing *Kiss* by Prince.

Brewster's nasty act, which is similar to what we remember from the polo game in the movie, couldn't happen at a polo game in my story, either. Although polo was indeed a sport during the Regency Era, it was not as widely recognized or played in England until later in the 19th century. Polo's major leap in history began in 1859 when English Army Lieutenant Joseph Sherer played his first "pulu" game in India and brought the sport back to England. Thus, I placed it at a horse race akin to the Royal Ascot, which was equally pompous and reserved for the elite, and I gave my Lola an equally gorgeous brown dress with white polka dots.

If you remember the scene in the movie where Vivien drives the stick shift Lotus Esprit SE and says, "It turns like it's on rails," you'll quickly see why I couldn't translate this easily to the Regency era, where trains were being developed, and cars hadn't been invented. I took artistic license with the part of the movie in which Vivien impresses Edward with her driving skills by allowing Lola to drive a phaeton.

It is my sincere hope that this story left you with a smile and warm feeling about the romance that unfolded between my pretty woman, Lola, and her hot duke, Edmund, in the spirit of the movie I love but also with my distinct style.

If you'd like to read more about the kind jewelers on Regent Street, including Raphi, who provided the gorgeous necklace for Lola's special date night at the opera, check out my other series at www.SaraAdrien.com. There's also a story for each of the doctors, including Alfie Collins, the apothecary in my series titled *Miracles on Harley Street,* and my spin-offs with more doctors from across the street in the *Lyon's Den* series. For more information about my books, trailers, new releases, and other perks, subscribe to my newsletter and check out my website at www.SaraAdrien.com.

Additional Dragonblade books by Author Sara Adrien

Miracles on Harley Street Series
A Sight to Behold (Book 1)

The Lyon's Den Series
Don't Wake a Sleeping Lyon
The Lyon's First Choice
The Lyon's Golden Touch

About Sara Adrien

Bestselling author Sara Adrien writes hot and heart-melting Regency romance with a Jewish twist. As a law professor-turned-author, she writes about clandestine identities, whims of fate, and sizzling seduction. If you like unique and intelligent characters, deliciously sexy scenes, and the nostalgia of afternoon tea, then you'll adore Sara Adrien's tender tearjerkers.

Sign up for her VIP newsletter to be the first to hear about new releases, audiobooks, sales, giveaways, and bonus content at SaraAdrien.com.

Catch up with Sara Adrien here:
linktr.ee/jewishregencyromance
saraadrien.com
instagram.com/jewishregencyromance
facebook.com/AuthorSaraAdrien
bookbub.com/authors/sara-adrien
goodreads.com/author/show/22249825.Sara_Adrien
youtube.com/channel/UCK9OLp1wN6IaGkXe7OugfHg

THE WORTH OF AN EARL

by Jude Knight

Jen, a waif from the slums, rescues a wealthy lady from kidnappers. Against the objections of her grandson, the Earl of Frome, Lady Eloise insists on taking Jen to London.

Against his will, Frome falls in love with Jen. Just when he is ready to throw his reputation away for the sake of love, he uncovers a secret that changes everything.

(Note: This story was inspired by the tale of *Aladdin*, but with the roles reversed.)

CHAPTER ONE

THE LADY SAID, "Thank you." It was an unexpected courtesy, and it changed the course of Jennifer Ward's life. Without it, Jen would never have left Bristol. She would never have discovered the value of the stones she had been playing with for the past several years. And she would never have discovered the worth of an earl.

Jen didn't want to help the lady at all. But Uncle Edgar had threatened Mammi if Jen didn't come to perform maid services for a lady who was staying in his house, no questions asked and all hush-hush. "You won't even speak to her, Jennifer," he ordered.

A mistress, Jen had assumed. Several times, Uncle Edgar had promised a house, a maidservant, and an allowance to a lady of negotiable affection. The house was a tenement block he had neither the wherewithal nor the persistence to restore. Jen was the maidservant. All the mistresses decamped as soon as they realized the allowance was as mythical as Uncle Edgar's good nature.

Jen had second thoughts about her assumption as soon as she arrived. For a start, the lady was old. Not decrepit old. Still as spry as a woman half her age, but well beyond the age that appealed to Uncle Edgar. She had a crown of flyaway white hair and laugh wrinkles enough to make it clear that smiling was her favorite thing.

She was also fashionably dressed in real silk, though she lacked the jewels that went with such attire. Perhaps the lady had had the sense to leave them at home before coming to a neighborhood like this? For the lady did not belong here. Jen recognized quality. She had seen it, albeit at a distance. What was a lady like this doing with a villain like Uncle Edgar?

It wasn't her business, of course. Jen did not want to be involved. Jen intended to leave the tray, carry off the chamber pot, and think nothing more about it. But then the lady spoke to her. "Thank you. That looks very tasty."

"It is just a simple cottage pie," Jen said. She had picked it up from the ordinary. That, and a jug of light ale. Peasant food, and she had expected Uncle Edgar's fancy woman to turn up her nose at it.

"It is very welcome," replied the lady, proving the point by pouring herself a glass of the ale and draining it before she added, "I have had nothing to eat or drink since supper last night. The kidnappers took me before I could eat breakfast."

Oh, horse feathers! What had Uncle Edgar got her into now?

Suddenly, his insistence that the lady could only eat with spoons made more sense. The vile old carbuncle. A kidnapper? Really? He would get them all hanged, and then what would become of Mammi?

"Then you had better eat the pie before we escape," Jen found herself saying.

The lady's look of surprise matched how Jen was feeling. Sweet pigeons of paradise! Never mind the constables! Uncle Edgar would kill her himself if he found her helping his captive to escape.

Jen would need to get the lady to a safe place, and then go back for Mammi, and all before Uncle Edgar had any idea that she had betrayed him. And then Jen would have to hide herself and her mother somewhere Uncle Edgar would never think to look for them.

"You are really going to help me?" the lady asked.

"Yes, of course," Jen replied. "I didn't know about the kidnapping, and I do not want any part of it. We shall have to be careful, though. My uncle has one of his men downstairs—he said to keep you safe, but I guess he meant to keep you in. Eat up, my lady, while I figure out how to draw him away from the stairs so we can get out."

"Eloise," said the lady.

"I beg your pardon?"

"My name is Eloise," the lady told her. "If we are going to be friends, you should know my name."

Friends. That was a laugh. A girl like Jen and a lady like this? The word was temptation itself, though. Jen had plenty of friendly acquaintances, but her last friend was Chris, an imaginary boy she used to talk to when she'd been a child—until Mammi began to believe in him, and Jen had to put him away with other childish things.

"I'm called Jen," she found herself saying. She slipped out of the door and down two floors to where Biff waited, overflowing a spindly chair that looked as if it would collapse under his weight at any minute.

"Biff, have you eaten?" she asked. "Would you like me to fetch you some of that pie I got for the lady?"

"That 'us be roight kind of 'ee, Jen," Biff replied in his usual deep growl.

"I won't be a minute. It's no trouble to get another helping, and then I can wait until you and the lady have both finished and take the bowls back to the shop."

Biff unlocked the door for Jen, and she legged it to the cook shop, casting an experienced eye at the sky to estimate the time. They still had a couple of hours before dark, which meant Biff would probably stay on duty at least that long, and Uncle Edgar was probably still sleeping off his night's work.

She had to use her own money to pay to fill a bowl for Biff, but she made sure it was a big bowl, and full to the top. Some sort of recompense for what Uncle Edgar was likely to do to the poor man when he discovered that Lady Eloise and Jen had escaped.

Biff was pleased. The poor man was usually hungry. He buried his nose in the bowl and Jen hurried upstairs. Now for the next part of her plan.

When she explained what she had in mind, Lady Eloise agreed immediately. She was less certain about descending all the way to the cellars, but Jen explained about the tunnels, which went right under the street and several buildings.

Jen had found the hidden entrance when Uncle Edgar had locked her in the cellar for several days. She'd explored and discovered where they came out. She figured the knowledge might come in handy someday, and today was the day.

Lady Eloise, wrapped in Jen's shawl and carrying the chamber pot as a weapon, went first. Jen watched, and Biff didn't even look up from his bowl as she passed on down the stairs. Jen followed with a second chamber pot. Biff was intent on scraping the last of the pie from the bowl and didn't see her, either.

Excellent. But sooner or later he would realize she had not come for the bowl, and then he might search the house. Or he might not. Biff had not been hired for his brains. Better, however, to assume they would soon be discovered if they did not move on.

She lit a couple of candles and handed one of them to Lady Eloise.

The entrance to the tunnel was a hole in the smallest room of the cellar, hidden behind a huddle of broken furniture and other detritus. Only someone as small as Jen or Lady Eloise could slip through the hole, and Jen had long since leaned a board up against a wall to hide it. It was the work of a moment to move the board—just far enough to allow entrance, but not so far Jen could not pull it back into place.

When she stood again, Lady Eloise was leaning back against the side of the tunnel with her eyes closed.

"Are you unwell?" Jen asked.

"I am old, Jen," Lady Eloise replied, "and unused to this kind of excitement. But I shall keep up. You need have no fear about that."

"Lean on me, Lady Eloise," Jen commanded, offering her arm. "We go this way." Some tunnels were dead ends. This one would take them nearly beyond the mean streets to the safer neighborhood where the hackneys could be found.

All went smoothly. The tunnel was narrow in a few places, but that was all to the good. Even if Biff found the hole in the cellar and was able to break the sides to get into the tunnels, he would never fit through the spaces that were but a squeeze for her and Lady Eloise.

"One moment," she said to the lady, as they passed the little room she had found the second time she had explored this hidden way. A shelf near the door held what she thought of as her "treasures": A tumble of dull stones that caught the candlelight in interesting ways. A pretty bracelet she had hidden here because Uncle Edgar would have taken it if she kept it where she lived. The locket she had worn as a little girl, was also placed here to keep it from thieves. An old-fashioned lamp she had always intended to find time to polish. Her foster father had called it his "lucky lamp", and Jen kept it as a memory of him, and because she hoped the luck would rub off on her someday. Maybe today.

She poured the stones into the lamp, added the bracelet and locket, and tucked the lamp into the bodice of her gown. She would not be coming back.

"Lady Eloise, after we exit, I will take you two streets over and find a hack to take you home," she said.

"You must come with me," the old lady insisted. "I cannot let you stay to be punished."

"I can't," Jen said, though the lady's kindness warmed her heart. "I need to fetch my mother before my uncle finds out you are gone. I want to be well on our way out of the city before dark."

"Where is your mother?" Lady Eloise asked.

"In the next street. I won't have to come back far. All shall be well, my lady. Eloise, I mean. I have enough put away for Mammi and me to take a stagecoach, and to give us a start somewhere else. I've always wanted to go to London."

"London, is it?" Lady Eloise commented. "I have a better idea. Let us fetch your mother then hire a hack. We shall use my carriage to go to London. I owe you my freedom, Miss Jen, and I would be very happy to repay my debt by helping you and your mother to safety."

As it turned out, it was just as well Lady Eloise was with her. Mammi became panicked when Jen began throwing their possessions into bags. Lady Eloise took Mammi's hands. "Mrs. Ward, you and your daughter are invited to join me in London," she said.

Mammi's eyes lit up. "London? Am I to go to London again? Will I dance?"

"Would you like to dance?" Lady Eloise asked, and she and Mammi chatted away about all the wonderful entertainments Mammi was certain she had enjoyed just a short time ago, for Mammi was having one of those days in which she believed she was only eighteen.

Perhaps Mammi had been a lady's maid in those far-off days, for she certainly knew enough about the life of a debutante. Jen had always assumed it was all made up, but as she whizzed around the two rooms in which they lived, Mammi and Lady Eloise exchanged stories from their debutante days. It sounded as if Mammi knew exactly what she was talking about.

Mammi came along happily, arm-in-arm with Lady Eloise, leaving Jen to carry the bags and keep a wary eye on everyone they passed, for fear Uncle Edgar might still prevent their escape.

They reached a street broad enough for carriages and Jen flagged down a hack. Suddenly, there was a shout. A horseman pulled up between Lady Eloise and Jen, and men appeared as if from nowhere, one of them grasping Jen by the arm, and another grabbing hold of Mammi.

"Grandmother," said the man on the horse, swinging to the ground. He tried to embrace Lady Eloise, but she was busy batting at the hands of the man who held Mammi.

"Please release my friend," she demanded. "Worth, this is Miss Ward, who rescued me from the kidnappers, and Mrs. Ward, her mother. Ladies, my grandson, the Earl of Frome. Worth, darling, the ladies are in danger from the kidnappers, so I am taking them to London with me."

The earl was a handsome man, but the frown he turned on Jen was not attractive at all. "I hardly think that is necessary, Grandmother," he growled.

"Oh, don't be a bear, Worth," said Lady Eloise. "Help me into this hack, dear. Come along, Mrs. Ward. Come along, Jen."

Frome was going to be trouble, but Lady Eloise was more than a match for him. Jen followed Lady Eloise and Mammi into the carriage.

CHAPTER TWO

I N LONDON, LADY Eloise soon realized that Jen had been raised to be a lady. Then the stones she had brought away in the lamp proved to be uncut gems. "You are a lady and wealthy," Lady Eloise declared. "We shall find you a chaperone, and you shall enter Society. Why not?"

Jen had grown up on her mother's stories of Society balls, and something in her must have believed them, even as she doubted, for she was thrilled to attend her first. It looked to an observer exactly like Mammi's stories. And an observer was what Jen was, at the first ball and each that followed.

No one asked her to dance. No one spoke to her except for Mrs. Bartley, the distant cousin of Aunt Eloise hired to be her chaperone. No one acknowledged her when she spoke, or in any way indicated they were aware she existed and was present.

One night, unable to sleep after yet another dismal and disappointing evening, she stomped downstairs. The library might have a book to distract her, and better yet, she knew there was brandy in a decanter on the sideboard.

It wasn't fair. Jen could have bought most of the other guests a dozen times over with the money from the stones she'd bundled into the lamp—they turned out to be uncut gems of a very high quality. But because she lacked august bloodlines—or any discernable family at all—she was invisible, except to men who were so obviously fortune hunters that she did not need Mrs. Bartley to warn her not to encourage them.

Frome was at the ball again tonight, which was somehow worse than all the rest. Repellent, miserable, squint-nosed worm!

Except only one of those words was true. Frome was even more handsome in evening dress than he was dressed for riding, and when he smiled—as he did to everyone, except Jen—he was utterly compelling.

He had charm, too. Jen had seen him applying it with a ladle to men and women alike, and they all adored him, from the newest debutante to the oldest dowager—from the youngest cub fresh on the town to the elderly uncles. Again, everyone except Jen.

Miserable numb-brain.

The library was in darkness except for a glow from behind the fire-guard and a shielded candle almost guttering inside its protective cover. Jen used the flame from her lamp to light the candles on the mantlepiece and then on the sideboard. She turned one of the waiting glasses up the right way and poured a finger of brandy. Then, with the lamp in one hand and the brandy in the other, she turned to the bookshelves.

She jumped when a voice spoke from the corner near the guttering candle. "Be careful with that lamp near the books."

Frome.

Her simmering anger at the man made her voice sharp. "See to your own candle, Lord Frome, and I shall see to my lamp."

Frome moved into the candlelight to glare at her. Why did the man have to be so Dag bland gorgeous? Even when frowning? Even when she was furious with him? Even when he had removed his coat and waistcoat so the neat darns on his shirt showed how hard he was trying to fool the ton into thinking that all was well with his estates?

Which wasn't the point, and Jen tried hard never to lie to herself. It wasn't the darns that had her attention, but all the hard muscle shifting under the shirt. To give the devil his due, Frome had apparently been working alongside his tenants ever since his brother died and left a reeking pottle of mess for Frome to inherit. Or so Lady Eloise claimed.

He spread his arms, his own brandy glass dangling from one hand. "Like what you see, do you, Miss Ward?"

She did, but she wasn't going to tell Frome that. "You think a lot of yourself, do you not, Lord Frome?" she asked.

"Not particularly. But I do think I belong here, and you do not."

"You have made that perfectly clear," Jen agreed. "However, in this house, your grandmother's is the opinion that counts." But not outside this house. Lady Eloise Ainsworth was Frome's mother's mother and the daughter of an earl. But she was also the widow of Henry Ainsworth the merchant. In the wider world, she was not nearly as important as a dozen twit-brained crows who happened to have married people with titles.

Frome, who possessed a title and plenty of charm besides, had more influence than any of them. Jen's indignation frothed up and overflowed. "Outside of this house, you have made certain I will not be accepted. Can you not be satisfied with that, instead of attacking me at every turn?"

By the look of affront on Frome's face, he had not expected the attack. "I have never said a word against you."

"Hah!" As if he did not know perfectly well what he had done. Jen would spell it out so he would see that she knew, too. "What conclusion did you expect people to draw when you, the darling of the ton, refuse to dance or even talk with the girl your grandmother is sponsoring? When you stay away from the few entertainments to which I am invited? When, if you cannot avoid being in the same room with me, you ignore me as if I do not exist? I never stood a chance."

She couldn't say anything else, for the hurt had bubbled up and was leaking from her eyes. She turned her back on him, facing the bookshelves, though she could not see them through the tears.

OH DAMN. THE little witch was in tears. Worth—he had been given the first name Ainsworth after his grandfather but had always been called Worth—was embarrassed enough at Miss Ward's accusations without that. What could he say? He *had* been avoiding her, but not for the reasons she thought. She consumed his mind and fueled some very specific dreams that led him to wonder whether she would consent to becoming his mistress.

Not that he could ask her. Not while she was a guest of his

grandmother. And she was correct about him attacking her, too. He had to hold her at arm's length somehow.

After all, who was she? Some relative or accomplice of the men who had kidnapped his grandmother—the authorities in Bristol had failed to run them to ground. She claimed to be the daughter of the sadly simple lady who had been with her and Grandmother when he found them, but the lady did not make the same claim. Most days, she thought Miss Ward was her sister or her maid, and some days, she did not recognize her supposed daughter at all.

To be fair, most days the lady did not know who Grandmother was, either. Nobody could doubt that Mrs. Ward was a lady born and bred, if fallen on hard times. The calluses on her hands support-ed Miss Ward's claim that Mrs. Ward's skills in embroidery had supported the pair until Miss Ward was old enough to earn money herself.

Furthermore, both Wards shared the same blue-green eyes with a slight tilt to them and the same brown hair with coppery high-lights.

Dash it. She was surreptitiously wiping those lovely eyes. If she had made a display of them, he would think it all a show, but... No. Probably he would not. He had seen her front up to a ballroom of harpies out to tear the flesh from any scandal she might represent, and do so without a tear or a tremor. Miss Ward might be a liar, a fraud, and—for all he knew—a thief. But she was not a manipulator.

Worth knew manipulators. He had been ignored in favor of his brother for most of his life, then pursued doggedly by the very harpies who'd dismissed Miss Ward.

"Is there something in my behavior that gives you cause to think I shall embarrass you or Lady Eloise?" Miss Ward asked him, her voice hitching, as if she was suppressing a sob.

The truth was that there was nothing. She had told Grandmoth-er that she had modeled herself on Mrs. Ward since she'd been a tiny child and that Mrs. Ward had scolded her if she failed to walk, eat, sit, speak, or otherwise behave like a lady.

"You know there is not," Worth admitted, with more truculence in his voice than he intended.

"Then you want me to fail because you do not like me." Miss

Ward sounded sad, and her voice hitched again.

He wanted to deny the accusation, but he did not want to explain that he was endeavoring to ignore his attraction to her.

"I apologize," he said, instead. "I did not mean to give people the wrong impression." On an inspiration, he explained, "You are living in my grandmother's house and so am I. I thought to protect your reputation." For if he let his true feelings for her show, everyone who saw them would assume he was bedding her.

She turned around at last and glared at him. "Do not think to lie to me, Lord Frome. I might not be of your class, but I am not an idiot."

There was not a lot of Worth could say to that since Miss Ward was in the right and he was in the wrong. Besides, her eyelashes still glistened with the remnants of her tears. Also, the candles on the mantlepiece shone behind her, and in their light, he could see the shadowy outline of her figure through the fine linen of her night-rail and wrap.

He shifted to ease the sudden constriction in his trousers and turned his gaze upward. "I will speak to you at the next ball. How is that?"

Miss Ward started to nod then stopped and looked thoughtful. "I wonder if we might negotiate something better than that. May I be frank, my lord?"

Worth inclined his head and flung out his unoccupied hand with the palm up. He took a sip of his brandy while his lovely nemesis frowned in thought.

"I will pay you two thousand pounds to bring me into fashion," she declared.

Worth choked on his brandy. "I beg your pardon?"

Miss Ward moved to sit in one of the fireside chairs. "You are fashionable and popular. You have, perhaps inadvertently, used that against me. I am unfashionable, unpopular, and unknown, but I am very rich. Think of it as an exchange of favors, if you will. Something of which I have plenty—money, in return for something of which you have plenty—social approval."

Worth did not appreciate the "perhaps." It *had* damned well been inadvertent. He had worked so hard at not looking in Miss Ward's direction, that he had missed seeing how she was being treated. Worse—he was remembering and reinterpreting some of the comments of the least pleasant-natured of Society's eligibles. And his responses.

"Is Miss Ward a member of your family, my lord? A poor relation, perhaps?" Lady Laura Pincheck had asked, and he had replied, "No relation to me at all, Lady Laura. She is a distant connection of my grandmother." Dear heavens. He had as good as fed her to the hyenas.

"Master Ainsworth," said his long-dead governess in the back of his mind, "you have not acted the part of a gentleman." It was her sternest reproach, and always brought him, at least metaphorically, to his knees.

"I will do my best," he decided. "Keep your money, though, Miss Ward."

"It is not ill-gotten, Lord Frome," she replied, looking anxious. "I expect your grandmother has told you how it came about, and it is the truth. I came across a double handful of pretty stones several years ago and collected them into a lamp I found in the tunnels. I brought them away with me when we escaped the kidnappers, thinking they might be worth something. I had no idea they were gems, and valuable ones at that. But your grandmother was wiser than I, and insisted on them being assessed by her jeweler."

The law might hold that the stones belonged to the property owner, but Worth was not inclined to dispute her ownership. Especially since the property belonged to Edgar Barton, whom Miss Ward called *uncle*. Mind you, she also claimed that the deceased Freddie Ward, Barton's half-brother, was not really her father. Edgar Ward was Grandmother's kidnapper and had completely disappeared from Bristol. If Miss Ward's story about discovering the stones was true—and Worth had to admit he believed her—then he'd far rather she have them than Barton.

"I do not want to be paid to do the right thing," Worth insisted. Though two thousand pounds was just what he needed to pay enough of the mortgage on the most at-risk estate to have a chance of keeping the bailiffs from his door. "Why did you suggest two thousand?" he asked.

It was an idle question until Miss Ward blushed.

CHAPTER THREE

J EN HAD PEEKED at Lord Frome's account books. Not peeked so much as studied a couple of them carefully. To be fair, he had left them lying open on his desk, which was in the corner of the library. She had meant to just have a quick look but had got caught up following a repeating pattern.

Frome was being cheated, and she ought to tell him. But then she would have to admit she had been snooping, and he had a low enough opinion of her already. Yet she owed a great debt to his grandmother, who had not only snatched her and Mammi from Bristol and given them a home but had encouraged her to have the stones assessed. And Lady Eloisa loved Frome. *Aunt Eloise*. The darling lady was insisting that Jen call her that.

Oh, sniveling barnacles! She was going to have to tell him. Perhaps the tent in his trousers might predispose him to be lenient. "I might have sort of glanced at some papers that were lying around on your desk," she admitted.

"You what!" Frome turned red. If steam had come out of his ears, she would not have been at all surprised. She shrank back in her chair so she would be harder to reach if he turned violent. Living soft had made her careless. The arms of the chair had her trapped, and she had chosen the seat herself, forgetting that the first rule of survival was to have an escape route.

She couldn't run. Fighting back would be stupid when he was so much bigger, and she had no room to move. *Curl up. Protect your head.*

Instead, he leaped to his feet and started marching. Up and down in front of her, talking all the time, ranting about hospitality and trust and impudent witches who didn't know their place.

In the middle of one of his marches, he spun around on her, leaning with one hand on the arm of her chair, his other hand, fisted, waving in the air.

Jen threw her arm up to protect her face and hunched herself into a ball.

Nothing happened. Frome went silent. After a moment he said, "I am not going to hit you, Miss Ward." His voice sounded strange as if he was forcing the words through a suddenly stiff throat. It sounded farther away, too.

She risked a peek over her elbow.

Frome had fallen back a few steps and his hands hung empty at his sides.

Cautiously, she unwound herself.

"I was not going to hit you," he repeated.

"I was wrong to read your papers," Jen admitted. "I apologize, Lord Frome. It was just..." She wanted to give him some honesty in return for his non-violence. "I was curious about why you looked so cross and anxious."

That was a mistake. The worried furrow between his brows deepened into anger.

"And I am not surprised," she added, deciding to push her way forward. "Whoever deals with the Chillington Court books has been cooking his accounts. In this year alone, he has marked down the income by at least two hundred pounds and increased the expenses by two hundred and fifty. Maybe more, but those were the altered figures I was able to find."

A succession of expressions crossed Frome's face, settling into the shape of determination. "Show me," he demanded, grabbing her by the arm and pulling her towards him. Perhaps he tugged harder than he intended, for she landed against his body, and he put a hand on her back, holding her against his hard torso.

She assumed his intention was to keep her from collapsing, which was good, for her knees seemed to have turned to jelly, and for a moment, she could not move. Her breasts, pressed against Frome's chest, felt heavier and more sensitive and disclosed a hitherto unknown connection to her groin.

Jen had managed to reach the age of nineteen still a maiden by being fast on her feet, quick with a knife, and quicker with her words, but she was not precisely an innocent. She knew what she was feeling was lust, even if she'd not herself experienced it until she met the pompous, toffee-nosed Earl of Frome.

After a burning moment, he moved his hands to her shoulders and set her back from him, but not before she detected the rigid evidence that his body was as attuned to hers as hers was to his.

"Show me," he repeated, stepping back, and pointing to the desk. The candelabra he collected from the mantlepiece cast its light on his red cheeks, which perversely calmed her own racing heart.

She fetched the other candelabra. The more light the better. Some of the alterations were hard to detect. His desk was clear, but he quickly found the folder with the Chillington Court accounts, and she just as quickly pointed to the first of the changes she had found.

"He could have been correcting a mistake," Frome said. She showed him another, and then another. More than fifty. Every single change increased the income or reduced the expenses.

Frome said nothing as the evidence mounted up.

"There are more, but they are harder to see by candlelight," Jen said, as she closed the book. "I can show you in the daytime."

The earl was silent for what seemed like forever. Jen studied his face, trying to read his mood, wondering if he would return to berating her. At last, he shut his eyes, sighed, and ran a hand through his hair. "Have the other books been altered in the same way?"

Jen shook her head. "I cannot tell you. The other set of accounts that was on the desk, Batterwick, was clean. Only one correction, and I think that had been to fix an addition error. It was crossed out and rewritten, not drawn over to hide the change like these are."

"Would you look at the rest?" He was already pulling them out of the drawer from which he'd pulled the Chillington Court books. "No. What am I thinking? It is—" he peered at the clock. "Good heavens! It is three in the morning! Miss Ward, we can take this up again after we have slept." He colored again. "That is, if you are willing to assist me?"

"Yes," said Jen, before she could think better of it. On the one hand, Frome was Aunt Eloisa's beloved grandson, and the dear old lady would want Jen to help him find out who was stealing from him. On the other hand, she should not be agreeing to anything that meant spending time in the company of the annoying, arrogant, and far too fascinating man.

It was too late now. She had agreed. "I will look at the accounts tomorrow. That is, later today. We should sleep."

"Yes. We should go to bed," said Frome, and blushed. "That is, you should go to your bed, and I should go to mine."

Jen nodded. It would be beyond foolish to say the words that popped into her head. Nonetheless, she repeated them in her mind as she climbed the stairs with Frome behind her. *Why, Lord Frome, whatever can you be thinking?*

She knew exactly what he had been thinking. The mention of "we" and "bed," had sent a succession of images through her own mind, even though she did not have the experience to add detail to the mental pictures.

He would show me the details if I asked. Jen growled the wanton inside her back into its cave and turned left at the top of the stairs when Frome turned right. "Good night," he said.

"Sleep well," said she.

⇶⇷

BY THE MORNING, Worth had decided he was mad to trust Miss Ward to go through his books. He had been keeping his financial condition secret for eighteen months, ever since his brother's sudden death. The secrecy was partly to keep from scaring his creditors and partly for his reputation. A stray word from her could make that effort pointless.

When she joined him in the library as promised, he said, "You must swear to me you will not tell anyone about..." he wasn't sure what to say.

"That you are broke?" She gave him the cheeky grin that had been driving him mad for weeks. He was desperate to kiss it from her face, and then see if she still found him funny.

"Lord Frome," she told him. "You have my promise. I would like to point out, however, that I figured out your financial state long before I looked at the books." She started counting on her fingers. "One, you are renting out your townhouse and living with your grandmother. Two, you wear black coats all the time, with buff pantaloons in the daytime and black breeches for the evening. This means you can wear the same clothing over and over because one black coat looks much like another."

Worth groaned. Miss Ward folded down a third finger. "Also, the fancy waistcoats you wear—different ones every time you go out—have been cut and made by your valet out of coats from the attic, and then recut and turned to serve again. That was three. Four, your shirts are darned and so are your stockings. Your valet, by the way, is a treasure. And your only servant, which brings us to five."

"Not quite my only servant," Worth protested. "I have servants at my estates." All those he could afford to hang on to, in fact. Family retainers who did not deserve to be cast out to fend for themselves. At least town servants had a chance of finding another position.

"I can't comment on that. But here in London, you live at your grandmother's townhouse, and you use her stables so that you don't have to keep servants. So that is five."

She held up the other hand, but Worth put his hand up in a stop signal. "Enough. You have made your point. I venture to say, Miss Ward, you are smarter than most. No one in Society appears to have noticed any of those things."

"If you do not mind my asking, Lord Frome, why do you care about people knowing? I am certain it is not your fault. I've heard enough from your grandmother to know your brother and father were all about gambling and wagering and wild parties, and that you are not. And one cannot open a newspaper without reading about bad harvests and reduced land incomes."

It was a good question. Smart, like Miss Ward. "Part of it is family pride, I suppose," Worth acknowledged. "But also, I've managed to keep the worst of the creditors satisfied with regular payments. I do not want to alarm them."

"If they are spooked, they might bolt," Miss Ward said, nodding, a thoughtful expression on her face. She was wise beyond her years, and even, her gender. He could only admire her more for it.

And so, Worth accepted the analogy. "And crash the carriage."

"Fair enough. Well, no one will hear anything from me. Shall I take a look, then?"

Weirdly, since he was still telling himself that he didn't trust the lady, Worth was reassured. He set her up at the desk in the window nook with the stack of folders and notebooks, one set for each estate, and retreated to give her space.

She called him back once to ask for writing materials to take notes, and he interrupted her twice to bring her tea, once with some of Cook's maid-of-honor tarts and once with a slice of fruit cake.

She was putting the accounts into two piles. One for those with suspicious amendments and one without. Worth itched to see which estates were in which piles, but he left her to continue and retreated across the room.

Mrs. Bartley came looking for her charge and was alarmed to find her alone in the library with Lord Frome. "Not that I have any fears for Miss Ward, my lord. You were on the other side of the library, and in any case, one cannot miss the fact that you and Miss Ward are..." she blushed and floundered. "Not friends," she finished.

Just as well the lady could not read minds. "Miss Ward is busy," he commented. "I suspect she is not aware of our presence."

Miss Ward, the minx, looked up from what she was reading and winked at him. More aware than he had thought, then. He moved the book he had been reading to cover his instant reaction to her cheeky intervention.

"I will just take a seat by the other window and do my sewing," said Mrs. Bartley. "I shall not disturb Miss Ward, my lord."

Late in the morning, two and a half hours after she had started, Miss Ward sat back and folded her hands. Worth, who had been only pretending to read, looked up as soon as she moved and met her eyes. She nodded.

Mrs. Bartley was bent over her sewing and did not notice.

The accounts were now all in the two piles, one slightly larger than the other. Miss Ward laid a hand on one of the piles and shook her head, then put it on the other pile and nodded vigorously. She then stood. "Mrs. Bartley, what a dear you are to wait so patiently. Is that the cap you have been making for your new grandson?"

The two ladies put their heads together to coo over a tiny piece of embroidered material, then left the room, Mrs. Bartley chattering about an imminent visit to the modiste and Miss Ward putting in a word here and there.

Worth waited until the door shut behind them and then examined Miss Ward's findings, carefully detailed in her notes, which she had also left.

"It requires more study to find everything, but whoever has had the handling of the accounts in the left-hand pile is lying to you, and is presumably stealing from you.

"As you undoubtedly know, the right-hand pile is fine. Did I pass the test, Frome?"

The little witch. He could not help a reluctant smile as he went through the left-hand pile, moving each estate's records in turn until he knew she had pinpointed every estate managed by one of his two factors.

The estates managed by the other factor were all in the right-hand pile.

How long had the theft been happening? That, too, required more study. Still, even if he could stop the level of loss, he had discovered this morning, estates he had been on the point of selling were suddenly looking viable again. If he could recover some of the money, he might even be able to reduce their mortgages!

And he owed it all to Miss Ward and her nosy ways. Tonight, he would begin to repay the debt he had incurred to the lady. In fact, he'd make a start at his club after the calls on his solicitor, the honest factor, and a magistrate—and then the dishonest factor.

CHAPTER FOUR

AUNT ELOISA WAS becoming anxious. "It is not like Worth to be late," she said, several times, peering at the clock as if responsibility for the tardiness of the Earl of Frome fell entirely on its clockwork shoulders.

Frome did not always eat with them, but apparently tonight, he was expected. "He told me this morning that he would be dining at home. He is always such a considerate boy. I wonder what on earth might have happened?"

The clock was five minutes past the hour appointed for dinner when a footman hurried into the room and whispered to the butler. "My lady," the butler then said to Aunt Eloisa, "his lordship has just arrived home. He will change and be down shortly. He said to begin without him."

"Nonsense," said Aunt Eloisa. "If he will be here shortly, we shall wait. Send to the kitchen and let them know they can send up the first service as soon as Frome comes down the stairs."

"Yes, my lady," said the butler and summoned a footman to take his message.

"Oh dear," said Mrs. Bartley. "I do hope that nothing unfortunate has occurred. Frome is normally so punctual."

Seeing the worry in Aunt Eloise's eyes, Jen reminded both ladies, "We know Frome is home, and if he is changing for dinner, he must be in one piece."

Aunt Eloisa brightened at the thought. "That is true, my dear." She changed the topic to the evening's entertainment and was distressed to hear that Jen did not have an invitation.

"Not even to the Beauchamp ball?" she exclaimed.

"I do not mind, Aunt Eloisa. Indeed, I am unaccustomed to the late nights, so it is a boon, really."

Mrs. Bartley sighed, deeply. "I am sorry to say, Eloisa, but Miss Ward is not having the social success that one might have hoped. Indeed, I do not understand it, for she is as pretty and as well-behaved a young maiden as one could hope to meet. But she is not asked to dance nor do the hostesses introduce her. One would hope Frome... but there. Young men seldom think of such things for themselves."

She turned to Jen. "I have been away from London for such a long time that I am of little use to you, dear Miss Ward. I hoped it would resolve itself after a few entertainments when people could see how well you conducted yourself. But I truly believe it is getting worse."

Aunt Eloisa looked distressed. "Jen, dear, why did you not tell me?"

"I did not want to upset you," Jen admitted. "You have been so kind, so good to me. I do not mind about not dancing, and if people do not want to speak to me, then I certainly do not want to speak to them."

"Dancing!" Mammi declared. "I love dancing. A pink gown with lace, and when I turned and turned it looked like a bell made from sugar, Anthony said. A sweet, sweet bell." She smiled into nowhere, and began to sway to and fro to music no one else could hear.

"Who is Anthony?" Mrs. Bartley whispered.

Jen shook her head. She didn't know. "Someone Mammi mentions now and then. A memory, perhaps? Don't ask her. It upsets her."

Jen had done so in the past when she was younger. Each time, Mammi had become agitated and would huddle on her bed, hugging her legs and crying. Left to live in the memory, if it was a memory and not imagination, she was happy.

Frome entered the drawing room just as the butler announced, "Dinner, my lady."

"Thank you for waiting, Grandmother," he said. "I am most sorry for my tardiness, but truly, it was unavoidable. I hope you and the other ladies will forgive me?" Frome was smiling. It was the sort of smile that attests to some internal source of happiness that could not be contained.

Jen burned to ask, but she kept her mouth shut, unsure if their fragile new accord allowed such curiosity.

As usual, Frome offered his arm to Aunt Eloisa and the other ladies followed the couple into the dining room. "Miss Ward," he asked when they were all seated and the first bustle of serving was over, "may I enquire about your plans for this evening? I have been invited to the Beauchamp ball, and I wondered if I might be permitted to escort you."

Aunt Eloisa beamed. "Of course, she will," she said. "This shall be just the thing for you, Jen. I am so pleased, Worth," she added, "that you have finally decided to do your duty by my guest."

Frome turned accusing eyes on Jen, but Aunt Eloisa added, "I had no idea she was being given the cold shoulder until Mrs. Bartley mentioned it this evening."

She turned her gentle scold to Jen. "You should have told me, my dear. Can you believe it, Worth? The child tells me that she did not want to upset me! Tonight, she was going to stay at home, and she tried to convince me that she would prefer it."

Now Frome's eyes were warm as he gazed at Jen, and she shivered, unsure of how to respond. "Perhaps she would, Grandmother. Miss Ward? Will you favor me by permitting me to escort you tonight? I promise that the ton will not turn away from you if you are on my arm."

Jen had conflicting feelings. On the one hand, she wanted, just once, to fulfill her childhood dream of dancing at an upper-class ball. On the other hand, it smarted that the very people who had been insulting her for weeks would accept her on the word of one of their own.

"Please?" said Frome. "How else am I to bring you into fashion?"

"We shall change after dinner," Mrs. Bartley declared. "Oh, Miss Ward, I am so excited!

After that, the two older ladies dominated the conversation through most of the dinner, with the occasional surprisingly apposite comment by Mammi. Talk of balls they had attended moved to comparisons of yesterday's ornate gowns with today's much simpler styles.

"The men looked so beautiful in their colorful brocade coats and matching breeches, with all the lace on their cuffs and their cravats," Mrs. Bartley mourned. "Today's fashion for plain dark colors is so melancholy."

"Yes, that scoundrel Brummel has much to answer for," Aunt Eloisa agreed. "Mind you, some took fashion to excess." And they were off again, exchanging stories of ridiculous flights of fancy by both men and women. Had a lady really attended a ball with a live bird as part of her hair adornment?

Aunt Eloisa had a dozen other stories about the wigs that had once been an essential part of the dress of both ladies and gentlemen. Mrs. Bartley was ten years younger, and wigs had already been falling out of favor by the time she made her debut.

When Aunt Eloisa rose to signal the end of dinner, Mrs. Bartley declared, "There is no time to waste, Miss Ward. Let us immediately to our chambers to prepare for the ball. Oh, I am so excited!"

"Can Mammi watch?" Mammi asked. "Please, Jen."

Frome, bless the man, looked at Jen. "Do you wish to attend, Miss Ward?" he said quietly.

It seemed to Jen that the whole room went still, waiting for the answer. Even the footmen who were clearing the sideboard stopped to listen.

Only one answer seemed possible, not just because the ladies would be so disappointed at a "no," but because Jen really wanted to see what it was like to be accepted. *Just once.* "Yes, Lord Frome. I would love you to escort me to Lady Beauchamp's ball. That is if you are certain she will not object?"

"Not," said Frome, with the arrogance that usually so annoyed her, "if you are on my arm, Miss Ward."

FROME WAS RIGHT. When they reached the reception line, Lady Beauchamp suppressed the questions that were seething in her eyes, and merely said, "Good evening, Miss Ward. So good of you to join us."

With time to wait before the first dance—which Frome had politely requested—he conducted her around the ballroom, introducing her to his friends. The reactions of some of them would have been demoralizing if Jen had actually cared. To be honest, she did care a bit, but the smart was reduced by Frome's indignation.

He even took up cudgels in her defense when Lady Laura Pinchbeck accosted them and attempted to turn an introduction to a cousin of hers into an opportunity to cut Jen off at the ankles. "Frome, how generous of you to be so charitable towards your grandmother's distant relative, but do you not think it unkind to take a person out of their place? Miss Ward would be more comfortable, I am certain, with shop owners and yeoman farmers, and that kind of person."

To which Frome replied, "Is that what you think, Lady Laura? I think I have been most remiss and have given my friends a false impression of Miss Ward. She is a lady to her fingertips, and I am proud to be, in some sort, a cousin. Not too close a connection, thank goodness."

"Why, Frome," said Lady Laura, tapping Frome's forearm with her fan, "it almost sounds as if you have romantic feelings for Miss Ward."

"Lady Laura," replied Frome, "it would be none of your business if I did."

"Really, Frome!" declared the lady. "That is hardly the way to speak to a lady."

"Speaking of my cousin with disrespect is hardly the behavior of a lady," Frome replied.

Lady Laura flushed and fell back a step. "Well, I never."

The revolting malicious turnip.

Frome said to Jen, "Shall we continue, Miss Ward? I have other people I would like you to meet."

When the musicians began to play, Frome swept Jen into the dance. Aunt Eloisa had hired a dancing instructor, so Jen was not afraid of disgracing herself.

She had known the basic footwork since she was a small child, practicing with Mammi while the man she had known as Da played for them on the harmonica. She knew how to apply the steps in the cotillion, the country dance, and the reel. With the dancing instructor, she learned the basics of the quadrille and the waltz.

This dance was a country dance, and the first time she had danced it with an audience would be right now. Creeping fish feathers! She was afraid of disgracing herself!

But after the leading couple had called a few figures and she and Frome had successfully danced them, she began to relax and even to enjoy herself.

In the dance, each couple danced in a square with the couple next to them, but when they'd danced the pattern set by the lead, the couple at the head of the line danced to the end, so each set of four constantly changed. Some, Jen found, were focused on the dance. Some were welcoming and cheerful. Some turned up their noses. But all had to follow the figures, whether they wanted to dance with Jen or not.

She and Frome worked their way forward until it was their turn to dance down the line to the rear. Frome must have been waiting for them to be inconspicuous, for when the next top couple began heading to the rear, he hastily said to Jen, "I must tell you what happened today, Miss Ward. Will you allow me a second dance? The supper waltz?"

Jen agreed. She did not expect any other partners and was, in any case, dying to know what Frome was so pleased about. At that moment, the couple who had been dancing down the line arrived to take up the rear, and it was time to form a new square.

There would be three sets before the supper dance, and Jen expected to watch them from the sidelines, but Frome's attention must have been a signal to other gentlemen, for two of them were waiting with Mrs. Bartley to ask her to dance, so she had a partner for the next two sets.

The first was a quadrille, which gave little chance for conversation, but the gentleman seemed pleasant enough. Frome was dancing, too, and Jen found herself sneaking glances at him, and wondering what he thought of his current partner.

He was waiting with Mrs. Bartley when she returned to her chaperone. Three more sets were spoken for before the music started up again, and her next partner escorted her into the dance.

The time passed quickly until Frome claimed her for the supper waltz.

"Are you enjoying yourself, Miss Ward?" Frome asked.

"Very much," Jen told him. "It is just as Mammi described. I always wondered if they were true memories or something she read. If she was a debutante once, she must have been as popular as I am tonight, Frome. Thanks to you."

Frome's smile was warm. "It is a small return for your help. Jen—Miss Ward, I should say—I had my dishonest factor arrested, and I believe we are going to be able to recover at least half of what was stolen."

"That is wonderful news," Jen said, and then added, "You could call me Jen in private conversation."

"If you call me Worth," he replied. "In private, or when it is just family."

They spoke little for the rest of the dance and then joined a table of his friends for supper. The group accepted Jen with warmth, and she thoroughly enjoyed a lively conversation that ranged over ridiculous fashion trends, tax reform, court news, the spring planting, and what was happening in Europe.

Even if Worth's magic touch did not have a permanent effect, Jen would have this night to remember.

CHAPTER FIVE

WORTH WAS IN trouble. Jennifer Ward had fascinated him from the moment he clapped eyes on her back in Bristol and charmed him more and more as he watched her interactions with her mother and his grandmother.

With the former, she was respectful, firm, kind, and loving. He could imagine her as a mother. He could, all too easily, imagine her with his children. A boy, perhaps, who had her coppery brown hair, and a little girl with her mother's dauntless spirit, determined to keep up with her older brother.

Once they were home again and Jen had gone up to bed, he sat in the library with a brandy, considering his next steps. To have that marvelous spirit at his side for his whole life. Mistress? No, never. Worth wanted Jen as his wife. His countess. She would be a magnificent countess. The problem was that he had given her no reason to look on him with favor. He had been horrid to her. Arrogant. Suspicious. Unpleasant. Unfriendly, as Mrs. Bartley had noticed.

He knew it was because he had been trying to keep his distance. Jen didn't.

At least he had apologized. He had started tonight to make up for it. But would it be enough? Well, if it wasn't, he would have to try harder, for he knew to the depths of his soul that she was his match. He could no more walk away from her than from his own arm.

Should he send flowers? Even though they were living in the same house? And that was another thing. Should he leave the house and stay at his club? It hadn't mattered when the whole of Society thought he resented her. But once it was known he was courting her, the pair of them being under the same roof might be a problem. He didn't want people gossiping about Jen. Not any more than they were because of her mysterious origins.

What a meal they'd make of it if they knew where Aunt Eloisa had found her, and under what circumstances! As for Worth, he no longer cared. She should be proud of all she achieved under very adverse circumstances. Looking after her mother. Retaining her integrity. Learning the skills of a lady.

"Frome. You are still up." There she was. The woman he had been thinking about, all but her face, hands, and feet modestly covered by a large shawl. Which didn't keep his imagination from picturing her in the night rail that was probably beneath the shawl, or better still, in nothing at all.

He grunted, all he was capable of as he fought his response.

"Are you upset with me, Frome?" she asked.

"Worth." See? He could still produce words. He proved it by managing a few more. "Call me 'Worth'. Like my grandmother does. After all, we are friends now, are we not?" He found himself holding his breath as he waited for her answer.

"If you call me Jen," she offered, blushing.

"Not Jenny?" he asked, prompting a somewhat wistful smile.

"No one has ever called me Jenny." The blush deepened. "You can if you like, Worth."

If he did not change the tenor of the conversation, he would kiss her. Which would probably frighten or anger her. Even if it didn't, it would be the act of a cad to take advantage of her when they were living under the same roof. Or at all. "Did you come down for a book? May I hold a candle for you?"

"Thank you. I wanted the next volume of *The Modern Griselda*. Here it is. Thank you."

She was almost burbling. Jenny never burbled. Worth felt a surge of pride and lust at her reaction to him. "I am about to go up to bed myself," he improvised. "May I light you up?" *And kiss her at her door. No! That would be wrong.*

"Thank you," she said again, and he had to be stern with his lust, which was certain her words were an answer to his thoughts.

He said a polite good night but found his feet unwilling to move him away after she had closed the door with him on the other side. Had he been farther away, he might not have heard the muffled sounds from inside the room. A shout, which shut off after the first yelp. Breaking glass or china.

Worth looked around for a weapon. Continued noises had him picturing a struggle, and the jangle of a key in the lock meant he was out of time. He turned the handle and hurled himself against the door. Someone on the other side pushed back, but the door gave, so it was not locked.

"Worth!" shouted Jenny. Worth's fear and anger gave him strength. He barged the door with his shoulder and pushed his way in. Jenny was struggling in the arms of a villain near the window, but most of his attention had to go to the younger villain who had given up the lost battle for the door and was on the attack.

Worth ducked under the club that was descending towards his head and managed a solid punch to the man's chin that knocked him backward. He snatched at the man's wrist. Jenny yelled again, this time a wordless protest, and again it sent a surge of energy into Worth's attack. He swung the man by the wrist, and the man hit the door and collapsed, unconscious.

Worth faced the other villain. The one who held Jenny with one arm around her waist holding her arms trapped and one hand over her mouth.

"Let her go," Worth demanded, taking a step towards them.

"Come any closer, and I shall break her neck," said the villain, "and neither of us want that."

Worth certainly didn't. He stopped where he was, looking help-lessly at the woman he loved. Yes, loved, and wasn't this a bad time to realize it?

"What do you want?" he demanded. Anything. Anything at all, for she was worth everything to him.

"My lucky lamp," growled the villain, and gave Jenny a shake. "She took it and I want it back."

Jenny tried to speak but it came out muffled.

"If I take my hand away, you'll not shout out," the villain said. "I have a gun, and I'll shoot yon earl if you speak too loud." He dropped Jen and stepped back several steps, one hand darting into his coat and reappearing and holding a gun.

"It was not yours," Jenny told him. "It had been thrown away in the cellar."

"It was too mine. Looked everywhere for it, didn't I, after Freddie died. It was his, and it brought him luck. Everything he had came to me, so it is mine. Come on, Jen. Hand it over. Besides, anything you found is mine by rights, to pay me back for keeping you and your Ma after Freddie died."

Jenny scoffed. "Ma and I kept ourselves. She sewed and I did the books at the inn and then several other places."

"You lived under my roof," argued the villain, who must be the nefarious uncle who'd kidnapped Grandmother.

"And kept your house clean and put meals on your table," Jenny replied.

She had been moving away from Worth as she spoke, and the uncle was so focused on her that he had forgotten about Worth. Worth took two steps to the side so that he was completely out of the man's view, then began to inch towards him.

"Stop arguing, girl, and give me the lamp. Here, is that it?" He pointed at the silver oil lamp Jenny had brought with her. "You've polished it. It's right pretty!"

Jenny put out a hand as if to stop him from stepping forward, and said, "It isn't yours, Uncle Edgar. Don't touch it." The clever girl was giving Worth his opportunity.

Worth was right next to the fire irons on the hearth. In one move, he picked up the poker and hit Uncle Edgar on the head, dropping him in his tracks.

He scooped up the gun and wrapped his arms around Jenny. "My love," he said. "Are you well? I have never been so scared in my life as when I saw you in his clutches."

"Your *love*, Worth?" asked Jenny, her eyes wide.

Greatly daring, since she had accepted his embrace and even snuggled into him, Worth dropped a soft kiss on her lips. "Indeed. It is why I was so grumpy. I was falling in love with you, and I was not prepared for it. May I court you, Jenny? Will you allow me to convince you I can make you happy?"

"Courtship would be nice," Jenny allowed. "I suppose I should tell you, though, that I am already in love with you, and very cross about it. I was, too, thinking you would never feel the same way about me. But Worth, you cannot have thought. I am not at all suitable to be your countess."

At that moment, the first villain groaned. "The only requirement is being married to an earl," Worth explained. "Besides, I think you will make a wonderful countess, but we had better tie these two up before we discuss the matter."

IN THE MORNING, after far too little sleep, Worth and Jenny met at breakfast. Aunt Eloisa, Mrs. Bartley, and Mammi were delighted to learn that Worth and Jen were betrothed. "Will you wear a new dress, Jen?" Mammi asked. Jen chatted to her about dresses, shoes, and bonnets, all of which seemed to Mammi to be an essential part of a wedding. It kept Mammi occupied while Worth told Aunt Eloisa and Mrs. Bartley about their nighttime visitors.

"I haven't questioned the leader yet," Worth said. "I didn't think he was worth losing sleep over. I had the footmen lock the pair of them in the cellar. They were both conscious and complaining."

"Leave questioning them to the constables," Aunt Eloisa demanded.

But Worth explained that the leader was Jen's Uncle Edgar, and he did not want anything said to constables or magistrates that might touch her reputation.

Aunt Eloisa agreed immediately. "Of course. We do not want a scandal. You question the horrid man. See if you can find out who Jen's real people are."

Jen would like to know the answer to that question. She suggested coming down to the cellars with Worth but was not surprised when the obstinate man refused outright. He was going to have to learn his protective instincts could cause problems between them.

Perhaps he already knew, because he attempted an explanation. "He thinks he knows you, Jenny, and will try to bully you, and then

I will have to punch him again, and we won't get any sense out of him. Besides, it upsets me to see you in the same room as that man. It makes me remember you were in his power for most of your life, and I can't bear it."

Given Worth's nature, Jen could see his point. "Very well then, darling. As long as you promise to tell me everything, good or bad. I want to know who I am, Worth, and how Mammi ended up married to Freddie."

He checked to see their elders were busy chatting and gave her a quick kiss on the lips. "I will tell you everything," he promised.

Worth was gone for a long time. Jen tried to busy herself with the ledgers he had asked her to review. She was going back through the records the crooked factor had presented to the previous earl over the last four years of his life, to see if he had been stealing then, and if so, how much.

She found it hard to concentrate this morning. Not only did the older ladies keep interrupting to ask her opinion about their plans for her wedding and her trousseau, but she kept wondering what Uncle Edgar was saying to Worth.

At last, Worth returned to the drawing room. He immediately crossed to where Jen was sitting and dropped to his haunches so he could hold her hands. "Jenny, the old villain told me an incredible tale, but I think the essence of it is true." He looked over his shoulders to Aunt Eloisa. "Grandmother, the villain in the cellar has told me how Jen and her mother came to live with him but claims not to remember any names. I suspect we need your knowledge of the London ton to make sense of it."

It was, indeed, an incredible tale. "Many years ago," Worth told them, "an earl married one of the loveliest debutantes of the season. He was a man in his late thirties, so the marriage came as a great disappointment to his younger brother. The marriage was brief. Some six months after the wedding, the earl was attacked in the street and died.

"The brother immediately claimed to be earl, but the widow's father, who had swooped on the grieving household and taken his daughter home, announced that the widow was with child. Some four months later, the news came out that she had given birth to the new earl.

"For several years, the widow and the baby earl remained at her father's country estate, well-guarded. But eventually, she accompanied her father to London, and the uncle took his opportunity. He hired three villains, half-brothers, to steal the baby away.

"They entered from the roof, using a rope ladder to get down to the nursery, and picked the lock of the barred gate that kept children from falling out of the window.

"Things went wrong almost immediately. They made it inside but found two railed beds, each with a child in it. As they frantically discussed whether to take both children, the mother interrupted them. She managed to scream once before Freddie, one of the brothers, clapped a hand over her mouth.

"With servants likely to arrive at any second, Freddie dragged the mother to the window by which they had entered and the two remaining brothers went for a child each. But only one brother, Edgar, exited the window with a child. The other, Bill, was shot by the guard posted by the mother's father to protect his household; he was the first servant through the door.

"Freddie pressed the mother's face into his chest until her struggles ceased. Edgar thanked his lucky stars that the infant he carried did not wake. With two inert victims presenting little challenge to their climbing ability, they soon escaped across the roofs and away.

"The hue and cry set up by the grandfather's household consumed the streets. They hid in a garden, Freddie keeping his hand over the mother's mouth and nose, so she did not make a noise. The baby continued to sleep.

"It was some time before they were able to make their escape. Edgar wanted to leave the mother, who was nearly dead from suffocation, but Freddie refused. Back among their own, they found the child they had was a girl. Also, Bill, who had survived being shot, had named his accomplices.

"Figuring that London was too hot for them, they left for Bristol, and Freddie insisted on taking the mother and the little girl with him, for he would not leave them unprotected in the wild part of London they called home, and they could not risk taking them back to their own part of London.

"And in Bristol, the mother and child lived until the day I met Jenny helping my grandmother to escape from her Uncle Edgar."

Aunt Eloisa looked at Jen with wide eyes. "I remember the kidnapping. The lost countess and her little daughter. The little earl left behind. Jen, darling, you are Lady Jennifer Sheffield, twin to the Earl of Brinkley. Oh, my goodness. That means your mother is Madeleine, Lady Brinkley."

"Maddie," said Mammi, in a dreamy tone. "Pretty Lady Maddie." Her voice deepened and her tone changed to a kind of gleeful sneer. "Poor Lady Maddie, such a pity. So young to be a widow." She blinked a couple of times. "I should sew. I need to sew." She picked up the embroidery that lay neglected in her lap and focused solely on that, ignoring Jen when she tried to speak to her.

"Mammi? Maddie? What do you remember?"

But Mammi would not reply.

"My locket!" Jen exclaimed. "It has pictures in it. Two infants. I always thought they were both me. Wait! I shall get it."

And when Lady Eloisa and Worth saw the locket, they both agreed.

"This crest on the back?" Worth commented. "It is the family crest of the Earls of Brinkley. I know the current Brinkley. Your brother. A good man. Shall I send him a message, Jenny? Do you want him to know?"

Jen shuddered to think of the baby left behind. At least she had had Mammi, even if a much-diminished Mammi with erratic memories and her intellectual abilities largely erased. "He should know, do you not think? He must have also spent a lifetime wondering what had happened to his family."

"His first name is Christopher," Aunt Eloisa said, helpfully.

EPILOGUE

THE RETURN OF the lost Sheffield ladies was the sensation of London. Undoubtedly, that was the reason for the crowd outside of the church when her brother, Christopher, helped Jen from the coach. The people cheered. Some threw flowers. Others called out blessings for the bride.

Christopher, who was fast becoming as dear to her as he must have been when they were infants, stopped on the steps. "Just remember," he said. "I am always here for you. I have missed you for most of my life, and I don't want to lose you now that I have you back."

Right there on the steps of the church, Jen threw her arms around her brother and hugged him. "You will never lose me," she vowed. "I love you, Chris."

He hugged her back. "I love you, too, Jen. But I guess you are going to insist on me sharing you with Frome. Are you ready?" he asked.

Jen nodded. Ready to marry Worth and spend the rest of her life with him? Absolutely.

She put her hand on Christopher's arm and he led her into the church. It might have been packed. The organ might have been playing. Mammi and dear Aunt Eloise might have been watching. Only one person mattered.

Worth stood at the head of the aisle, his eyes fixed on hers, and Jen smiled as she walked toward her future.

The End

This story is part of my series, *A Twist Upon a Regency Tale*, in which a folk tale inspires a Regency-era story, with the magic elements becoming natural happenstance and the roles reversed. In *The Worth of an Earl*, my inspiration was *Aladdin*.

Additional Dragonblade books by Author Jude Knight

A Twist Upon a Regency Tale, The Series
Lady Beast's Bridegroom (Book 1)
One Perfect Dance (Book 2)
Snowy and the Seven Doves (Book 3)
Perchance to Dream (Book 4)
Weave Me a Rope (Book 5)
The Sincerest Flattery (Book 6)
Inviting the Wild (Book 7)

The Lyon's Den Series
The Talons of a Lyon
Hook, Lyon and Sinker

About Jude Knight

Have you ever wanted something so much you were afraid to even try? That was Jude ten years ago.

For as long as she can remember, she's wanted to be a novelist. She even started dozens of stories, over the years.

But life kept getting in the way. A seriously ill child who required years of therapy; a rising mortgage that led to a full-time job; six children, her own chronic illness… the writing took a back seat.

As the years passed, the fear grew. If she didn't put her stories out there in the market, she wouldn't risk making a fool of herself. She could keep the dream alive if she never put it to the test.

Then her mother died. That great lady had waited her whole life to read a novel of Jude's, and now it would never happen.

So Jude faced her fear and changed it—told everyone she knew she was writing a novel. Now she'd make a fool of herself for certain if she didn't finish.

Her first book came out to excellent reviews in December 2014, and the rest is history. Many books, lots of positive reviews, and a few awards later, she feels foolish for not starting earlier.

Jude write historical fiction with a large helping of romance, a splash of Regency, and a twist of suspense. She then tries to figure out how to slot the story into a genre category. She's mad keen on history, enjoys what happens to people in the crucible of a passionate relationship, and loves to use a good mystery and some real danger as mechanisms to torture her characters.

Dip your toe into her world with one of her lunch-time reads collections or a novella, or dive into a novel. And let her know what you think.

Website and blog:
judeknightauthor.com

Subscribe to newsletter:
judeknightauthor.com/newsletter

Bookshop:
judeknight.selz.com

Facebook:
facebook.com/JudeKnightAuthor .

Twitter:
twitter.com/JudeKnightBooks

Pinterest:
nz.pinterest.com/jknight1033

Bookbub:
bookbub.com/profile/jude-knight

Books + Main Bites:
bookandmainbites.com/JudeKnightAuthor

Amazon author page:
amazon.com/Jude-Knight/e/B00RG3SG7I

Goodreads:
goodreads.com/author/show/8603586.Jude_Knight

LinkedIn:
linkedin.com/in/jude-knight-465557166

Made in the USA
Columbia, SC
23 May 2025

58385090R00222